A Girl with No Name

Also by Carola Dunn
in Large Print:

Crossed Quills
The Improper Governess
Rattle His Bones
The Case of the Murdered Muckraker

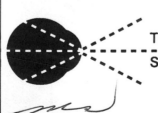

A Girl with
No Name

Carola Dunn

Thorndike Press • Waterville, Maine

Published in 2004 by arrangement with Carola Dunn.

Thorndike Press® Large Print Candlelight.

The tree indicium is a trademark of Thorndike Press.

The text of this Large Print edition is unabridged.
Other aspects of the book may vary from the original edition.

Set in 16 pt. Plantin by Minnie B. Raven.

Printed in the United States on permanent paper.

Library of Congress Cataloging-in-Publication Data

Dunn, Carola.
   [Toblethorpe Manor]
   A girl with no name / Carola Dunn.
     p. cm.
   Originally published under title: Toblethorpe Manor.
   ISBN 0-7862-6341-5 (lg. print : hc : alk. paper)
   1. Yorkshire (England) — Fiction. 2. London (England)
— Fiction. 3. Amnesia — Fiction. 4. Large type books.
I. Title.
PR6054.U537T58 2004
  823′.914—dc22   2003071174

A Girl with No Name

National Association for Visually Handicapped
---------------------- *serving the partially seeing*

As the Founder/CEO of NAVH, the only national health agency solely devoted to those who, although not totally blind, have an eye disease which could lead to serious visual impairment, I am pleased to recognize Thorndike Press* as one of the leading publishers in the large print field.

Founded in 1954 in San Francisco to prepare large print textbooks for partially seeing children, NAVH became the pioneer and standard setting agency in the preparation of large type.

Today, those publishers who meet our standards carry the prestigious "Seal of Approval" indicating high quality large print. We are delighted that Thorndike Press is one of the publishers whose titles meet these standards. We are also pleased to recognize the significant contribution Thorndike Press is making in this important and growing field.

Lorraine H. Marchi, L.H.D.
Founder/CEO
NAVH

* Thorndike Press encompasses the following imprints: Thorndike, Wheeler, Walker and Large Print Press.

Chapter 1

A ruthless hand flung back the bed-curtains and its owner looked down in amused distaste at the recumbent figure sprawled on its back with its mouth open, an unlovely sight. He poked it in the ribs.

Lord Denham awoke with a yelp and sat up abruptly, his nightcap awry.

"What the devil?" he roared, his usually placid face wrathful. Then he saw his attacker and subsided. "Damme, Carstairs, what do you mean by waking me in the middle of the night?" He slid down under the covers and winced as Richard Carstairs threw open the draperies at the window, allowing a flood of sunlight to assault his half-closed eyes.

"It's a glorious morning, Tony, and we are going for a ride. We don't often have a day like this in Yorkshire at this season, and I'll not miss it for my slugabed friend!"

"Go without me, Richard, by all means go without me. I shall be perfectly happy to miss it. I came here for a rest, not to be routed out of bed at cockcrow." Tony pulled the quilt close about him.

"You rested in the chaise all day yesterday and the day before," Richard pointed out. "And you can, and do, sleep till all hours in town. Come on, there's a good fellow. I have already sent Willett to wake your man, and ordered the horses saddled. Chocolate in the breakfast room in ten minutes."

"Oh, very well," groaned Lord Denham. "I can see I shall have no peace unless I comply with your outrageous demands. I'll be down in twenty."

Satisfied, Mr. Carstairs left him to the ministrations of his valet, who looked quite as sleepy as his lordship.

"Like master, like man," he commented to his own servant with a grin that lightened his dark, somewhat saturnine face.

"Something of the sort might be considered appropriate, sir," replied Willett primly. He himself had answered his master's bell at dawn, immaculately dressed and without a hair out of place. Richard sometimes wondered if he ever slept.

Returning to his own chamber, he pulled on his glossy riding boots, and Willett helped him into a tight-fitting coat. Tailored by Schultz, it had no need of padded shoulders to set off his tall figure to perfection.

"I shall need a greatcoat, Willett," Richard ordered. "It will be cold in spite of the sun. I expect there is still snow on the moors, though not drifted too deep for riding, I hope."

"There is frost on the lawn this morning, sir, but I believe most of the latest snowfall melted during our absence. A beautiful day for an outing, if I may say so, Mr. Richard."

"Well, I think so. However, his lordship took some persuasion. He's a regular townsman and seems to prefer smoky slush to our fresh moorland air."

"I trust Lord Denham will not be distressed by the chill, sir. There is hot chocolate waiting in the breakfast room."

"So I told him, and I rather think that was the clinching argument. Pierre's chocolate is a rare concoction, and Tony is a rare trencherman." Richard grinned. "Thank you, Willett."

He made his way below stairs. His mother and sister had not yet risen. Maids scurried about laying fires to warm the old stone mansion that had been the home of the Carstairs family for generations. They bobbed curtsies to the master, noting that

9

he was looking cheerful. Though Mr. Richard was a fair and generous employer, he was not noted for lightheartedness. The servants were glad to see his stern face relaxed and set it down to Lord Denham's good-humoured presence.

That gentleman shortly joined his friend in the breakfast room, still grumbling. A few sips of Monsieur Pierre's hot chocolate soon restored his spirits.

"I don't suppose your chef would tell my Alphonse the secret?" he asked wistfully.

"He might, if Alphonse would reciprocate with his wild duck recipe that you guard so jealously."

"Ah, who would come to my shooting parties if they could eat that duck elsewhere?" sighed Lord Denham. "I shall just have to keep visiting you. It is ambrosial, positively ambrosial. Bedford! my compliments to Monsieur Pierre."

"Certainly, my lord," assented the butler.

Tony insisted on a second cup before Richard could drag him out into the crisp morning. At last they were mounted and riding up the lane, a new panorama exposed to their view at every twist and turn.

A light crust of snow sparkled in the sun as the two gentlemen galloped along a moorland ride. They pulled to a walk and the steam of the horses' breath hung in the still, bright air.

"Well, Tony?" drawled Mr. Carstairs, grinning at his friend's scarlet complexion.

"Oh, I'll admit it is a beautiful morning, but damme if my nose is not frost-bitten," complained the fair young man. "You Yorkshiremen are bred hardy. If you want to ride before breakfast tomorrow, zounds! You can go by yourself!"

"Tomorrow it may be raining, or foggy. This is too good to miss. We shall go a little farther; I want to see if there are any sheep on Daws Fell." His tanned face did not appear to have felt the biting frost and his hair, cut short in the fashionable Stanhope crop, had fallen neatly into place, unlike Lord Denham's tousled mop, after their wild ride.

"Dash it, Richard," said Tony in annoyance, "do you never look anything but elegant?"

"Not if I can help it," Mr. Carstairs replied firmly. "Come on now. Another ten minutes and we shall turn back."

His chestnut mare and his friend's grey gelding were now picking their way daintily between snow-rimed heather bushes.

"I must have this ride cleared as soon as

it thaws," muttered Richard. "I don't come up here very often, and my agent seems to have . . . What's that?"

Standing in his stirrups, he pointed at a blue grey heap half hidden by a gorse thicket to one side of the path. Tony peered in that direction but had no answer.

"Here, hold my reins while I investigate." Richard dismounted and strode toward the bundle, which revealed itself as a motionless figure.

"Good Lord, Tony, it's a female! What the devil . . . ?"

Lord Denham hastily dismounted and, leading their horses, made his way among the snowy tussocks of grass to where his friend stooped over a huddled form.

"Dead?" he queried succinctly.

"I don't believe so," said Richard Carstairs, as he gently turned her over. "But look, she's been hit on the head."

The brown-stained hood of the girl's blue grey cloak had fallen back, revealing a deathly pale face with a red crescent on the temple. Her copper-colored hair was matted with blood, and the snow where her head had lain was crimson.

"Horse kicked her," proposed Tony. "The snow is all trampled around. Must have taken fright at something."

"You could be right. It must have been a glancing blow or she'd not be alive now. She has bled a lot though, and we cannot guess how long she has been lying here. Let's get her home quickly."

He mounted and held out his arms to receive the young woman. As Tony laid her in them, she moaned. Her eyes opened and she looked up into Richard's face. Her body tensed, her lips parted and she seemed to want to speak, then she was limp again, eyes closed. If it were not for the slight rise and fall of her breast, he would have thought her dead.

"Do you ride ahead, Tony, and warn my mother. She must send for Dr. Grimsdale and prepare a chamber."

"A guest room?" asked Lord Denham.

"How the devil should I know?" was the impatient reply.

Tony raised his eyebrows, but said no more.

Richard Carstairs, walking the mare so as not to jolt his burden, studied the girl in his arms. A thin face, a little too long for beauty, soft, delicate lips contrasting oddly with a strong chin. Red gold hair, where it was not sticky brown with blood, pulled back smoothly from a high forehead, but trying to escape at the sides. Her eyes, he

13

thought, grey or green? Odd, I don't remember. About twenty-six or twenty-seven, he decided.

He transferred his gaze to her clothes. The cloak was thick and warm, but old-fashioned and a little shabby. One leather glove, too large, probably a man's. Where had she lost the other? The ungloved hand was square and capable, but with long sensitive fingers. It did not seem to be work roughened. Icy cold. He somehow managed, with his one free hand, to remove his own glove and work her hand into it.

She wore a riding dress and leather boots, again shabby, though they had once been of good quality. Probably a lady, then, unless they were castoffs. Perhaps she was a governess. Guest room or servants' quarters? He'd leave his mother to decide, he thought, impatient now with himself.

He bent his mind to a more significant question. What had she been doing riding alone on the moor, and so early in the morning? Judging by the tracks, her horse had galloped off by itself after throwing her. He wondered briefly whether he should send someone to search for it. It could be miles away now, heading for home. Where had she come from and where was she going? He knew most of the

14

families in the West Riding and he was certain he'd never met this girl. She must have ridden far.

There was no way to find out the answers until the young woman woke. Richard pondered more practical problems. What was his mother going to say? She was planning to leave for London in a week's time, weather permitting, to introduce his young sister to Society. A smile lit his eyes as he remembered Lucy's excited planning for her first Season, her endless questions and her attempts to practise behaving as a young lady should. Well, doubtless she would be equally excited by the surprise he was carrying home, but the unknown girl must not be allowed to spoil his mother's plans. For a moment he almost wished he had not seen her cloak, obscured as it had been by the bushes. Then he looked at her white face as she rested so helplessly in his arms, and could only be glad that he had forced Tony to ride those few furlongs farther.

His left arm, supporting her shoulders, was growing numb, and he shifted a little to ease it. The movement brought another moan, though the girl did not rouse. Damn, he thought, she must have injured her back. Thank heaven we are nearly there.

15

They had passed the home farm, and Richard could see the slate roofs of the village of Toblethorpe in the valley below, streamers of smoke rising straight from the chimneys. The drystone wall of the park was on his left, winding along the lane down the treeless hillside. The gates were open and old Matthew Braithwaite stood at the door of the gatehouse, scratching his head.

"Eh, lad," he said, "it's a graidely mornin', an' thy gran' Lunnon friend in such a hurry he near jumped t'wall a'fore I could open. 'Leave it for Mr. Richard,' he says, so open it be yet, sir. Should I be a-closin' of it now?"

"No, Matt, there will be more coming and going shortly. You may leave it as it is. Did someone ride for the doctor already?"

"Nay, Master Richard, but here come Jem now. He'll be after t'doctor, I daresay. Is tha hurt then, Master Richard?"

"Not I. We have found a young lady injured in an accident on the moor."

"Oh, aye. That be who tha has in thy arms, then. Come, Jem!" the old gatekeeper shouted, "there's a wee bitty lady hurt hersen up t'moor. Tha mun ride faster, lad."

"Hush thy noise, Matthew!" cried the

16

young groom. "Mornin', sir. I be off after t'sawbones." He dashed past and down the lane on the big cob, obviously delighted with the urgency of his errand.

The carriage drive led around the side of the hill and approached Toblethorpe Manor from the west. The steep slope to the north protected the old stone house from winter winds and provided shelter for a wood of chestnuts and beeches, now leafless, which had been planted by Richard's great-grandfather. The weathered limestone looked warm and cheerful in the low rays of the eastern sun, and smoke pouring from many chimneys promised snug warmth inside.

Wide steps led up to the massive front door, and on them stood a lissome brunette of seventeen, shivering in a thin wrap. Seeing her brother ride around the corner of the house, Lucy raced toward him in a most unladylike manner.

"Richard, who is it? Is she badly hurt? Mama is having the Blue Room prepared, and she sent Jem for Dr. Grimsdale. Tony — I mean Lord Denham — was practically incoherent when he arrived. It was so funny!" She giggled, and then stood on tiptoe and peeked at her brother's burden.

17

"Oh!" she gasped, "she is so pale! Come, bring her into the house quickly."

"If you would hold the horse while I pass her to Tony, I might be able to do so," said her exasperated brother. "Get out of the way, chit."

Lucy pouted but obeyed. Lord Denham hurried down the steps to help and soon the injured girl lay on a sofa in the drawing room before a roaring fire, while the butler, a footman and two maids hovered, oohing and aahing

"Bedford, where is my mother?" Richard demanded of the butler, who came to his senses, shooed the other servants out, and replied with unimpaired stateliness.

"I believe she is instructing Mrs. Bedford concerning the preparations to be made for the young lady, sir. I will inform her of your return."

Richard knelt by the sofa and drew the gloves from the cold hands. Lucy was busy unlacing the boots.

"Come help me, Tony, er . . . Lord Denham," she ordered.

"Very well, Lucy, er . . . Miss Carstairs," answered Tony obediently. She looked at him suspiciously, but his face was straight.

Richard chafed the icy hands of the unconscious girl. Already the warmth of the room seemed to be having an effect. A tinge of color, barely perceptible, crept into the white cheeks. She opened her eyes (grey-green, he thought, like the sea) and gazed up at him.

"Where am I?" she whispered.

"Oh, just like a novel!" crowed Lucy and clapped her hands.

The girl looked at her with a puzzled frown, then at Tony and back to Richard.

"Who are you?" she asked painfully. "I don't understand . . . What has happened? My head hurts so." She raised one hand to her forehead, and Richard hastily released the other, which he was still holding.

"My name is Richard Carstairs. This is my sister, and a friend, Lord Denham. You are safe at my house, Toblethorpe Manor."

"But why am I here? I was . . . How did I get here?"

"We found you on the moor, near Daws Fell. You had had an accident. We think your horse must have thrown you and kicked you."

Lucy pressed forward.

"Who are you? Where did you come from? Why were you on the moor so early?"

The girl looked at her blankly.

"Hush your chattering, child," commanded Richard. He turned back to the girl. "We must inform your family of your whereabouts," he said gently. "What is your name?"

She looked up at him helplessly, a sudden fear in her eyes.

"I . . . don't know. I don't understand. Who . . . who am I?"

Richard frowned.

"Where do you come from? Where is your home?"

"I can't remember. I can't remember anything."

Chapter 2

It was nearly noon when the family at last gathered in the breakfast room. Dr. Grimsdale had come and gone. His diagnosis had been exhaustion, loss of blood, and exposure, which might lead to an inflammation of the lungs. The only evidence of concussion was amnesia.

"There's no telling how long it may last," he had declared with unwonted loquacity. "Such total loss of memory is rare. Occasionally it may clear up spontaneously, but usually some encounter with a familiar person or object or situation is the only hope. There is no way we can deliberately bring that about, so we shall have to rely on time and chance."

Richard had mentioned a possible back injury.

"No, nothing serious," replied the doctor. "Considerable bruising, I would guess from a recent severe beating. No sign of previous beatings. Such things usually leave permanent marks."

Dr. Grimsdale had left a sleeping

draught and a concoction to be administered in case of fever. The stranger slept deeply, watched over by Lucy's old nurse.

Richard and Tony sat down to plates piled high with ham and eggs, kidneys, muffins and smoked haddock. Their hot chocolate at dawn seemed long ago. Lucy's plate was only slightly less heaped, but Lady Annabel contented herself with a piece of toast and a cup of weak tea.

"Lucy, my dear," she protested, "it is most unladylike to eat such an amount."

"But, mama, I am so hungry. You would not have me starve, I am sure." Her mother sighed.

"Richard," she said, "I cannot continue to refer to the young woman above stairs as 'the young woman above stairs.' We must decide what to call her before I can discuss the matter any further."

"Clarissa!" cried Lucy. "She is just like the heroine of a novel."

"I cannot think it necessary to provide her with a Christian name that she might well dislike excessively," reproved her brother. "For the present a surname will be adequate. Any suggestions, Tony?"

Lord Denham disposed of a mouthful of muffin. "What was the name of that place where we found her?"

"Daws Fell."

"Why not call her Miss Daws, or perhaps Miss Fell?"

"Such dull names," protested Lucy.

"Lucy!" Lady Annabel called her wayward daughter to order. "Either name seems unexceptionable, Lord Denham."

"Clarissa Daws, that sounds so common," remarked the irrepressible Lucy, considering the choice. "Clarissa Fell has a more . . . a more romantic sound."

"Miss Fell let it be then," decided Richard, "but I beg you will drop 'Clarissa.' Well, mama, now you are able to put a name to 'the young woman above stairs,' let us by all means discuss the situation."

"I cannot fault you, Richard, for rescuing Miss Fell, but it does complicate our plans. Lucy and I must go to London next week or there will be no time to order new clothes before the first parties of the Season. We have already received invitations, you know, as I informed dear Maria Allenby of Lucy's coming out, and she is the greatest gossip in town."

"I would not for the world have you alter your plans, mama. I think Lucy would never speak to me again."

"But Miss Fell is very ill and needs a great deal of care, and how can I leave a young lady alone in the house with only the servants?"

"We do not know that she is a lady. Certainly her clothes would suggest otherwise. I suspect she may be a governess or something of the sort."

"No, Richard, how can you be so prosaic," said Lord Denham, grinning. "I am sure Miss Carstairs has recognized in Miss Fell a princess in disguise, or at the least, the daughter of a duke."

"You are teasing, my lord," said Lucy crossly. "Richard, I do not wish to seem unfeeling, but I could not bear it if my first Season were to be spoiled. I have been waiting seventeen years for this moment."

"I shall send for Florence," declared Lady Annabel in a voice that announced the ultimate solution.

"Do you think my aunt would come?" queried Richard. "I cannot like asking her to nurse a stranger who, after all, was found in the most ambiguous circumstances."

"I shall not ask her to do any nursing. I hope my housekeeper and Nurse are capable of that! Your Aunt Florence has often mentioned to me how she would enjoy being invited to an empty house for once, with no necessity for entertaining or being entertained. Of course, she was funning," (Richard and Lucy here exchanged speaking glances: Miss Florence Carstairs had never been known to joke) "yet I am sure she would find it restful after living in my brother-in-law's house with his six children."

"I daresay you are right as always, mama. Jem can ride to Arnden with a note and return with an answer tomorrow so that we may arrange the matter. If all goes well, I shall return here after escorting you to London, to check that everything is in order."

"You'll not persuade me to accompany you again, especially with your sister settled in London," said Lord Denham. "Miss Carstairs, if you are not occupied elsewhere, perhaps you would favor me with a stroll around the shrubbery. I believe the sun has dried the grass, and I find myself recovered from my enforced early ride."

"I shall be delighted, my lord," replied Lucy demurely.

At that moment the butler entered and bent to murmur in Lady Annabel's ear.

"Oh dear!" she exclaimed, "Miss Fell is in a fever and Nurse wants my advice. Lucy, wrap up well if you are going out. Richard, pray do not leave the house for a while, I must speak with you. Lord Denham, do not let my daughter become a nuisance."

"Mama! I am not a child anymore. You must not speak so," said Lucy in indignation.

"I beg your pardon, dearest. It is difficult to remember that you are a young lady already."

"Behave like a young lady or you shall not be treated as one, Lucy," threatened Richard with a grin, and a wink at Lord Denham.

Lucy cast him a darkling glance and flounced out of the room on his lordship's arm.

"Oh dear, Richard," said Lady Annabel with a sigh, "I do not believe I shall ever teach her to behave as Society will expect."

"Come, mama, you would not wish her to be missish or tongue-tied. Do not let her worry you, she will be a great success."

"Indeed I hope so. Well, I had better see how Miss Fell does."

"I will be in the library when you want me. I beg you will not let Miss Fell worry you, either. I could wish her in China!"

Lady Annabel smiled up at her tall son and patted his cheek. As she left the room, she was thinking that her biggest problem was not her daughter, nor even the stranger who had appeared in her household so unceremoniously. She hoped Richard did not know how much he worried her.

Lady Annabel, in her late forties, was still as blond as she had been when she had caught the eye of Mr. Christopher Carstairs during her second Season. Her husband had had light brown hair and a ruddy complexion; her father, Lord Mortlake, had been as blond as his daughter, but her mother had been an Italian contessa, dark as a Gypsy. Both Lady Annabel's children had taken after their grandmother. Lucy was a glowing brunette, Richard so dark-skinned he could have passed as a savage from the colonies. He had been a happy child, mischievous but not difficult, and then at the age of thirteen he had been sent away to school. She was still not very clear as to exactly what had happened. She and Kit had been absorbed in their newborn daughter, a miracle after so many barren years. And then Kit had been killed hunting. It still hurt her to think of the dreadful moment when they had borne his body home on a hurdle.

Richard had been at Eton for two years before she had realized that something was seriously wrong. The charming small boy had become a withdrawn adolescent, hiding his hurts under an arrogance justified to himself by pride in his family and birth. A lecture on manners, after he had been insolent to a neighbor, had led to an agonizing session during which she learned that he had been christened "the Indian" by the older schoolboys and ostracized by his fellows.

She had suggested that he finish his studies under a tutor. But the tall, painfully thin boy with the haunted eyes had told her, "The Carstairs do not run away."

After another year of misery, his last two years at the school had been not unhappy, she thought. Richard had proved himself highly successful in both studies and sports and had at last made a few friends. But the damage had been done. He found it difficult to socialize, and the idea that had saved him, the importance of birth and breeding, was too much a part of him to be relinquished.

Three years at Cambridge and a couple

of seasons in London under the aegis of his uncle, Lord Mortlake, had smoothed the corners of his character. He was able to hold his own in any society, though he relaxed only among close friends and family. His essential arrogance was blunted by courtesy, but it was not diminished, nor, indeed, would Lord Mortlake, a high stickler, have approved of anything less. He had introduced his nephew to the ton and made sure that he frequented only the best society. He had watched indulgently as the young man had gone through the usual discreet liaisons with opera dancers, but when Richard had seemed to be attracted by a most ineligible young person, the daughter of some obscure country gentry, he had promptly nipped the affair in the bud.

Not that it was necessary. Richard was perfectly aware of the unsuitability, and was merely being kind to the distant cousin of a particular crony.

Lady Annabel could not complain that Richard was not kind. He was a perfect son and brother and always ready to come to the aid of anyone in distress. He spent a good deal of time at home, supervising and improving his estate, and was on easy, though far from intimate, terms with the neighbors. He had friends to stay occasionally, especially Lord Denham, and went visiting in the hunting season. Lady Annabel would be perfectly satisfied with him for months at a time.

Yet she had listened in repressed horror as he had discussed cold-bloodedly whether Miss Fell were well born or not, as if it were the only important point, as if she were not desperately ill a few feet above his head. Hurrying up the stairs, she wondered what revelations lay in store for her in London. She had not seen her son in Society, and rather dreaded the prospect. Finding a husband for Lucy, she suspected, would be a far easier task than finding a bride who would satisfy her son's stringent requirements as to birth. She did not begin to know what he might expect in the way of beauty or character. However, she was determined to find a wife for him. Her mother's eye had pierced the shell of self-sufficiency surrounding him and saw within the loneliness and lack of assurance that were so well masked by his arrogance.

"He must marry," she decided, "and he must marry for love."

The door of the Blue Bedchamber was ajar. It had not warranted its name for years, being decorated in cheerful yellow and russet. The bed hangings of buttercup silk were pulled back, and Nurse was sitting on the edge of the bed, bathing with lavender water the hot face that tossed and turned on the rumpled pillow. She rose and bobbed a curtsy as her mistress entered.

"She'm bin this way a half-hour, my lady. So quiet and still as she was to start, then all of a suddenlike she were a-mutterin' away, an' the flush come to her face. I give her the doctor's medicine, but it don't seem to do no good."

"What did she say?" asked Lady Annabel eagerly.

"Well, I can't rightly tell you, my lady. I couldna make out the words till she cried out: 'Oh pray, uncle, don't!' then she were incohairem again."

Lady Annabel sat down and felt the burning forehead, careful not to touch the court plaster on the left temple.

"Nurse, have Mrs. Bedford tell Cook to make some barley water."

"Indeed, my lady, that Cook is a great ignomalous. Them furriners don't know how to prepare a nice barley water for a sick young lady. I better make it wi' my own two han's."

"Now, Nurse, you know how upset

Monsieur Pierre gets if anyone invades his kitchen. Just give the message to Mrs. Bedford, and then I will need your help here. You had better call one of the maids; Mary will do."

"Very well, my lady. As you says." Nurse heaved a heavy sigh and went on her errand.

Lady Annabel was at last able to turn her full attention to the patient. The thin face was not that of a young girl. The red hair and firm chin suggested a certain strength of character, belied by sensitive lips and fluttering hands. "Miss Fell" was breathing fast and shallow, painfully, and seemed to be growing too weak to continue her restless motion. Suddenly Lady Annabel realized she might die and wondered if somewhere her mother were waiting for her, praying for news of her. How would she herself feel if Lucy disappeared and fell sick among strangers? She resolved that unless the young woman was truly out of danger, Lucy must go to her Aunt Blanche for the start of the Season. She and her Cousin Jennifer would probably live in each other's pockets anyway.

Nurse returned with Mary, followed by Richard.

"May I come in, mama? I wanted to see

how you go on." He caught sight of the sick girl and was alarmed to see how the already thin features were hollowed out. The hectic flush was fading; for a moment it presented almost a picture of health, then the face was pallid again, the brow bedewed, and Miss Fell's body was seized with uncontrollable shivering.

Her eyes opened, appearing huge in the wasted face.

"Cold," she whispered, "I'm so cold."

"Since you are here, dearest, do you lift Miss Fell so that the bedding may be changed."

Richard picked her up gently and Lady Annabel tucked a blanket around her while Nurse and Mary remade the bed. The burden seemed pounds lighter than when he had carried her on horseback. He gazed down into her face, then raised his eyes to his mother.

"Will she live?"

"I do not know. We must do the best we can, but now that the fever has broken there is little to be done. Do not look so despairing, Richard, there is yet hope."

"I feel responsible for her, I suppose because I found her. She is so . . . helpless."

He had felt the same, thought his mother, at the age of twelve when he had

33

saved a puppy from drowning and nursed the feeble thing back to health.

The housekeeper came in with warm barley water. Richard propped Miss Fell up with his arm while Lady Annabel held the glass to her lips. She had scarcely strength enough for a few swallows.

"I will watch her for a while, Nurse. You had better get some rest, there may be a long night ahead. Mrs. Bedford, I will send for you when I need you. Richard, I cannot talk with you now."

"Mama, I shall ride up to the moors and see if I can learn anything from the horse's tracks. We were in too great a hurry to consider it before, but there may be some clue."

"Certainly, dear. I suppose Lucy will keep Lord Denham tolerably entertained."

Miss Fell's gaze followed Richard as he left the room. In this nightmare into which she had woken, his dark face, constantly recurring, was a landmark to which she clung. It was the first thing she could remember seeing, the only thing that stood out in a haze of other faces, coming and going. She was too tired to think about it, too tired to try to understand what was happening, too tired to sleep, but too tired to keep her eyes open. As they closed she felt as if she were sinking into a dark whirl-pool that sucked her down and down. Someone took her hand in a firm, gentle clasp; it seemed far away; she must hold on or she would drown in the blackness that grasped and pulled at her.

Lady Annabel sat by the bed in a rocking chair, the cold, still hand clasped in both hers. She had felt the feeble, desperate clutch, and though the girl's hand was limp now, she would not let it go. The winter sun sank in the west, its ruddy rays turning the silk draperies to flame.

"Like her hair," Lady Annabel thought drowsily.

Lucy peeked in and, seeing that all was quiet, went to warn everyone to stay away. Richard had told her that her heroine might not live, and the sight of the pale face so still on the pillow was enough to suppress her usual exuberance.

At dusk Mrs. Bedford brought the doctor. The sound of their arrival roused Lady Annabel, who had been dozing. Miss Fell lay motionless, but a slow pulse beat at the base of her throat. Dr. Grimsdale laid his hand on her forehead and took her pulse.

"Sleeping," he grunted. "She'll do. To tell the truth, I'm surprised. Must have an excellent constitution. Main thing now is to keep her strength up."

He changed the dressing on her head. The cut was already showing signs of healing, though there was a dark bruise and some swelling.

"I'll drop in in the morning," he said as he left. "She should sleep all night, but someone should watch. Try and get her to drink some broth this evening even if you have to wake her. She's half starved and very weak."

The housekeeper went to fetch Nurse and Lady Annabel hurried to tell the others the good news. She found them in the music room gathered round the piano-forte, singing mournful ballads about death and forsaken lovers. The result was not entirely felicitous. Lucy's playing style ran more to verve than to sensitivity or accuracy; and while Richard's light baritone sounded pleasantly, the fervor of Lord Denham's tenor did not make up for his inability to carry a tune.

Richard noticed his mother's entrance and broke off in the middle of a plea for branches of yew to be strewn on his coffin.

"Mama! You look happy! What is the news?"

"Oh, my musical children, Miss Fell is

sleeping and Dr. Grimsdale considers her out of danger, though still very ill and weak."

Richard felt as if he had unknowingly been holding his breath for hours and was only now able to breathe freely again. Lucy, frozen at the piano, relaxed with a small sigh, and Tony turned to inquire, "Then may I stop singing these dreadful songs?"

"Mama, that is wonderful!" cried Lucy, throwing her arms about Lady Annabel and giving her a hug. "You must know that Richard would have us indulge in music because he said I looked as though I were going into a decline. But I could not bear to play anything cheerful while Clarissa was dying upstairs."

"Not 'Clarissa,'" groaned Richard, and they all laughed as if he had voiced the wittiest of bon-mots.

Lady Annabel caught sight of the clock on the mantel.

"Oh dear, it is past five, and I suppose Cook will have prepared dinner for six o'clock as usual. Lucy, we must dress immediately. Richard, you shall tell me at dinner what you found on the moor. Excuse us, Lord Denham."

The two young men were left alone for a

moment, occupied in closing the pianoforte and putting away the music books.

"Tony, I really must apologize for the musical interlude. It was all I could think of to distract my sister."

"It is for me to apologize, Richard. You are a musical family, and I cannot hold a note. Lucy plays as charmingly as she smiles."

"Indeed, if you think so you are undoubtedly tone-deaf. She does well enough with a gig or a hornpipe, but she mangles anything requiring sensitivity of touch!"

"Oh, you are an expert. I sometimes think we should never see you in London were it not for the concerts and the opera. I insist, for us tyros who enjoy a good tune, Miss Carstairs does an excellent job."

Laughing, Richard led the way upstairs.

Some thirty minutes later, the party assembled in the small salon. Lucy pointed out to her mother a bowl of snowdrops she had picked that afternoon.

"May I put them in Miss Fell's chamber?" she asked. "Flowers always make me cheerful, and I am sure she needs them more than anyone."

"I cannot promise she will notice them, Lucy, but you may take them to her this evening."

The dinner gong rang. Lord Denham gave his arm to Lady Annabel, and Lucy followed with Richard. He offered her his arm, and she was about to refuse scornfully when she saw the twinkle in his eye and remembered what he had said earlier. Mindful of her mother's lessons, she inclined her head regally and laid her fingers lightly on his sleeve. Then she looked up inquiringly into his face, so much like a sparrow that he laughed and patted her hand.

"Excellent," he approved. "Almost I think you are ready for London."

Monsieur Pierre had outdone himself in honour of the noble guest, a noted gourmet. *Caneton à l'orange* followed braised kidneys in white wine, Brussels sprouts au gratin succeeded a succulent sirloin surrounded with elaborate side dishes. Richard noted with amusement that Lucy confined herself to small helpings of a few dishes and ended her meal with an apple, which she delicately peeled and sliced instead of munching it down to the core. The child was really trying.

"Come, Lucy," he said, "time enough to stop eating when you get to Town." He cut her a large slice of gooseberry tart and piled it with whipped cream. Throwing him a grateful look, she demolished it rapidly.

The ladies left the gentlemen to their brandy. Lord Denham, replete, suppressed a belch and remarked, "My mother was always on at m'sisters about their appetites. Of course they did put on weight easily, especially poor Agnes. But your sister don't seem to, mustn't let her waste away just to be fashionable."

"Oh, if I know Lucy, she will spend half her time pestering the cook for bread and jam. She had as lief eat that as anything."

"No, how can you say so?" exclaimed Tony, revolted by such philistinism. "Pretty girl like Miss Carstairs should live on strawberries and cream."

"She would if she had the chance," said her brother cynically. "I remember when she was twelve . . ."

"Devil take it, Richard," protested his lordship, "don't ruin any more illusions! Let us join the ladies."

Meanwhile, Lucy had carried the bowl of snowdrops up to the Blue Room. Nurse was knitting in the rocker, and Miss Fell appeared to be sleeping peacefully.

"How is she?" whispered Lucy.

"The better for your asking, dearie," said the old woman. "Brought some flowers, have you then? Proper cheers the place up, don't they?"

Lucy hung over the bed, examining the patient.

"She's still awfully pale, Nurse."

"Well, Miss Lucy, as I hear it, she'm lost a mint o' blood. Takes a while to make it up, it do. Now, you go tell my lady as Miss Fell be doin' fine. Me and Mrs. Bedford'll give her some o' that there comsonny broth in a while."

"I believe mama wishes to be here when Miss Fell awakes. I expect she will come up shortly. Do you wait for her."

"Right you are, dearie."

When Lucy returned to the drawing room, Lady Annabel was sitting at the desk, writing the letter to her sister-in-law that she had not had time for earlier in the day. Richard and Tony were setting up a game of backgammon.

"Lucy, will you come and play with Tony? I must talk with mama. Do not let her off easily, Tony, she plays excellently, much better than at the piano."

Uncertain whether to be more pleased at the compliment than indignant at the slur, Lucy ignored him pointedly and sat down to play. Richard pulled up a chair beside Lady Annabel and said in a low voice,

41

"The longer I consider this situation, the more difficulties I foresee. Even supposing that my aunt will come, and that Miss Fell recovers quickly, what do we do then? Of course, she may suddenly regain her memory, but Dr. Grimsdale seemed to think it unlikely."

"I have thought about it, dearest," said his mother. "When Miss Fell is strong enough, she shall join us in London. There will be far more chance in town of her meeting someone who recognizes her. I suppose you found no clue on the moor as to her origin?"

"No, mama. The sun had melted all the snow, and the ground was hard as a rock, so there were no tracks. You are right, of course, about the possibility of her being recognized in London, though that is only true if she is fit to go about in Society. Even if that is so, it will be most awkward to introduce to the ton someone who has no family or background and whose name even is unknown. This is a devilish coil! Excuse me, mama."

"I shall introduce her as the daughter of an old school friend. She is not of an age to be formally brought out, but she may perhaps be able to chaperone Lucy. I am sure there will be occasions when I had rather not accompany her, and Richard, I do not think I am partial when I say that I expect it will not be long before Lucy is sought in marriage. Of course, it is what one most wishes for one's daughter, but I shall be sadly lonely without her. Miss Fell may yet turn out to be the perfect companion for an old woman."

"Mama, I will not have you put yourself out so for a stranger with no claims upon you. I am sure we will be able to find a post as a governess, or something of the sort, for the young woman."

"Indeed, dear, since I sat with her this afternoon I feel toward her as to a daughter. It is true that we cannot yet know aught of her character, but she has a sweet face."

"She does, does she not? I wish . . . no matter. I cannot like it that she was riding alone on the moor, and at night. I can think of no explanation that will satisfy the requirements of respectability. Miss Fell is probably a thieving abigail or the like!"

With these harsh words, Richard rose and began pacing up and down before the fireplace. Every time he saw the girl, or pictured her face, he was conscious only of a desire to protect her. Yet as soon as he considered her situation and the problems it seemed likely to precipitate, he was certain that she could be no lady. He felt that in some subtle way she was taking advantage of him and his family; then her sea green eyes swam before his vision, lost and frightened, and he despised himself. He resolved to put her out of his mind as much as possible. Surely further acquaintance would resolve his dilemma. He went to watch the backgammon game.

Lady Annabel had studied the play of emotions on her son's face and interpreted them with fair accuracy. She sighed gently. It had been easier with the puppy. Since it was an obvious mongrel, there had been no question about its place in Society.

She finished her letter, signed and sealed it, and rang the bell. When Bedford came, she instructed him to give it to Jem, who must leave at dawn to ride to Arnden and wait there for an answer.

"I shall go to Miss Fell now," she said; "See that the broth is brought to her room. When I come downstairs again, you may bring in the tea."

"Very well, my lady." The butler bowed and left, and with a word to the players, Lady Annabel followed.

Her return, half an hour later, went unnoticed for a few moments. She paused in the doorway and saw Richard and Lucy helpless with laughter and Lord Denham considering them with the smirk of a raconteur whose story has met with unexpected success. He was the first to notice Lady Annabel's presence and he rose from his chair.

"You must excuse us, ma'am. Had I known these two were so easily amused, I'd not have tried to cheer them up."

Lady Annabel advanced with a smile.

"Oh, mama," cried Lucy, gasping for breath, "he is so funny. He must tell you . . ."

"No, no, Miss Carstairs. It has been my experience that a story repeated so soon always falls flat. You cannot desire me to spoil my reputation."

Bedford brought in the tea tray, and as Lady Annabel poured, she told them of Miss Fell's progress.

"I truly think that she has taken no harm from lying in the snow. She was half asleep, but she drank all the broth one could wish. She is so weak from loss of blood and exhaustion that her recovery is bound to be slow; however, I don't think we need fear for her."

Chapter 3

Morning brought Dr. Grimsdale, who agreed absolutely with Lady Annabel's prognosis. His one warning was that Miss Fell must not be worried about her loss of memory.

"Time enough to discuss that when she is stronger," he advised. "I am sure, ma'am, you will know how to reassure her, should she ask any questions. I shall not call again unless I am sent for."

Miss Fell had breakfasted on some more of Monsieur Pierre's *consommé* — to call it broth was an insult — and was now lying drowsily in that state between sleeping and waking where all one's problems vanish in a haze of half-dreaming fantasy. She was warm and comfortable; her hurts were fading; and the fact that she did not recognize the motherly woman who appeared now and then to check on her, seemed unimportant. Floating in sunshine, she was at peace.

The sunshine was an illusion produced by firelight on her chamber's yellow hang-

46

ings. It was in fact a grey day, with a damp blustery wind blowing fitfully from the west, the sort of wind that after a spell of hard frost can make spring seem possible even in February. Lucy and Lord Denham had decided to ride after breakfast. Richard, occupied by business with his agent, was unable to accompany them. His mother, busy about the tasks that fall to the lot of the lady of the house in even the best-run establishments, found time between consultations with Cook and instructions to Mrs. Bedford to look in periodically on Miss Fell. So much improved was she that Nurse, who had spent the night on a trundle bed in her room, was sent home to the cottage she managed for her widowed brother-in-law.

In the library, Richard was discussing lambing with Jeremy Denison, the young man to whom he entrusted his estate during his absences. Jeremy, the younger son of a younger son of distant relatives of the Carstairs, worshiped his employer. Some three years before, coming down from Oxford with no prospects, he had been enabled by the offer of his present position to exchange the probability of solitary penury for a comfortable, spacious cottage and marriage to his childhood sweetheart. They now had two small children, and in their eyes Mr. Carstairs could do no wrong, though he was a demanding master. He was always ready to try new farming methods and expected his agent's knowledge and understanding to equal his own. The problems of his tenants must be dealt with immediately, and the land must be cared for constantly and thoroughly.

Toblethorpe Manor had belonged to the Carstairs family for generations. It was mentioned in the Domesday Book as a gift from William I to Sieur Reynald de Carresteyr, knighted on the field at Hastings. The family records were incomplete, having suffered during both the Wars of the Roses and the Civil War, but it seemed likely that the property had descended from father to son in unbroken line until the reign of Charles I, when Sir Roger Carstairs, who had no heir, had died fighting for the king. The manor was inherited by a cousin, and the title was lost under the Commonwealth, yet how many families in England could trace their ancestry half as far! Dukes themselves appeared upstarts viewed from such a perspective. Perhaps Richard did not consider himself superior, at least in birth, to many dukes, but he had good reason for his pride of family.

Such things were far from his mind at present. Jeremy had just given him some most unwelcome news.

"Sir Philip?" he groaned. "Not that business of the thirty-acre field again! How did he know I was returned, Jeremy?"

"Oh, the usual gossipers, sir. You know how news travels. I tried to persuade him that you would be too busy to receive him, being here for so short a period, but he is one who will not take no for an answer. I fear you must see him, unless you smuggle yourself out the back way."

"What, and meet his groom on the way to the stables? I had almost rather give the fellow the land than be persecuted every time I show my nose in Yorkshire!"

"You are not serious, sir! That field has been in the family since 1587."

"I bow to your superior knowledge, Jeremy. You shall stay and support me through this trial. It is eleven o'clock. I suppose he will be here on time at least."

Twenty minutes later Bedford appeared to announce, with deep disapproval, Sir Philip Rossiter, and received permission to show him into the library.

Sir Philip was a stout gentleman in his early forties who affected a bluff heartiness that accorded ill with his sly, rather porcine eyes. His wife, a meek, faded woman, was much pitied in the area both because of his bullying and his notorious womanizing in town, whither he repaired alone every winter. However, since his conduct was otherwise unexceptionable, if unattractive, and he did not bring his libertinage into his home county, he was everywhere received with the complaisance due his baronetcy and his large fortune.

For some months Sir Philip had been trying to persuade Richard to sell him some land that he had decided was necessary to his estate. Not only would he not accept repeated refusals, he was becoming increasingly abusive and had recently threatened to go to law, a step for which he had absolutely no justification. He obviously hoped that the prospect of a lengthy, troublesome and expensive lawsuit would change Richard's mind.

Richard, however, had been assured by his lawyer that the case would be thrown out of court without a hearing, so the threat did not dismay him in the least. In fact, he would welcome such a definite decision if only to enable him to escape the constant visits of a man whom he could find no reason to like or admire. He was unwilling simply to refuse to see him, as he would be bound to meet him at the houses of his neighbors and would not for the world embarrass them, so he was forced to endure the unwelcome attentions and rudeness with what patience he could muster.

This morning Sir Philip seemed in a good humour, though his hard eyes belied the expression on the rest of his face. Always inquisitive, he had heard rumours that distracted him momentarily from his more serious purpose.

After greeting Richard and pointedly ignoring Jeremy, as beneath his notice, he continued, "So, Mr. Carstairs, what is this I hear of your finding some female on Daws Fell? Pretty chit, is she? Perhaps I'll take her off your hands."

"The young lady is very ill," said Richard shortly, suppressing his disgust. Whatever his own feelings about Miss Fell's origins, he would not expose her to the attentions of this gross rake. Then, remembering his mother's suggestion, he added, "She is the daughter of an old friend of Lady Annabel's. She was on her way to visit us when she had an accident."

"Strange that she should come alone on horseback, and at this season," mused Sir

Philip, "and Lady Annabel about to leave for Town." He wondered what Richard was concealing.

Richard did not feel it necessary to answer. Almost with relief, he turned to the business of the sale, or rather the non-sale, of the thirty-acre field. Sir Philip's assumed good humour vanished, and Richard and Jeremy spent a very unpleasant half-hour before their visitor took his leave in a furious temper.

As he left, Lord Denham strolled in.

"Phew!" he said, "was that Rossiter? I was prepared to find a couple of dead bodies in here. You could hear him in the front hall."

"Let's forget him," proposed Richard firmly. "I am in need of sustenance. Jeremy, will you join us for luncheon? I have worked you hard this morning and you must have breakfasted even earlier than I."

The butler appeared miraculously with sherry.

"Luncheon will be served shortly, sir."

"Ah, Bedford, sometimes I think you read my mind. Tony, where is my sister? You did not lose her on the moors, I trust?"

"One female lost in that wasteland is

enough for a lifetime! Miss Carstairs decided to sit awhile with Miss Fell, I believe. She is a most intrepid rider; I was hard put to keep up."

"There speaks the man who broke the London to Brighton record not three years ago. You grow old, Tony. Indeed, Lucy is a neck-or-nothing rider. I know my mother expects her to be brought home with a broken neck any day, but it is dull here for a girl her age, and I cannot bring myself to forbid her to ride."

"I daresay she would not obey you if you did," replied Lord Denham, amused. "She has a strong will of her own." Then, hastily turning the subject, he commented on the excellence of the sherry.

"Jeremy is in charge of my cellars, in addition to all the other duties I pile on his shoulders."

"Superb, Mr. Denison. Where did you find this?"

"My uncle is in the wine trade, my lord. The family has second choice, after his most favored customers."

"That is why Jeremy is in charge of my cellars," said Richard smugly.

Lucy and Lady Annabel were awaiting the gentlemen in the breakfast room. A cold collation was spread on the buffet, and Lucy, after her exertions of the morning, forgot her good resolutions and helped herself to a huge plateful. Noting her mother's reproving look, she apologized.

"I'm sorry, mama, but I am simply ravenous. We rode for miles, and then seeing Clarissa — Miss Fell — take only a cup of soup made me even hungrier. Richard, I helped Mrs. Bedford feed Miss Fell and then I read poetry to her. She fell asleep," she added ingenuously.

The gentlemen laughed.

"What did you read her, Miss Lucy? Not Cowper, I trust, for then it is no wonder she fell asleep."

"Well, Jeremy, I did not think Macbeth suitable."

Mr. Denison, whose devotion to the bard was a byword, gracefully accepted the laughter directed this time at him.

In the afternoon, Richard and Jeremy rode out to inspect the flocks and call on one or two tenant farmers. Lord Denham was persuaded to go with them, grumbling loudly that he had had more exercise in a week in Yorkshire than in the rest of the year.

Lucy was sent to practice upon the pianoforte. Her last governess had left in despair some eighteen months previously, quite unable to make Lucy mind her. Since that time, Lady Annabel had instructed her. Lucy's intelligence gave her a quick grasp of such subjects as French and geography; but though she obeyed her mother, she was totally uninterested in such ladylike accomplishments as drawing and embroidery, and only practiced the piano assiduously because she enjoyed it. Her liveliness made her both a rewarding and an exhausting pupil, and after a busy morning and half an hour of supervising her playing, Lady Annabel retired for a nap.

From this she was called by her abigail, with the news that the Vicar and Mrs. Crane were come to see her. The Reverend Mr. Crane was another neighbor who would not take no for an answer. He and his wife were busybodies and great gossips, considering anything that occurred in their parish to be their business. The Carstairs tolerated them but were not intimate with them, though naturally they went to morning service every Sunday.

The Cranes had, of course, heard about Miss Fell. Lady Annabel found Lucy trying manfully to cope with a flood of nosy questions and delighted to be rescued even to be sent back to the pianoforte. Lady Annabel, more adept in the ways of the world, had no trouble stemming the tide and sending the couple on their way satisfied with a minimum of information. She even managed to persuade the vicar that her "old friend's daughter" was in no immediate need of spiritual consolation, yet was too ill to receive visitors.

In fact, that evening Miss Fell was strong enough to eat some chicken and a custard instead of the broth, which, however excellent, palled as a constant diet. Lady Annabel was delighted to see a little color in her cheeks, and though she was tired after sitting up to eat, she was wakeful. Eager to avoid a conversation that would be certain to lead to subjects better left alone for the present, Lady Annabel suggested that Lucy might read to Miss Fell again.

"But perhaps not Cowper," suggested Miss Fell with a twinkle in her eye. "I'm afraid I fell asleep this afternoon."

Lucy was happy to find that Miss Fell would enjoy hearing a chapter of the novel she had recently received in the mail. This coincidence of taste, however much due to her own obvious preference for such literature, confirmed Lucy's determination to make a friend of the heroine so conveniently delivered to her. If Miss Fell's lips twitched at the more lurid passages, it was because a real heroine must know so much better than any novelist just how an adventure should go.

Miss Fell's strength proved equal to only a single chapter. "Thank you, Miss Carstairs," she said with real gratitude. "Perhaps, if you are not otherwise occupied, we might have chapter two tomorrow."

"Of course," assured Lucy. Then she added hesitantly, "Won't you call me Lucy? I should like it of all things."

Miss Fell crimsoned.

"Thank you," she whispered, "but I . . . I cannot reciprocate. I have no name."

"Oh, forgive me," cried Lucy. "I should not have . . . Please, let me call you Clarissa?"

Amusement overcame embarrassment.

"Oh, not Clarissa, I beg of you!" Then seeing Lucy's disappointment, "Perhaps you could call me Clare, or Clara, then you might think of me as Clarissa if you wish, but no one else need know."

"Of course, dear Clara. Now you had better sleep." And Lucy, surprising herself as much as Miss Fell, stooped and gave her a motherly kiss on the forehead. Blushing at her own forwardness, she left hurriedly, calling "Good night!"

What a charming child, thought Miss Fell, newly christened Clara. As good-hearted as her mother. Her amusement faded. Who were they? Who was she herself? Suddenly the awkwardness, the helplessness and embarrassment of her position overwhelmed her. What could she do? She was totally dependent on strangers; and however kind, they had their own plans, and she must be upsetting them dreadfully.

She did not even know how long she had been here. Time blurred into a succession of vignettes, of faces appearing and disappearing, dominated by one dark, pitying face, which she had not seen today. Feeling lost and alone, Miss Clara Fell slipped into uneasy sleep.

Late that evening when Jem returned with an answer from Arnden, he received a sovereign for his pains. Miss Florence Carstairs was happy to be of service to her sister-in-law. Since Lady Annabel had informed her that Miss Fell was the daughter of an old friend, she expressed no qualms about that young lady's doubtful gentility.

"But oh, Richard," exclaimed Lady

Annabel, "I should never be able to face your aunt again if Miss Fell should turn out to be not quite elegant!"

Chapter 4

Another three days passed before Miss Fell was allowed to leave her room. By this time Lady Annabel's doubts were quite laid to rest — Miss Fell was a lady. Lucy, of course, had never had any doubts. Clara was her best friend and by way of becoming her confidante, which amused her mother and dismayed her brother. In spite of Lady Annabel's assurances, Richard still had his misgivings; it was a relief that at least the young woman was not vulgar, but only time would tell whether she knew how to go on in Society, and they might never learn her background.

It was a rainy Monday morning, gloomy and chilly. Richard and Lord Denham were playing billiards in a desultory way when Lucy bounced in.

"Richard, mama desires that you will carry Miss Fell to the morning room. She is well enough to come down; is not that delightful?"

Richard looked annoyed.

"Surely one of the footmen . . . ? Oh,

very well. I shall be there directly. Tony, let us finish the game in a few minutes."

"Certainly not. I am most anxious to make the acquaintance of Miss Fell and shall be happy to abandon a game that you are winning for the fourth time. I shall await you in the morning room."

Unwillingly, Richard followed his sister upstairs. His feelings were confused. Used to regulating his conduct toward strangers and slight acquaintances according to rigid rules laid down by his uncle, Lord Mortlake, he had no idea how to approach a young woman whom he had saved from death, yet of whose position in life he was totally ignorant. He supposed she must be grateful, but deep in the hidden places of his mind a hurt child looked out and thought: *She will look at my face and she will despise me.* That child had kept him from ever allowing himself to have serious intentions toward a woman. Indeed, he was never at ease with any female outside his family. Now, he unconsciously armored himself in his arrogance, and his mother's heart sank as she saw his cold, stiff face.

Miss Fell sat in a chair by the fire, with her back to the door. No less nervous than Richard, she nevertheless seemed calm and composed; and no one could have guessed from her appearance that she felt like an intruder. However warm and accepting the ladies were, she was sure her presence must be less than welcome to the master of the house. Indeed, Lucy had dropped several hints as to her brother's feelings, vaguely hoping to lessen the shock to her dear friend in case he should let her see his disapproval.

At least, Miss Fell thought, there is a vast improvement in my appearance. Lucy had described her pallid, bloodstained arrival with ghoulish enjoyment. Now she was dressed in a green wrapper of Lady Annabel's ("It does not become me in the least, my dear, but green is quite your color"). Her hair had been vigorously brushed by Lucy's maid and arranged simply in a loose chignon. The scar on her brow was now a thin white line, scarcely visible, and her hair covered the bruise, which was fading rapidly. Lucy thought she looked charming, interestingly pale, and only her tightly clasped hands suggested to Lady Annabel that she was not at ease.

Lady Annabel led her reluctant son forward. "Miss Fell, I must make known to you my son, Richard Carstairs."

Miss Fell held out her hand and raised

her eyes to his face. Richard, prepared to bow coldly, met her eyes, shyly smiling, and took her hand in both his.

"I am delighted to see you so much recovered," he stammered.

"I owe you my life, Mr. Carstairs," she said simply. "There is no way I can ever thank you."

"Pray do not try, Miss Fell. I could hardly have left you lying in the snow."

Lucy giggled. "Last year he brought home an early lamb that was half frozen to death."

"I am properly put in my place," declared Miss Fell, chuckling.

It was the wrong thing to say. Richard stiffened and let go her hand, which he had forgotten he was holding. She cast him a quick glance of appeal, but he was not looking at her. Her hands again clasped tightly in her lap.

"Well," said Richard with an effort, "if you are to go below stairs this morning, let us have done with it."

Lucy helped her friend to stand. Awkwardly, and furious with himself, Richard picked her up in his arms, carefully avoiding her eyes. She blushed to feel him holding her and trembled a little with tension and embarrassment.

Richard felt her shiver and looked down at her. She smiled up at him timidly and apologetically, and there was a lost look in her eyes. He cursed himself for distressing her. Had she not enough troubles without his adding to them? He should rather be solving her problems than causing new ones. His arms tightened about her involuntarily.

"I shall not drop you," he reassured gently, and his eyes now begged her forgiveness.

Miss Fell relaxed and watched his face as he carried her along the passage and down the stairway. How strange, she pondered; as long as he can think of me as a sick lamb, he is kindness itself; yet as soon as he considers my position, he becomes as haughty as a duke. He is very handsome in a stern sort of way. I wonder if he ever smiles? Lucy seems very fond of him and she is so lively. He must be a good brother. If I have any brothers, I hope they are as kind as he, she thought wistfully, and that I may find them soon.

Richard set her down on a sofa close to the fire in the morning room, and she was introduced to Lord Denham.

"Delighted to see you up and about, Miss Fell. I daresay you will not have to

64

endure Miss Carstairs' reading poetry to you any longer."

"My lord, Miss Carstairs has been reading me a most intriguing novel, and I trust we shall finish it together. But I must thank your lordship for your help in rescuing me."

"Ah well, *noblesse oblige* you know. Besides, I could not bring myself to stand aside and let Richard reap all the glory. Have you still no idea why you were in that godforsaken place at that godforsaken time?"

Lady Annabel cast him a reproving glance and looked anxiously at Miss Fell.

"Lucy told me," she said hesitantly, "that the doctor thought I had been beaten. I can only suppose I may have been running away, though from whom or what or where I cannot guess. I find it hard to believe that I can have come so far that none of you recognizes me, nor has even heard of someone being missed. It is a very strange feeling not to know who you are."

She put her hand to her head and Lady Annabel stepped swiftly forward.

"My poor child," she soothed, "you are not to think of the business until you are quite well. Lord Denham, that was ill done."

He looked like a guilty small boy.

"Lady Annabel, Miss Fell, my apologies. Here we have a heroine and a mystery in our midst and I find it irresistible, but I will curb myself."

"Indeed, ma'am, I am quite well. I cannot help but think of it often. Lord Denham is not to blame."

"He is, he is," crowed Lucy, "and you shall give him a forfeit, Clara, for being so thoughtless."

Lady Annabel and Richard exchanged looks of despair. Lord Denham was equal to the challenge.

"Shall you rap my knuckles with a ruler, Miss Fell?"

"I shall rather sentence you to listen to Miss Carstairs reading poetry for half an hour."

Lady Annabel and Richard applauded; Lucy laughed, and Lord Denham drew back in mock horror.

"What, so fair and yet so cruel? At least allow me to choose the poet. Not Cowper, I beg of you."

It was impossible not to like Lord Denham. Comfortable in any company, he quickly put others at their ease. Indolent he might be, but always good-natured, and his ready wit made him a welcome guest wherever he went. He spent most of his time in London, except for a stay at Brighton during the summer months and visits to his many friends. His father, the Marquis of Hendon, despaired of ever persuading him to take an interest in the vast estates that would be his one day, consoling himself with the thought that Lord Denham would be sufficiently wealthy to hire a dozen agents to take care of them for him. Mamas with eligible daughters had been chasing him for near a decade with no luck. It was generally said, waspishly, that he was too lazy to trouble himself to marry.

Lady Annabel, seeing his expression as he laughed with Lucy, wondered if he had been caught at last. Lucy obviously enjoyed being with him. She did not think there was any warmer feeling on her side, but, after all, the child was not even out yet.

Let her have a season of fun in London without any thought of marriage. She was pretty, of good birth, and would have twenty thousand pounds; sooner or later she would fall in love, and she was good enough for anyone. She would be more troubled by the need to beat off fortune hunters than to catch a husband, she thought proudly. But the warmth in Lord Denham's eyes should not be dismissed lightly. Lucy might be as happy with him as she herself had been with Kit.

Richard was inquiring about the plot of the novel that Lucy had been reading to Miss Fell. Lucy related with glee the bloodcurdling tale of mysterious counts and sinister castles on remote peaks in Transylvania. Miss Fell listened with a quiet smile, now and then adding a detail. She seemed to have recovered completely the self-possession that appeared, on short acquaintance, to be a fixed part of her character. Lady Annabel slipped away to see Mrs. Bedford. The journey to London was to begin the day after next, and there was a great deal to be done.

One task that must be finished was the altering of several gowns to fit Miss Fell. Lady Annabel and Lucy had gone through their wardrobes and picked out suitable items. Lucy was somewhat shorter than Miss Fell and her clothes were designed for a schoolroom miss, while Lady Annabel was her height but quite different in build, and her clothes were designed for a widow. In spite of this, Miss Fell had adamantly refused to accept any new garments to be made up by the dressmaker in the village, so the two abigails and a maid had been set to work to alter and retrim enough of a wardrobe to make her at least presentable, if not elegant.

Miss Fell had also adamantly refused to join the Carstairs in London, until the alternatives were pointed out to her. She could not be left alone at Toblethorpe, nor could Miss Florence be expected to chaperone her for several months. Loath though she was to impose, she realized that she was not in a position to take care of herself. The clinching argument was the possibility of meeting in town someone who knew her.

"You will be of use to me in London," Lady Annabel had assured her. "Lucy is a darling, but an exhausting companion, and you will be able to help me chaperone her. She loves you already."

"No one could help loving her," Miss Fell had replied. "My lady, without your kindness . . ." Her voice was suspended by tears.

Lady Annabel had held her close until she mastered herself. "You shall be a second daughter to me," she had declared firmly. "I always wanted a larger family."

Having inspected the progress on the clothing alterations, Lady Annabel made her way back to the morning room. Richard had gone off to consult with Jeremy Denison, and Lucy and Lord Denham were teaching Miss Fell to play backgammon, which she either did not know or had forgotten. She looked tired, and Lady Annabel told Lucy to fetch Richard to carry her back to her chamber.

"It is my turn," Lord Denham protested.

Lady Annabel was a little startled. Then she reflected that, after all, both gentlemen were strangers to Miss Fell, and while she could not have asked Lord Denham to do it, it was not a bad idea that he should, making such attention from Richard seem less particular. So she agreed, and Miss Fell was borne back to bed.

That evening she was again slightly feverish and Lady Annabel would not let her come down the following morning. In the afternoon she felt so much better that Richard was called on again to assist her. He seemed to have decided to treat her as he might any friend of Lucy's, and was able to relax and be natural. Miss Fell was grateful, both for his help and for his forbearance. Considering his reactions the previous day, she realized that he was making a deliberate effort to accept her and to forget her lack of family. She did not understand why it was so important to him, but it obviously was, and she appreciated his effort.

In fact, Richard had found it remarkably easy to put aside his prejudices, at least for the moment. The half-hour he had spent with her the day before had shown him that she must be gently bred. He had seen how his rejection had hurt her, and was ashamed of himself for injuring one who was so wholly at his mercy, and already in distress. His mother and sister had welcomed her into the family, could he do less? If she turned out to be a nobody, no harm had been done, and there was time enough to consider the matter when and if it arose.

He looked down at her as he carried her into the drawing room, and she smiled at him with gratitude. "Nobody" was the wrong word, he thought. With those eyes, that hair, she could never be that.

Miss Fell looked extremely well. The westering sun, shining again at last, lit her hair like glowing embers. Lady Annabel, busy at her embroidery, thought she and Richard made a charming picture as they bent over the backgammon board. Lucy and Lord Denham had ridden out as soon as the sun had showed itself, but Aunt

Florence was expected at any minute, so Richard had stayed home. He was smiling at something Miss Fell had said, and Lady Annabel hoped further acquaintance would reconcile him to the necessity of her remaining with them.

Miss Fell observed how much that smile changed his face. She had seen him laughing with his sister and his friend yesterday, but today his smile was for her alone, and it made her heart turn over. Dismayed by her own reaction, she silently took herself to task as Richard pondered his next move. Nothing, she thought, could be so fatal as to fall in love. Besides, was she a schoolroom miss to fall for a charming smile? She turned her attention strictly to the game.

The sound of carriage wheels crunching over gravel broke the silence.

"Florence!" exclaimed Lady Annabel. "Come, Richard, we must go and greet her. Miss Fell shall study the board so that she may demolish you on your return."

Richard pulled a face and followed obediently, whispering to Miss Fell, "I am afraid we are to leave you in the clutches of a veritable Gorgon."

Miss Florence Carstairs, sister of the late Mr. Christopher Carstairs and of Mr.

Geoffrey Carstairs, with whom she usually resided, was a tall, spare, elderly woman. Her face was severe; but while she disapproved strongly of males of all ages and of females under the age of twenty-five or so, she could be perfectly cordial to the remainder of the human race. Her nieces and nephews were all greatly in awe of her, and it was a constant source of amazement and gratitude to Richard and Lucy that she had chosen to make her home with her younger brother in spite of his six offspring. The choice was at least partly due to the fact that Mr. Geoffrey was almost as much in awe of his sister as were his children, while Mr. Christopher, with three years' advantage, had been unable to forget pulling Flo's pigtails in his youth. Both Blanche, Geoffrey's wife, and Lady Annabel had always found her a tower of strength in time of trouble.

Thus it was that, in spite of Richard's warning to Miss Fell, Miss Carstairs received a warm welcome from his mother.

"Florence, I am delighted to see you. How kind of you to come, and at such short notice. Richard, come and make your bow."

Richard did so, feeling ten years old again as he usually did in his aunt's presence.

"How do you do, aunt?" he greeted her. She ignored him.

"Well, Annabel," she said, "you look very well. And how is this Miss Fell I have come to chaperone?"

"Much improved, but still easily tired. I am sure you must be exhausted or I should ask you to let me present her to you at once. She has been out of her bed quite long enough, and I must send her back shortly."

"I am not at all fatigued, Annabel. By all means, introduce Miss Fell now so that she may retire."

The ladies proceeded to the drawing room, followed by Richard, who would far rather have hidden in his library. He would be needed to carry Miss Fell up again, however.

Miss Fell rose as they entered. She was presented as the daughter of a mythical Charlotte Fell, nee Davis.

"I do not remember a Charlotte Davis," remarked Miss Carstairs as Miss Fell curtseyed rather shakily. "Sit down, child, before you collapse."

"Oh, she was married from home, immediately she left school. A childhood sweetheart she was forever talking about. She never did come up to Town; her husband's father was an invalid, and then she had children. I don't suppose you ever met her; but she was my dearest friend, and we have corresponded constantly." Lady Annabel, startled by her own powers of invention, hated lying to her sister-in-law, but to tell her she was being asked to chaperone a stranger who had been found alone at dawn on the moors was unthinkable.

"Indeed," pronounced Miss Carstairs, bowing her head regally. "Most generous of you to sponsor her daughter for a Season, my dear Annabel."

"Oh, no, Florence, Miss Fell is past the age of being brought out in form and presented. She will merely visit us in London and help me take Lucy about."

"I see. Well, child, you look to be exhausted. You had best take Richard's arm and retire to your bed. How unfortunate that you should have had an accident at such a time."

Miss Fell was indeed looking white and tired. She had just realized that she must spend ten days or two weeks alone with this formidable old lady, and how was she to answer the questions that must inevitably come?

Lady Annabel was not worried. Miss

Carstairs was little interested in other people's affairs and not at all inquisitive. She generally divided her time between endless *petit point* and the perusal of equally endless books of sermons. She was more likely to discourse on missionary work in India than on anything closer to home. Unfortunately, Lady Annabel had not thought to reassure Miss Fell on that point, and it was a nervous young woman who murmured, "Thank you, ma'am, my lady," and took Richard's proffered arm as instructed. With his aunt's eye upon him, Richard did not dare to pick her up, but lent her as much support as he could to the door.

Fortunately, it was not far. As he closed the door behind them, she swayed and he turned just in time to catch her. Full of concern, he furiously, if silently, damned his aunt and picked up the burden that was becoming so familiar to him.

Miss Fell was not unconscious, merely dizzy.

"I should not have let you walk," Richard said ruefully. "You can see how terrified I am of my aunt."

She gave him a wavering smile.

"It is good of her to come all this way to care for me," she replied, "but I am a little afraid of her also."

"I shall not let her eat you," he promised lightly.

A maid was waiting in her chamber, alerted by the butler. The bed was folded back and Richard laid Miss Fell upon it, then tucked her in. He remembered doing the same for Lucy when she was four or five, and the deed made him feel very brotherly.

"Sleep," he ordered, "and do not let anything worry you."

Sleepy already, she watched him leave the room and wished, very deliberately, that she had a brother like him. She could not allow herself to wish for anything more.

The following morning, Lucy popped in to see her early.

"I've brought you *Count Casimir's Castle*, Clara," she said after inquiring whether she had slept well. "I fear I shall not have time to read to you today. There are a thousand things to be done, for we depart tomorrow. So I will leave it for you to read."

"Oh no, you must take it with you. Indeed, I believe that if you do not continue reading of her adventures you will lie awake nights wondering what fearful events have befallen the fair Melisande. You shall write and tell me the end of her troubles."

"I do not see how she is to escape the wicked Count. Clara, do you think you were running from such a sinister fate?"

"I cannot think so. This, after all, is England and the nineteenth century, not Transylvania in the fifteenth. Our time is much more prosaic, I fear. I shall miss your reading, Lucy dear, and your cheerful presence. What shall I do without you?"

"Shall I bring you some other books? If you are unoccupied, my aunt may offer you her sermons, and I am sure I can find you something more amusing. I shall ask Richard if there is anything in the library you might like. What kind of reading do you prefer?"

"That is more than I can tell! Lucy, do not bother Mr. Carstairs. He must be very busy today."

"Well, I shall tell Tony to select you some volumes."

Miss Fell's protests were unheeded. Lucy went off to help her mother prepare for the three-day carriage ride and several months' absence from home. Midway through the morning she reappeared with an armful of novels and poetry, followed by Richard and Lord Denham each bearing a load of histories, biographies, travelers' tales, books of prints and a variety of other volumes.

"Here you are," announced Richard cheerfully. "Whatever your taste, you must find sufficient reading matter here to last for months."

"Indeed, you should not have troubled, Mr. Carstairs."

"Miss Lucy painted such a pathetic picture of your lying in your sickbed surrounded by sermons," explained Lord Denham, "that we could do no less."

Lucy surveyed the scene with disapproval.

"We cannot leave these all over the floor. I think there is an unused bookshelf in the room beside yours, Lord Denham. Pray come and help me find it."

They departed.

"You are very kind, Mr. Carstairs," Miss Fell thanked him. "I confess I cannot appreciate Count Casimir as I ought without Lucy's exclamations and comments as leavening. These will be a most welcome alternative."

"We shall place them where you can reach them from your bed," said Richard seriously, "but I trust you will soon be strong enough to make use of the library. When you are able to be about, I beg you will treat this house as your home: the library, the music room, the gardens. I believe my mother has instructed Mary to wait on you, so if there is anything you need, tell her. I shall return in about a fortnight; and if you are well enough, I shall escort you to London. In the meantime, do not let my Aunt Florence browbeat you."

"Miss Carstairs came to see me this morning and she was most cordial and sympathetic. Everyone is so kind to me. I cannot hope to repay it; I must study to deserve it."

"Be a friend to my sister and a companion to my mother, and we shall be your family as long as you need us. The Carstairs do not abandon those in trouble."

So, thought Miss Fell sadly as he left her, I am nothing to him but a family obligation. Well, I am lucky to be that, in truth. I could have been found by anyone. Or no one.

Her reverie was interrupted by a heavy tread in the passage, a crash, and a thump on the door, which heralded Lord Denham and a footman, James, bearing between them a large carved oak bookcase, hideously ornate. Moving a chair, they placed it by the bed. Lord Denham sat down on the chair with a groan and wiped his forehead, while James started putting books on the shelves.

"Whew! That must weigh half a ton!" complained his lordship, fanning himself. "I hope only that it will not give you nightmares, Miss Fell. Look at those devilish dragons climbing the sides!"

"Lord Denham, you should not have been carrying that. Surely there is another servant . . ."

"Lucy's orders." He grinned. "Thomas was called away to sit on a trunk that could not be closed and since he was to take it downstairs thereafter, I decided the bookcase would be lighter. I do not think it is, however. What a frightful piece of furniture! But Lucy would have it that you could not have books cluttering up your chamber a moment longer. I'd have made her do it had her mama not summoned her."

Miss Fell laughed.

"Lucy cannot have been serious, my lord. Though she is so excited about going to London that I am sure she cannot think straight. I believe she has not sat still for a

81

moment all morning."

Richard popped his head round the door.

"There you are, Tony. Let us get out of this madhouse before my mother finds me anything else to do. Begging your pardon, Miss Fell. Your room is a haven of quiet in Bedlam, but we are not safe even here. You will excuse me if I take Tony to inspect the stables before we are caught."

"Certainly, Mr. Carstairs. I give you my word I will not reveal your whereabouts. My lips are sealed."

They had not been gone five minutes when Lucy reappeared. "I thought Richard was here," she said crossly. "I want him to persuade mama to let me ride part of the way instead of traveling in that stuffy carriage."

"He is not here, as you see, my dear. I daresay you will find him shortly. Are you still very busy?"

"Mama says I am just in the way," was the disconsolate answer. "Only because I cannot decide whether to take my blue riding dress or the brown one with yellow trim. I shall have new ones when we reach London anyway, so I cannot see that it matters. Oh, Clara, have you ever been to Town? I suppose you do not know. I cannot wait to see the shops and theatres and the wild beasts at the Exchange. To go to proper balls instead of parties with just three or four couples in someone's drawing room, or those stuffy assemblies at York. Oh, do not tell Richard I said that. He does not know that when mama and I went to stay with my Aunt Blanche last winter, we went to the balls at York. Mama said he would disapprove of mixing with hoi polloi, but what the eye doesn't see the heart doesn't grieve over. You will not mention it?"

"I am very good at keeping secrets, chatterbox," assured Miss Fell. "Tell me about the ball gowns you will have made up."

A discussion of silks and satins and sarcenets ensued, of the relative merits of matching and contrasting ribbons, of embroidery and lace. Lucy fetched copies of *La Belle Assemblée* and brown head and copper bent together over the fashion plates in earnest consultation.

Before they had grown tired of this occupation, Mary arrived with a tray for Miss Fell.

"There be luncheon in the breakfast room, Miss Lucy," she announced. "My lady says tha mun come soon, if tha wants to eat."

"Thank thee, Mary," said Lucy. "I'll see thee later, Clara."

"Oh, Miss Lucy do be a caution," giggled the maid. "Does tha want owt else, miss?"

Miss Fell dismissed her and turned to her tray. Her appetite was returning rapidly, and indeed Chef Pierre's creations would have tempted the most jaded of palates. Every tray she received bore new delicacies, yet contrived to offer nothing that might offend an invalid's touchy appetite. She thought it fortunate that the master of the kitchen would be traveling to London on the morrow, or she would soon grow quite plump.

After luncheon Lady Annabel came to see her and was delighted to see the empty tray.

"My dear," she said, "I am so pleased to see you eating well. You were nothing but skin and bones when Richard found you, you know. When Dr. Grimsdale examined you, I could count every rib."

"I am so well fed, Lady Annabel, I shall grow fat if I am not soon able to exercise."

"You must rest and grow strong. I hear you had visitors all morning. You had better sleep for a while now. If you should not dislike it, Miss Carstairs will come and sit with you after her nap. You need not fear that she will ask you questions you cannot answer, she has the greatest horror of gossip and of prying into other people's concerns. I daresay she will read you a sermon or two, but you will bear that."

"May I get up later, ma'am?"

"The house is all at sixes and sevens at present. You shall come down after dinner, on condition that you allow Richard to carry you. He told me that you fainted yesterday."

"If Mr. Carstairs does not object . . ."

"Of course he does not, child. After today, however, you must rely on Thomas to help you about. Let that be an inducement to you to recover quickly. Now rest."

By dinnertime the entrance hall was piled high with trunks and boxes and bundles. Richard had always kept only a skeleton staff at the house in Cavendish Square, as his mother had not ventured to London since his father's death. Besides Monsieur Pierre, two abigails, a valet, a maid, a footman and two grooms would precede or accompany the party, not to mention Old Ned, the coachman. The huge old traveling carriage, once the height of elegance, had been reupholstered and polished till it shone.

"It is quite out of date," stated Lucy disparagingly. "I shall be ashamed to ride in such an old-fashioned contraption. I should think it would need six horses to pull it."

"It was good enough to take you to Arnden, and it will get you to London," said her brother without sympathy. "Unless you had rather postpone your journey until I can order a new vehicle from the coach-builder?"

"It is not very comfortable, nor fast," Lady Annabel agreed with Lucy. "Perhaps when we reach Town we might look at some of the newer carriages, Richard?"

"As you please, mama. Had you suggested it several months ago, we might have had one by now."

"Oh, a London carriage would be far more elegant, I am sure," cried Lucy. "In Leeds they only know how to build hideous things like this. Let us find a new one at once in London, and then Richard may fetch Clara in it."

"I hope you will find my town carriages unexceptionable, Lucy, or you will be so busy at the coach-maker you will have no time for the dressmaker."

The evening seemed endless to Lucy who was full of impatience to be off.

Richard also found it passing with excruciating slowness. He had been ordered to take a hand at piquet with his aunt, who had no reticence about criticizing his play in acid tones.

Miss Fell watched them both with amusement, which was shared by Lord Denham.

"I do not know how Lucy will survive till bedtime," he whispered to her, as Lucy jumped up and wandered restlessly around the room. "And as for Richard, he is generally considered an excellent player at piquet."

"It is strange, is it not, how Miss Carstairs sets him all at sixes and sevens? To me she has been perfectly amiable."

"She is not your aunt, Miss Fell. I have just such an aunt myself. She would put the fear of death into the devil himself."

"Lucy, you had better go and play the pianoforte if you cannot sit still," said Lady Annabel crossly. "Tomorrow will come no sooner for your jumping up and down."

"I should like to hear you play," Miss Fell said. "Lord Denham, perhaps you would help me to the music room. No, do not carry me, I must try to walk. It is not far."

Richard watched anxiously as she moved

shakily into the next room, leaning heavily on Lord Denham's arm. His inattention to his cards drew a biting rebuke from Miss Carstairs.

When Miss Fell was guided to a couch and settled on it, she seemed none the worse for her effort, though she could feel her heart beating rapidly. She thanked Lord Denham, who said, "You must excuse me, if you please. I am no musician, as Miss Lucy knows, so I shall go and sit with Lady Annabel."

Lucy pouted a little, but she was not vain about her performance and did not protest. She played several lively tunes with great vigor and considerable charm and then started on a pavane. The slow, stately dance emerged mangled from her fingers. Miss Fell winced. In the next room, Richard and his mother exchanged despairing glances, and Miss Carstairs looked up in outrage.

"Annabel, if your daughter can play only gavottes and gigs, she should not offend our ears with such distressing incompetence. Let her cultivate a light style and leave pieces requiring sensitivity to those who are sensitive!"

"Indeed, Florence, I constantly remind her to play only lively pieces in company.

There, it is nearly over."

Lord Denham, though unable to comprehend their horror, went over to the piano and said tactfully, "Let us have a jolly tune, Miss Lucy. Such solemn stuff does not suit your sparkling eyes."

"Fie, Lord Denham," she replied, looking up at him archly through her lashes. "You said yourself you are no connoisseur of music."

"But I am a connoisseur of young ladies' eyes, and yours make me think of waltzes, not dirges. Come, will you promise me your first waltz at Almack's?"

"La, sir, I daresay the lady patronesses will not permit me to waltz."

"What, with every gentleman in the room bogging for an introduction?"

Lucy blushed. The evident admiration in Lord Denham's face was very flattering, but used only to the clumsy compliments of provincial beaux, she was unsure how to answer.

Lord Denham, amused, accepted the blush as sufficient reply. "I shall haunt Almack's so as not to miss the fateful moment." He lifted her hand and kissed it lightly. "Now play me a waltz that I may dream we are dancing already."

Miss Fell had followed the conversation

with interest. She wondered if Lord Denham had serious intentions. They would make a charming couple, she thought, but she had been acquainted with Lucy long enough to know that she needed a strong hand on the reins to check her liveliness at times. She suspected Lord Denham was far too lazy to curb her high spirits, and sooner or later that might lead to trouble. However, it was not her problem, though she must take an interest in the fate of one who was becoming as dear to her as Lucy undoubtedly was.

Richard, his game over to his vast relief, watched the *tête-à-tête* with very different feelings. Lord Denham would be an extremely eligible husband for his sister, and how delightful to have his best friend become his brother-in-law. He had always stood as much in the position of father to Lucy as a brother, and though her vivacity sometimes led her into mischief or beyond the line of what was pleasing, he had always been able to quell her with a word. He made his way into the music room now with unalloyed pleasure in the hope of her marrying the heir of a marquis and such a good fellow.

"Do you waltz, Miss Fell?" he inquired, sitting down beside her. "Oh, I beg your pardon, I suppose you do not know."

"I have no memory of waltzing, Mr. Carstairs," she answered, "but my toes have been twitching and I rather think they have a better memory than my head." She did not mention the fact that all the time Lucy had been playing, her fingers had seemed to want to join in. She resolved to attempt to play as soon as she was able and no one was by to hear.

Lady Annabel rang for the tea tray, and she and Miss Carstairs joined the young people in the other room.

"We must rise betimes if we are to reach Doncaster tomorrow night," she said, apologizing for the early hour. "It is only sixty miles, but there are always so many things to be done at the last moment and the days are short. Besides, until we reach the post road at York, it is very slow going."

Richard would not permit Miss Fell to attempt to walk up the stairs. As he carried her up, she said shyly, "The house will seem very empty when you are all gone."

He heard the forlorn note in her voice and looked down at her. For a timeless moment he lost himself in the sea green eyes raised appealingly to his, then he caught his breath.

"I will come for you soon," he promised

with a catch in his throat that made speaking difficult.

To both of them the words seemed pregnant with meaning, and each fought the impression. As Mary helped her prepare for bed, Miss Fell forced herself to realize that Mr. Carstairs was referring only to her journey to London.

Making his way to his room in the other wing, Richard assured himself that he was merely full of pity for her. Her situation was most unenviable, and she needed his protection. But how did she come to be in that situation? What was she doing alone on the moors? No one knew what sort of person she really was. Did she really deserve his sympathy? He had taken her into his house; his mother, a Carstairs, had personally nursed her. Whoever she was, she could not complain of her treatment.

By the time he reached his chamber, he had managed to make himself angry with her. Reproachful green eyes haunted his dreams.

Chapter 5

Morning came, as mornings do. It was a foul day. Icy rain blew in sheets from the east, soaking the servants as they struggled to load the vehicles. Lady Annabel was almost persuaded that they should postpone their departure. One look at Lucy's anxious face changed her mind. She sighed, and went to bid farewell to Miss Carstairs and Miss Fell.

Lucy had already taken leave of her dear Clara. Bubbling with excitement, she had bounced in and flung her arms around her, drawing a protest from Mary.

"Now give over, Miss Lucy. Tha's near upset Miss Fell's chocolate. And lookee, tha's got marmalade on thy gown!"

"Oh, Mary, stop fussing. You're as bad as Nurse. You make sure you take good care of Miss Fell when we are gone. She must be quite recovered when my brother comes for her."

Mary bobbed a curtsy, and Lucy, looking at her, did not see the quick, faint blush that covered her friend's face and then ebbed as quickly.

I must not be so sensitive to those words, Miss Fell scolded herself. They mean nothing. Yet she felt hurt when Richard did not come to say good-bye. She started every time she heard footsteps in the passage, but, except for Lord Denham, and then Lady Annabel, they always went on by. Though once she thought they hesitated outside her door, they continued in spite of her wishing. At length she heard the jingle of harnesses and the rumble of wheels, and gave up hope.

She managed to get to the window and watched as the three loaded carriages rounded the corner of the house. It had stopped raining, and a hand emerged from the foremost vehicle and waved to her. Lucy's hand. She did not know how much effort it cost Richard, now cantering past the procession, to stop himself from turning back and rushing up to her room for a last word. Determined to consider her as a mere dependent, he would not show her any particular attention, and in his resolution he lost sight of the fact that to say good-bye was common courtesy.

Miss Fell returned to her bed, wondering sadly what she had done to offend him. She rang her bell, and when Mary came in she said, "I shall dress this morning. If I do not make an effort, I shall never grow stronger."

"Yes, miss. What'ud tha like to wear, miss?"

That gave her pause. She knew she had been brought here in a riding dress, which was not at all suitable.

"I believe Lady Annabel's abigail altered a gown to fit me, Mary. Was it finished?"

"Oh yes, miss. Me an' Miss Vane an' Miss Lucy's maid, Molly, we did ever so many gowns. They mun be in t'sewing room yet. I'll fetch 'ee one on 'em."

She ran off and soon returned with a morning gown of fine warm merino, dove grey, and an armful of petticoats.

"This were my lady's visiting dress last winter, miss. It's a right treat to touch it, so soft it is. I sewed this one. Will it be a'right for now?"

"Yes, indeed. What a fine needlewoman you are, Mary."

"Thank'ee, miss, but let's see if it fits proper."

The gown fitted perfectly. Miss Fell sat gazing at herself in the mirror while Mary brushed her hair vigorously and tied it back in a loose knot. She had not looked at herself since her arrival at Toblethorpe and she felt strange. Her face was familiar to her, yet she did not precisely remember it. Had she been asked a few minutes earlier, she would not have known the color of her eyes. She studied herself. Forehead too high, she thought disparagingly. Mouth too wide, and that great masculine chin. What a fright! No wonder Richard — Mr. Carstairs — was not interested. Then her hair was finished and she could see her whole face at once. Well, she mused, perhaps not so bad. Not exactly pretty, but I don't think I am quite an antidote.

"I think I had better wear a cap," she said to Mary.

"Oh no, miss! Tha's pretty as a picture. Caps is for old ladies and servants."

"You are an excellent abigail, Mary. Thank you."

"Does 'ee think so, miss? Ee, I'd like to be a lady's maid, but Mrs. Bedford says I don't talk right."

"That can be remedied. Would you like me to teach you? If you are free after lunch, we could start then."

" 'Ee, miss, I'd be that grateful. I'll have to ask Mrs. Bedford though."

"Of course. I shall just sit here and rest for the present. I find I am a little tired after dressing."

With much solicitude, Mary settled her

in a chair by the fire with a pile of books and went out.

Not ten minutes later there was a knock at the door, and Mrs. Bedford appeared. As jealous of the Carstairs' pride as they could possibly be, she had resented Miss Fell from the first, and was most suspicious of her right to be treated as a member of the family. Ready and willing to take affront and consider herself put upon by a nobody, she advanced on her victim, glaring like a turkey cock.

"What's this I hear about Mary learning to be an abigail?" she demanded. "The lower servants are in my charge, and I'll thank you not to meddle, miss."

"Lady Annabel instructed Mary to wait upon me," said Miss Fell coldly, hiding her dismay. "If you have work for her when I do not need her, of course she will do it. I am sure you must be very busy with half the staff gone."

"Well, it's not so much trouble looking after just you and Miss Carstairs, miss, but I'm sure I don't know what to do about meals. That Gladys says she don't know how to go on without the Frenchie to hold her hand. I'm at my wit's end, and I can't be running off after the maids all the time." Mrs. Bedford ran the gamut from condescension through complaint to belligerence in one short speech.

"Indeed, you cannot," said Miss Fell soothingly. "I shall speak to Gladys. I do not think Miss Carstairs should be bothered. And Mary shall come straight to you whenever I am finished with her, so you see you need not chase her. Surely you'd not deny her a chance to better herself?" she added cajolingly.

"She's a good girl," pronounced the housekeeper grudgingly. "If you're sure she won't be a bother, Miss Fell? She's my own sister's child; I'd like to see her rise above housemaid."

"So you are a Yorkshirewoman also, Mrs. Bedford? I would not have guessed it from the way you speak."

"Ah, Mrs. Geoffrey taught me, Mr. Richard's grandmother, that is. She was a proper lady, Miss Fell. She was a Lucy, too, Miss Lucy Arnden. That's where young Mr. Geoffrey's property came into the family."

"You have been with the Carstairs a long time, then."

"Oh yes, Miss Fell, and many's the tale I could tell — Oh, there's a rhyme, something lucky's on the way."

"Tell me a tale, Mrs. Bedford," coaxed

Miss Fell. "I find I am not well enough to read much."

Some time later, Mrs. Bedford descended to the kitchen to announce to all and sundry that Miss Fell was a proper lady, and she'd have something to say to anyone as said she wasn't.

"And she wants to see you right away, Gladys," she added ominously.

Gladys scurried out, and after a brief interview returned full of confidence to prepare luncheon. The transformation set the seal on the approval of the servants' hall, except for one aged gardener who prophesied disaster in a gloomy voice.

"Oh, get on wi' yer," snorted Gladys in disgust. "How an owd curmudgeon like you can grow food as won't curdle the stomach is beyond me!"

Miss Fell, meanwhile, was far more exhausted than if she had spent the morning reading. She lay back on her bed, sadly crushing the grey merino, and closed her eyes. Her head was aching slightly and she hoped fervently that she would not have to deal with any more servants' squabbles for a while. When Mary brought her lunch tray she was fast asleep.

"Poor soul," she reported back to the kitchen, "she'm pale as t'moon an' I'll thank 'ee, auntie, not to go upsettin' my young lady no more."

"Watch thy tongue, young woman," said Mrs. Bedford indignantly. "Don't tha come the high and mighty wi' me. Poor soul!"

When Miss Fell woke her headache was gone, and she rang the bell. She ate luncheon and gave Mary a language lesson. The girl was very quick except in the use of "you" for "thee."

"It don't — doesn't — seem right, somehow. 'You' is a cold sort of word to call a body."

Miss Carstairs' abigail came to convey a request for the pleasure of Miss Fell's company in the drawing room, if she were well enough. She trod her way slowly to the head of the stairs, then Thomas was called to carry her down. Outside the drawing-room door, she made him put her down. She could not feel it dignified to arrive in the arms of a footman. She thought she could manage without his arm, then decided that discretion was the better part of valor. She was glad of it before she was halfway across the room.

"You are still a little shaky on your feet, my dear," remarked Miss Carstairs kindly.

"A little, ma'am. I feel very well, however."

"Should you object to helping me sort my silks? I find they become thoroughly tangled for no apparent reason, and if they are not sorted daily they are very soon inextricable."

The afternoon was passed in sorting silks, discussing embroidery patterns and remarking upon the weather, which had abruptly turned unseasonably warm for February.

"There will be sickness in the village," declared Miss Carstairs. "I shall see what simples Mrs. Bedford has on hand and consult the vicar as to who is in need."

Miss Fell was relieved to find that her companion displayed no curiosity whatever about her own history. It was a very soothing afternoon.

At five o'clock Miss Carstairs put away her embroidery.

"I shall dress for dinner now, Miss Fell. You had better dine in your room today. I shall hope you may be well enough to join me tomorrow. You will not, I trust, think me impertinent if I say that you are a very pretty-behaved young woman. I am happy that dear Annabel should have found such a companion. She has been too much alone, I fear, since my brother's death."

Miss Fell blushed and murmured a disclaimer. A word of approval from such a formidable old lady was flattering, and the confidence she showed in discussing her sister-in-law, when she had such a distaste for personal remarks, was an even greater sign of approbation.

"Do not get up, my dear," said Miss Carstairs. "I shall send Thomas for you. Until tomorrow, then."

Sitting snugly wrapped before the fire in her chamber, Miss Fell attacked her dinner with a hearty appetite. Though it could not compare with the French chef's master-pieces, Gladys had done her best. The best sauce, however, was the realization that she had won over two such stern critics as Miss Carstairs and Mrs. Bedford. She wondered wistfully whether anything she could do would make Richard wholeheart-edly approve of her. If she turned out to be a duke's daughter, or at least an earl's, per-haps, she thought; but she did not feel like a great lady, and, besides, she might never know who she was.

Her appetite had faded, and she strug-gled manfully with a huge slice of apple pie. Giving up after a few bites, she rang for Mary.

"My compliments to the cook," she in-structed, "and, Mary dear, explain that the pie was delicious but I am growing fat. I am sure Gladys would not wish to make you alter my gowns again."

Mary giggled.

"Oh no, Miss Fell, I'll tell her. Tha was . . . you was so thin when Master Richard found 'ee. Now tha's . . . you are just right and I'll not let Gladys spoil my young lady's looks."

"I shall go to bed now, Mary. Leave me a pair of candles and I shall read for a while."

Lying propped up on the pillows with a book of poetry open in front of her, she found herself unable to concentrate on her reading. The question of her origins seemed to loom larger now that the house was so quiet, the family gone.

They all treat me as a lady, she thought. Surely so many people could not be mistaken. Yet, Richard does not believe it. Is there something about me that only he has seen, something that proves I am not of gentle birth? Would he not have pointed it out to his mother? Oh, I do not understand him. One minute so stiff and disapproving, the next so kind and thoughtful and gay.

She shivered as she remembered the feel of his arms around her, then sternly put such thoughts away and turned to her book.

The next few days passed uneventfully. Miss Carstairs spent a good deal of time in the village, where sickness had broken out as she had predicted. The weather continued unseasonably warm, and by the fourth day, Monday, Miss Fell was able to take a brief stroll in the shrubbery, well wrapped up by Mary, and with Thomas hovering near at hand. Here she won over her last critic. She stepped around a beech hedge, crinkly brown leaves still clinging to the twigs, and found herself facing a stone wall against which flowered a fountain of forsythia.

"Oh, how beautiful!" she exclaimed aloud, startling old John, who was leaning on his spade with his back to her, contemplating the sight. He turned slowly to face her.

"Ar," he said.

"Is it not early for forsythia?" she asked. "And oh, look! Scilla and crocuses already!"

" 'Tis a sheltered spot," the gardener muttered unwillingly. "Gets all t'sun. T'warm weather do bring 'em on. We calls 'em squills," he added belligerently.

"Yes, of course," soothed Miss Fell. "I

have heard that name. You must be Mr. Carstairs' head gardener?"

"Oh, aye. Bin here fifty year, man an' boy. 'Ud 'ee like a bunch o' that there yaller stuff?" he inquired grudgingly. "Some outlandish foreign name, but it do last well in a vase."

"How kind of you. Would you cut me some?" The conquest was complete.

Miss Fell's next trial was the vicar, Mr. Crane. She had been ten days in the neighborhood without attending church, and Miss Carstairs' habit of going every morning to early service pointed up her absence. Mr. Crane felt she must be in need of spiritual sustenance, and, besides, his curiosity had been sharpened by Miss Carstairs' total, though tactful, refusal to satisfy it. In spite of her devotion to the Church, Miss Carstairs could not bring herself to approve of clergymen — after all, they did belong to the despised male sex.

On Tuesday morning the wind turned chill and clouds started to gather, but Mr. Crane was undeterred. It was his duty to visit the mysterious Miss Fell, and he was not to be put off by the threat of rain. He understood that Miss Carstairs would be visiting old friends at some little distance, so he would be free of a presence he found rather overwhelming.

Mr. Crane called for his horse and set off up the hill. He regarded without pleasure the prospect of the village below and the towering moors beyond it, revealed now and then by a twist in the road. Lincolnshire bred, he had never been able to reconcile himself to having to go up or down to get anywhere, and the treeless slopes and rocky outcrops made him shiver. He was, in fact, even now negotiating for a living in his home county. It would be worth slightly less, but he felt oppressed by the gloomy hills and the cold courtesy of his patron, Mr. Carstairs. The hills grew gloomier as his horse plodded upward, and large drops of icy rain began falling.

By the time the vicar reached the manor, his coat was soaked and he was in a very bad humour. The servants greeted him without enthusiasm. ("Nasty, nosy creature, even if he be a man of God.") Thomas took his coat and Bedford showed him into the back parlour, a chilly, formal room used by the family to entertain visitors they did not wish to encourage.

"I shall inform Miss Fell of your arrival," said the butler, and left him to kick his heels.

It was at least twenty minutes before Miss Fell hurried in.

"I beg your pardon, sir, for keeping you waiting. I was not dressed to receive visitors." Her apology in no way effected a thaw in Mr. Crane's demeanor. While waiting, he had been reflecting on this nobody who had been taken into the bosom of the family that barely tolerated him. He proceeded to preach a sermon on the danger to the soul of avoiding regular churchgoing, brushing aside her explanations about the state of her health.

He was just embarking upon a detailed interrogation, nearer to inquisition than to catechism, when the door opened and a slight young man entered. He took in the situation at a glance. The vicar towered like an avenging Fury over the young woman, who sat, composed but pale, with her hands folded in her lap. They both looked at him.

"Good morning, Vicar," he said quietly. "The rain has momentarily ceased. I think you should seize the opportunity to ride home without getting wet. There is so much grippe about."

Mr. Crane glowered at him. "Oh, good morning, Denison. I have not . . . well, I daresay you are right. I shall see you again, Miss Fell."

With that threat, he stalked out, muttering.

Miss Fell rose to greet her deliverer. "You must be Mr. Carstairs' agent," she said. "How do you do? I am Miss Fell. I cannot guess how you disposed of that dreadful man so quickly, but I am most grateful."

"Do not thank me, Miss Fell," Jeremy Denison demurred with a grin. "I believe Mr. Crane can hardly have had time to open his mouth before the housekeeper sent Davy, the groom, after me. The message I received was, 'That there Reverend be a-bullyin' of the young lady an' Miss Carstairs from home an' please to come help!' How could I resist such an appeal?"

"Indeed it was good of you. He was asking me such questions! I . . . I daresay you may wonder . . ."

"Not at all, Miss Fell. Richard has told me the whole," he explained gently. "I should tell you that Mr. Crane was most unpleasant to my wife when first we came to Toblethorpe. Then he discovered that her uncle has an excellent living in his gift, so now he crawls to us in a most objectionable way, though as you see it can prove useful. Incidentally, my wife is as much inclined to see you a heroine as is Miss Lucy. Might I tell her she may visit you one day?"

"Of course, Mr. Denison, I should be very happy to receive her. Pray tell her to come at any time, only Miss Carstairs generally sleeps after lunch, so perhaps . . ."

"After lunch it shall be," promised Jeremy.

Mrs. Denison came to call on the following afternoon, and Miss Fell found her delightful. She was a quiet, gentle little woman who adored her husband and her children and was quite happy talking about them for half an hour at a time. Miss Fell encouraged her, envious of her placid, comfortable life, where a scraped knee was an event and a loaf that failed to rise a crisis. Mrs. Denison — they were soon Clara and Susan — was flattered by her interest and sympathy and thought her no less a heroine after meeting her than she had before.

"I shall never again be satisfied with a heroine who is blond or dark," she declared later to her husband. "There is something very romantic about Titian hair."

"I prefer blonds," he said, kissing her yellow curls.

After Mrs. Denison left her, Miss Fell was restless. Miss Carstairs had risen from her nap in time to greet the agent's wife as she departed, and then went out visiting. Many of the friends of her girlhood still lived in the neighboring villages and she thoroughly enjoyed the opportunity to renew old acquaintances. She would have been happy to take Miss Fell with her ("A most presentable young female," was her description to Lady Venables); however, Dr. Grimsdale, when consulted, advised caution.

"Stroll around the shrubbery," he grunted, "if the weather permits. Otherwise, no outings till next Monday at the earliest."

Rumours of Mr. Crane's attack on Miss Fell had reached him, and he was delighted thus to stymie his adversary. He made sure his prescription was known to all and sundry. It was not difficult. He had only to mention the matter to his housekeeper, an inveterate gossip who, in taking up cudgels on her master's behalf, had developed a running feud with the vicar's wife.

So Miss Fell was alone that Wednesday afternoon. It is true that her footsteps were dogged, as she wandered round the house, by Mary and Thomas, the former pleading with her to rest herself, the latter ready to lend his arm, or catch her if she swooned, or run for the doctor. Irritated, she snapped at them and was stricken with guilt at the sight of their disconsolate faces.

"Indeed, Mary, I am quite well," she said apologetically. "I know, I shall go to the music room and sit at the pianoforte. Then you and Thomas may go about your duties with easy minds. I thank you for your concern for me."

The anxious pair escorted her to the music room, opened the piano, built up the fire, drew the curtains at a drafty window, and at last left her in peace. For a few minutes she sat with her fingers resting lightly on the ivory keys, gazing dreamily out of the French windows at the sodden lawn and the bare trees beyond. Then she began to play, almost without volition. It seemed to her that her fingers chose the piece, that they performed it without any effort on her part. It was a quiet, rippling prelude by Bach, though she could not have put a name to it. The intricate harmonies wound together into a delicate tapestry that had a wholeness and rightness, which in some obscure way completed her being. She still had no memory beyond the past two weeks, but she no longer felt the aching void that had been a part of her for that fortnight.

She played for an hour and more, drugging herself on the music. The notes came to her fingers without stumbling or dragging as long as she did not consciously think about them. Then a sudden noise startled her, a coal falling in the grate, and she lost her place. It was like waking from a deep sleep. For a moment she sat confused. Unable to regain the almost trancelike state she had been in, she sighed and flipped through Lucy's music books. A Mozart minuet caught her eye, and she played the piece with enjoyment; but her total submission to the music was gone and with it her total peace of mind

As she finished, she heard footsteps behind her and turned; Miss Carstairs was entering the room.

"My dear, that was delightful. What a pity that Lucy cannot play with such charm."

Miss Fell smiled and rose to bob a curtsy. Suddenly she was exhausted, drained. Palefaced, she put a hand to the instrument to steady herself. Miss Carstairs moved swiftly to her side.

"Sit down, child. I daresay you have been playing too long. I shall ring for the servants and you shall go to bed."

"Oh no, ma'am. A momentary dizziness;

perhaps I should not have stood up so quickly."

"Well, if you are certain you should not retire, Thomas had best help you into the drawing room and we shall have a cup of tea. That will revive you."

The hot drink brought the color back to her pale cheeks, and she was able to dress for dinner without any unusual feeling of fatigue. That evening, as she sat at her daily task of sorting Miss Carstairs' tangled silks, she looked back on the day with pleasure. She had found a new friend and a new occupation, both of which promised delight.

The days passed more quickly now. She spent a good deal of time at the piano, though she was unable to abandon herself completely to the music again.

Miss Carstairs often listened to her playing, which improved with constant practice, and complimented her on it.

"You must have had a superb master," she pronounced. "I do not know when I have heard such excellence, though the Carstairs are a musical family. It is a pity that you do not sing."

"Indeed, ma'am, I would be happy to sing in a family party, but I have a horror of standing up before strangers and facing their indifference or scorn. When I play the pianoforte I may turn my back on the audience."

Now, how do I know that? she wondered. She could not precisely remember such a situation and yet it seemed to her that was how she would feel.

After that exchange, the two ladies were occasionally to be heard singing duets, Miss Carstairs' strong soprano mingling with the warm low voice of Miss Fell in ballads and folk songs.

"It do be a proper treat to hear 'em," declared Mary, "but my young lady do get tired a-singing, more nor playing."

Miss Fell's health was improving rapidly. She still tired very easily though, and more than once she had to retire before dinner, or Thomas had to carry her up in the evening.

Mrs. Denison visited her regularly, and she grew very fond of the unassuming young woman. When the doctor permitted at last, she repaid her visits and met her children, an adorable two-year-old boy as blond as his mother, and a baby girl whose lack of hair was more than compensated for by a pair of huge blue eyes that solemnly studied everything in sight.

On Sunday she went to church with

Miss Carstairs. The villagers stared mightily, but in a friendly way, which owed much to the reports of the manor's servants. The Reverend Crane preached a lengthy diatribe on the sin of pride, glaring at her the while. His own pride took a fall after the service when Miss Carstairs, pointedly ignoring him, invited the Denisons to join them for dinner that evening.

"Jeremy Denison," she announced firmly in the carriage on the way home up the hill, "is a young man of culture and sense, and Susan is a pretty-behaved creature. I am happy to see you have made her acquaintance."

Gladys was thrown into a panic at the thought of cooking for guests.

"More hair than wit, that one," said Mary with acerbity. "Auntie says, would 'ee speak to her, miss, or there won't be no dinner," she amended conscientiously.

Miss Carstairs could not approve of any other than sacred music on the Sabbath, or of the reading of novels or poetry. She presented Miss Fell with a copy of Miss Hannah More's *An Estimate of the Religion of the Fashionable World*, with which she spent a long afternoon. Truth to tell, she spent more time gazing out of the window at the clouds scurrying past in the cold grey sky, wondering if it would snow and if that would prevent Richard's return.

On Monday a letter from Mr. Carstairs was delivered to his Aunt Florence, announcing his intended arrival on the following Wednesday. He trusted Miss Fell was much recovered. There was no personal message for her.

Don't be gooseish, Miss Fell told herself severely. Why should there be?

Chapter 6

Lucy had sent all sorts of messages to her dear Clara, but Richard had refused to add them to his note.

"You will see Miss Fell in a few days," he said, "and besides I would not inflict such twaddle on my aunt. You may write yourself if you wish."

Lucy had just sat down to do so when the knocker below announced a visitor, and Lord Denham appeared to take her driving in the park.

Life had been hectic since the Carstairs' arrival in Cavendish Square a week earlier. After enduring for three days Lucy's grumbling every time a faster vehicle overtook the old traveling carriage, Richard had insisted on taking her to the coach-builder at the first opportunity.

"The mantua-makers will have to wait, mama," he told Lady Annabel. "If Lucy decides the coach is to be upholstered in purple velvet, it will take some time; and if I am to buy a new carriage, I would wish to use it on my return to Toblethorpe next week."

His sister moderately chose a cotton plush in royal blue. "I am sure the old coach must be fifty years old," she explained, "and if we are to have this one as long, it had better be fitted to last well."

The mantua-makers' turn came: muslins and jaconets, sarcenets, silks and satins; walking dresses, riding dresses, morning gowns, ball gowns; laces, ribbons and spangles; gloves, slippers, boots and bonnets. Lucy emerged dazed from fitting after fitting.

"I am sure I shall never wear the half of them," she confided to Richard. "At Toblethorpe such a quantity of clothes would last for years. It seems a wicked waste."

"I agree absolutely," he replied gravely. "We will send everything back and return to Toblethorpe at once."

"Oh no, Richard," she exclaimed, "I did not mean . . . Oh, you are bamming me, you odious wretch! I did not mean to be ungrateful, and, of course, I do not wish to miss my coming out. Only it is such a bore standing still while mama and Vane cluck around me, and I shall never have time to see the wild beasts at the Exeter Exchange."

"We shall go this afternoon," was the

prompt reply. "If you have no engagements?"

"Oh, mama will not take me visiting until I have suitable clothes. I have seen no one but Aunt Blanche and Cousin Jennifer in three days."

"Did I not see Tony here this morning?"

"Yes, but he is your friend, and I have known him forever. You know, Richard, Cousin Jennifer talks of nothing but clothes, and I daresay you may not believe me, Cousin Edward is the same! Jenny says he spends hours tying his cravat, and when he is done, his collar is so high he cannot turn his head. He wears such strange waistcoats, too. Yesterday he had one with pink and orange birds embroidered on it!" She giggled.

"I am not surprised, then, that you should hold elegant dress in such scorn. Come, go fetch a wrap while I order the curricle, and we'll be off to see the animals."

Lucy was enthralled by the strange beasts on view at the Exchange. It was a damp, chilly Tuesday, and few people were there, so they had an excellent view. They were studying a huge tiger huddled miserably in the back of its cage when someone tapped Richard on the shoulder. He turned.

"Harry!" he exclaimed. "When did you return home? I thought you were in India or some such godforsaken hole. Let me present you to my sister. Lucy, this is Captain Lord Harry Graham, Tony's brother, and he seems to have some of the younger ones with him. Colin, is it not, and Edwin?"

Lord Harry bowed over Lucy's hand, and the boys followed suit.

"Beg leave, ma'am," he said, "to introduce my friend. Richard, don't think you know him, either. Major Charles Bowen. Charles, this is Richard Carstairs and Miss Carstairs."

How-do-you-do's were exchanged.

"We are just returned from India," Lord Harry explained. "I merely went there and back with dispatches. Charles had been there three years and was sent home by Richard Wellesley with news of a victory. He has been telling the children such tales of tiger hunts that we had to bring 'em to see for themselves."

Major Bowen bowed to Lucy. He was a fair man of medium height and solid build. Where Lord Harry's face had been reddened by the glare of southern climes, the major's had been exposed long enough to develop a deep tan, which made a startling contrast with his sun-bleached hair and white teeth. Lucy thought he looked as exotic as the wild beasts.

"How do you do, Miss Carstairs," he said smiling. "I fear these sorry creatures bear little resemblance to the cats one sees in the jungle."

"They look very unhappy, do they not, sir? I am sure they should be left at peace in their own country. It is supposed to be educational to display them so," Lucy explained wisely. "I daresay it is more enlightening to see them in their natural state, but one cannot travel to India as easily as to the Exeter Exchange."

The major laughed. "Irrefutable, ma'am," he agreed.

Lord Harry and Richard were talking politics, and the boys had wandered off, so Major Bowen went on to tell Lucy about the excitement of tiger hunts on elephant back and the sadness of seeing such a noble creature shot.

"Though indeed it is sometimes necessary," he added. "In general, tigers do not attack people, but when they turn maneater, they are extremely cunning and dangerous."

They passed on to other subjects, and half an hour went by without their noticing it. Major Bowen thought Lucy charming, and refreshingly ready to announce her own opinions. He had, before he went to India, met many young ladies as pretty, but none as delightfully free from vanity, missishness, insipidity or flirtatiousness. When they parted, he asked her permission to call on her, and she agreed with alacrity.

Lucy was fascinated by the major's thrilling stories and flattered that he had taken her opinions seriously, even when he disagreed. Richard, and even Lord Denham, so often laughed at her. And yet he has a sense of humour, too, she thought. He laughed when she was funning. She hoped he would call soon. Her first London beau!

Richard had not observed his sister's long conversation with Major Bowen. His discussion had turned into a heated debate on the Spanish declaration of war, now three months old. After that, Lord Harry had set aside argument to relay a juicy on-dit he had just heard.

"You know the king opened Parliament last month?" he began in a low voice. "It seems that after the ceremonies he went home, threw the Princess of Wales on a sofa and tried to rape her. She escaped only because the sofa had no back and she rolled off."

"Where did you hear that?" asked Richard skeptically. "King George has always been a faithful husband, unlike his son."

"The story came from Princess Caroline herself. She is a strange one, but even she would hardly invent such a thing. Mark my words, we'll have a regency soon."

As they chatted about their distaste for Prinny as a prospective ruler, Richard suddenly remembered his sister and was relieved to see her some way off, apparently chatting to Lord Harry's friend and examining a hippopotamus. He listened with one ear to an apocryphal tale he had heard before and then excused himself.

"My mother will be wondering where Lucy has got to," he explained. "I had not intended to be gone so long and I suppose the chit must see all the rest of the animals. Shall I see you at Almack's tomorrow?"

"Lord no," said Harry frankly. "Too prim and proper for my taste. Cribb's Parlour is more my line. Daresay m'brother will be at the Marriage Mart. Seems to have taken quite a fancy to Miss Carstairs, though he's not in the petticoat line in the regular way." He winked.

"I'd as soon not be there myself," Richard disclaimed, "only I promised to escort my mother and Lucy. It will be her first time there."

"Nervous, is she? M'sister was terrified of those old biddies."

"Lucy nervous? Good God, no. I don't believe she knows what the word means!"

Dressing the next evening in her new ball gown of primrose yellow gauze over white silk, Lucy was indeed not at all dismayed at the prospect before her. Her mother's old friend, Lady Cowper, had sent vouchers for Almack's without being asked. Lord Denham had driven her in the park that morning and reminded her to save him her first waltz, and the second, too. Major Bowen had called with Lord Harry and engaged her hand for the cotillion and the supper dance. Her Cousin Jennifer would be there, and if she did not quite expect, as a newcomer, to dance every dance, she was sure she would enjoy herself.

"I know it is usual to begin the Season with rather more intimate parties," said Lady Annabel apologetically to Richard. "However, our first engagement is tomorrow, and Lord Denham insisted he could not wait another week to waltz with your sister. I thought it best to acquiesce.

Lucy does not know many people yet; but she is not precisely shy, you know, and it will not hurt her to sit down for a part of the evening."

"Devil a chance of that, mama! Tony and this major of Harry's have taken two dances each, and the minx has engaged me for two more. With only one or two new acquaintances she will be busy all night."

"Major Bowen seems an unexceptionable young man. I suppose Lord Harry has known him for some time?"

"Oh, forever, I believe, though that means nothing. Harry has some mighty strange friends. You had best keep an eye on the major, mama."

"I will, dearest. However, I daresay once Lucy has met more people, she will be less interested in him."

"Have you had that all day, too? 'The major says this and the major says that!' I wish the fellow would go back to India."

" 'The major says' he has several months' leave due to him and a good deal of personal business to attend to."

" 'The major says' India is most interesting but three years is enough."

They both laughed and went to dress for dinner.

A few minutes later, Lady Annabel entered Lucy's room. Her abigail, who was brushing her hair, retired. Lucy turned to greet her mother and saw that she was holding a small, velvet-covered box.

"Dearest," said Lady Annabel, "I have brought you my pearls." She took them out and clasped them around Lucy's neck. "Your father gave them to me when we were betrothed. I have not worn them since . . . since you were a baby. They are yours now."

"Mama, how beautiful. I do thank you and I will take the greatest care of them, I promise."

"They are just the thing for a young girl making her debut," said Lady Annabel practically. "I shall wear my diamonds, which would never do for you."

"Oh, mama, I shall be quite the thing! And look, Lord Denham sent me flowers." She showed her mother a posy of primroses in a silver holder. "Richard said he thought I might carry them."

"Yes, indeed. It will be quite proper. I am glad you had the sense to inquire. It will not do to be accepting gifts from just anyone."

"I knew it would be unexceptionable from Tony. Richard said he inquired about the color of my gown, so as to match it.

Was not that charming?"

Lord Denham had been invited to dine, and when Lucy descended the stairs a half-hour later he had just arrived. He regarded her with such evident admiration that she blushed. Richard looked at her with approval and came to take her hand.

"I have something for you, Lucy," he said, and presented her with a tiny box.

"What is it, a beetle?" inquired Lucy suspiciously, and the gentlemen roared with laughter.

"What a memory!" exclaimed Richard. "That must have been ten years ago! Don't be bacon-brained, Lucy. You are a young lady now, not a schoolgirl."

Lucy flushed. "I beg your pardon, Richard," she said stiffly. "May I open it now?"

"Of course, child. Go ahead."

The box contained a pair of the daintiest pearl earrings. Offended sensibilities and genteel reserve alike forgotten, Lucy flung her arms round her brother.

"Oh, Richard, they are lovely. I am truly grateful and I did not really think it was a beetle."

"Next time it may be," said Richard wickedly.

Turning to Lord Denham, Lucy thanked

him prettily for the flowers.

"I shall wear them tonight," she promised.

"Better check them for beetles first," he replied with a grin.

"You are both odious," pouted Lucy.

Providentially, the butler entered to announce dinner. Bedford had been left in Yorkshire. The Carstairs' London house was presided over by the supercilious Bell, who had regretted for years his young master's dislike of entertaining. With the arrival of the ladies of the family, he foresaw the opportunity for a more adequate display of his talents and had gone so far as to unbend to Mrs. Dawkins, the housekeeper, "I thinks it 'ighly likely, Mrs. Dawkins, as we shall 'ave the honner of h'entertaining the 'ighest in the land," he had pronounced regally. "Miss Lucy is a fetching young lady and h'I do believe as 'ow she will Bring 'Em In, Mrs. Dawkins, if you gets my meaning. I thinks it 'ighly likely."

He had even condescended to say to Lucy, when she thanked him for some service, "H'it's a pleasure to 'ave you in the 'ouse, miss, you and m'lady."

Now, as Lucy and Richard followed Lady Annabel and Lord Denham to the dining room, he bowed to her and said in a ponderous, fatherly tone, "Begging your pardon, Miss Lucy, but being as it's your first Lunnon ball, me and the servants was wishful to tell you as 'ow you looks beautiful and to 'ope you 'as a 'appy h'evening."

Lucy dimpled up at him.

"Why, thank you, Bell. I am sure I shall."

"My, what condescension!" whispered Richard in her ear. "He is never half so complaisant to me. I do believe you have made a conquest."

"At least he is not likely to speak to me of beetles," she retorted, her good humour restored. She was so delightfully gay during dinner that Lord Denham was inclined to think his suspicions were correct – he was in love.

In town they ate dinner at a fashionably late hour, so afterwards there was little time for the gentlemen to sit over their brandy before the carriage was at the door. Lucy was in an agony of impatience. It would never do to be late, for once the doors were shut, the patronesses of Almack's would allow no one to enter.

At last Richard and Tony appeared. Lucy thought her brother looked very fine in his knee breeches, black coat and snowy white linen. Richard made no attempt to ape the extremes of fashion, modeling himself rather on the quiet elegance of Beau Brummell, with whom he had been at school. Constantly conscious in public of his dark complexion, he had taken to heart the Beau's tactful and kindly advice. Observing an exquisite who had a large wart on his nose and wore a candy-striped waistcoat, he had pointed out that to draw attention to one's appearance in such a case was shockingly unwise. Never a fop, Richard had since studied to give no offence with his clothes to add to the offence caused by his face.

Lucy knew none of this. Lady Annabel had an inkling, though she did not know of the occasion in his youth when a reigning beauty, known for the liberality with which she granted her favours, had turned from his request for a dance and giggled behind her fan to her companion that she could not possibly dance with a blackamoor. That had been the last time he had danced at any but small private parties where he knew everyone. He was determined that tonight his sister should be his only partner.

His resolution was soon broken. The first people they saw upon entering the already crowded rooms were their Aunt

Blanche and their cousins. Edward hurried up and claimed Lucy's hand. He was a sight to behold, in an orange satin coat and mauve waistcoat, his collar so high and tight that his eyes were popping with semi-strangulation.

"Do you think you should dance, cousin?" asked Lucy solicitously, not daring to look at Richard or Tony lest she burst into laughter. "The exercise might spoil your finery."

"Do you like it?" he preened. "I am surprised that no one has previously thought of combining orange and mauve. A particularly felicitous combination, do you not think? I am sure no one has done it before."

"I feel certain you are right, Edward," reassured Richard. "You had better take Lucy to dance now, the sets are forming."

He, too, avoided Lord Denham's eye, but in fact Tony was wondering if Edward was not right. Perhaps a little too extreme, he decided. He himself was very fine in green, with a primrose waistcoat in compliment to Miss Carstairs.

Richard introduced Lord Denham to his other cousin, who was sitting disconsolately by her mother. Miss Jennifer Carstairs was a plump blond in her second

Season. She had had a moderately successful first Season, and this year she had been fired by emulation of her brother's finery. Her pink gown was so embellished with lace and frills and knots of ribbon that the color could barely be seen. Mrs. Geoffrey Carstairs looked despairingly at her sister-in-law as Lady Annabel, scarce recovered from Edward's appearance, was newly stunned by her niece Jenny.

Lord Denham, always well-mannered and obliging, requested a dance and Jennifer gratefully complied. She now wished she had heeded her mama's warnings, and resolved ruthlessly to strip away all the decorations her abigail had painstakingly sewn on her gowns. Not without sense, she had realized as soon as she saw her cousins how much more elegant their simpler clothing appeared. She decided Edward looked like a popinjay, but a lingering taste for frills made her think Lord Denham quite a Pink of the Ton.

In spite of providing a partner for his cousin Richard could not in all decency avoid putting his name down for a country dance, and he knew that if she remained a wallflower he would be forced to exert himself further. Having seated his mother, then conversed for a few minutes with his aunt, he spotted Brummell across the room and left the ladies to a comfortable cose.

The Beau was the one crony of Richard's of whom his uncle, Lord Mortlake, could not approve. His father had been a clerk, his grandfather, it was rumoured, a valet. Educated at Eton, he had made the acquaintance of the Prince of Wales and on entering the Fashionable World, had quickly become its arbiter of fashion. His membership in Prinny's set did him no service in the eyes of high sticklers like Lord Mortlake, who was quite unable to understand Richard's friendship with him, especially as Richard had no interest in frequenting Carlton House. However, the friendship had started at Eton and showed every sign of continuing.

"Who was that charming child who entered with you?" Brummell accosted Richard.

"My sister, George. With your accolade there will be no further need for me to exert myself on her behalf. Will you let me present you to her?"

"By all means, my dear chap, provided your cousins are not in the vicinity. You cannot expect me to lend them countenance."

Richard laughed ruefully.

"I fear not," he said. "Come, let us take a hand at piquet until this dance is over, then I will attempt to separate Lucy from Edward."

Lucy was thoroughly enjoying the dance, in spite of her partner's wheezes and alarmingly purple face, which clashed distressingly with his clothes. It ended not a moment too soon for Edward, who mopped his forehead and conducted her back toward her mother. As they made their way through the crush, Lucy found a familiar figure beside her.

"The next dance is mine," claimed Major Bowen.

Lucy presented her cousin, wishing suddenly that he did not appear such a figure of fun. The major shook hands gravely and turned back to her with a twinkle in his eye.

"Is your brother here?" he inquired.

"Yes, but I do not know where he is. My mother is over there with my aunt, and there is Lord Denham with Jennifer, my cousin. Pray let us not go there. I fear we will be drawn into some tedious conversation." Lucy impulsively pulled at his arm.

"I must make my bow to Lady Annabel," he said calmly, ignoring her ill-judged outburst. He was a major at the early age of twenty-six because, while insisting on firm discipline and obedience to orders, he had been able to make allowances for the untutored waywardness of his native soldiers. He had ignored behaviour of which they, eager to please, were already ashamed, while expecting them to act correctly next time. His expectations had rarely been unfounded, his sepoys had worshiped him and happily risked their lives for him. Now, looking with well-hidden amusement at Lucy's guilty face, he could almost imagine he had a sepoy on his arm. Not quite.

Lucy knew she had transgressed and was grateful for his forbearance. Richard would have reproached her, her mother would have chided, but this almost stranger seemed to understand that she was already repentant and did not need to be scolded. She found it hard to believe that she had met him only the previous day. She looked up to find him gazing at her with such serious intentness that she felt a little breathless.

She managed to smile and to ask with creditable composure, "Have you had many partners already, Major?"

"Partners? Oh, yes, I have danced once

or twice. I was waiting for you."

He said this in such a matter-of-fact tone that she hardly knew whether it was a compliment. Uncertain how to answer, she was silent until they reached her mother. Then she was busy introducing the major to her aunt, her cousin, Lord Denham. The latter shook his hand.

"Ah, yes, friend of Harry's, ain't you? Think we must have met before. You must tell me about General Frazer's engagement at Delhi some time. Miss Lucy, the next dance after this is a waltz. I am off to find Lady Cowper, to ensure that you cannot break your promise."

Major Bowen led her on to the floor for the cotillion.

"Will you waltz with me?" he asked when the dance brought them together.

"I cannot!" Lucy exclaimed. "We are engaged for the supper dance, and mama would never permit me to dance more than twice with the same gentleman."

"I beg your pardon. I have been so long out of the country that I have quite forgot the rules."

"Then I shall have to remind you so that you may observe the proprieties." Lucy twinkled at him.

He laughed. "Touché! You will save me a

waltz at the next ball?"

"Of course," she said lightly.

Her waltz with Lord Denham passed in a dream. The dance was still considered slightly indecent in Yorkshire and Lady Annabel had not permitted her to take part at the York Assemblies. However, with Emily Cowper approving, there could be no objection now. Lucy had been looking forward to it for months. At first it felt strange to have a gentleman's arm about her waist, then she reminded herself that after all she had known Lord Denham for years — he was almost a brother to her. She gave herself up to the music and the motion, and no one watching her could have guessed that she had learned the dance in three brief sessions, crammed between shopping and fittings.

Lord Denham was an excellent dancer when he decided to make the effort. He swung her round the room, intoxicated by her closeness. At the end of the dance, they found themselves beside the draped alcove of a window.

"I am so hot," declared Lucy. "Let us open that window."

"I would not dare. We should have all the old biddies crying 'inflammation of the lungs!' "

"Well then, let us go closer and draw the curtains and no one will know."

Lord Denham knew he should scotch the scheme, but he was too lazy to protest. He followed her into the bow and opened a pane while Lucy closed the curtains tightly. She stood by the open window, fanning herself.

"I enjoyed waltzing excessively, Lord Denham," she said.

"Surely you could call me Tony, after we have known each other for so long," he protested.

She smiled. "I often do so by mistake," she agreed. "It would be so much simpler. I am not sure if I should ask you to call me Lucy. Would it be forward in me?"

They were discussing the matter when the curtain was pulled back and Richard appeared with a thunderous face.

"Lucy!" he hissed, "what the devil do you think you are doing?"

"I was very hot, Richard, and Tony said people would object to the air," she explained innocently.

"I'll talk to you later," he promised grimly. "Here is my friend Brummell. You must go and sit with him and we must hope that no one has noticed your lack of conduct."

An amused Brummell bore Lucy away. Richard turned on Tony.

"Oh, I cry quits," he apologized hastily. "Indeed, Richard, Lucy only wanted some air. I should have stopped her, but damme if I can be always contradicting the chit."

"Of course, I know you would not take advantage of her, Tony," said Richard, somewhat mollified. "I suppose I am up in the boughs because that dashed major had the infernal impudence to tell me where Lucy was. Said he felt it was not his place to intrude upon you. Dash it, Tony, how could you be so confoundedly thoughtless? I only hope Lady Cowper may not have noticed."

The guilty Lord Denham apologized again and the two went off to play cards.

No more contretemps marred Lucy's evening. Beau Brummell sat with her for quite twenty minutes, assuring her success. She waltzed again with Tony, avoiding windows, and enjoyed a gay supper with Major Bowen, Jenny, and her partner. So many young men begged to be presented to her that Richard had not had to do his duty after all. As the carriage rolled home through the quiet streets, she was too sleepy to worry about the lecture she was bound to receive from Richard on the morrow.

Chapter 7

Lucy's scolding was not very severe. The few people who had noticed her imprudence had then seen Richard and Lord Denham stroll off arm in arm while Lucy chatted happily to Beau Brummell, the last man to countenance any havey-cavey goings-on. Lady Annabel had seen nothing, and nobody had brought it to her attention, so Richard could not even accuse his sister of worrying their mother.

"Do try to be a little more circumspect," he said with asperity. "You were lucky this time. If it happened again you might easily gain the reputation of being fast."

"Fustian!" Lucy declared. "When we have known Tony forever! Of course I should not behave so with a mere acquaintance." She was tempted to try it with the major, but suspected that he would not permit anything so improper.

"You must remember that not everyone knows on what terms we stand with Tony. Indeed I should call it unwise with any man other than myself. Lucy, try to think before you act. You will not wish to distress mama."

"Oh, Richard, I promise I will try," she cried in penitence. "I do not mean to fall into such scrapes. It would be odious in me when you are such a good brother and mama is at such pains to give me a wonderful Season." She hugged him, and he dropped a kiss on her brow.

"Very well then, goosecap, we shall forget it. I hear the knocker. Surely it is early for even the most ardent of your admirers."

They had just finished breakfast, Lady Annabel having eaten in her room. Shortly, Bell appeared to announce that a hackney piled high with bandboxes had arrived from Chez Lisette.

"My new gowns!" crowed Lucy. "Have them taken up to my chamber, please, Bell. Madame Charmaine promised my hats for this morning, also. Richard, only wait and see how elegant I shall be."

"Did not a vast number of packages come home with you yesterday?"

"Yes, but they held only stockings, shawls and gloves. And the gown I wore last night, which was completed in a hurry for me. Just wait till you see my riding dress."

"I cannot wait!" said Richard dryly. "Off you go, now. I hear another carriage drawing up."

Lucy had barely time to open half the boxes before Lord Denham arrived. She scrambled into the new royal blue velvet riding dress, and hurried downstairs.

"Good morning, Tony," she greeted him, unabashed by the memory of the night before. "Do you like my new habit?" The train over her arm, she pirouetted before Richard and Tony.

"Charming," said the latter, "though not half so charming as the young lady wearing it."

"How charming of you to say so," giggled Lucy.

"Charming weather, is it not?" said her brother.

Tony laughed. "I am come to ask if you will give me the pleasure of your charming company in the park, as the day is so charming."

"I should be charmed, only that I am engaged to ride this morning with Major Bowen. Perhaps we shall see you in the park?"

At that moment more visitors were announced. Miss Maria Allenby had called to see Lady Annabel and had met on the steps with two of the young sprigs of fashion who had been made acquainted with Lucy the previous night. Each had brought her a large bouquet and they were glaring at each other like a pair of tomcats.

"Thank you so much, Sir Percy, Mr. Haselton." Lucy tried to soothe their ruffled feelings. "It is charming of you, I do love flowers."

"Charming flowers," murmured Lord Denham provocatively in her ear, and her gravity was nearly overcome.

The next arrivals were Cousin Jennifer and a friend, Miss Melville, escorted by Cousin Edward, whose sartorial magnificence, though stunning to behold, did not compete with his array at the ball. The drawing room was growing crowded and the sound of conversation masked Bell's announcement of Major Bowen and Captain Lord Harry Graham.

Lucy being much occupied with her two youthful admirers, the officers made their way to Lady Annabel. Miss Allenby had known Harry from the cradle and she and Lady Annabel engaged his attention. Major Bowen went to speak to Richard, who greeted him stiffly. *What a damned persistent fellow,* he was thinking. *A fortune hunter, I'll be bound.* He had better make inquiries.

Finding no welcome, the major decided to interrupt Lucy's circle. She was in any case looking rather hunted. He noted that she was wearing a riding dress, very becoming, and hoped that she remembered their engagement.

She smiled up at him as he approached. "Major Bowen," she said thankfully. "Let me present Sir Percy Driscoll and Mr. Haselton. The major is just now returned from India, gentlemen, with news of a great victory."

The youths gazed at him in awe, and started to question him about the fighting, their quarrel forgotten. Lucy sighed with relief.

"I have not forgot our ride," she murmured. "Only there are so many people here and I have not spoken to the half of them. Will you wait a little?"

"Forever," he replied, with such a look that she was breathless once more. He turned what would be a meaningless compliment on the lips of another man into an avowal, she thought.

Seeing her confusion, he rescued her. "However, I trust you will not make me wait so long!"

"Indeed I will not. I must speak with my cousins and then I will come. The horses must have been standing this half-hour."

Another half-hour found them in the park. Lucy being but lately come to town and the major recently returned after a long absence, neither had much acquaintance to interrupt their talk. The horses picked their way between phaetons and curricles, strollers and riders, until they came to a clear spot.

"I must have a gallop," cried Lucy. "Poor Star has not stretched her legs since we came to town."

"I think we had better not, Miss Carstairs," said the major quietly. "A short canter would be unexceptionable, however."

Lucy looked rebellious, and he wondered for a moment if he would have to catch her rein. She saw in his face that he would not hesitate to do so and gave in gracefully.

"There are so many rules of conduct in London," she observed in disgust. "It is a wonder there is anything left to do that is proper."

He laughed. "Many people consider there is a vast choice of occupations in town, and find it dull in the country."

"I never was bored at Toblethorpe. You have lived mostly in the country, have you not, until you went to India? Did you not find a deal to occupy you?"

"Oh yes, Miss Carstairs, I prefer a rural life, though I enjoy a few months in fashionable society now and then."

"Then we are quite agreed. Indeed, I do not mean to complain, I am enjoying London excessively."

"I think you are not the complaining sort. I do not know which to admire most, the spirit that makes you wish to gallop, the good-natured way you give up an unwise project at a hint, or the picture you present on horseback. Come, let us canter before anyone blocks our path."

He let Lucy lead by a head, happy to watch her enjoyment, and was relieved to find that his hired hack had not too bad a pace. She drew rein as they again approached the thronged mass of High Society taking the air.

Lord Denham, accompanied by his brother, appeared on his grey mare. "Aha," called his lordship. "We thought we should never find you. What a crush!"

"Is it not, Tony? Major Bowen and I found a little space and have managed to canter."

The major was dismayed to hear Lucy addressing Lord Denham by his nickname. He was not left to brood.

"Charles," said Lord Harry, "you are wanted urgently at the War Office. We met a messenger on the way."

"Dash it, it must be that meeting with the Prime Minister they warned me about. Miss Carstairs, I shall have to escort you back immediately."

"Do not trouble yourself," advised Lord Denham. "Harry and I will see Lucy home."

The major thanked him, most unwillingly. He turned in the saddle to say goodbye to Lucy and found her close beside him, holding out her hand.

As he bowed over it, she said softly, "Shall I see you again soon, sir?"

He raised his eyes to her face and she had so much the appearance of a hopeful puppy begging for a walk that he had to smile as he replied, "I do indeed trust you may. However, I fear that I am going to be kept very busy for a few days. Shall you be at Lady Exeter's ball?"

"Oh yes, I shall save you a dance."

"Two," he proposed, "and one of them a waltz. I dare not ask for the supper dance again so soon," he added wryly.

She blushed, but answered, "You are too modest, sir. It is yours."

He pressed her hand, and she withdrew it quickly. She had not realized he still held it, she told herself; then, being an honest young lady, had to admit that perhaps she had known.

Major Bowen bowed to their lordships and rode off.

Tony and Harry had been greeting acquaintances, and now their group was joined by several others. Lucy renewed her acquaintance with a Miss Harvey whom she had met at Almack's, and was introduced to her brother and two or three other newcomers. How delightful it would be, she thought as she chatted happily, to have a large circle of friends in town. Some of the gentlemen asked her to put their names down for dances at Lady Exeter's ball, and she was glad the major had already spoken for his two. She wished she dared write him down for a third, but by now she knew him well enough to be sure he would not take it.

Lord Denham rode up beside her. "Are you not tired, Lucy? You have been out for some time."

"Tony, you know I ride for hours in Yorkshire."

"In Yorkshire you do not stay out until three in the morning dancing. However, I take it you are not yet ready to return."

"Well, I am enjoying myself famously but we are to go out visiting this afternoon, so perhaps mama would wish me to go home."

"Come, then. Harry, do you accompany us?"

"You will excuse me, Miss Carstairs. I believe you will be moderately safe with my brother." Harry was occupied in flirting with Miss Harvey, a diminutive blond with sparkling blue eyes.

Lucy and Tony made their farewells and departed. The crowds were thinning now. The morning sun was hidden by threatening clouds and the park did not look so inviting.

When they reached Cavendish Square, large drops were falling. Lord Denham hurried her up the steps and kissed her hand warmly.

"I shall call tomorrow," he said. "If this continues we shall not be able to ride, however."

"I suppose not. Thank you for your escort, Tony." Lucy was in a pensive mood. Tony was a delightful companion, amusing and good-natured, so easygoing that he would never try to hold her back from whatever she wanted to do. She was beginning to suspect that he might hold warmer feelings for her than could be accounted for by her being the sister of his bosom-bow. Yet he was too much the gentleman to put her to the blush. Suppose he had taken advantage of her foolishness last night? She wondered if he wanted to marry her. He was rich, heir to a marquis; as his wife she would lead a fashionable life with every luxury.

Yet she felt she had rather follow the drum with a certain gentleman of whom, she feared, her brother disapproved. Entering the drawing room, she heaved a deep sigh.

"My dear!" exclaimed her mother, "are you in the mopes? Come, tell me what is wrong."

Lucy nearly opened her heart to Lady Annabel, then remembered Richard's strictures against worrying her mama. "Oh, it is nothing. Simply that it is raining and I shall not be able to ride tomorrow if it continues. It makes the streets look so grey."

"What, five days in town and already blue-devilled?" asked her brother. She had not noticed him, as he had been standing in the window embrasure, gazing out at the

150

wet square. How lucky she had not explained her sigh!

"You do not look so cock-a-hoop yourself," she retorted sharply.

"I was thinking of Toblethorpe," he said. His mother, watching closely, thought that a slight flush colored his dark cheeks as he added hurriedly, "It may be snowing in Yorkshire, you know, and the early lambs will be in danger."

"I am sure Jeremy and the shepherds are taking good care of them," said Lady Annabel soothingly. "Lucy, you had better have a bite to eat. We are to call on your Aunt Blanche and Emily Cowper this afternoon, and this evening there is a dress party for Vanessa Arby's daughter. I do not think you have met her, but I was at school with Lady Arby."

Lucy brightened. "I had forgot. May I wear the pink sarcenet with cerise ribbons?"

"That would be most suitable, my dear. Richard, do you come?"

Richard was once more gazing moodily out of the window. "No, mama," he said impatiently, "unless you particularly need my escort. I detest such affairs. I am engaged to dine with Tony and Sir Andrew Gibbons."

"Very well, dear. I hope you will join us for Her Grace of Devonshire's musicale tomorrow?"

"I would not miss it for the world. I hear she has engaged an entire orchestra to play some symphonies, instead of the usual caterwauling soprano or amateur hopefuls." Richard was roused to enthusiasm. Lord Denham had spoken truer than he guessed when he suspected his friend's chief enjoyment in London was the music.

"Yes, I believe they will play something by this Viennese, Beethoven is it not? Maria Allenby's cousin was in Austria in 1802 and was most impressed by him. I wonder if we could find some music of his for the pianoforte that Lucy could play. She has been neglecting her practice shamefully since we left home."

"Oh, do, mama. I should like something new to play. The waltz is from Vienna, is it not? Perhaps Monsieur Beethoven has written some waltzes."

"Herr Beethoven, chucklehead. Indeed, I believe it is Herr van Beethoven. I am off now, mama. Enjoy your party, Lucy, if I do not see you before."

The ladies went to change for their round of visits. In spite of the rain the streets were full of carriages, and they were far from being the only ones visiting either Aunt Blanche or Lady Cowper. While Lucy chattered with several young people at the latter's house, Lady Annabel, mindful of Richard's words, tried tactfully to find out something about Major Bowen.

"A dashing young man, is he not?" observed Lady Cowper. "I know little about him. I believe Sally Jersey gave him vouchers for Almack's. She had ever a soft heart for a soldier, and Harry Graham introduced him. I suppose he is unexceptionable. He certainly seems a gentleman, though one never knows these days."

Lady Annabel decided Richard would have to pump Lord Harry if he wanted any further information.

The dress party that evening was a great success, honoured by the description "a shocking squeeze," than which no higher praise could be given. Lucy was lovely in a gown of the palest pink, relieved by knots of cherry ribbon. Her hand was solicited for every dance.

Lord Denham turned up in the middle of the evening, saying he would never forgive Richard for expecting him to play cards all night when there was an opportunity to waltz with his sister. He was very merry, and Lucy suspected he must be a little "on the go." When he found out that Lucy was engaged for all the waltzes, he waxed very indignant and threatened to call out all her partners.

Lucy, giggling, offered to console him with a country dance, which he accepted with the proviso that they should sit it out.

"Not too steady on m'feet, y'know," he confided. "Wouldn't have drunk all that brandy if Richard had come clean a bit earlier. 'Sides, wanna talk to you."

When his turn came, he flirted outrageously with her. The alcohol did not seem to have impaired his wit, and he kept her in fits of laughter for half an hour. Several people noticed them, and a rumour began to circulate that Lord Denham was dangling after Miss Carstairs.

"A chit just out of the schoolroom," whispered envious mamas of hopeful daughters. "Much too young to marry. And he one of the most eligible bachelors. He never was in the petticoat line before. Maybe he has just decided to hang out for a wife. It might be worth . . ."

Lord Denham was indeed hanging out for a wife; but only one wife would suit him, and the lures cast his way went unheeded. He found himself uncharacteristically uncertain of the best course of action. Had he followed his heart, he would have asked for Lucy's hand immediately. Though he could not doubt that her family would welcome him as a suitor, he was less certain of Lucy's feelings. He rather thought she regarded him as an elder brother, and was at a loss how to act to dispel that image. He wished he had exerted himself more in the past in the pursuit of young ladies, and felt himself sadly in need of practice. In any case, he decided, it would be unfair to propose when she was so lately come to town. She should have a chance to meet more people before she had to choose.

So he postponed the matter, exerted himself to make her laugh, and took her to Gunther's the next morning for an ice.

"Though why anyone should wish to eat ices in this weather is beyond me," he frankly admitted to Richard.

Saturday evening came at last, and Lady Exeter's ball. It was to be Lucy's first grand private ball, and she told herself that was why she felt so fluttery. After all, she thought, if he cared for her he would have found a way to see her. Three whole days! Well, she admitted, two and a half, and he said he would be very busy. *Don't be bacon-*

brained, she scolded herself vulgarly, *you have known him only a week. He has forgotten you by now.*

She could not decide which gown to wear. No fewer than three nosegays had arrived, two yellow and one pink. One was primroses from Lord Denham, with a clever message involving "Wednesday," "waltz" and "charming."

"I cannot wear my pink dress again so soon," she said crossly to her abigail, "and I do not feel like either of the yellow ones. How silly people are, thinking one must forever wear the same colors."

There was a knock at the door. Molly went to it, and returned with yet another bouquet.

"Ooh, look, Miss Lucy," she cried. "This 'un's purple. How'd anyone find violets this early?"

Lucy took the flowers and slowly opened the accompanying card, heart in mouth. Then suddenly she was all gaiety.

"Molly, I shall wear the lilac taffeta with the cream silk underdress. Hurry, I shall be late."

Lucy danced on air that night. The first thing she saw when they arrived at Exeter House was a tan face with startlingly blue eyes that filled with joy as they noted her bouquet. So great was the press of bodies that she could not come near the major for some time, and then only to exchange a hurried word.

"I missed you," she said simply.

"You are wearing my flowers." His look was full of gratitude.

Partner after partner came up to claim her. She danced in a dream, unaware of whose hand held hers, answering at random. At last came the waltz she had saved for him, and he appeared at her side.

Major Bowen's dancing could not be compared with Lord Denham's elegant precision. He was a soldier, and India had held little opportunity for balls and routs. But Lucy noticed only the strong arm supporting her, the blue eyes looking down so warmly into hers.

Due to her careful planning, their waltz was followed immediately by the supper dance. They were joined at their table by a gay group, and Lucy talked and laughed with the rest, yet she could not afterward have named one of them, and Lady Exeter's chef would have been shockingly insulted had he known how little interest she had in the delicacies the major set before her. That is not to say that she did not eat. It would have taken more than love to destroy Lucy's appetite after three hours of dancing. But she did not notice whether she was consuming lobster patties or *crème aux fraises*, strawberries smuggled in from Spain at vast expense, and her favorite dessert. The only thing she was conscious of was that he held her hand under the table. As for him, he quite forgot to eat.

At last she saw her next partner bearing down on her. "Shall I see you tomorrow?" she whispered.

He shook his head gravely, and winced at her puzzled look. "I must attend the Chapel Royal," he explained, "and then I am to see His Majesty to describe the fighting in India. And on Monday I expect to be all day with my lawyer. I have not yet had time to begin on my private business, and it cannot in conscience be put off longer. Are you engaged Monday night?"

"We go to the play," she pouted.

"I shall try to be there. In any case, I will call on Tuesday morning. Will you walk with me if it is fine?"

"Of course." Lucy melted at his anxious look. "I shall try to understand that you are a busy man. I do not mean to tease."

He kissed her hand. "Until Tuesday, then." He bowed, unsmiling, to the Tulip who was waiting to lead her out, and left the ball.

Walking to his lodgings, he began to think seriously about selling out of the army. He tried to put out of his mind the thought that he could not ask Lucy to become a soldier's wife. After all, perhaps she was merely flirting with him.

He dismissed that idea at once. Yet she was very young and he had every reason to suppose that he would not meet her family's approval. From all he had heard, they were a very toplofty lot, and though he had sufficient fortune to support her in comfort, and a good-sized estate in Northumberland, they might well object to his birth. His mother had been a baronet's daughter; but his paternal grandfather had worked for his fortune, and he knew all too well how the whiff of trade sent the *haut ton* scurrying.

Thinking of his family, he wondered, not for the first time, why he had not had a reply from his Cousin Rosalind to the letter he had sent on his arrival in England, two weeks earlier. In India he had never been surprised by the dilatory, or even disappearing, mail. Surely in England in the nineteenth century he might expect better service. He was torn. Should he post up to

Northumberland to assure himself that all was well? It would mean an absence upward of a week, and even if Lucy would forgive him, he doubted that the Minister for War would do so. He decided to wait. For all he knew, the county might be under six feet of snow.

His thoughts returned to Lucy, and he prayed that it might be fine on Tuesday.

It rained all day Sunday and it rained all day Monday. Richard nearly put off his intended departure for Yorkshire, but filled with an impatience he could not explain, he held to his original plan to leave on Tuesday.

"I told Aunt Florence I should arrive on Wednesday," he told his mother. "I do not dare be late."

"What a bubble! Richard, can you really make it in two days? You will have the travelling carriage, you know, not your light chaise."

"The new carriage is to be delivered today. I am sure it will be much faster than the old. I shall leave early, and the evenings are lighter now, so I can travel longer. Do not fret, mama."

"You will not expect Miss Fell to make the journey at such a speed!"

"What do you take me for, mama, a slave driver? We shall spend Sunday at Arnden and from there make three easy stages. You may look for us early on the first Wednesday in April."

Richard bade Lady Annabel and Lucy farewell that night after the theatre. Willett woke him at dawn the next day, and in the early light he could see that the skies had miraculously cleared. Thinking of the new team he had purchased in honour of the new coach, prime cattle if he knew his horses, he was sure he would have no trouble in reaching Toblethorpe the following day. He set off as the sun rose, whistling merrily in an ungentlemanlike way that had servant girls, busy scrubbing steps, gaping at him in surprise.

Lucy was no less pleased to see the sun. She put on her walking dress immediately, making her mother protest at her appearance at breakfast.

"I beg your pardon, mama. I know I should have worn a morning gown, but I get so tired of changing clothes all the time. I am to go walking early, you see." She hoped the major would arrive before the inevitable stream of visitors who turned up rain or shine.

After breakfast, she sat down at the pi-

161

anoforte. She found herself quite unable to concentrate on Herr van Beethoven's sonata. In a very few minutes the knocker was heard, and she listened with bated breath as the firm tread ascended the stair.

"Major Bowen, my lady," announced Bell.

For the next week, Lucy's busy life became hectic. The major was occupied every morning but was with her every afternoon for as long as Lady Annabel would spare her. Lord Denham, roused from his comfortable lethargy by the appearance of a rival, danced attendance on her every moment that she was not otherwise engaged. It was rumoured that Lord Alvanley, wagering odds on the Carstairs chit being married before the Season's end, had found no takers. He was also willing to sport his blunt on Lord Denham being the lucky man, and there he found one or two gentlemen willing to take him on. However, the general opinion was with him.

"Devil take it," he said, "you can't expect her to turn down a title and fortune for some unknown redcoat, even if she does make sheep's eyes at him. My lord had best watch out though, once he's tied the knot. She's a lively one!"

Word of the wagers came to Lord Denham's ear and encouraged him. Alvanley's devilish lucky, he thought, and he thinks I'll win Lucy. Yet, he had his misgivings. He resolved to ask Richard's permission to address her as soon as his friend returned from the wilds.

Major Bowen was not a member of White's, and the rumours did not reach him. They would hardly have disturbed his bliss in any case. Lucy had confessed, on that memorable if muddy Tuesday, that she held him in high regard. Unable to restrain himself, he had avowed his love. She had reciprocated, and they had plighted their troth with a chaste kiss, while Molly tactfully flirted with an errant groom. Afterward he felt, guiltily, that he had taken advantage of her innocence. He knew he should have spoken to her brother first. However, Lucy seemed to have no qualms, so he cast his doubts to the winds and rejoiced in every sweet moment he could spend with her. He went about his morning duties walking on air, and sadly neglected his lawyer, who called on him several times, always finding him from home.

The weather changed abruptly the day before Richard's return. Overnight, yellowish clouds and an icy wind replaced blue skies and gentle breezes. Lucy and the major, now "Charles" in private, spent a shivering half-hour walking briskly in the park. It began to snow, so they gave up and returned to Cavendish Square. Lucy loved snow in the country, but in London it was grey before it landed and dirty brown five minutes later.

"Ugh!" she exclaimed. "You wouldn't think it was the same stuff.

"Charles," she went on seriously, "pray do not speak to Richard for a few days. He is so starchy sometimes, though he is the dearest of brothers, and he will be tired from travelling. Besides, I want to prepare him first."

"I cannot like to deceive him, dearest."

"It will be only for a short while, I promise. Please?"

"Oh, very well, my sweet. I suppose he is more likely to believe in our love if we do not tell him at once. We have only known each other two weeks, after all, though it scarce seems possible to me."

Chapter 8

Richard had had no trouble in reaching Grantham on Tuesday evening while it was still daylight. He and Ned, the coachman, had taken turns driving the light, elegant new carriage, and he had several times ridden his chestnut mare, Flame, rather than relaxing in the luxury of the well-padded vehicle.

On Wednesday they stopped at the Angel in Doncaster for lunch and to bait the horses. The weather was glorious — cloudless blue skies with a nip in the air that made one want to be up and about. They left the Great North Road at Doncaster, heading northwest toward Leeds. The road was in fair condition, and they passed through that town in midafternoon. As always, Richard noted with regret how fast the sleepy old wool-market town was becoming a grey, smoky city. Mills were rising on the hillsides all around, three- and four-story buildings, rectangular, with monotonous rows of windows all alike.

As the four matched bays pulled up the hill out of town, the road gradually deteriorated. Badly rutted, pot-holed, and deep in mud, it slowed them so much that when they reached Ilkley, with twelve miles still to go, the sun was sinking behind the high fells. The western sky was gloriously painted with reds and oranges and pinks but the horses were sweating, almost staggering from the weight of dirt clinging to their fetlocks and hooves.

"I'll not take 'em no further tonight, sir," asserted old Ned. "We'm best put up at t'inn."

"You shall, Ned, and bring them on tomorrow," agreed his master. "I'll take Flame and go ahead. It will be light for another hour yet. You know Miss Florence."

The two men grinned at each other.

"Aye, Mr. Richard. She'm a holy terror, an' she were t'same afore ever tha was born."

They pulled into the inn-yard. Richard unhitched Flame's bridle from the back of the carriage and mounted. He waved to the old man and set off through the mud. Soon he left the road for a well-known moorland track. The going was easier and he turned his attention to the spectacle in front of him.

The hills rose ahead, range upon dark range. His heart lifted at the sight, as it always did when he approached his beloved home, and this evening it must have raised the spirits of any person of the slightest sensibility. Beyond the rolling horizon the sky was the color of fire above banks of crimson clouds far in the west. The red light kindled the mare's coat to a blaze, and Richard thought of Miss Fell's hair shining in the sun. He had avoided thinking of the errand that had brought him home, still unsure of his feelings toward his protégée, but suddenly he was glad he would be seeing her again.

As Flame cantered onward, the sky paled to pastel; the clouds were a soft rose, and a band of pure clear green faded gradually into darker and darker blue. He was nearly at Toblethorpe village when the evening star appeared, and as he trotted up the drive of the manor, it was joined by a myriad others.

Riding around to the stables, he turned Flame over to a groom with a word of praise and a sugar lump. He entered the house by a back door, happy now to be out of the chilly night.

As he passed the billiard room, Richard became aware of the sound of the pianoforte. A Mozart minuet, played with a sure yet delicate touch, very unlike Lucy's. He listened with pleasure. Surely not his aunt . . .

At the door to the music room, he paused to study the charming scene within: Miss Carstairs sat in an easy chair, her back to him and her inevitable embroidery lying idle in her lap; at the instrument, half facing the door, wholly concentrated on her playing, was Miss Fell. In the candlelight, her hair had a soft sheen as vivid as the sunset but gentler, which contrasted delightfully with her gown of dark green silk.

The dainty piece came to an end. Richard clapped his hands. "Bravo!"

Miss Fell looked up in amazement, which quickly turned to a glad welcome. "Rich . . . Mr. Carstairs! We had almost given up hope of seeing you today. I did not hear the carriage."

"It is at Ilkley. I rode the last few miles. Your servant, Aunt." He bent to kiss the cheek presented to him.

"So, Richard. Miss Fell insisted on holding back dinner until seven. I trust you mean to divest yourself of your filth before sitting down?"

Richard and Miss Fell exchanged

glances brimming with amusement.

"Indeed I do, Aunt Florence. I beg your pardon for appearing before you with half the county on my boots and breeches. I heard the music as I entered and could not resist it."

"Miss Fell is an admirable player," stated the old lady.

"Say, rather, superb." He bowed over Miss Fell's hand as she blushed. "Are you quite recovered, ma'am?"

"Thank you, I am very well."

"You are much improved," said Miss Carstairs magisterially. "However, you still tire too easily."

"If my aunt thinks it wise, perhaps you would indulge me with a little music after dinner, Miss Fell? I must thank you for preserving that meal for me."

She laughed.

"I doubt whether we could have prevailed upon the servants to serve it before that hour, when you were expected. I was told very firmly that my lady always waits for Mr. Richard."

"How fortunate that I did not stay at Ilkley, or you must have gone fasting to bed! Yes, Aunt, I am going to change immediately."

He was met in the hall by a reproachful

Bedford, "I did not hear your arrival, sir," he said disapprovingly. "I shall have hot water sent up at once and Thomas will help you."

"Thank you, Bedford. It is good to be home."

Over dinner, Richard regaled the ladies with the story of Lucy's success in London. "She hardly knew a soul that night at Almack's," he said proudly, "yet she stood up for every dance. I was prepared to do my duty, but there was no need. You would not believe all the new gowns she has."

"The modern fashions are very simple," pointed out Miss Carstairs disparagingly. "In my young day we wore hoops and powdered wigs and yard-high ostrich feathers. It took two hours to change one's dress. I remember the gown in which I was presented at Court . . ." Her detailed description of the formal dress of forty years ago fascinated Miss Fell and nearly sent Richard to sleep. At last she ended with a sigh. "Of course, King George was a young man then. We had no idea of the troubles that would follow."

Richard wished he dared tell them the story he had heard about His Majesty and the Princess of Wales. Instead, he described the two tulips who had appeared on the doorstep the morning after Lucy's first ball.

"However," he added, "Cousin Edward is finer by half, a regular Bond Street Beau. Have you seen him in his town rig-out, Aunt Florence?"

"If he could only be persuaded to confine it to town! He appears at Arnden in a cerise coat, having taken an hour and a half to tie his neckcloth. Making a cake of himself and all the while thinking himself monstrous fine."

"Oh, he's a veritable man-milliner, bang up to the knocker. Let me tell you, his ball dress is like to blind you. Uncle Geoffrey asked me to have a word with him, but I cried craven. I quite long to introduce him to you, Miss Fell."

"I'd as lief forgo that pleasure, sir, judging on your description. Is that how Beau Brummell dresses? Lucy told me that he is a friend of yours."

"I daresay the Beau spends as long or longer over his cravat, but his mode is rather characterized by quiet elegance than by display. My cousin would do well to follow his lead."

"Edward never had the slightest common sense," said his aunt austerely.

171

"Jennifer also spends more time on her dress than I consider justifiable."

"There is no fear of Lucy doing so. She enjoys appearing elegant, to be sure, but she is not truly interested in fashions and modes. After a day of shopping she was better pleased to visit the Exeter Exchange than another mantua-maker."

"I suppose Lucy has had little time for reading," observed Miss Fell. "I quite expected that you would bring word of the fate of Count Casimir and the unfortunate Melisande."

"Oh, Lucy charged me with a thousand messages for you. I told her I should remember only one, so I am to tell you that she cannot wait to see you again. Mama is also looking forward to receiving you in Cavendish Square."

"You wrote that you will accompany me to Arnden and spend the Sabbath there," said Miss Carstairs. "An excellent arrangement. I do not approve of the modern habit of traveling on the day of rest. Also, you will want to take the journey in easy stages, as Miss Fell is still convalescent."

Richard did not linger over his brandy. He was tired after travelling two hundred miles in two days, and before retiring he was anxious to hear Miss Fell play again.

When he entered the drawing room, she was reading. At his request she went willingly to the piano. He watched her walk, remembering the times he had carried her. Her movement had elegance, he thought, yet it was purposeful somehow, unlike the languid fatigue adopted by so many fashionable ladies. Her figure was full, but she was tall and did not appear plump.

She turned to ask what he would like her to play, and found him gazing at her. He flushed and apologized.

"I beg your pardon, Miss Fell. I did not mean to stare. I was wondering at how much your appearance has changed. When I found you, Lucy quite thought I had brought home a skeleton. Oh, my cursed tongue! That is not very complimentary!"

"As you are saying that I no longer look like a bag of bones, I will take it as a compliment," she assured him with a smile. Her eyes smiled, too, and he thought of all the faces he had seen that smiled only with the lips. Her eyes were her best feature, he decided. A man could lose himself in their sea green depths.

She called him back to reality.

"What would you have me play, Mr. Carstairs?"

"Something restful," he answered. "It

has been a long day."

She chose the Bach that was the first piece she had played in his house. Her fingers moved lightly over the keys, interweaving strands of melody that somehow built a towering castle in the air, a magic castle which enchanted her listener and then faded softly away. There was a long silence when she finished.

"Thank you," he said simply. "You have a great talent."

Miss Carstairs brought them back to earth this time. "I am unable to understand," she declared, "why gentlemen nowadays think it not the thing to play an instrument. Your grandfather, Richard, was an excellent violinist, and even your father played the clarionet in his youth. We were used to have delightful musical evenings. Today it is a wonder if a gentleman can read music well enough to sing."

"I can do that much, Aunt, though I'll not boast of any great ability."

"You shall show your paces tomorrow. Miss Fell and I are wont to sing ballads together and have sadly felt the lack of a deeper voice to join us."

"Yes, ma'am," Richard submitted.

"Now, come and drink your tea, children."

"Yes, ma'am," they chorused obediently.

The next day dawned fair. Miss Carstairs had gone to early service in the village as usual, so Richard and Miss Fell met alone at the breakfast table.

"Red sky at night, shepherd's delight," Richard greeted her.

"Did you see the sunset yesterday?" she queried. "Oh, of course, you must have been riding right into it. I watched from my chamber. It is fortunate that dinner was put back, or I should have been late for it. I do not remember having seen a more beautiful sky."

"Have you remembered anything?" he asked gravely. "It is three weeks today since we found you."

"No, nothing. Unless you count the music — and I do not precisely remember having played before. When I sat down at the pianoforte, it just seemed to come to me." She looked at him helplessly. "I have tried to think about my childhood, but I just get the headache and no memories. I am sorry."

The distress in her face shook him.

"You are not to worry about it," he said hurriedly. "Tell me what you have been doing since we left."

Miss Fell described her encounter with

the Reverend Crane and Jeremy's timely rescue. "I was quite at point non plus when he appeared," she said. "However, I am grateful to Mr. Crane, for if he had not seen fit to visit me I might never have become acquainted with Susan Denison, and she is such a dear person . . ."

"A happy outcome, to be sure," agreed Richard, laughing. " 'Tis an amusing story, but I must apologize for the vicar's lack of manners. It must have been a painful experience. He was given the living by my Uncle Mortlake before I attained my majority, and unfortunately I cannot dismiss him. He is not popular in the parish. He crawls to the great, comes the mighty over the villagers, and tells spiteful tales of all."

"Mr. Denison told me he is angling for a living in Lincolnshire, so perhaps you will soon be free of him."

"I can only hope so. Jeremy has a brother in orders to whom I would be happy to offer the parish."

"They are relatives of yours? I thought so. It is good of you to take such an interest in their welfare."

"I have done little enough. The elder brother, William, is a soldier, and the two sisters have both made good marriages. Indeed, I should hesitate to say that I have obliged Jeremy more than he has obliged me. He is a first-class agent, and I would trust him with my fortune."

"Miss Carstairs agrees with you, I am sure. She described him as 'a young man of culture and sense,' a rare encomium from her, is it not?"

Richard whooped. "She has never said anything half so complimentary about me!" he exclaimed, "and you heard her strictures on Cousin Edward. Did you tell Jeremy?"

"I told Susan," she said. "I am sure she passed it on."

"You have seen a good deal of Mrs. Denison, then?"

"Yes, nearly every day since we met. She came here several times, and then when Dr. Grimsdale permitted, I visited Rosebay Cottage."

Richard was pleased. He had a high opinion of Susan Denison's common sense, and if, as it appeared, she liked Miss Fell, it was definitely a point in that young lady's favor.

Miss Carstairs returned from church and came in for a bite to break her fast. She soon retired to the morning room with several volumes of sermons, and Richard asked Miss Fell how she usually occupied her mornings.

"I am quite at your disposal," he said.

"Would you care for a stroll in the gardens?" she asked. "It must sound very flat after the entertainments of London, but it is a beautiful day. Your gardener told me another day like this might bring on the daffodils in the sheltered spots."

"That sounds delightful." Another point. If John, the old grouch, was willing to discuss with her his beloved flowers, that was praise on a par with Aunt Florence's of Jeremy. It was hard enough to get a civil word out of the old man.

Helping her on with her wrap, he had to suppress an urge to kiss her neck. Suddenly he felt ashamed of the way he was totting up points for and against, as if she were a game of cards. He wished he could simply accept her for herself, as a sister.

She confused him with so many different emotions that he could not think straight. Some he recognized. He knew he felt protective toward her, though she was less in need of his aid now. Her music delighted him, as did her sense of humour. He admired her composure in the difficult situation in which she found herself, yet that same situation was appallingly unclear.

Could she be an adventuress? He loathed himself for his suspicions but could not altogether suppress them. His desire to hold her, to kiss her, he distastefully recognized as lust. Well, that could be dealt with. He was not in the habit of keeping a mistress, but there were other, more temporary, remedies.

He refused to consider the possibility that he might be falling in love. Doubly afraid — of rejection and of making a fool of himself over a soubrette with no claim to gentility but her manners — he could not entertain the thought.

Nor did he wonder what her feelings might be. He had closed himself away from the idea that he could be personally attractive to women. She might be grateful, indeed she ought to be grateful, and appeared to be. Otherwise, he knew his only advantages were birth and wealth. The latter he had exploited not infrequently in casual liaisons with opera dancers who cared naught for his family or his face.

Unknowingly, deep in thought, Richard had escorted Miss Fell out of the house and toward the shrubbery. Regarding his stern face, she wondered, a little fearfully, what he was thinking. A strange man this,

179

one minute laughing with her, the next lost in a reverie that did not seem to be pleasant. One moment strong and masterful, she thought, the next minute a hurt small boy. She longed to comfort the small boy, and even more to submit to the man. She suspected that the best she could hope for was the friendship of the kind, considerate person in whom the two were united. Unsure that she had yet earned that friendship, she decided wistfully that it would not be something to be scorned and sternly suppressed her deeper feelings.

At this point, Miss Fell stumbled over a low step in the pathway and instantly Richard's hand was beneath her elbow.

"Take my arm," he urged. "I beg your pardon, I was dreaming. It is amazingly warm outside, is it not?"

"I have high hopes of the daffodils," she replied, "although March is early in the North."

"It has been a mild winter and John has made all sorts of nooks and crannies that catch all the sun and no wind. Besides, tomorrow is the first of April."

"Coming in like a lamb. I fear it cannot last."

"I wish it may last until I have you safe in London."

They were on a gravel walk between long beds of shorn rosebushes. Miss Fell nearly expressed a wish to see them flowering, then decided it might sound encroaching. Her companion was so relaxed and charming now, she desperately wanted to avoid anything that might make him stiffen. They came to the stone wall that supported the forsythia. It had lost its flowers and tender green leaves were appearing on its thin, spiky branches. At the foot of the wall was a drift of crocuses, purple, gold and white.

Miss Fell had watched them come out over the past two weeks. She felt an almost proprietorial pride in them, and was gratified when Richard drew a deep breath and said, "Beautiful! A promise of spring even if it should snow tomorrow."

Walking on, they found a niche holding a huge alabaster urn. In it grew a score of daffodils at various stages of budding. None were fully open, but half a dozen showed yellow.

"Let me pick them for you," suggested Richard. "They will soon bloom in the house."

"I should not dare. What would John think?"

John appeared round the nearest corner.

"Go ahead, missy," he invited. "There's plenty, an' only me to see 'em when tha's gone up to Lunnon-town." He disappeared again.

"Why, he was positively cordial!" exclaimed Richard in a low voice. "He is barely polite to my mother!"

Miss Fell laughed.

"Such an invitation cannot be refused. Will you gather some?"

Half an hour later they returned to the house. For the last five minutes Miss Fell had been leaning increasingly heavily on Richard's arm, and he realized that she was not as strong as he had supposed. He took her to the morning room, where she sank wearily into a chair. He looked down at her pale face with concern.

"Are you sure you will be fit to travel on Saturday?" he asked rather harshly.

"Oh yes. I shall rest on Sunday at Arnden. We shall go by easy stages, shall we not?"

"I had intended to stay in Newark Monday night. That is not too far. Then I was hoping to get to Hitchin on Tuesday so that we might arrive early the next day in Cavendish Square. However, now I think that will not do. We shall aim for Huntingdon instead. If necessary, we may spend a day there."

She looked up at him timidly. "Please, do not change your plans for my sake. I shall do very well. I expect you have engagements on Wednesday?"

"Nothing of importance," he said absently, his mind on the journey. Then he noticed her worried face. "Don't worry, goosecap," he reassured her in a brotherly manner. "It will not be the end of the world if I miss a card party. In fact, it will no doubt be good for both my pocket and my liver. You must not think I am addicted to play. Now if it had been a concert . . . However, at present I can get as good a concert here as any in London!"

"Tell me about the London concerts," she begged eagerly.

He described the Duchess of Devonshire's musical evening. "Half the ton attends only to see and be seen," he explained. "One must shut one's ears to the whispering and fidgeting of the Philistines. In fact, Her Grace is not a noted music lover. Of course, the opera is worse. The audience is full of cits aping the Fashionable World.

"The duchess had hired an entire orchestra, the best of course. They played Mozart, Haydn, Handel, and a symphony by Herr van Beethoven. It is said he had dedicated it to Bonaparte; then the Corsican declared himself emperor and Beethoven changed his mind. A wonderful piece, rich and complex, yet full of melody."

"Are not the orchestras on the Continent much superior to ours, Mr. Carstairs?"

"Every princeling has his court musicians, so there is certainly more opportunity to hear orchestral music. I do not know if the quality is superior. I believe Vienna has an exceptional orchestra. When Boney has been put out of the way, I should like to tour the musical centers of Europe."

"That sounds delightful," said Miss Fell wistfully. "Think you the French will invade our shores?"

"I think it unlikely. Our navy is too strong for Monsieur Napoleon. However, I believe there will be a deal of fighting yet. Russia and Austria are gathering armies even now."

Bedford entered. "Mr. Richard, a message from Mr. Denison. The boy is waiting for a reply."

Richard perused the note.

"He wishes to see me on some minor

matter of business. Should you like to visit Mistress Susan this afternoon, Miss Fell?"

"Yes indeed."

"Tell the boy that Miss Fell and I will do ourselves the honour of calling at Rosebay Cottage this afternoon, Bedford."

"Very well, sir." The butler departed.

"Perhaps we might ride over, Miss Fell, if you do not think the exertion would be too great. It is not above a mile."

"I should like that, but I have not ridden since . . . that day."

"I have an ambling old hack that will give you an easy ride. If you find it tiring, Jeremy shall send you home in his gig."

Miss Carstairs appeared, and they told her their plans, which she approved. So after luncheon Miss Fell changed into her riding habit, the only gown she felt was truly hers, and joined Richard at the stables. He was holding the bridle of a placid-looking grey, stroking its nose, while a groom held Flame.

"This is Horace," he greeted her. "Come, let me help you mount."

Suppressing her unexpected agitation, Miss Fell set her foot in the stirrup and Richard swung her up. He adjusted the stirrups.

"Are you comfortable?" he asked, and

glancing up at her was horrified to see her white, panic-stricken face.

"I cannot!" she cried. "Please . . ."

At once he lifted her down and she burst into tears on his shoulder. He held her, while the interested groom looked on.

"Hush," he said. "Of course, you need not ride. I had not thought it would upset you so." He gave her his handkerchief.

"I beg your pardon," she gasped through her sobs. "I do not in general act like a watering pot." She moved away from him and blew her nose. "I don't know what came over me," she apologized. "I was simply terrified."

"Your last experience on horseback was deuced unpleasant. Even if you cannot remember it, I suppose we might have expected something like this," he reassured her. Realizing that the groom was drinking in every word, he turned to him. "Harness the trap, we shall drive."

Miss Fell quickly recovered her composure, and Richard drove to Rosebay Cottage. As he helped her out, the Denisons appeared on the doorstep to invite them in. After a few minutes of general conversation, Richard and Jeremy went off to discuss business, and Miss Fell told her hostess of her horrid experience.

"Clara, how distressing!" exclaimed Susan with ready sympathy.

"I feel much better for having told you," declared Miss Fell. "It is a great relief to me to have someone in whom I can confide."

"I hope you will always turn to me," said Susan warmly.

Meanwhile, the gentlemen, sprawling at ease in the tiny back room which served Jeremy for an office, had finished their business.

"I want to consult you on another matter," said Richard. "Was not William in the Nth Foot at one time?"

"Yes, until they were sent to India. Having recently married, he transferred to a home regiment."

"Did you ever hear him speak of a Major Charles Bowen?"

"Charlie? Why, yes, only he was then a new-made captain. A very good fellow. He stayed with us in Kent before embarking, as his home is in the north. What did you want to know about him, and why, if I am not prying?" asked Jeremy curiously.

"I know I may trust you to see that this goes no further. The major is dangling after Lucy, and he is not well-known in London, so I must needs find out whether he is a fortune hunter and so on."

"No fortune hunter he!" Jeremy assured him. "I believe he has a comfortable income; certainly he owns a very pretty estate in Northumberland. William visited him there. As I remember it, he was brought up by an uncle who manages the land for him."

"What of his birth?"

"I will tell you what I know, though I would not have you take my word for it. As I understand it, his grandfather was a ships' chandler in Newcastle, joined the East India Company and made a fortune. A regular nabob. He bought the estate from a Scots gentleman whose family was ruined after the Forty-five. Been hanging on to it by the skin of their teeth for years, I gather. Stuart, the name was. Then the Stuart heir married the nabob's daughter. That, I fancy, is where the uncle comes in."

"A royal name," said Richard dryly.

"Charlie's father inherited the estate and married some squire's daughter. They died and the Stuart uncle took over until Charlie's majority. He had always been hot for a pair of colors, so he joined up and left the uncle in charge. There, you have wrung me dry. I never would have thought I remembered, or even knew, so much."

"Not as bad as I feared," Richard admitted, "but quite ineligible for a Carstairs who might look to marry the heir to a dukedom."

"Charlie is an officer and a gentleman, and a damned good fellow to boot. I hope you will not give him too severe a setdown, Richard."

Richard hesitated, then replied, "I think I need not speak to him at all. It may well have blown over by the time I return to town. If not, I shall simply forbid Lucy to see him."

Jeremy wondered whether that would answer with a high-spirited young lady like his employer's sister, but he did not venture to express his doubts. Richard changed the subject.

"I saw Rossiter in London, parading down Bond Street with a very fancy piece on his arm who looked most discontented. I suppose he would not buy her some brooch or bracelet."

"The man's a shocking screw," agreed Jeremy, laughing. "I had a letter from your lawyer the other day. He thinks Sir Philip will have to drop the case because he is too clutch-fisted to pay to take you to court. It seems he has approached several lawyers and been frightened off by their fees. They charge high for a hopeless suit."

"You think my thirty acres are safe, then? I trust you are right."

"I think so. However, I beg you will watch out for Rossiter. He will surely hold a grudge and I believe he might be dangerous."

"If he wishes to call me out, I shall be happy to meet him."

"Oh, not that! He is as fat as a flawn! No, he is more like to come at you from behind in a dark alley."

"I cannot think so. Well, I will keep an eye on him, since you are concerned. Come, let us join the ladies."

The rest of the day passed pleasantly, and the next day likewise. Nothing happened to mar the growing accord between Richard and Miss Fell; he managed not to incur his aunt's displeasure more than twice; and the weather remained fine.

Chapter 9

On Saturday morning, after a leisurely breakfast, they set off for Arnden, which was not more than forty miles distant. Richard rode Flame, as the new carriage was fully occupied by the two ladies, Miss Carstairs' abigail, and Mary, who was so excited that but for her awe of Miss Florence, she would have chattered all the way. She had never before been farther afield than the fair at Harrogate. The sight of the City of York in the distance, with the Minster towering over the old stone walls, finally overcame her ability to hold her tongue.

"Ooh, miss, be that Lunnon?"

"No, Mary, that is York. London is much larger."

Mary, her eyes popping, looked disbelieving.

"Be we a-goin' to drive through that there City o' York?" she queried.

"Not today, I believe. On Monday, we shall do so."

"Ooh, miss!" A disapproving glare from the very proper abigail silenced her, but as the turn of the road hid the city from sight, she craned her neck out of the window to catch a last glimpse.

The lane wound down the eastern flank of the Pennines. Arnden was situated on the plain of York, some five miles from the city, near the pleasant village of Otterwold. A charming brick-built house, considerably smaller than Toblethorpe Manor, it seemed to erupt with children and dogs as they drew up before the door.

"Cousin Richard!" shouted a fresh-faced youth of sixteen or so, "may I ride Flame? You promised!"

Other voices joined his, contradicting and expostulating, and, not to be outdone, the dogs chimed in, barking madly. A harassed governess stood at the top of the steps, ineffectively trying to calm the chaos.

Aunt Florence had only to show her face for quiet to descend. As she was introduced, Miss Fell realized that there were only four children present, and the canine mob resolved itself into a spaniel and two terriers. They seemed to be the responsibility of ten-year-old Tommy, judging by Miss Carstairs' strictures.

The boy shook her hand gravely. "Will you shake hands with the dogs?" he asked appealingly. "I have just taught them how."

Miss Fell agreed and Patch, Silky and Amos were solemnly presented to her.

She did not feel at all fatigued. They had stopped for an hour at noon, taking luncheon at a hotel in Harrogate Spa. The wagon with their baggage, having left at dawn, had already arrived, so she allowed herself to be led to her chamber by Anna and Lydia, and after changing her clothes and parrying their eager questions, she went down to the drawing room.

Richard had been dragged off to the stables by the young man who had hailed him. The other children, under the eagle eyc of their aunt, were removed by the governess. Miss Fell and Miss Carstairs relaxed over a tea tray.

"The young people seem very fond of Mr. Carstairs," observed Miss Fell.

"He spoils them abominably," said Miss Carstairs with disapproval. "Christopher positively worships him. One can only hope that it will dissuade him from the sartorial excesses of his elder brother."

"Indeed, I am most anxious to meet Mr. Edward Carstairs. The man who dares to appear in a cerise coat in such comfortably rural surroundings must be brave indeed."

"Counter-coxcomb," snorted his aunt.

Richard and Miss Fell spent a restful Sunday at Arnden. Miss Fell was delighted with the family and the house. Mary was not so easily pleased, in fact she was most scornful of the household arrangements; however, she did not seem at all homesick.

They set off again early on Monday morning. Miss Carstairs kissed Miss Fell's cheek, much to that lady's surprise, and bade her not permit Richard to go too fast.

"For though he is in general a most considerate person," she added, "gentlemen are always in a hurry."

Miss Fell could not wait to relay to Richard his aunt's unwonted praise.

The sky had clouded over, and there was a chill wind from the north, so Richard was glad to join Miss Fell and Mary inside. He debated leaving Flame to be brought on later by his uncle's groom, then decided he could not involve him in such expense. Geoffrey Carstairs had a large family and only a moderate income, but he would never accept any assistance from his nephew. The most Richard could do was to keep his cousins supplied with horses of a size suitable to their changing ages, and pay occasional tailor's bills for Edward.

It was fully sixty-five miles from York to

Newark. The road was in good condition after nearly a week of fine weather, so they made good time. At Doncaster they paused for an hour to eat and rest the horses. Richard asked Miss Fell if she would like to stay longer.

"It is early yet," he said. "You may lie down for a while."

"Thank you," she replied gratefully. "However, I am not at all fatigued and had rather arrive early in Newark."

As they drove through Nottinghamshire, Miss Fell was silent, staring pensively out at the flat plain to the east. It was lushly green and dotted with fine oaks and elms, yet uninteresting after the high moors they had left behind.

After some time, Richard asked her what she was thinking.

"Oh, simply that this is excellent pasture, but I prefer the fells. I think I must have lived in the north."

Richard cast a warning glance at Mary, who was glued to the opposite window, anxious not to miss any detail of these foreign parts.

Miss Fell understood his look. "The servants all know the truth," she said. "They would not spread it, I am sure. You have a very loyal staff."

"No doubt you are right," he admitted. "Was it difficult to keep it from Aunt Florence?"

"Not at all. Anna and Lydia are another matter!"

"A pair of chatterboxes, as bad as Lucy, and inquisitive also."

"I found your cousins charming. It must be delightful to have such relatives."

"They have their points," Richard conceded. "However, before you praise them too highly, I should tell you that Christopher had been sent home from school for spreading glue on half the pews in the chapel!"

"How reprehensible! It must have been very funny."

"I felt it my duty to give him a scold, but when he described the ripping sound that ensued when the congregation arose, I must confess I could not keep a straight face."

"Will his papa be very wroth?"

"Oh, Uncle Geoffrey is no heavy-handed father. In fact, he is shockingly easygoing or he would not permit Edward to make such a cake of himself."

"I mind Mr. Edward," volunteered Mary. "Him that come at Christmas last? He be a real dandy, fine as fivepence."

Richard and Miss Fell laughed.

"My curiosity to see Mr. Edward Carstairs grows by leaps and bounds," she said.

They reached Newark before dark, and Richard ordered dinner in their private parlour.

"I hope you think it unexceptionable," he apologized. "You look a little tired, and I would not expose you to the racket in the coffee room. Mary shall stay with us."

"You are very thoughtful," she thanked him. "I am a trifle weary. I shall retire early."

Richard was concerned to see that she barely touched her food. He made her drink a glass of wine, which brought the color back to her cheeks. She ate very little though, and retired shortly after dinner.

Worried by his charge and bored by his own company, Richard joined a convivial party in the coffee room and drank a good deal of brandy. Wakened early the next morning, he found he had a headache and his temper was not improved when he looked out and saw that the dark mass of cloud overhead had a yellowish tinge that threatened snow.

He had half a mind to remain in Newark for twenty-four hours, but the idea of a day of inaction, coupled with the possibility of being snowed in, persuaded him to carry on. He hoped the storm would not follow them southward.

Entering the private parlour, he found that Miss Fell was down before him. He was glad to note that she looked rested. To his inquiry she replied that she had slept extremely well and was ready to go.

"We had better leave as soon as possible," she added. "I do not like the look of the sky."

He grunted.

"You do not look at all the thing yourself," said Miss Fell candidly. "Are you unwell?"

"I overdid the brandy last night," he confessed wryly. "Just a trifle on the go, but I have a devilish head this morning." He wondered why he had told her. Never would he have admitted such a thing to his mother or sister.

She smiled at him with sympathy. He looked like a guilty small boy. "Have some black coffee," she suggested, and poured him a cup.

She had recovered her appetite and he forced himself to eat, but breakfast did not take long. They were soon on the road again, driving toward Stamford at a good pace. Richard rode for a while, which helped clear his head, but the icy air soon forced him inside to the comfort of hot bricks and fur rugs.

Their breath fogged the windows so that they could not see out. Richard produced a pocket chess set and he and Miss Fell became so engrossed in their game that the thirty miles to their next stop passed unnoticed. As they rattled over the cobbles of the inn-yard in Stamford, Miss Fell looked up.

"We'm stopping, miss," announced Mary.

"Saved in the nick of time! Another five minutes and you had my king, Mr. Carstairs."

When they descended from the coach, they discovered it had been snowing for some time. The air was warmer, but a white carpet a good inch thick covered the ground. Old Ned, climbing slowly down from the box, had a layer of snow on his cap and each shoulder. His nose was cherry red.

"Go warm yourself, man," said Richard, "and be sure they dry your coat. We'll not stay long. I've no mind to be caught here, and it's only twenty-five miles to Huntingdon."

"Don' 'ee worry, Mr. Richard," answered the old man gamely. "What's a bit o' snow to a Yorkshireman?"

They left within the hour. It had stopped snowing and the clouds thinned enough to show a trace of blue sky.

"Bain't enow to make a sailor a pair o' breeches," said Mary forebodingly, but Richard was optimistic.

"Maybe we should push on to St. Neots," he proposed. "We shall see how you do at Huntingdon, Miss Fell."

Shortly after they passed through the village of Wansford, Mary was proved right. Without warning they were surrounded by whirling snowflakes. The road was well marked, so they continued. Within half an hour the horses were struggling through drifts eighteen inches deep. Richard consulted Ned.

"They'll do," said the coachman. "Take us mebbe two hours 'stead o' one, s'all."

So they plowed on. Richard, unwilling to sit doing nothing, saddled Flame and rode a little ahead. They were barely three miles from Huntingdon when there was a sudden jolt and a cracking sound. Slowly the carriage tipped to the right and settled at an angle against the hedgerow. Old Ned had driven into a ditch.

Heart in mouth, Richard galloped back. He clambered up onto the side of the coach and opened the door.

"Miss Fell, are you hurt?"

"I do not think so," replied an uncertain, muffled voice. "But I am very uncomfortable. Mary is on top of me."

"I'm tryin' to move, miss, but everythin's topsy-turvy like."

There was a sound of scuffling, then Miss Fell said in a more normal voice, "We are so well bundled up that we are just a little shaken. Can you get us out?"

"If you are not injured, I must see to the horses first. Forgive me."

"Of course. I hope they are not hurt."

Ned had landed in a deep drift; he had already extricated himself and was cutting the bays free. "I dunno what to say," he muttered. "I ain't niver done sich a thing afore."

"We should have stopped earlier," said Richard. "You could not see the road. You are not to blame."

"If the 'osses are 'urt, I'll niver forgive mysen."

"There, that is the last of them. No broken legs at least."

They examined the team. Amazingly, none were so much as scratched. The snow had padded their fall.

Richard and the coachman next pulled Mary and Miss Fell out of the carriage, and Ned studied the damage.

" 'Tain't serious," he pronounced. "Just the spokes. Howsomever, we won't be movin' wi'out they're mended."

"We are not far from Huntingdon," said Richard. "Should you and Mary mind waiting here, Miss Fell, while I ride to fetch another conveyance? Ned could stay with you, though he ought perhaps to start leading the bays after me."

"We shall be perfectly all right, shall we not, Mary? No one is like to disturb us, I think!"

"No one of sense," admitted Richard. "We should have stayed in Stamford. Well, useless to cry over spilled milk. I'll be off and return as quickly as I may."

Miss Fell watched him gallop off down the road, Flame's gait apparently unaffected by the snow. Ned and the team followed more slowly. She and Mary found some shelter against the tilted coach. Spreading a rug, they sat down with their backs against it, huddling in the furs.

It was not long before melting snow soaked through the rug beneath them. They began to feel the chill and decided to walk up and down. The blizzard was thinning and soon the snow ceased to fall. It suddenly became much colder.

Mary was rosy-cheeked and bouncing with energy after being cooped up in the carriage. She chattered excitedly until she noticed that Miss Fell was not responding.

"Be you aw'right, miss?" she asked anxiously.

"Yes, Mary, only I am so cold and I cannot walk any farther."

"Sit tha down, miss, an' I'll wrap my rug around thee. I be warm as toast."

"Thank you, Mary." Miss Fell was grateful, but the extra wrap did not seem to help. She was shivering convulsively and she could barely speak.

Mary went to the center of the road and looked down it, shading her eyes against the glare of the snow. "There be a carriage a-comin'," she called. "It'll be Mr. Richard for sure."

He was beside them in a moment with a gig driven by an ostler from the White Hart. He had been gone scarce half an hour and he was appalled to see the state Miss Fell was in. She was pale as a ghost and unable to stand.

Richard took a flask from his pocket and forced her to swallow some brandy. "What a fool I am," he groaned as he lifted her up. "I deserve anything my aunt could say about me, and worse."

"No," she whispered, smiling faintly. "I shall be all right. I am only cold."

He held her all the way back to Huntingdon, and gradually she stopped shaking. There was a great to-do when they reached the White Hart. The landlord's wife came bustling out and hurried them into a private room where a blazing fire roared in the hearth. Richard set Miss Fell down on a sofa. He knelt beside her, pulled off her gloves and began to chafe her hands, thinking of the other occasion on which he had done that. This time she was at least conscious, thank heaven.

A bowl of hot soup was produced on the instant, and Miss Fell was able to feed herself. In fact, by the time she had finished it, the landlady was saying, in motherly if slightly disappointed tones, that the poor young lady looked to be well on the way to recovery.

"A nice bite o' dinner and a good night's sleep, and I'll warrant you miss will be as good as new come morning."

Looking at her, Richard thought with relief that the good woman might well be correct.

In fact, by the time she had rested on her bed for an hour and eaten her meal, Miss Fell felt as fit as ever. She even proposed to stay up for a couple of hours to keep Richard company.

"You must not tax your strength," said Richard firmly. "I promise I will not indulge in an excess of brandy."

"Mr. Carstairs, you know I meant no such thing!" She laughed. "However, I daresay you are quite right. I do have a slight headache."

"Brandy!" said Richard in a sepulchral voice.

"Wretch! I had scarcely a mouthful!"

"Ah, but you are not used to it."

"And you are, I take it?"

"Wretch!" he said in his turn, and wished her good night.

She did not sleep well, and woke in the morning heavy-eyed. Her headache was worse, but she did not mention it to Richard, fearing that he would postpone their departure. If she was going to be ill, and she could not dismiss that possibility, she had much rather be settled in London than in a posting house en route.

Mary was so thrilled that today she would see Lunnon-town, and Richard so preoccupied with wondering whether to send ahead a message cancelling his engagement, that neither noticed Miss Fell had only a cup of tea at breakfast. The sun had returned and was sparkling on the new-fallen snow. Richard decided to ride. Mary was spellbound at the window, greeting every distant village with, "Be that Lunnon-town, miss?"

"Is that London," corrected Miss Fell irritably. The glare from the snow worsened her headache.

"Is that London," repeated Mary obediently. "Is it, miss?"

"No, it is not. You will not need to ask when we arrive."

At their noon stop in Hitchin, she was glad to lie down for half an hour. She still did not feel like eating, but seeing Richard's worry, she forced down a morsel of chicken. When she rose to return to the carriage, her head was throbbing so that she could hardly see, but again Richard, paying the reckoning, noticed nothing. He settled her in the hired chaise with no more than his usual solicitude. Her cheeks were flushed with the beginnings of a fever, and he even thought she looked very well. He rode Flame again.

The roads had been cleared between Hitchin and London, and they had fresh horses. They sped along, passing through Hatfield no later than three o'clock. Miss Fell lay back against the cushions and wished she could die in peace.

Mary's first sight of the streets of London was ruined; she turned from the window to gasp, "This is London-town!" and found Miss Fell holding her head and weeping. Trying to comfort her, Mary discovered she was half delirious. She was muttering and moaning and now and then she would cry, "I want to go home!"

All the while tears poured down her face.

Mary did not know what to do. She did not dare let go of Miss Fell to rap on the glass that separated her from the coach box. She managed to let down the window and through it she could see Mr. Richard, but he was out of earshot, and she could not make the coachman hear her through the terrible din of the London streets.

Weeping herself, she tried to soothe her mistress.

"We be in Lunnon a'ready, miss," she kept repeating. "We'll soon be there. Don' 'ee give up, miss."

At last, when she was despairing, they pulled to a halt in a fine square outside an imposing row of houses. Richard had already arrived. He ran down the steps and opened the door of the chaise.

"Tha'll have to carry her, Mr. Richard," said Mary in a frightened voice. "She'm terrible sick agin."

Chapter 10

"How could you, Richard!" said Lucy severely. "Mama warned you not to tire Clara and then you leave her sitting in the snow for half an hour!"

"You cannot blame me more than I blame myself," he answered wretchedly.

Lucy relented.

"Mama does not think she is as ill as last time," she reassured him. "Dr. Knighton will be here shortly, and he is the best doctor in London. He attends the Prince of Wales, you know."

"Prinny may go to the devil! Does mama really say that?" He paced restlessly up and down the drawing room, halting now and then at the window to stare blankly at the muddy slush in the square.

"Indeed she does. And she also says you are to calm down and eat something. She does not want two patients on her hands."

"Lucy, this will upset your entertainments. Perhaps you should remove to Aunt Blanche's for a time."

"As though I could when my dearest

friend needs me! I shall nurse Clara, of course."

"You are a darling," he said, and hugged her. "I wish I could do so also."

"To tell the truth, Richard," she admitted candidly, "I find the balls and routs not near so exciting as I had expected. I'd as lief go to a small party and dance with friends I know well, as we do at Toblethorpe."

"Silly puss. What of all your new admirers?"

"Most of them are quite dull. Oh, I am glad we are here, and I have met some amusing people. I like your friend Brummell very well — we go on famously together. But I should not wish to spend every winter in town, just an occasional visit to keep up with the fashions and the latest *on dits*."

"Then you had better find a husband this Season, if you do not mean to have a second!"

She was about to tell him that she *had* found a husband, when the knocker was heard. They both rushed to the window and craned their necks to see who was at the door.

"I am sure it is Dr. Knighton!" cried Lucy. "I shall go back to Clara." She ran out of the room in a manner that her Aunt Florence would have stigmatized as hoydenish.

A few minutes later she returned. Richard was pacing again, fists clenched, head bowed. He looked up eagerly as she entered.

"Mama would not let me stay," she said disconsolately.

This time her chatter did not distract Richard from his worry. Lucy soon gave up trying to obtain an answer, and remembering Lady Annabel's advice, went to order some refreshment for her brother. Then she slipped upstairs to see if she could glean any news.

Shortly, Bell entered the drawing room with a tray of tea and cakes. "Miss Lucy," he declared ponderously, "h'intimated as 'ow you'd h'appreciate a little sustenance, Mr. Richard. H'I took the liberty of fetching up a bottle of brandy h'also, h'it being a chill sort of day."

"Thank you, Bell, I'll drink a glass," said Richard absently.

The butler poured some, and set it on a side table, as Richard was still pacing. By the time Bell left the room, Richard had forgotten about it.

At last Lucy burst into the room. "It is

merely the grippe!" she announced. "Dr. Knighton says she will be well in a few days. Mama says I am to go to Aunt Blanche, for fear of infection. Must I, Richard?"

"You will do as your mother says. You are sure those were the doctor's words?" he asked eagerly.

"Well, he is still talking to mama, but Mary came out to tell me as soon as she heard that much. She has become very attached to Clara, you know."

A heavy tread was heard on the stair. Richard hurried out and greeted Dr. Knighton. "Will Miss Fell recover, sir?" he asked anxiously.

"She'll do, she'll do," replied the great doctor with assurance. "Lady Annabel has my instructions and will send for me should there be any untoward symptoms. Otherwise, I shall be back in a day or two to check the young lady." He went on his way.

Richard ran up the stairs and knocked softly on the door of Miss Fell's chamber. Mary opened it, her finger to her lips.

"How is she?" Richard whispered.

"She'm better already, sir. Not tossin' an' turnin' like. 'Ee's not to fear."

Lady Annabel appeared. "Miss Fell is

asking for you, dearest. You can come in, but stay only a moment. I shall come down presently and tell you what the doctor said."

Richard approached the bed with bated breath. He had to bend to hear her pitifully weak voice.

"Not your fault," she murmured. "Only thing to do. You took good care of me." She tried to smile.

He pressed her hand.

"Thank you," he said in a low voice. "You are too generous." Lifting her hand to his lips, he kissed her fingers. "You will get well soon?" He looked into her eyes and saw in them the smile that was too much effort for her lips.

"Off you go, Richard," ordered Lady Annabel. "I will be with you in a few minutes."

He turned at the door, and found that Miss Fell's eyes were still on him. Then Mary moved between them.

Returning to the drawing room he found the glass of brandy and sat down to sip at it. The cakes were half gone, and he surmised that Lucy had demolished them. Lady Annabel soon joined him.

"Whatever were you about, Richard, to leave poor Clara sitting in the snow? No, dearest," she hushed him, "you do not need to explain. Mary has told me what happened and it seems you had little choice."

"Lucy has already read me a scold, mama."

"And I daresay the worst scolding is the one you gave yourself. Well, she is not seriously ill, unless she takes an unexpected turn for the worse. Dr. Knighton sees no sign of inflammation of the lungs, which is most to be feared. He says she would not be near so ill now had she not been still convalescent from her previous illness. You are not to blame yourself. *She* does not blame you."

"I know, mama. She is the most generous soul in the world."

"You have been generous to her, child, and she is grateful."

"I don't want her gratitude," he said roughly. He hesitated, and Lady Annabel thought he was going to open his heart to her, but he changed his mind.

"This situation is intolerable, mama," he continued. "Not knowing who she is or anything about her. How can we introduce to the ton someone who is an imposter, however unintentional?"

"We know a great deal about her,

Richard. We know she is generous and capable of gratitude. We know she is pretty-behaved, modest, unassuming. I have also learned a great deal from Mary — that girl never stops talking! Miss Fell is a stoic, the servants all think her a lady, your Aunt Florence approves her, and she plays the pianoforte 'ever so nice.' "

"She plays like an angel. If she is not a governess or an abigail, she is probably a professional musician," he said gloomily.

"If you are determined to be negative, I have no more to say to you," said Lady Annabel with dignity. "I shall go and dress for dinner. Lord knows what Monsieur Pierre thinks of all these disruptions."

"And she sets us all at sixes and sevens!" was Richard's parting shot.

After dinner, much argument, and a great deal of to-and-fro of servants with messages, Lucy was packed off to stay with her aunt, who would escort her to Almack's that evening. Richard found himself too exhausted to consider turning up at his card party, and Lady Annabel confessed she should be glad of an early night.

"For you would not credit how we have been gadding about while you were gone, Richard. I believe we have not dined at home above twice this past week."

She looked in on Miss Fell when she retired, and found her sleeping peacefully. Mary, who had not left her for a moment since their arrival, was curled up on a pallet on the floor. She looked up drowsily to say, "Don' 'ee worrit thysen, my lady. I s'll take care o' my young lady."

On Thursday morning, Lord Denham called to welcome Richard back and to ask after Miss Fell.

"Saw Lucy last night," he said cheerfully. "She told me all about it. Of all the bacon-brained things to do, Richard!"

"I'd like to know what you would have done in the same situation," answered Richard belligerently.

"Why, set her on the horse and taken her with me!"

Richard told him what had happened when Miss Fell had mounted on horseback at Toblethorpe.

"The devil!" exclaimed his lordship. "What a coil! Well, I'm off to take Lucy driving. Shall I see you at White's this afternoon?"

"No, I shall stay in, lest my mother has need of me," said Richard shortly.

Lord Denham gave him a shrewd look. He had intended to speak to Richard about paying his addresses to Lucy, but he could see that the time was not ripe.

"Any message for your sister?" he inquired.

"Tell her Miss Fell had a good night and seems a little recovered this morning."

"I will," promised Lord Denham.

Richard hovered around the house, getting in the way of the servants and irritating his mother unbearably.

"If you can find nothing else to do," she said crossly, you may come and lift Miss Fell while the bed linen is changed."

His eyes brightened. "Of course. I feel so useless. I fear men are not much needed in a sickroom."

"Men are not apt to wish to help in a sickroom."

"I do, mama. You will tell me if there is aught I can do?"

"I will, Richard, you may be sure. However, at present there is little for anyone to do. As at Toblethorpe, it is now a matter of time and rest."

"I shall see that this time she does not go gallivanting across half the country when she should be in her bed!"

"There is no need for her to go anywhere, dearest, but I hope you do not mean to shut her up in the house when she is enough recovered to go about a little."

"Since she is in London only to meet as many people as possible, that would be foolish beyond permission."

"And are you never foolish, dearest?" asked Lady Annabel wickedly.

"Mama, you are a complete hand! Do you expect me to confess to such an impossibility?"

Miss Fell was indeed much improved. Her fever was abated, the headache gone. She felt only an overwhelming lassitude, which made her unwilling to eat or speak, or move a finger unnecessarily. Dr. Knighton had expected the loss of appetite.

"She is in good frame," he had said. "As long as she takes plenty of liquids, do not press her to eat."

When Richard entered the chamber, she turned her head and smiled, but it was obviously an effort.

"Do not stir," said Richard. He lifted her, and her head rested against his shoulder. He decided she had not enough strength to sit in the wing chair by the fire, so he sat there himself, holding her. Every nerve in his body thrilled at her closeness. The sweet scent of her hair was in his nostrils, and he felt her heart beating. Her eyes were closed, so he studied her face in silence while Lady Annabel directed the

218

remaking of the bed.

It was done too soon for him. As he stood up, she stirred in his arms and opened her eyes. He smiled down at her, the smile that transformed his face and made her heart jump within her. She shut her eyes again quickly, lest he should read her thoughts in them.

"Sleepyhead," he said in a teasing, caressing voice as he laid her on the bed.

She did sleep most of that day. Faithful Mary watched beside her, busy the while with her needle. Downstairs, Lady Annabel sat down to write a letter to Miss Florence, and bade Richard do likewise.

"Need I, mama?" he groaned. "You must know that I actually had a word of praise from her." He told her what Miss Fell had repeated to him. "I fear this start will blacken me irremediably in her eyes."

"The more reason to write and present your excuses," said his mother severely.

"Yes, ma'am," he meekly submitted.

In the afternoon he went riding in the park for a short while to get some air and exercise. When he returned, Dr. Knighton was just leaving.

"A fascinating case, Mr. Carstairs," said the doctor. "Fascinating!"

"Has Miss Fell suffered a relapse?"

asked Richard in alarm.

"No, no, nothing of the kind. I must not keep you. Good day, sir."

Richard ran up the steps and went to find Lady Annabel. "What did Knighton mean?" he demanded. "He kept on about a 'fascinating case.' Is something wrong? I thought it was just the grippe."

"I told him about the loss of memory," admitted Lady Annabel. "He was asking Clara all sorts of questions about past illnesses, and of course she could not answer."

"Has he upset her? I'll have his liver for this!"

"He was merely doing his job," soothed his mother. "Clara was not upset. Indeed, I think she is too languid to be much concerned over anything."

"What did he say about the amnesia?"

"He would not say anything definite, but he wishes to return tomorrow with a colleague who specializes in the brain, a German, I believe. I thought it best to concur. He may be able to help her. I daresay there have been advances in treatment of which our Dr. Grimsdale knows nothing."

"I suppose so," agreed Richard reluctantly. "But I'll not have her bullied. I want to be present when they talk to her."

"I don't see why you should not."

"What of the grippe?"

"Oh, she is quite out of danger. He agrees with Dr. Grimsdale that she has an excellent constitution and doubted that she had ever been seriously ill before. However, she is not to leave her bed for a week. He said that repeatedly interrupted convalescence will undermine the stoutest constitution."

"I am glad I was not there when he spoke so. I should not have known where to look!"

The next morning, Miss Fell was able to sit up, propped by a mound of pillows, and take a morsel of breakfast. She was glad to lie down again after twenty minutes, her head swimming after two days without food.

Dr. Knighton arrived early, bringing with him a short, square Teuton in an old-fashioned wig. While Dr. Knighton examined Miss Fell and pronounced her well on the way to recovery, Richard entertained Herr Doktor Holzkopf, or rather was entertained by a long and totally incomprehensible disquisition on illnesses of the brain. Then he accompanied him above stairs.

The Herr Doktor was introduced to Miss Fell, who was looking somewhat nervous. Richard resolved to protect her to the death.

"Ach, zo! Ziss iss die jung lady zat nozzink can remember? Zese cases *sind* rara, ve haff liddle experientz, *aber* ve vill *machen* vass ve can, *nicht wahr?*" He asked Miss Fell several questions, which Richard did not hear, as Dr. Knighton was addressing him.

"There are two types of amnesia, as explained by my worthy colleague," said that gentleman. "In many cases the patient can remember nothing, not even how to speak or walk. *Tabula rasa,* so to say. One is left with an adult with the mind of a newborn child. The other type is a selective memory loss. In Miss Fell's case she appears to be unable to recall any information of a strictly personal nature. The chances are that there is some good reason for this.

"The treatment and prognosis are much the same in both cases. Usually the patient remains in a familiar environment and will gradually regain his memory as he is faced with well-known people, places and situations. When the patient is separated from all that is familiar, there are two possibilities. A sudden shock, such as a blow to the head or an unexpected meeting with, for instance, a family member, may restore the memory wholly or in part. Or the memory may never return. The patient must then take up a new identity and give up all hope of finding the old."

"Thank you, sir," said Richard grimly. "Now I know what we are up against, it seems unlikely that Miss Fell has much chance of recovery."

"Do not despair, young man. The Herr Doktor has some new ideas. You may have heard of Anton Mesmer?"

"The animal magnetism man?" asked Lady Annabel, in puzzlement. "He was in London in my youth, in the eighties, was it not?"

"You are correct, my lady. Herr Doktor Holzkopf has studied with Anton Mesmer at his retreat in Switzerland, and has applied his knowledge to several disorders of the brain with varying degrees of success. He would be happy to try its effect on an amnesiac patient."

"I'll not have him upsetting Miss Fell," insisted Richard.

"I know little of his methods. You had best request an explanation direct from him. Well, I have other patients to see; you will excuse me, Lady Annabel. I think Miss

Fell has no more need of me, but you will call me if necessary. Your servant, Mr. Carstairs."

Richard advanced upon the unfortunate Herr Doktor with a scowling face. The little man was perched on the edge of the bed chatting away with Miss Fell. Seeing that she appeared far from distressed, in fact rather amused, he relaxed.

"Well, Herr Doktor, will you explain to me what you propose to try?"

"*Natürlich!* mein Herr. I vill Miss Fell in a deep trantz put, zen I vill her some qvestions ask. Simple, *nicht?* I vould it *mit* pleasure immediately do, *aber der gut* Herr Doktor Knighton say she first several days to rest must."

Lady Annabel looked blank. The guttural accent, combined with the strange word order, were beyond her comprehension. Richard had difficulty understanding, but he got the gist of the speech.

"In that case, I suggest you return this time next week," he proposed, "and if Miss Fell is willing, you may try your experiment. I shall be present throughout, of course."

"Iss understoodt!" beamed the Herr Doktor. "I vill next Friday in ze evnink ze attempt *machen*. Farevell, Miss Fell. I see you again. *Gnädige Frau,* mein Herr, your servandt." He bowed himself out.

Richard and Miss Fell's eyes met, and they burst into laughter. Lady Annabel joined in.

"Oh!" cried Miss Fell at last, "my sides hurt! What a dear little man. I shall not in the least mind him putting me in a trantz."

"The trantz will not help if you cannot understand his qvestions," pointed out Richard.

"Do not make her laugh any more," said Lady Annabel severely. "Clara, I am glad you like him and I hope he can help. Now you must try to sleep before luncheon, my dear, or you will have a relapse." She shooed Richard out.

Miss Fell found she was more than willing to sleep. She woke ravenous in the middle of the afternoon and, as Mary reported proudly to Lady Annabel, ate a slice of boiled chicken and half a custard. She felt she would soon be able to appreciate Monsieur Pierre's genius once more.

A little later Richard came in and asked if she would like him to read to her. She had been lying gazing out of the window at grey clouds streaming past the chimney pots of the neighbouring houses, and she welcomed a diversion.

"That will be delightful," she said gratefully. "Something soothingly rural, with trees and streams and cows in it."

"Not Cowper, however! I'll see what I can find."

He returned in few minutes bearing a pair of volumes.

"I hope you like Mr. Wordsworth's verse," he said. "I find it has a charming freshness and simplicity."

He read a number of poems in a clear and natural tone, which allowed the beauty of the verse to speak for itself, then he turned to Blake and chose several of that odd gentleman's less apocalyptic offerings. He paused. She was watching his face, a slight smile on her lips.

"I am not tiring you?"

"Oh no. Pray go on. This is just the sort of poetry I was speaking of. It presents such a clear picture of beautiful things without all the classical imagery to distract one's attention, or depressing reflections upon the transitory nature of life."

" 'The curfew tolls the knell of parting day,' " quoted Richard. "I know just what you mean. The cows are there in the next line, but so overhung with a pall of doom that one cannot tell if they be in milk or no."

"Precisely," she agreed, thinking that if he were to read her the entire Book of Revelations, she would not tire of the sound of his voice.

There was a knock at the door, and Mary went to answer it. It was James with a tea tray. She took it, and said to him, "Tha'd best bring anither cup, I'm thinking. Mr. Richard is reading to Miss Fell an' he'll be wanting some too."

"Gi' us a kiss, Mary, an' I s'll go fetch it."

"Get on, ye great gowk. I'm an abigail now, not a housemaid, an' I'll thank 'ee to keep thy kisses to thysen. Ladies' dressers don't consort wi' footmen. 'Twouldn't be proper."

"Much tha knaws. Miss Lucy's Molly's bin an abigail a sight longer nor thee."

"An' no better than she should be, that Molly. Go fetch a cup afore t'tay's cold."

This exchange was carried out in low voices, but Richard and Miss Fell heard every word. They exchanged amused glances. Miss Fell resolved to warn Mary not to be so high and mighty; there was no knowing how long a third abigail would be needed in the Carstairs household and she might find herself a housemaid again any day.

Mary set the tray down and poured a cup for Miss Fell. James returned in a few minutes. "Tha'll come drink a cup in t'kitchen, Mary?"

"Nay, I canna. Summun must stay wi' Miss Fell long as t'master's here."

"Pour me some tea, Mary, and I'll be gone the sooner," said Richard.

Abashed, she hastened to obey, and passed a plate of macaroons. "Begging your pardon, sir, I didna mean to rush you."

"I know, Mary, but it is time Miss Fell lay down anyway. Enough of poetry for today."

Miss Fell nibbled a macaroon.

"Are these not delicious, Mr. Carstairs? Poor Gladys could never produce anything so light."

Mary was heard to snort.

"You are acquainted with Gladys, Miss Fell?" inquired Richard.

She described to him how she had had to deal with panic in the kitchens when Monsieur Pierre had left for London.

"Have my mother tell you what she had to cope with when he arrived here and usurped Mrs. Tupton's position! Monsieur Pierre is a late addition to my staff, and Tuppy has been ruling here forever. I remember how she used to feed me sugarplums and scraps of pastry when I was a child. Truth to tell, I thought last time I came up to town that she was growing too old for the position, but it would break her heart to be pensioned off."

"Perhaps now that Monsieur Pierre has relegated her to second place, she would not be so unwilling."

"That is possible. I will try again if I cannot persuade her. I wish she would retire to Toblethorpe, it is so much more healthy than London, but she is a Cockney through and through."

"I canna make out a word she says," interjected Mary.

"Mary, you must learn not to join in our conversation," said Miss Fell in kindly reprimand. She was loath to scold her before Richard, yet Mary must learn to behave as a lady's maid while she could.

Richard was thinking how gently she had corrected the girl. Servants would find a good mistress in her, and she would be a wonderful mother. He flushed slightly at the thought.

Miss Fell saw his cheeks color and wondered in dismay if he was thinking again about her own ambivalent status. He had been such a charming and considerate companion since he had returned to Toblethorpe to fetch her that she had almost forgotten the way he would stiffen at any mention of her situation. She could not, however, dismiss Lucy's hints from her mind. She had gathered that he was excessively proud of his birth and all too ready to look down upon those he considered encroaching.

Supposing her family were in trade, she thought, almost in a panic, or yeoman farmers, say. He could not then continue to regard her as a sister, or even a friend. She dreaded losing him so entirely.

Richard took her silence for fatigue. He quickly finished his tea and gravely took his leave, wondering how he could be so foolish as to keep her so long from her rest. He was finding it more and more difficult to be long away from her. He decided he must get out of the house and went off to dine at his club.

His solemnity and hurried departure seemed to Miss Fell to confirm her fears.

Mary helped her lie down and went to have her tea. "I'll just grab a jam buttie and be right back, miss."

"I shall not need you till dinnertime, Mary," she said. "I am no longer so ill that I must always have someone by me."

As soon as the girl had left, she turned her face to the pillow and wept. She wished she had not scolded Mary in such a way. It was so difficult to guess what might upset Richard. She resolved to be extra careful until Friday next. She might never see him again after that day. Why had she so eagerly agreed to the German doctor's plans? She might otherwise have put off the evil day indefinitely. Perhaps she had in any case so disgusted Richard that he would not speak to her for the next week. Exhausted and unhappy, she cried herself to sleep.

When Mary brought her dinner tray, she was still sleeping, so Mary ventured to consult Lady Annabel, who said she should not be disturbed.

"I daresay she will waken later, and she may eat then. I shall be at home this evening, and I shall visit her."

Miss Fell woke at nine-thirty, and Lady Annabel sat with her while she ate. They laughed together about Herr Doktor Holzkopf, and Miss Fell inquired about Mrs. Tupton's disgruntlement. Lady Annabel described the uproar.

"She won the argument, if not the kitchen. ' 'Eaven 'elp me,' she said, 'if I kin see 'ow yer kin let one o' they murtherin'

231

Frenchies prepare yer wittles. I'd as soon marry Boney as eat anythin' 'e'd made. Mounsewer Peer, indeed! I'll Mounsewer 'im, not 'arf I won't!' "

Lady Annabel had the Cockney accent perfectly. Tears of laughter running down her cheeks, Miss Fell asked, "How do you do it, ma'am? Are you not Yorkshire bred?"

"Not I. The Mortlake estates are in Somerset, but I was brought up mostly in London, and almost all the servants, including my nurse, were Cockneys. My mother was Italian, you must know, and did not at all like the English countryside."

"Would you like to live in town still?"

"Oh no. When my dear Kit first showed me Toblethorpe he was afraid I should be bored in such a remote place. I soon learned to love it, though we usually spent some of the winter months in London. When I lost Kit, his home, as well as his children, became very important to me."

"You still miss him, do you not?" Miss Fell asked hesitantly.

Lady Annabel nodded, her eyes bright with unshed tears.

"He must have been a wonderful person to make you love him so much. You must have been very happy together," said Miss Fell wistfully.

"I pray that Lucy and Richard may find such happiness," answered Lady Annabel with fervor. "And now, dear Clara, I hope the same for you." She took Miss Fell's hand in hers, and they sat a moment in silence, both, had they but known it, with much the same thoughts.

At last Lady Annabel sighed and stood up. "You have scarce eaten anything," she said. "You are not to be wasting away."

"I had luncheon very late," Miss Fell apologized. "I seem to feel more need of sleep than food."

"Sleep well, then, my child." Lady Annabel stooped and kissed her forehead.

Chapter 11

When Miss Fell awoke, the sun was shining. Mary flung the curtains wide, and she could see the blue sky with white puffs of cloud scurrying before the breeze.

"Open the window a little, Mary," she ordered. "What a glorious day!"

The air was cool and refreshing, and she found that the previous day's distress loomed less black in her mind. She ate a hearty breakfast and then wondered what to do next.

Lady Annabel dropped in and was delighted to find her so well. "I'll send you some books, if you feel in need of an occupation," she offered. "I would keep you company for a while but I must drive over to Orchard Street and see how Lucy goes on."

"Lady Annabel, I ought to write to Miss Florence and thank her for her care of me."

"If it will not tire you, Clara. You shall have paper and pen and see how it goes."

Miss Fell wrote her letter and started on

one of the books. She was amused to find it was a novel very like *Count Casimir's Castle*, and she wondered if it was one of Lucy's or if Lady Annabel had similar tastes in literature.

The book bored her, and she grew restless. The shadow of a cloud fell across her window, cutting off the sun, and she was just deciding that, after all, it was a perfectly horrid day, when Richard requested permission to enter.

"Come in!" she called eagerly, then added shyly, "I was afraid you were angry with me."

"With you? Lord no, whatever made you think that? With myself rather, for tiring you. I have the best intentions, yet I seem fated to retard your recovery."

"Oh no!" she cried with a joyful heart. "I am very well today, and I enjoyed your reading amazingly."

"Shall I read to you again? What is this you have? *The Ruins of Adelstein Abbey*. It does not sound very amusing."

"I find it rather dreary," confessed Miss Fell. "Your mama kindly lent it to me. It is full of mad monks."

"Yes, mama has a taste for such stuff, though she frowns on Lucy's reading it. I am surprised she should confess it to you,

235

for it is a dark secret and I found out quite by accident. Pray do not let Lucy guess!"

" 'Twould be shockingly treacherous in me to do so."

"Shall I read you some more poetry?"

"To tell the truth, Mr. Carstairs, I am too full of energy for such a passive occupation. Should you object to a game of chess?"

"Not chess," he said firmly. "Too much mental exertion by half. Backgammon is more the mark."

"Very well, sir," she submitted, "let it be backgammon."

"I suppose Mary will not go fetch the board as it would mean abandoning you to my tender mercies. I shall be back in a trice."

That day set the pattern for several to come. Richard would go riding after breakfast, and then play at backgammon or chess with Miss Fell until luncheon. He taught her piquet and they wagered vast amounts of totally imaginary money on the turn of a card. After luncheon, she would sleep for an hour or two, and then he would read to her, or they would discuss the latest news. In the evening he would go to White's or dine with friends, while Lady Annabel sat with her, reading or sewing or simply chatting companionably.

Miss Fell was blissful. Determined not to suffer in advance whatever the future might bring, she gave herself up to the enjoyment of Richard's company. Happiness speeded her recovery, and she argued when Lady Annabel insisted on her obedience to Dr. Knighton's recommendation of a full week in bed, but a word from Richard quashed her rebellion. When she was able to rise, he would no longer feel obliged to entertain her, she realized suddenly, and pondered a relapse. It would have been useless — the bloom in her cheeks announced her returning health.

Lady Annabel had never seen Richard so happy and at ease since he was a small boy. The hopes she had hardly dared admit to herself seemed less and less outrageous. She deliberately absented herself from the house in Cavendish Square, calling on people she had not thought of in years and finding every day some ribbon that must be matched or book to be returned to Hookham's Circulating Library. Richard, on the rare occasions when he noted her absence, lovingly called her a regular gadabout and failed to notice her conscious look. In the evenings she furthered her acquaintance with Miss Fell, and grew more and more certain that that young lady, whatever her birth, would be the most delightful daughter-in-law.

The day arrived at last when Miss Fell was permitted to leave her bed. Her legs trembling from lack of use, she leaned heavily on Richard's arm as she walked across the chamber to the wing chair by the fire. However, she very quickly recovered from the effort and stayed up for two hours. It was decided that if she slept after luncheon she might venture to the drawing room for a short while later on.

"For if Mr. Carstairs would be so good as to carry me," she pointed out, blushing, "it would be no more tiring than to sit in my chamber; and while it is a charming room, I have been confined to it for a whole week and it would be positively restful to have a change of scenery. Besides, Herr Doktor Holzkopf is coming tomorrow and I should wish to try my strength a little before I see him."

"We had better put him off," protested Richard. "You are not ready for such exertion."

No less than Miss Fell did he dread the morrow and the revelations it might bring. He was very ready to postpone it, but she now felt she wanted to know the worst and get it over. Richard would never be more in charity with her and if his regard was not now strong enough to survive the truth, whatever that might be, it never would be. She was adamant that she would see the German physician.

"I shall be there to take care of you," conceded Richard. "If necessary, I shall simply stop the wretched experiment."

Lady Annabel had stayed home to watch that Miss Fell did not overstrain herself. She was completely satisfied with the results of the expedition to the drawing room.

"She is very much improved, dearest," she said to Richard. "If we can but see her completely recovered, I daresay she may never have another day's illness in her life. As both doctors have admitted, her constitution is excellent."

Richard, preoccupied with thoughts of the morrow, did not reply. His face had the stern expression that had not been seen on it for several days. He went off to change, as he had an engagement that evening.

Lady Annabel dined in Miss Fell's chamber, as was her wont when Richard was out for dinner. Miss Fell was sleepy, so she left her early. She had just decided to put away her novel and retire when

Richard came storming in looking thunderous.

"Where is Lucy tonight?" he demanded.

"Whatever is the matter, dearest? What is today's date? The fourteenth? I declare I do not know where the days disappear to."

"Please, mama! Where is Lucy?" repeated Richard savagely.

"At Lady Twistleton's rout, I believe. A dreadful woman, but her parties are all the rage. Richard, what has occurred to put you in such a tweak?"

"I cannot stop now. Excuse me, mama."

Without another word, he rushed out.

I love Lucy dearly, thought Lady Annabel, *but if some outrageous prank of hers has ruined everything, I shall wring her neck.*

She sighed, and went to bed.

Richard came home after midnight and sat drinking brandy in the library far into the early hours of the morning.

"H'I disremember when I've seen Mr. Richard so top-heavy," remarked Bell disapprovingly to Willett as they helped him up the stairs.

"Mr. Richard has Things on his Mind," replied Willett with equal disapproval.

Richard woke in the morning with a splitting head. When his mama requested that he assist Miss Fell to her chair, he growled at her, an event so unprecedented that Lady Annabel quite forgot to ask what had upset him the night before. He did not growl at Miss Fell, but scowled at her so ferociously (and quite unknowingly) that she hardly dared to take his arm. He departed immediately, leaving both ladies wondering desperately how they had offended.

Lady Annabel quickly conquered her own dismay and decided to see Lucy as soon as possible. Miss Fell had more reason to fear his displeasure. She worried all morning, and when Herr Doktor Holzkopf arrived and Richard had not yet reappeared, she was feeling distinctly unwell.

He came unexpectedly in the middle of the afternoon. When Lady Annabel pointed out that he had mentioned the evening, he roared with laughter.

"Ev'nink, ev'nink!" he repeated with gusto. *"Verstehen Sie, gnädige Frau, auf* Spanish is ev'nink *'tarde'; auf Deutsch,* iss *'tarde' Abend.* Iss *auch Nachmittag! Ich habe* many years in Spain lift. I mix up mein lenkvitches, iss all!"

Having no idea what he was talking about, Lady Annabel was powerless to protest. Miss Fell gathered the gist of his speech and treasured up his last sentence, feeling that Richard would appreciate it — if he ever spoke to her again.

She was almost glad, now that the time had come, that Richard was not present. It might be just as well if she had time to adjust to the knowledge of her origins before she had to face him. Of course, she might yet turn out to be the daughter of — well, perhaps not a duke — but an earl, say. Unlikely, she thought ruefully; if she had been, her disappearance would have been widely noised abroad by now. No one seemed to have missed her, she realized, her depression deepening.

Herr Doktor Holzkopf had the room arranged to his liking at last. He sat her in a deep chair with wings that hid from her the banks of candles on either side. The curtains were all pulled close against the daylight. Lady Annabel, in the absence of her son, sat slightly behind Miss Fell, out of her sight. The little German perched on a high stool, hastily carried up from the kitchen by a puzzled James, directly before her. He took a gold watch from his pocket.

"Zo, Miss Fell, you regard ziss vatch. I svink it slow, zo slow, before ze eyes. Back and fort' it go, back and fort', back and fort'."

Miss Fell watched, fascinated, as the glittering circle swung more and more slowly. She wondered when she would fall into the expected trance.

"Zo slow it go, slow, slower, slower. Now ze head feel zo heavy, you are fallink to sleep, fallink, fallink, fallink. Your eyes are closink, closink."

She was not doing anything of the sort, but did not like to tell him so. Obediently she closed her eyes.

"Zo, my lady," he observed with satisfaction, "ze patient iss to sleep. Now I will ze qvestions to ask. Miss Fell, can you to hear me?"

"Yes, doctor."

"Very gut. You haff anozzer name, you are not Clara Fell. Vot iss your name?"

"I'm afraid I still don't know, doctor," said Miss Fell apologetically, and opened her eyes.

"Ach, zo!" cried the Herr Doktor in amazement. "You are not in ze trantz, Miss Fell?"

"I am very sorry. I did everything you told me."

The doctor was very excited. "I haff only two ozzer people known," he explained, "who half ze resistance zo shtrong. Lady Annabel, I fear ze eggsperiment iss not a

243

success. I vill try vunce more, if you vish?"

There was no answer from Lady Annabel. Miss Fell pulled herself out of her chair in alarm and looked at her. She was sitting bolt upright, her eyes closed, her face blank. Herr Doktor Holzkopf was overcome with raucous mirth.

"Ach, mein gootness!" he exclaimed. "Hier iss die gut lady in a trantz, ze wronk lady haff I in ze trantz put!"

His laughter was so infectious that Miss Fell found herself giggling. With an effort she forced herself to gravity.

"Can you do something about it, sir? Pray bring her round at once!"

"I do. *Gnädige Frau,* you hear me?"

"I hear you."

"I count to zree, zen I snap mein finkers und you vill avake. Vun, two, zree." He snapped his fingers. For a moment Miss Fell feared that Lady Annabel would not admit his extraordinary numbers, then her eyes opened and she looked around.

"Are you ready to begin, Herr Doktor?" she asked.

Great was her amazement when Miss Fell explained what had occurred. She refused absolutely to permit a second attempt.

"It seems to be a shockingly unreliable

cure," she said severely. "I cannot think how Dr. Knighton came to recommend it."

"It vork, it vork," insisted Herr Doktor Holzkopf as he was remorselessly ushered out of the room by Bell. "It is zat ze junge lady a head ze most shtrong haff. *Ausserordentlich, ausserordentlich!*" He went away muttering to himself.

"What did he say?" inquired Lady Annabel suspiciously.

Miss Fell started giggling again. "I do not know what that last word was, Lady Annabel, but before that he said that I have a very strong head."

"Oh dear! I suppose that means that *I* have a weak head. What a dreadful little man! I am so glad Richard was not here, Clara."

Miss Fell suddenly found she was exhausted. James had to be called to carry her above stairs, and she retired to bed with relief. Nothing had been settled, she thought with despair. She still might be a baron's daughter or a butcher's. The way she felt at that moment she would bet on the butcher.

When Lady Annabel described the fiasco to Richard, he was not at all amused.

"We might have guessed our problems

would not be solved so easily," he said gloomily. "I beg your pardon, mama, for not being here. I'd have thrown the fellow out on his ear."

"You must beg Clara's pardon, Richard. She was quite distressed by your absence."

"I shall do so. I fear I was unconscionably rude to both of you this morning. The truth is, I was blue-devilled."

"Is Lucy in a scrape, dearest?" asked Lady Annabel, trying to hide her anxiety.

"Oh no, mama. It is all settled. Pray do not speak to her about it."

She might have pressed him, but she suspected she knew what the trouble was. She did not feel up to tackling Richard about Major Bowen, even for Lucy's sake. If Lucy were truly in love, her brother's disapproval would not change her feelings, and sooner or later her mother must find out. She would deal with her difficult son at that point, she decided, a little guiltily.

Richard apologized stiffly to Miss Fell the next morning. He did not try to avoid her, and willingly aided her still stumbling steps, but their free and easy intercourse was at an end. Lucy's misdeeds had returned his thoughts to the question of eligible and ineligible birth, and he, too, would now have bet on the butcher.

Miss Fell suffered in silence. Her health did not improve as fast as Lady Annabel considered proper, and Dr. Knighton was called in again. After submitting patiently to a scolding for introducing the German quack, he was permitted to prescribe an iron tonic, which Miss Fell swallowed three times a day with many protests and grimaces.

However unpalatable, the tonic appeared to be efficacious, unless it was her improving relationship with Richard that was responsible for the return of roses to her cheeks. She spent an increasing length of time each day at the pianoforte, and he listened in silence as she played. They were still not on their old basis of familiarity, but every time he saw her he was more inclined to give her the benefit of the doubt. Her sad eyes bewitched him, and he longed to make them smile. She, however, was the one to make him laugh, when she judged the time ripe to tell him about her head "ze most shtrong."

"As though I were a confirmed tippler!" she said in mock indignation, and went on to explain why the Herr Doktor had arrived several hours early. " 'I mix up mein lenkvitches, iss all,' " she quoted.

"Good God, and we expected that . . .

247

that monkey to cure you!" gasped Richard, helpless with laughter.

Lady Annabel watched the reconciliation with joy marred by a feeling of lethargy. Her back ached, she could not concentrate on her needle, the candlelight was too bright. Firmly she pulled herself together. Lucy was coming home tomorrow, as Dr. Knighton had pronounced all danger of infection past. She must keep her wits about her and attempt to discover the truth about her daughter's feelings. Irritably, she wished Lucy could be satisfied with Lord Denham, a most unexceptionable match.

On Wednesday Lady Annabel woke with a fever, and aching in every limb. Dr. Knighton was sent for again.

"It is the grippe, of course," announced Miss Fell, entering the drawing room where Richard awaited the verdict.

He turned on her savagely.

"More trouble to be laid at your door!" he snarled. "I wish I had never found you!" He flung out of the room.

Miss Fell was shattered. Whatever his mood, he had never before reproached her directly. She wanted to burst into tears, but she was far too busy to indulge in the vapors. She told herself sternly that she could not possibly be interested in the opinions of so unstable a gentleman and sent James off to the apothecary.

Returning to Lady Annabel's chamber, she found the abigail, Vane, in tears.

"Oh, miss," she wailed, "I can't bear to see my lady so ill, tossing and turning so and burning up with the fever. Whatever shall I do?" She wrung her hands, and the question was evidently rhetorical.

"That one never were the least use in a sick room," observed Mary dispassionately. "Best send her to her room, miss. I'll nurse m'lady. Got plenty of experience, I have."

"Thank you, Mary, we shall care for her between us," said Miss Fell gratefully. "Vane, you may leave, and do not come back unless you are able to be of assistance."

Between caring for her patient and running the household, Miss Fell was kept fully occupied for two or three days. She was happy to be able to give some exchange for all that Lady Annabel had done for her and, feeling herself to be of real use for the first time, found that she was only mildly fatigued at the end of each day. She had no time to think of her own problems. She did not see Richard at all. He visited his mother only when Mary was on duty and dined out every day.

Lady Annabel was a docile patient. The grippe did not hit her as hard as it had struck Miss Fell and by the third day she was able to sit up for a while in the afternoon. The next day she expressed a desire to go below stairs.

"I think a little music would be good for me," she declared. "Will you play, Clara?"

"The doctor is coming this morning, Lady Annabel. If he allows it, I will certainly play for you."

Richard entered as she sat down at the pianoforte. She looked at him questioningly as he kissed his mother. He came over to her, and while opening her music he said in a low voice, "I must speak to you, Miss Fell."

She looked up at him gravely. "When Lady Annabel returns to her room?" she suggested. She could not read his expression.

"Very well." He went to sit by Lady Annabel, and they conversed quietly while Miss Fell played. Once she glanced at him and found him gazing at her longingly, but with something strange in his look that puzzled her.

Richard helped his mother upstairs. Miss Fell saw her settled comfortably in her bed and repaired to the library, where he awaited her. He was leaning on the mantel, staring down into the fire. As she came in he turned. He stepped toward her and took both her hands.

"Miss Fell, what I said on Wednesday was inexcusable," he said painfully. "I beg you to forgive me."

Her heart went out to him, but she pulled her hands from his clasp and answered with reserve.

"Indeed I forgive you, Mr. Carstairs. It was said in the heat of the moment when you were worried by your mother's illness."

"You have been very good to her. She calls you her angel of mercy."

"I did no more than she had done for me. Less rather, for I am nothing to her, and she has been like a mother to me."

Richard was silent. He was about to speak again when she turned and ran from the room.

His mind was in a turmoil. Watching from a distance as she had abandoned the role of invalid and become the nurturer, he had been forced to realize that what he felt for her was not a blend of protectiveness and desire, but love. It warred in his head with his pride and his lack of self-confidence until he thought he would go mad. He feared that he had irredeemably offended her and was almost glad, since that would solve his dilemma. He groaned aloud and rang for some brandy.

Miss Fell had run from him because she must otherwise have burst into tears or flung her arms round him. Or both. She had decided that she must never again relax her guard with him. It hurt too much when he rebuffed her. Conquering her tears, she went to discuss dinner with Monsieur Pierre.

Chapter 12

Richard stayed home for dinner. He dined alone, as Miss Fell had a tray in Lady Annabel's chamber; however, she joined him later at his request, and they played a quiet game of chess. Each had resolved to keep his emotions to himself and to treat the other with impeccable courtesy. Almost in spite of themselves they fell into the easy interchange that had been so precious to them, but now each was conscious of feelings held back, of a certain caution.

Lady Annabel recovered rapidly. At least partially satisfied by the relations between Richard and Miss Fell, she was anxious to have Lucy back under her care and to try if she could to discover how sat the wind in that quarter. A week after her collapse she was pronounced fit ("Thanks entirely to dear Clara's nursing," she insisted), and Lucy was to be permitted to return two days later, provided certain precautions were observed. One or two of the London servants had succumbed to the grippe, but Mrs. Dawkins had packed them off home with a basket of comforts, so as not to endanger the rest. The Yorkshire servants regarded them with scorn, as proof of the decadence of London life in general. *They would not dream of so discommoding my lady.*

Lucy returned home on Friday afternoon. She seemed subdued, though happy to be back in the bosom of her family after three weeks' absence. She quickly resumed her friendship with her dear Clara, but did not confide in either her or Lady Annabel.

Saturday brought their first visitors in weeks. Aunt Blanche came to see her sister-in-law, bringing Jenny and Edward in her train. Richard was privileged to see Edward introduced to Miss Fell, and her reaction was all he could have wished. Taking in the violently flowered waistcoat, the striped neckcloth, purple coat and positively yellow pantaloons, she remarked with a choking gasp, "I see you are a very Nonpareil, Mr. Carstairs. What a pity Mr. Richard Carstairs is not a little livelier in his dress."

Edward cast a glance of triumph at his cousin, saw that gentleman laughing, and turned back in suspicion.

"I see you are bamming me, Miss Fell, just as Richard and Lucy do," he sighed.

"None of you understands the exigencies of Fashion."

Lord Denham arrived and bowed over Miss Fell's hand. He complimented her on her return to health. He chatted with her for a few minutes and then retired to a corner with Lucy, who flirted with him outrageously.

Jenny came to sit by her and regarded her with evident admiration. "Lucy told me all about you," she opened, to Miss Fell's alarm. "How your mama was at school with Aunt Annabel, and how you were thrown from your horse and rescued by Cousin Richard. It is so romantic!"

"It was very uncomfortable," said Miss Fell prosaically.

Lady Annabel, after consulting Richard, invited everyone present, including Lord Harry, who now appeared, and Mr. Geoffrey Carstairs, to take potluck in Cavendish Square that evening. Lord Harry was about to plead another engagement, having no taste for a family party, when he caught his brother's minatory eye and meekly accepted.

"It will be in the nature of a celebration," announced Richard. "My mother and Miss Fell are both recovered safely, and Lucy is restored to us.

"I shall broach the '87 brandy," he added privately to Lord Harry, at least partially reconciling that young gentleman to his lot.

The dinner party, after much anxious last-minute preparation in the kitchens, was a great success. As the gentlemen rose from the table to join the ladies, Lord Denham pulled Richard aside.

"Like a word with you later," he mumbled self-consciously.

"Pot-valiant, eh?" grinned Richard. "Of course, Tony. We shall retire to the library when the rest leave."

Miss Fell was persuaded to entertain the company with a performance upon the pianoforte. Lucy, entrancing in sky blue muslin, joined her in a song or two. The unmusical Lord Denham gazed at her throughout in uncritical devotion. Conscious of his gaze, Lucy blushed and giggled like a schoolgirl. The young people played a game of speculation, in which Lord Denham unashamedly robbed everyone else to ensure that Lucy won. She seemed to be in high spirits, but Miss Fell thought she detected unhappiness in her eyes and wished she had her full confidence.

The party broke up; guests went their

several ways; the ladies retired to bed, and Richard accompanied Tony to the library. Their interview was brief. Lord Denham formally requested permission to address Lucy and, not unexpectedly, received it.

"You gudgeon, Tony," said Richard affectionately, "as though I could have any objection. You are the most eligible bachelor in town, I only hope she'll have you."

On Sunday afternoon, Lady Annabel and Miss Fell went off in the town carriage to pay some calls. Many people had left their cards when Lady Annabel was unwell, and she decided to repay their visits and seize the opportunity of introducing Miss Fell to as many people as possible. Lucy, unaccountably depressed, complained of a headache and refused to accompany them. Her mother feared the grippe, but she did not want to fuss.

When they returned, Miss Fell was in the mopes. She had been made acquainted with at least twenty people and not one had even said she looked familiar. Lucy, on the other hand, had thrown off her depression and her headache. She seemed to have made up her mind about something, and there was a determined look in her eye that made Lady Annabel wonder, with a sigh, what she would be up to next.

In the morning, Lucy disappeared early, taking only Molly, her maid. Lady Annabel, who had planned a shopping expedition, was vexed.

"I fear Lucy is become a sad romp. Well, she will have to go without her new ribbons. We can concentrate on your purchases, Clara."

Miss Fell was to receive new gloves, stockings and footwear. Her vehement objections had been overborne.

"Clara, I cannot take you about looking like a dowd. Made-over gowns are acceptable, indeed you look charming in them, though I should dearly like to see you in a new one. However, I understand your unwillingness. But gloves and slippers *never* fit properly if they had been purchased for someone else. It will not answer. The silk stockings shall be a little extra present from me, because I am so fond of you. Come, kiss me, my dear, and do not cry. You will make your eyes red. It is All Fools' Day, so humour a foolish old lady."

Miss Fell was beginning to wish the London scheme had never been mooted. By Tuesday evening she had met fifty members of the Fashionable World and more. Not one had recognized her. She felt she was becoming deeper and deeper in debt to the Carstairs and was oppressed by her total inability to repay them. That night, however, she decided she must put aside her crotchets. Richard was taking them to the theatre.

They went to see a comedy in deference to Lucy's tastes. It was a new production, and the theatre was quite filled up. In the boxes sat the Quality, ready to be amused but more interested in noting who was present, waving and bowing to acquaintances, or studying each other's dress, than in the performance. The pit held many single gentlemen, and hoi polloi; a raucous hubbub rose thence to join the discreet murmur of the ton.

Miss Fell was fascinated to observe the audience, but Lucy sat back fanning herself languidly. After six weeks in London, she considered herself an habituée and refused to show any excitement. When the show began, however, she was glued to the stage and laughed as readily as any shop-girl in the pit, whereas Miss Fell decided the play was far from extraordinary and heard few lines that made her smile.

In the interval, their box became crowded with Lucy's admirers and friends of Lady Annabel. Richard proposed that he and Miss Fell should step out for some air. It was almost as crowded in the corridor, and Richard was constantly being greeted by acquaintances. Some of these he presented to Miss Fell, others he passed with a word. Then he was accosted by a stout, florid gentleman with porcine eyes.

"Ho, Carstairs," he accused, "so this is the ladybird you've been hiding. A real bird of paradise." He winked, and looked Miss Fell up and down in a most disagreeable way.

"Miss Fell is sponsored by Lady Annabel, Sir Philip," said Richard coldly. "You will excuse us."

The leering baronet was not at all discomposed. "Greedy dog. Want to keep her all to yourself, hey? I'll be seeing you, my pretty. *I* know all about riding on the moors early in the morning!"

Richard turned his back and led Miss Fell away. She felt a little faint.

"What a cursed position to be in, when Rossiter can so insult you," Richard said savagely. "Come, we will return to my mother at once. This is an abominable crush."

Miss Fell found it difficult to concentrate on the second act. She suspected it was not a very good play anyway, though the audience was laughing heartily. When the second interval came, Lucy and Lady Annabel proposed to take a stroll, but Miss Fell could not face the possibility of seeing Sir Philip again, so she chose to remain in their box. Richard offered to fetch her a glass of lemonade, and she gratefully accepted.

He had scarcely been gone a minute when she was horrified to see Sir Philip entering the box. Summoning up her courage, she told him that Mr. Carstairs was not present.

"The jealous lover is out of the way, is he? Well, my beauty, don't be shy, give me a kiss."

He moved toward her and she jumped up from her seat. She backed away, realizing too late that he would have her pinned in a corner. He seized her wrist and bent toward her. Not daring to cry out for fear of drawing curious eyes, she struggled desperately as he pressed himself against her.

Suddenly the baronet felt his shoulder seized in a grip of iron.

"Let go her wrists!" hissed Richard, "and turn around if you dare."

Sir Philip swung around, his hand reaching for his cane. He had scarce touched it when Richard's fist caught him on the chin and he went over backward, his flying arm hitting Miss Fell on the shoulder as he struck the wall and slumped to the floor.

"That was a clumsy bit of work," apologized Richard ruefully. "Did the swine hurt you? I'll see he is thrown out of all his clubs!"

"Oh no," whispered Miss Fell shakily, looking in distress at his bruised and bloodied knuckles as he helped her over the recumbent baronet. "You came in time. Pray do not punish him any further. It would only create a scandal."

"You are right," agreed Richard regretfully, "though Lord knows it is something I have been wanting to do this age." He looked around. "I don't believe anyone noticed, it is dark here at the back of the box. I must take you home immediately; you are shaking. Only how to dispose of the body?"

"When the next act begins, the corridor will be empty, and you may leave him out there with no one the wiser. Except, of course, Lady Annabel and your sister." Her voice trembled. "You are right: I bring nothing but trouble on you."

"Come, sit down. Do not distress yourself. My mother has as little liking for

262

Rossiter as I and will be happy to see him come by his just deserts. We shall do as you suggested and then I shall take you back to Cavendish Square."

"Might it not be remarked if we should leave early?"

"What, with this devilish play? I am surprised there is anyone left in the audience. Besides, you and mama are known to be convalescent."

Willingly accepting his reassurances and soothed by his calm, matter-of-fact manner, she laughed shakily. "I am glad your opinion of the play coincides with mine. It is dreadful, is it not? It seems to arouse such enthusiasm that I hesitated to criticize it."

"Your taste is impeccable, Miss Fell," he answered, with more warmth in his voice than he had intended to display. His admiration for the courageous way she put the unpleasantness behind her, together with the new evidence of her need for his protection, made him want to take her in his arms and kiss her. He might have done so, but for the realization that she had just fought off one such attempt. What assurance had he that his embrace would be any more welcome to her than Sir Philip's? He let her bind his bleeding hand with her handkerchief.

Lady Annabel and Lucy returned to the box, gasped at the sight of Sir Philip, who was stirring and groaning, and were regaled with the story. They were full of solicitude and agreed that they must go home at once. Richard, with Lucy's unnecessary but gleeful assistance, dragged the baronet into the corridor and dumped him unceremoniously, then they departed.

Lady Annabel insisted that Miss Fell should retire as soon as they arrived home. She was more than ready to comply. Besides the lingering shock of the baronet's attack, she was oppressed by the truth she had uttered to Richard, the echo of what he had said to her. She brought only trouble on her benefactors. What if Richard did love her, as she sometimes suspected he might? She could not allow him to ally himself to a nobody, and an unlucky nobody at that. The butcher was high on her list again, but she was beginning to feel that she would never know who her parents were.

She had been entertaining the thought that she might be able to earn her living as a musician. Now it appeared to her to be of the utmost importance that she should become independent and cease to be a burden to her dear friends.

After shedding a few tears, she slept.

Morning brought no new counsel. Miss Fell did not go down to breakfast but was too restless to stay in bed.

Hoping for solitude, she went into the library to think out her first move on the road toward finding employment.

As she stood by the window, gazing out unseeingly, Richard entered the room. As she did not look at him, he came to stand behind her, supposing that something in the garden held her attention. Deep in thought, she did not realize his presence until he was close to her. She turned, and found him so near that she lost her balance. He reached to steady her, his hands gripping her shoulders, and then suddenly his arms were around her and his lips were on hers. She resisted a moment, then gave in to the wave of feeling that surged through her. His mouth pressed on hers in a long, sweet kiss.

Miss Fell was the first to recover her senses. She pulled away from him and unwillingly he let her go. He took both her hands in his and his dark eyes gazed deep into her grey-green ones.

"Will you marry me?" he asked simply.

She drew a deep breath. Thinking that she was hesitating, he rushed on, "You must know that I have long admired you. It is my dearest wish to have the right to protect you from such insults as you received last night."

He had better not have spoken. He gave her time to think, even unknowingly reminded her of her resolve. Even now, had he told her of his love she might have cast caution to the winds, but he was too used to suppressing his emotions. *He thinks of me as a cross between a musical genius and a lost puppy,* she thought. It would not be long before a nameless wife became a burden to him.

"I cannot," she answered.

The hurt puzzlement in his eyes nearly made her break down. She could not stay to explain her decision. Once again, she ran from him.

Chapter 13

Lucy was quite unaware of the complex currents of emotion that joined her brother and her dear friend. When the two arrived from Yorkshire she had been very distressed that she was not to be permitted to nurse Miss Fell. However, her aunt had insisted that she accompany them to Almack's that very evening.

"Lucy, I will not have you indulging in the sullens. Your poor mama has enough to cope with, without my report that you are repining."

"I beg your pardon, Aunt Blanche," Lucy apologized. She obediently dressed for Almack's and soon forgot her disgruntlement in Charles's arms. Having been impressed all her life with the idea that gentlemen are not interested in sickbeds, she barely mentioned her friend's indisposition to him, though she discussed it more fully with Tony, who, after all, was acquainted with Miss Fell and her story.

She danced two waltzes with the major. He would not take her to supper, fearing that his constant attendance might be noticed and lead to comment.

"I care for nothing the old cats can say," objected Lucy scornfully.

"Nor I," he answered pacifically. "But if your friend is seriously ill, I shall not be able to speak to your brother for some time, and I cannot like it that he might hear rumours before I have seen him."

Lucy, who dreaded that interview, would have done anything to postpone it. Sorry as she was that Clara was taken with the grippe, she could not but see the advantages of living with Aunt Blanche for a while. Richard would not be looking on disapprovingly every time she spoke to Charles.

In fact, she saw very little of her brother for a full week. He was home most of the day with Miss Fell, and their evening entertainments did not coincide. Occasionally she met him in the park if she went out early riding or driving. However, Charles was still busy in the mornings with his military duties, so he and Richard did not meet. Lord Denham was her usual escort at that time, though there was generally a crowd of friends and acquaintances surrounding them.

Lucy spent the greater part of every afternoon with Charles, with only her cousin Jenny or her maid as chaperone. If the weather was fine, they met in one of the parks and wandered for hours up and down secluded paths, followed at a discreet distance by maid or cousin, each of whom had her own beau to attend her. When the weather was inclement, Charles would come to Orchard Street and Lucy would have the butler deny her to other visitors. Her aunt was usually out visiting her many acquaintances, and she rarely insisted on Lucy's presence at her side. Lucy made no secret of the fact that she saw Major Bowen frequently, but nor did she allow Aunt Blanche to know just how frequently, or how intimately.

The major, in seventh heaven, had no objections. He would quickly have pointed out the absence of a chaperone and condemned any attempt at secrecy, as Lucy knew well, so she did not resort to such measures though greatly attracted by their romantic aspect.

They usually met in the evening also, for while Charles was not invited to the small, intimate gatherings of the Carstairs' close circle, he had entrée to all the balls and dress parties, masquerades and routs. Hostesses quickly opened their doors to such a personable young gentleman, sponsored by Lord Harry Graham and with a fortune, too, according to rumour. High sticklers might ask who were his family, but the greater part of the Fashionable World was happy to welcome an officer who had fought for his country at a time when most of the British Army was lounging at home expecting an invasion.

Boney was sitting across the Channel building vast fleets of troop carriers and awaiting the time when favorable weather and a moment of inattention on the part of blockading fleets should give him his chance. Gentlemen and commoners alike were running to join the reserves, for fear of being mustered into the Regular Army; and, equipped with ancient pikes and halberds, the reserves were desperately in need of officers with some knowledge of military matters.

When Charles told his superiors he was seriously considering selling out, he was immediately offered the rank of acting lieutenant colonel in the reserves. He discussed it with Lucy.

"What would you have to do?" inquired that young lady cautiously.

"At present, nothing. The authorities are far from sure just what they want the reserve army to do and are simply signing them up and sending them home again. If they ever get around to starting a training program, I should be posted to a regiment near my home. Of course, in case of an invasion I should have to fight, but if I simply sold out, I should volunteer again then anyway."

"Then take it," said Lucy decisively. "When we are married, I shall be able to go with you if you are a colonel, shall I not?"

"Yes, beloved, or if I remain a major."

"I think I should like to be a colonel's wife," said Lucy, considering carefully.

"Only acting lieutenant colonel," Charles pointed out, amused. "They do not make full colonels of men my age."

"How silly of them," cried his prejudiced sweetheart, "when you are quite the best officer in the whole army."

How could he help but kiss her, after a swift look around to be sure.

They did not always meet unobserved. Thus it was that at White's the odds were fluctuating; Lord Denham and Major Bowen were running neck and neck in the Betting Book. My lord's obvious advantages of birth and fortune no longer looked so impressive when the major had been seen holding hands with Miss Carstairs on a bench in Green Park for quite half an hour.

Inevitably the news of the wagers came at last to Richard's ears, in spite of his friends' efforts to shield him. He was playing cards at the club one evening when a piercing voice at the next table caught his attention.

"I hear Major Bowen has overtaken Lord Denham in the Carstairs 'stakes," he heard. "I've half a mind to bet on him myself, you know."

The man's companions hushed him, and Richard's fellow players looked embarrassed. Seeing his icily furious face, they were ready to jump up and soothe ruffled feelings before it came to a duel. However, Richard finished the hand with iron control, paid his small debts, and excused himself. He rushed home, discovered Lucy's whereabouts, and set off again for Lady Twistleton's rout.

By the time he reached the brilliantly lit Twistleton house, he was somewhat calmer and was reconsidering his precipitate actions. Unfortunately, the first thing he saw was Lucy waltzing with the major. His fury reanimated, he approached his aunt.

"Aunt Blanche, I must speak to Lucy

immediately. I shall take her back to Orchard Street. Will you make her excuses to her partners? Plead a headache or some such thing. You will know what is best."

She looked up, alarmed. "Oh dear, is Miss Fell suddenly worse, Richard? Pray do not tell me Annabel has caught the grippe!"

"No, no, nothing like that. I must simply have a word privately with my sister, and at once."

"You will have to wait until she has finished her dance. It would be shockingly bad *ton* to interrupt it," said his aunt disapprovingly. "Do you have your carriage? Well, you had better take ours and send it back again. Is this really necessary, Richard?"

"I believe so, ma'am," he answered curtly, and restrained his impatience as best he could until Charles led his glowing sister back to her aunt.

"Richard, how delightful to see you!" she cried.

Her brother bowed coldly to her partner.

"Lucy, you must come with me immediately. I have a great deal to say to you."

Lucy pouted. "Why must I, Richard? I am enjoying myself excessively."

A reproving look from Charles changed

her mind. Secretly, she was rather afraid of the expression on her brother's face. She had never before seen him so angry.

"Oh, very well," she sighed.

When they were settled in the carriage, she said pettishly, "Well, what is it, Richard, that you should drag me away from a party?"

Richard explained what he had heard at White's. "I blush to think that the conduct of a sister of mine should give rise to such gossip and speculation."

"This is the outside of enough! You men are all odious with your endless wagering! I have done nothing to deserve such a reproach, nothing I should be ashamed for the world to see!" Lucy was near tears.

"I forbid you to see Major Bowen again," said Richard sternly.

"Don't be bird-witted. When I am forever meeting him at parties! Would you have me cut him dead? And are you going to demand that my aunt close her doors to him, pray?"

Richard had grasped at the easiest solution without considering the difficulties, nor had he realized that to be logical he must forbid Lucy to see Tony also. Fortunately for him, his sister was in no state to be logical.

"Very well," he conceded, "you will not give him more than one dance in any evening, and you will not walk or ride with him in the park. You can always plead another engagement, and I will see that Aunt Blanche takes you with her whenever she goes out."

"You are quite hateful!" stormed Lucy, but a part of her mind was already working out ways around his prohibitions. He had not, after all, said that she could not sit out with Charles as many dances as she pleased, had he? And there were places to meet other than in the parks.

His suspicions lulled by her outburst, Richard was satisfied when he at last received her reluctant promise that she would observe his restrictions. He thought his threat of sending her back to Toblethorpe had persuaded her, and hoped that her future discretion would scotch the rumours and put paid to the wagering. He would have liked to have called the major out, but that would give rise to even greater scandal; and, besides, the damned upstart had not really done anything that would justify a challenge. Curse the encroaching mushroom!

Richard left Lucy at their aunt's house, sent the carriage back to Lady Twistleton's, and, still raging, walked home, where he drank too much brandy. Unacknowledged to himself was the fact that he was rapidly falling in love with someone who might prove as ineligible as the major. The effort of suppressing that fact did not improve his temper.

When Mrs. Carstairs and Jenny arrived home, Lucy was in bed. They both repaired to her room at once. Aunt Blanche assured herself that nothing serious was amiss, shook her head over her nephew's strange behaviour, and retired. Jenny and Lucy spent the next hour in conspiratorial whispering and giggling.

The next morning, Richard, his head throbbing, took both girls driving. Unaware of Major Bowen's daily schedule, he was unknowingly cutting out Lord Denham. Since he drove in morose silence, the cousins chattered to each other and ignored him. He was glad to be rid of them, and went on to White's, where he hid behind a newspaper in the Reading Room and fell as sound asleep as any of the elderly gentlemen snoring in their wing chairs.

Lucy had already sent a message to the major, and in the afternoon, he escorted her and Jenny on a shopping expedition.

Unlike Richard, he enjoyed the girls' chatter and joined in helping to match ribbons and choose shawls. He bought them each a pair of gloves. Aunt Blanche had no qualms about letting her niece go out without her escort, as Richard, fearing to appear to criticize her chaperonage, had not opened his budget to her. He simply told her that he and Lady Annabel would be happy if she would take Lucy about with her more to meet her friends.

"The chit becomes a sad romp," he had explained. "She is always with young people. It would do her good to have more experience at dealing with the older members of the ton."

Aunt Blanche, noting his bloodshot eyes and the way he winced at the slightest noise, privately wondered what was going on but placidly agreed that it would indeed be good for Lucy. Whenever it was not fine enough for the girls to go out walking, she would take her.

So instead of meeting Lucy in the park, Charles found himself accompanying her to Hookham's Circulating Library, to Gunther's for ices — even to see the Elgin Marbles. They paid a nostalgic visit to the Exeter Exchange. Jenny insisted that the menagerie at the Tower of London was more impressive, so they went there and examined the crown jewels, taken for their benefit from a dusty cupboard by a crabbed and cobwebby old man.

In the evenings, Lucy became expert at finding private corners that could not be stigmatized as improper, and she would sit out two or three dances with Charles. She also granted Lord Denham three dances more than once.

"To throw Richard off the scent," she explained to Jenny.

She had not told Charles what Richard had said to her. Much as she hated concealing anything from him, she knew that he would have insisted on approaching her brother immediately, and the time was most unpropitious. Instead, she told him that Richard had wished to tell her that Miss Fell had had a relapse.

"He told me this morning that she is much improved again," she added airily, "but he is excessively worried about her, and you will not wish to speak to him while he has unpleasant matters on his mind."

Charles, knowing that Richard disapproved of him, could only agree that the time was not ripe. He felt it was incorrect behaviour to have a secret understanding with Lucy; but his intentions were honourable, and, after all, it was just a matter of awaiting the right moment.

Meanwhile, Lady Annabel fell ill. Lucy cried for an hour when she was told she might not go home and nurse her mama. Richard spent a great deal of time with her for three days and was so comforting and supportive that for the first time Lucy felt guilty about deceiving him. She had already lied to Charles, and her double guilt weighed heavily on her. Had it been possible, she would have confessed all to her mother.

So moped was she that Richard became alarmed and redoubled his attentions, not only increasing her guilt but cutting her off from Charles. Fortunately, before matters came to a head, Richard brought the news that Lady Annabel was well on the road to recovery.

"Dr. Knighton saw her this morning," he said, "and she is able to be up later today. I shall stay at home to help her downstairs, so I shall not see you this afternoon."

Lucy cheered up somewhat. At least one burden was removed from her. No sooner had Richard left than she sent a note to Charles's lodgings, arranging to meet him as soon as possible.

Neither of them was in a happy mood. Though greatly relieved that her mother was better, Lucy felt as guilty as ever, and was upset that she would not be able to go home for another week. Charles was disturbed by the implications of the fact that he had not seen his betrothed for three days simply because of the presence of her brother. He was beginning to think that there was more impropriety attached to his position than he had suspected, yet he could not justify disturbing Richard while he was worried about his mother's health.

Lucy and Charles saw little of each other that week. The weather took a turn for the worse and threatened a return to winter. Aunt Blanche took Lucy visiting with her every afternoon and Charles was busy wrapping up his affairs at the War Ministry. He also saw a good deal of his lawyer. There was still no news from Northumberland and he was growing worried. He told Lucy he would have to go home to investigate, and she was cross with him for proposing a protracted absence when their affairs were so unsettled.

Lucy went to an unconscionable number of private parties in the next few days. Lord Denham was usually there, and thinking her dismal face due to her mother's illness, he was particularly charming. Lucy began again to consider the advantages of becoming a marchioness.

That Wednesday at Almack's, Charles became aware that Lucy was responding with unwonted pleasure to Lord Denham's attentions. She was offhand with him, giving him only one dance; and his jealousy was aroused. He had not seen her for two days, and, too distressed to be reasonable he was unable to give due consideration to the fact that her brother was present.

The following morning they had a raging quarrel, in whispers, in a dark corner of Hookham's where the books of sermons were stacked.

"I shall marry Tony!" hissed Lucy in the end.

"If he comes up to scratch," retorted the major unforgivably.

She stalked off in a dignified rage, and his heart stood still. He would have called after her, but the library was full of people, and they had already attracted several curious stares. Cursing himself for a bacon-brained ninnyhammer, he followed her. The crowd, which had obligingly parted to allow passage to the beautiful young lady with the stormy eyes, was not at all willing to give way before him. It was several minutes before he reached the door, and there was no sign of her.

All afternoon he hoped for a word from her. By the next day he was ready to risk sending her a note, and had it reached her she might have relented; but she was busy packing to return to Cavendish Square, and the *billet* was misplaced by a careless housemaid.

Lucy felt her long-awaited return home was an anticlimax. Though she was happy to see her mama and Clara again, the world seemed grey. Praying for a message from Charles, she was not yet willing to give in and write to him. When no word came, she decided he was hateful, and she would marry Tony just to punish him.

On Sunday morning, Richard told her that Tony had requested permission to ask for her hand. He was disturbed by her obvious depression; but his own affairs were much on his mind and he dismissed her attitude with the thought that she was just in the crotchets.

"I do not mean to put any pressure on you, Lucy," he said, "but I must tell you that mama and I would be delighted if you were to accept him. We are agreed that you must be happy with such an amiable husband, and of course he is in every way unexceptionable, indeed highly eligible."

"I suppose I shall have him," answered Lucy discontentedly.

Richard was far from pleased with her reply but forbore from pressing her.

By the time Lady Annabel and Miss Fell went out that afternoon, Lucy was so miserable that she could not face being polite to her mother's friends, so she pleaded a headache and stayed at home alone. Brooding on her wrongs, she became more and more angry with Charles, and had quite made up her mind to marry Lord Denham when that gentleman was announced.

" 'E would wish to 'ave a word with you privatelike, Miss Lucy," said Bell in a fatherly manner.

Now that the moment had apparently come, Lucy put her doubts behind her. "Tell Lord Denham I shall see him in the drawing room in a few minutes," she ordered firmly. Calling Molly, she prepared herself to dazzle her suitor.

"Hallo, Tony," she greeted him, entering the room.

"Lucy! You look beautiful as ever. Er, has Richard spoken to you?"

Lucy lowered her eyelashes modestly.

"Yes, my lord," she said.

"Ahem. Will you . . . Lucy, I shall be very honoured if you will accept my hand in marriage." Dash it, he thought, as she was silent. He'd made a mull of it.

Faced with the reality of giving up Charles forever, Lucy had a complete change of heart. "I'm sorry," she faltered.

"I love you, Lucy," he muttered at the same time.

She burst into tears and threw herself against his shoulder.

"Tony, I am so very sorry. I really meant to say yes, only I cannot. I love Charles so desperately, and we have quarreled, and I may never see him again ever, and Richard does not like him, and I did not mean to hurt you, for I am truly fond of you, and whatever shall I do?" she wailed.

Disentangling her from his brocaded coat, Lord Denham sighed philosophically and gave her his handkerchief.

"Was afraid that was the way of it," he admitted. "Come, dry your eyes and tell me all about it."

Sniffing, she obeyed. The whole story came out bit by bit, and after a few adroit questions Lord Denham thought he understood the chief problem.

"Don't like to be advising young ladies," he disclaimed. "Not at all in the way of it. But if you ask me, you are bein' dashed goosish. How can the fellow write to you with your wicked brother lookin' over your shoulder all the time? Stands to reason he can't. If you love the fellow, by all means write to him — the sooner the better before he takes off for the godforsaken ends of the kingdom."

"He's not a wicked brother," contradicted Lucy, "but you are right. I will write to Charles at once. Tony, I am truly grateful for your patience and your advice. I never knew you were so wise."

"No, am I?" exclaimed his lordship, adding wryly, "I am not so sure of that." Sighing again, he mended a pen for her and took his leave.

"Won't have me," he admitted to Richard later, tactfully omitting all mention of Major Bowen. "Daresay I am a bit too old for her, don't you know. Might be a good thing she turned me down. I'm too dashed lazy to make a good husband. Quite happy for Harry to inherit."

Richard was struck by a thought that had not crossed his mind in an age. If he himself did not marry, that chuckleheaded fop, his Cousin Edward, would be his heir!

285

Lucy, meanwhile, had sent off a brief note to the major. She was not so lost to pride as to beg him to meet her; she merely suggested a time and place for an encounter "to discuss matters of mutual interest." The footman returned without an answer.

"T'major weren't at home," he reported.

Taken aback, Lucy was afraid he might have left for Northumberland. Seeing her alarm, James ventured to reassure her.

"Don 'ee worrit, miss. T'landlady said he'd be back soon."

Well, thought Lucy, even if he refuses to see me, I shall find a way to let him know Tony *did* offer for me.

She was not to be required to exercise her ingenuity to that end. Shortly before dinner, James discreetly knocked on her chamber door and handed Molly a twist of paper. There was only a single word on it: "Agreed." Lucy recognized the writing and hoped that the briefness of the message was caused by caution and not by disinclination.

In the morning Lucy made sure to leave the house early, before her mother was come down and could demand her attendance. Ignoring Molly's grumbling at the drizzle, she hurried to the rendezvous, heart in mouth.

One look at Charles's face and she knew all was well. Under the interested and benevolent gaze of the shopkeepers arranging their window displays, she flung herself into his arms and wept with as much abandon as she had on Lord Denham the day before.

"Forgive me, my dearest," whispered the major hoarsely in her ear.

"Charles, I did not mean all those horrid things I said," she replied into his shoulder in muffled tones.

It was some time before they returned to rational conversation; but at last the fears were dried, and they sat in the Royal Academy before one of Mr. Turner's pictures, which Lucy generally much admired, though she did not even notice it this morning.

"We cannot continue to meet in this havey-cavey way," said Charles gravely. "I must speak to your brother. Surely he would not be so cruel as to forbid you to see me."

"N-no," Lucy agreed, her voice doubtful, "but Charles, I have not yet had a chance to talk to mama. Will you not give me just a few days to see if I cannot persuade her to take our part?"

The major could not like the new postponement, nor could he at present refuse her anything she desired.

"As you wish, my love," he conceded. "Just a few days."

Lucy had no chance to speak privately to Lady Annabel until after the theatre on Tuesday evening. She would have happily included Miss Fell in her confidences but for two considerations. The first was that her dear Clara seemed unhappy. The second was that she did not wish to give Richard any opportunity to call her indiscreet, and she was afraid he would not think Miss Fell sufficiently a member of the family to be party to the secret.

When they returned from the theatre, Miss Fell retired immediately, after her unpleasant experience with Sir Philip Rossiter. Richard was very restless, and after telling his mother the full story of the baronet's attack, he retreated to the library with a bottle of brandy, which, however, he did not drink.

Lady Annabel proposed that she and Lucy should retire early for once.

Lucy agreed. "May I come and talk to you in your chamber, mama?" she added.

"Of course, dearest. It is such a long time since we had a comfortable cose together." Lady Annabel was delighted. She did not want to force Lucy's confidence, but she had been increasingly worried by her daughter's moodiness, though she had seemed much happier the last two days. Now, she sensed, she would hear the whole.

Seated on her mother's bed in her nightgown, Lucy poured her heart out and begged Lady Annabel to intercede on Charles's behalf.

"You are quite sure you love him?" she asked slowly. "You have not known him very long."

"Precisely six weeks. Is not that long enough, mama? You always say you knew you should marry papa after half an hour in his company. It was so with me and Charles. I was so miserable when we had quarrelled that I wished to die. And the only thing that Richard holds against him is that his grandfather was a nabob and not quite a gentleman, but I do not wish to marry his grandfather, I want Charles."

"Lord Denham also wishes to marry you, Lucy."

"I know. He proposed to me on Sunday when you were out. I did not like to tell anyone lest he should feel uncomfortable, for I turned him down. Tony is a dear, mama, but I do not wish to spend my whole life with him. And it is *my* life after all, not Richard's."

"You are right, my child, and I will not let your brother spoil it, you may be sure. Only you must be a little patient, dearest. Richard has troubles of his own, which make it hard for him to see yours clearly. If he should send your major away, will you forgive him and wait until he can be reasonable? You are very young, and a few months' wait would prove your love. Can you not count on Charles to remain faithful?"

"Of course I can! And if Richard should do such an odious thing, I should try to forgive him, but I do hope he will not. It would be very hard not to see Charles for months."

"I will do what I can and we must hope for the rest. God bless you, dearest, and make you as happy with your Charles as I was with your papa."

Lucy hugged and kissed her, and went to her own chamber to dream of wedding bells.

Lady Annabel had no opportunity to speak to Richard the next day, as he went out soon after breakfast and did not return until late at night, when he was carried home in a hackney and had to be helped up the stairs again.

"Gettin' to be a reg'lar 'abit," was Bell's censorious comment.

Miss Fell was also unavailable. She sent word that she had the headache and would prefer to be left alone.

So, as no other engagements superseded, Lady Annabel was taken to meet the major. She had met him extremely briefly before and was now charmed by his courteous manner to herself and his obvious worship of Lucy. Nor did her watchful eye overlook the way Major Bowen's slightest frown could correct behaviour in Lucy that must have drawn a reprimand from herself or Richard.

The major had business in the afternoon, but was to meet them at Almack's in the evening. He sent bouquets to both ladies, a delightful gesture that pleased Lady Annabel enormously. However, when they arrived at the Rooms he was not yet there.

Lucy, with newfound philosophy, accepted his absence with a sigh and went to dance. She looked more and more frequently at the door as the hour wore on toward eleven, when the doors would inexorably close. Just as she was beginning to fear that he must have met with an accident, he appeared, scraping through by the skin of his teeth. Lucy saw him approach her mother with a grave face. Lady Annabel excused herself to her companions and gave him her full attention.

Seeing her mother's face grow solemn, Lucy could scarce restrain her impatience to be done with the dance. At last it ended, and brushing aside her partner's offer of lemonade, she hurried to Charles's side.

He had bad news. Since he had left them that morning he had at last received word from Northumberland. Something was desperately wrong, and he must leave the next day without fail. Lucy looked at him reproachfully, and he seized her hands, not caring who might see.

"I cannot tell you why I must go," he said in a tormented voice, "there are others involved. Can you trust me? I shall return as soon as I can, but I do not know when that will be."

"Of course, I trust you," Lucy reassured him. "I shall not tease." She looked up at him bravely, and he was hard put to restrain himself from kissing her before the flower of the ton. He came to a sudden decision.

"One or two hours will make no difference," he said. "I shall see Mr. Carstairs first thing in the morning. I cannot leave you with such a secret on your mind. Now

I must go and prepare for my departure. I hope I shall see you in the morning, my beloved, but in case I should not, farewell, and do not grieve over your brother's decision, should it go against us. I shall wait for you."

With that promise Lucy had to be content. She could see that it would be useless to argue with him and did not attempt it. Bidding him godspeed as he kissed her hand, she watched him leave the room, then asked Lady Annabel if they, too, might depart.

"It would give rise to comment," said her mother gently. "You will not wish to draw unfavorable attention to Major Bowen when he is already facing such difficulties."

So Lucy languidly danced another two sets before she could go home and retire to her room to indulge in a bout of apprehensive tears.

Lady Annabel did not know what to do; Miss Fell was still confined to her room with the headache, though Bell said she had been out for an airing in the afternoon; Richard, who had left without a word, had still not returned; Lucy was weeping in her chamber and her betrothed was about to leave town on an unspecified errand that evidently had him greatly worried. To cap it all, before he left, he was to ask for Lucy's hand, and doubtless further upset himself and Lucy and Richard in the process.

She went to bed with a novel, and decided that the problems of Melisande in Count Casimir's evil clutches were positively restful compared to her own.

Chapter 14

When Miss Fell left Richard after he asked her to marry him, she ran straight to her chamber. She wanted to fling herself on her bed and cry her heart out, but Mary was there, tidying the room. She forced herself to be calm.

"Mary, dear, I should like to be alone. Do you go and make my excuses to Lady Annabel — say I have the headache. I shall ring if I need you."

"Tha's . . . you're not falling sick again, be you, miss?" asked the maid in alarm.

Miss Fell managed a smile.

"No, no, I shall be quite well shortly, but I must be quiet for a while."

By the time Mary bustled out, taking an armful of mending with her, the urge to weep had passed. She sat gazing out of the window, unaware of the inappropriately sunny day. A single thought chased itself round and round in her head: He wanted to marry her, and she had refused him. For some time she was quite unable to consider the implications. She was in a sort of trance, which would have delighted Herr Doktor Holzkopf. As that gentleman was not there to snap her out of it with a "vun, two, zree," she had to await a flock of sparrows, flying twittering past her window, to distract her.

She began to think again. It seemed to her essential to leave the Carstairs as soon as possible. She did not know how she would ever face Richard again. Either he would still want to marry her, in which case she was afraid she would give in and live to see him regret it, or else he would have changed his mind, and that would break her heart.

She would be sad to leave Lady Annabel and Lucy, and she hoped they would remember her with kindness. If she had felt the slightest chance remained of finding out who she really was, she might have reconsidered her decision. However, since she had already met scores of people, and no one had recognized her, she was quite sure she could never have been a member of the Fashionable World. There was no alternative but to try to earn her own living.

She hoped she might be able to join an orchestra and make enough money to support herself by performing upon the pianoforte. Failing that, she would try to obtain a post as a music teacher. Perhaps she could gradually find enough private pupils to become independent. If both those avenues should prove closed to her, she must turn to Lady Annabel for assistance in attaining a position as governess or companion. She dreaded that possibility, foreseeing objections, questions, and an eventual disclosure that Richard had wanted to marry her and she had refused him. Could she ever explain why she had done so? Imagining the bliss of being his beloved wife, she wondered if she could really explain her refusal to herself.

Then she remembered that she had no reason to believe he did love her. A lost piano-playing puppy, she reminded herself firmly, and the image even conjured up a faint smile.

She turned to practical matters. Whom should she approach in her search for a job? Richard had described to her all the musical societies and theatre orchestras in London, not that there were any great number. The London public was not notably enthusiastic about serious music, and most professional musicians eked out a livelihood that was meagre at best by playing at dances. Momentarily the thought struck her that she might not be near so talented as her kind and partial critics had led her to believe. She put the doubt behind her. Dwelling on the possibility could only sap her courage and self-confidence.

She decided to go to the leader of the orchestra that had played at the Duchess of Devonshire's musical evening. She had received glowing reports of their performance from both Richard and Lady Annabel. How wonderful it would be to play with them a concerto by Herr van Beethoven, whose sonatas she had been practicing assiduously since she had found them among Lucy's music books! Such passion and fire, quite unlike anything she had played before. She would play one of them for Mr. Runabout, the concert-master. If she could find him and if he would listen to her.

In her severely practical mood, she made up her mind to tackle these new problems as they came along. For the first, she would consult Mary. The girl was as much a stranger in London as Miss Fell herself, but she had a characteristic Yorkshire shrewdness and might be able to suggest a way to go about finding an orchestra. Miss Fell knew Mary had given in to James's pleading and allowed him to escort her about the city in her spare time. She could hardly know less of it than did her mistress.

She rang the bell. When Mary appeared with a luncheon tray, she realized that several hours had passed.

"Cook's made your fav'rites special, miss," announced Mary. "Cold chicken an' some mushroom fritters an' macaroons."

Miss Fell burst into tears.

It was not long before Mary had heard the whole story, excepting only Richard's proposal. She did not presume to question Miss Fell's decision to seek employment.

"Now don't 'ee fret, miss," she said soothingly. "Tha's sure to get a job piano-playin', an' you an' me we'll find a nice place to live an' tha'll go an' make music an' I'll do for 'ee an' mebbe take in washing if it be needful."

"Oh, Mary, even if I do find a position, I cannot suppose I shall be able to pay you."

"Who said owt o' brass?" Mary queried belligerently. "A fine critter I'd be if I s'd abandon my mistress a'cos o' a few poun's."

"Lady Annabel is your mistress."

"Her's got servants aplenty. Come, miss, eat thy lunch an' we'll be off to find this Maister Runabout. Just so be he's not a-

299

runnin' too quick for us."

Miss Fell obediently tackled her tray, thinking that it would be time enough to persuade the loyal maid when she had found a post.

"What we s'll do," explained Mary as Miss Fell ate, "is take a hackney. Them jarveys know where everyone in London is, near as makes no odds."

"I have no money to pay for a hackney, Mary."

"Money, money, money! And haven't I a few sovereigns put aside? I knowed 'ee mought be facing trouble one o' these days, not but what us in t'servants hall did think . . . but 'twas not to be, seemingly," she sighed.

Miss Fell blushed and hoped she had misunderstood. Of course, they probably simply wished that she might find her own family. It was kind of them to wish her well.

"Well," said Mary, "if tha's done, I'll take t'tray an' get my wrap an' see if t'coast's clear. Do 'ee get thysen ready, miss."

She returned in a few minutes.

"Mr. Richard's still out, an' my lady an' Miss Lucy went shopping. Let's be off while t'going's good."

Miss Fell, amazed at Mary's understanding of her unwillingness to meet the family, followed her downstairs.

James was at the door. "I got 'ee a hackney, miss," he announced. "Made sure t'driver knows this Runabout fella."

She thanked him, wondering if all the servants were privy to her private affairs. Bell was nodding at her in a stately but reassuring way from the far end of the hall.

Noting her bemusement, Mary explained as the hackney set off through the busy streets. "We wasn't a-goin' to tell t'London servants, miss, but that Molly as can't keep her mouth closed let it drop. Don't 'ee worrit, they're all on your side."

Miss Fell was torn between amusement and a strong desire to burst into tears again. She saw Mary feeling in her pocket for a handkerchief and laughed.

"How kind you all are. Do you all know everyone's business?"

"Oh, aye. We'm all rooting for Miss Lucy's major, too. Maybe he been't good enow for a Carstairs but Miss Lucy loves him an' that's enough," she said firmly. "I hadn't ought to've said that. We don' discuss t'gentry's affairs wi' t'gentry in general, only I'd not want 'ee to think we was just nosing into thy business."

301

"H-how reassuring!" Miss Fell gasped through her laughter.

Mr. Arthur Runabout lived in a tiny flat on the third floor of a most respectable building, the ground floor of which was occupied by a music shop. His sitting room was filled, almost to the exclusion of all other furniture, by a huge walnut grand piano, beautifully polished. Miss Fell and Mary heard it long before they saw it, as he was playing something very fast and loud with all his windows open. They were no longer surprised at the jarvey's knowledge of his address.

Miss Fell grew nervous as they climbed the stairs. Had Mary not been right behind her she might well have turned back. However, when Mary's brisk knock on the bottle-green door was answered, Mr. Runabout appeared just as nervous as she, or more so. He was a tall, thin, cadaverous man, wearing a coat of the same shade of green as his front door. Appalled at the prospect of permitting two young women to enter his room, he stuttered in alarm, "W-what c-can I d-do for you?"

"I wish to speak with you on private business," answered Miss Fell soothingly.

Mary was making slight shooing motions

and they had the desired effect. Mr. Runabout moved aside out of the doorway.

"Well, well, I suppose you h-had b-better come in," he invited, his voice somewhat tremulous with doubt.

Miss Fell explained her errand.

"Oh dear," exclaimed the musician. "We seldom need a pianist, and when we do, I generally play myself. And I know of no one else in the business who is looking for one. However, they do need someone who can play a little to work in the shop down below. Perhaps you noticed it?"

"I had not considered working in a shop," said Miss Fell unhappily. "I . . . I think I had better look about a little more. Thank you for your time, sir." She turned to leave.

"Wait a bit, young lady! I had quite forgot. There is a Herr Umlauf in London who is looking for musicians for the orchestra of one of those foreign princes — Prince Esterhazy, I believe, who was Haydn's patron, or his son perhaps. I wonder if he would be interested?"

"Are you acquainted with the gentleman, Mr. Runabout? Perhaps you could introduce me?"

"Well, well, I cannot do that unless you are an exceptional player, ma'am. Would you be so good as to let me hear a little something?"

Miss Fell sat down at the instrument and played a couple of scales. It had a superb tone and deserved a far grander setting than the cramped little room. She began the *Moonlight Sonata* — as always, losing herself in the music. At the end of the first movement she looked up. Mr. Runabout gestured to her to continue, so she played on to the end.

"Delightful, my dear. I have seldom heard it as well done. Well, I think I may safely recommend you to Herr Umlauf. Shall you not mind living in Austria? Have you no family to prevent your removal?"

"No, sir, none."

"Well, well, well. Well, I shall send a note to Herr Umlauf at once. I am not certain how long he will be in the country. Where shall I send his reply? And, my dear young lady, I do not believe I have your name."

"Clara Fell. I . . . should you mind if we waited here a little for the answer to your letter? Or perhaps in the music shop, or I could return tomorrow?"

"By all means stay a while. I shall request an immediate answer."

He went to a tiny table, which evidently served many purposes. The note was soon

304

written, and to Miss Fell's fascination, he went to the window and shouted in stentorian tones, "Boy!"

A moment later he opened the door to an urchin of nine or ten.

"Well, boy," he said, "take this letter to a certain Herr Umlauf at Grillon's Hotel and wait for an answer and you shall have sixpence."

"Airoomlowf? Wot sorta name's that?"

"Well, well, we shall say Mr. Umlauf then. Run quickly, boy."

The child caught sight of Miss Fell and Mary. "Ooh, lookee! A real lady. Cor, she ain't 'alf pretty. Red 'air an' all!"

"You will be doing the young lady a favour if you will just take this letter, boy."

"Yessir! Corblimey if I don' 'ave 'er a anser inside of 'alf a hour, if I 'as to write it meself." The latter part of this came floating up the stairwell.

"It is very kind of you to let us remain here, sir. Pray do not let us interrupt your occupation," said Miss Fell.

"Not at all, not at all. I have no engagements before six o'clock. May I offer you a cup of tea?"

"I should like it of all things," said Miss Fell, "if it is not a great deal of work."

"I always have a cup about this time myself," he assured her, setting the kettle on the hob. He was taking down a large teapot and a canister of tea when Mary said, "Don't 'ee trouble thysen, sir. I s'll do it in a jiffy."

"Well, well, a Yorkshirewoman!" cried Mr. Runabout in delight. "My mother was from Yorkshire." He questioned her eagerly until he found out that her village was not twenty miles from his late mother's hometown. Miss Fell was concerned lest he should connect her also with Toblethorpe, but he did not appear to do so.

"Well, bless my soul, it's a small world," he said at last.

The kettle started whistling merrily; tea was made, poured and consumed. Miss Fell managed to avoid those of his questions that she could not answer, a problem she had not considered. The boy at last returned with a heavily sealed missive, received his sixpence and a smile from Miss Fell, which he treasured equally, and was dismissed. Mr. Runabout struggled with large blobs of still soft sealing wax and finally managed to open the letter.

"Well, well," he said, peering at it. "I find this Germanic hand extremely hard to read. Where are my spectacles?"

They were found, after a brief search, on a pile of music under the pianoforte. Even with their help, it took Miss Fell's assistance to decipher the Gothic script.

"Well," declared Mr. Runabout cautiously, "it seems to me that Herr Umlauf will hear you play tomorrow morning at nine, at his hotel. I trust you will be able to attend him at that time?"

"Oh, yes, I should not miss it for the world. Herr Umlauf invites you also, as far as I can make out. Shall you come?" Miss Fell asked timidly.

"You would like me to be there? Well, then, I shall meet you in the lobby shortly before nine. My dear Miss Fell, it has been a pleasure meeting you and I look forward to hearing you play once more. Mistress Mary, I bid you good day."

The boy was waiting below to see the young lady again, and he willingly found them a hackney. Miss Fell was touched by his evident admiration and persuaded Mary to give him a penny instead of the farthing she had fished from her purse.

"Cor, ta, miss," he thanked her with a grin.

Miss Fell apologized in the cab. "I quite forgot it was not my money, Mary. When I am a famous pianist in Vienna, I shall pay you back every ha'penny."

"I dunno as how I can come to they furrin parts wi' you, miss. Why, I heard tell as they don't even speak English like."

"I shall not expect you to come, Mary, if I obtain the position, which is by no means certain. Indeed, I cannot think it wise that you should leave the Carstairs, even should I remain in London."

"Well, well, we s'll not argufy about that now, miss. There, if I haven't catched Mr. Runabout's way of speaking!"

Miss Fell laughed, but she was pensive the rest of the way to Cavendish Square. She had not had time to consider the difficulties attendant upon removing abroad, and now they loomed large. When the hackney pulled up before the Carstairs' house, she dismissed them from her mind. Time enough to worry if she was offered the post. Now she must decide what to say if she met Lady Annabel or Lucy. About Richard she did not dare to think.

Bell opened the front door to her and bowed as he took her pelisse. Not by so much as a quiver of an eyelid did he betray any curiosity about her errand. She supposed he would find out the result soon enough from Mary.

She met no one else on the way to her

chamber. Mary helped her change out of her walking dress, and then brought her a tray, but she found she could not eat much. After a couple of hours of trying to distract her thoughts with a book, she went to bed. She dreamed she was trying to waltz with Richard around Vienna to the strains of the *Moonlight Sonata.*

She woke early, and she and Mary slipped out of the house before any of the Carstairs arose. They reached the hotel at half-past eight and had to wait an endless time, enduring the impertinent stares of maidservants and early risers, before Mr. Runabout joined them.

Herr Umlauf was informed of their arrival and came downstairs to greet them. He was a dark, suave gentleman and Mary, prejudiced by Herr Doktor Holzkopf, was astonished to hear his clipped, correct English. He ushered them into the hotel's Grand Salon, as it contained an adequate pianoforte, at which he had been conducting auditions.

"I desire to hear you perform, madam, before I say anything concerning the position," he informed Miss Fell. His manner intimidated her as much as Mr. Runabout's had put her at ease. He was perfectly polite, yet there was something sneering in his tone. Feeling uncomfortable with his penetrating eyes on her back, she sat at the instrument, played some scales to loosen her fingers, and then launched into the *Pathétique* sonata. As the notes flew from beneath her hands, she forgot her nervousness. She would have played the whole piece, but Herr Umlauf, who had been surreptitiously glancing at his watch, stopped her at the end of the second movement.

"Bravo!" he cried with a kind of artificial excitement. "You play most excellently, Fräulein. And I believe you are pretty enough for His Highness. However, I ask that you stand up that I may examine once more your figure. Prince Esterhazy prefers plump women."

Miss Fell sat in horrified silence at the piano. Mr. Runabout's mouth opened and closed like a fish, and no sound emerged. It was left to Mary to sweep forward, her face a study in indignation.

"My young lady bain't that sort, I'll thank 'ee," she announced. "Come on, miss. Better work in a shop 'n for a furriner prince wi' no morals." She urged her mistress to her feet and hurried her out, casting a scornful glare at the speechless Umlauf as she passed him. Miss Fell was equally speechless. Mr. Runabout at last found his tongue and trotted after them, trying to apologize for his part in the affair.

Once more Miss Fell was torn between hysterical laughter and tears. Only the sight of Mr. Runabout living up to his name in his distress inclined her to the former. He looked so hurt that she quickly stifled her amusement, but they only just managed to bustle her into a hackney before she started weeping.

"Pray bring her to my house," Mr. Runabout suggested anxiously. "I shall send out for some wine. What a terrible shock for a gently bred lady. Well, I cannot too much regret my introduction. Who would have thought it, who would have thought it!"

"Thank 'ee kindly, sir," said Mary grimly, "but I s'll take her home. This business has gone farther nor it ought. There's those as ought to know what's a-goin' on."

The hackney dropped Mr. Runabout at his lodgings, and the sight of his worried and apologetic face made Miss Fell take hold of herself.

"Pray do not be distressed," she hastened to say as he stepped down. "You must not blame yourself. How should you know that Prince Esterhazy expects more talents of his musicians than one? I must thank you for your kind efforts on my behalf."

"Not at all, not at all, my dear. Well, well, I daresay it was all a misunderstanding. That Germanic writing, you know. Such talent to be so insulted! Will you let me know," he added shyly, "if you find a position? Anything I can do, anything at all. Dear me, grown quite attached — well, well, well." Fumbling for his spectacles, he disappeared up the stairs.

Seeing new signs of tears, Mary hurriedly ordered the jarvey to drive on. He and the young errand-boy had both been interested spectators of Mr. Runabout's farewell, and she now told him sharply to keep an eye to his horses.

"For my young lady has enow troubles on her plate wi'out being overset by a rascally Lunnon cabbie!"

He grinned and obeyed.

By the time they reached Cavendish Square, Miss Fell was restored to a semblance of calm. She knew she must soon see Lady Annabel at least, but dreading a meeting before she had put her thoughts in order, she decided to go into the house by the back way.

She and Mary entered by the back door. As they passed the library, its door ajar, she heard talking ahead of her in the entrance hall. Unwilling to face even the servants, she slipped into the library, while Mary went on.

The morning had gone almost as badly for Major Charles Bowen. After a late night, he had woken early. He was all packed and completely prepared to leave for Northumberland by the time the clocks struck eight. He had breakfasted, the post chaise was waiting, and he suddenly realized that he could not possibly call on Richard Carstairs at such an unconscionably early hour, especially on such a delicate errand.

He kicked his heels for an hour and then decided he could brook no more delay. Telling the coachman to pick him up in Cavendish Square at ten o'clock, he set off on foot for the Carstairs residence, hoping thus to waste another few minutes without further exacerbating his impatience.

Bell opened the door. The butler was trying so hard to infuse his face with both approval and warning that he succeeded

313

only in looking more wooden than ever.

The major asked for Mr. Carstairs.

"Mr. Carstairs h'is still h'above stairs, sir. Would you be wishful to 'ave 'im h'awoke?"

"Damn! And Lady Annabel?"

"Not yet down, but h'I believe she is taking breakfast h'in 'er room. H'I shall h'inform 'er ladyship that you are 'ere, sir. Would you be so kind h'as to step into the library?"

Bell sent James scurrying to inform her ladyship. "And not a word to Miss Lucy, nor that Molly neither. We don't want 'er h'upset h'unnecessary."

Lady Annabel, sipping her chocolate and half expecting the news, sent Vane to fetch Willett.

"He must be woken," she told the valet.

"I very much fear, my lady, that Mr. Richard will have something of a head," objected Willett primly.

"In his cups? I feared it. But do not tell me that Mr. Christopher's Plimton did not pass on a certain secret recipe to you. He did? Try it."

"Yes, my lady. I shall inform Major Bowen that Mr. Richard will be with him shortly."

For the third time in a month, Richard

awoke with a hangover. This was the worst of the three, and so devilish did he feel that he dared not even attempt to remember why, abandoning his usual sober habits, he had overindulged.

Willett handed him a glass containing a revolting-looking concoction and looked at him so disapprovingly that he drank it down. It tasted as frightful as it had looked, but miraculously his head seemed to be joined to his body again, though he still winced when Willett spoke.

"There is a gentleman to see you, sir, and her ladyship insists that you go down."

Richard decided that the sound of his own voice would be even more painful, so he did not ask who the devil wanted to see him at such a devilish hour and why the devil his mother cared.

By the time he had limply thrust his arms into the coat held for him by the valet, James had appeared with a pot of coffee. Willett poured a cup.

"Drink this, sir," he ordered, and Richard meekly obeyed. To his surprise it did not fight with the mess already in his stomach, but cleared his head still further. By the time he had staggered downstairs, he was able to straighten his cravat and brace his shoulders without more than a barely perceptible shudder.

He walked into the library and saw Charles.

"You!" he exclaimed in a voice of utter loathing. "*You* got me up at this ungodly hour! You had better have an exceptionally good reason, Major Bowen, or . . . or . . ."

"I have," answered the major quietly but firmly. "I must leave today for my estate in Northumberland, and before I go I wish to ask for your sister's hand in marriage."

"I thought I had nipped that affair in the bud. Lucy promised to obey me!"

"Oh, she did," the major said dryly. He explained just how Lucy had evaded her brother's prohibitions.

"I assure you that I discovered this only yesterday, or I should have done something about it."

"It is none of your business to enforce my orders!" Richard shouted. His own voice hurt his head so much that he listened almost with relief to the major's quiet response.

"I hope to make it my business." He paused. Richard said nothing, so he continued, "I shall lay my circumstances before you and hope that you may reconsider your animosity toward me. I cannot feel that I have done anything to deserve it. My intentions have never been anything other than honourable, and I love Lucy very much."

The sincerity in his voice silenced Richard once more, so he went on to give details of his estate and his income.

"I can support Miss Carstairs in elegance if not in luxury. I shall make any settlement on her that you may suggest," he finished.

"And what of your family?" Richard demanded dangerously. "What of your birth? What of your grandfather?"

"You know of my grandfather, or you would not ask," said the major, his voice so low that Miss Fell, coming in by the back passage, heard nothing. "He was an honourable man, a fine, hardworking man. I am not ashamed of him. Allow me a moment to collect my thoughts, and I will tell you about my family."

He turned to the fireplace and leaned against the mantel for a minute, deep in thought. Richard stood watching him grimly, his back to the door. At that moment, Miss Fell pushed it open and entered the room.

She saw Richard at once and started back. "I beg your pardon. I did not know anyone was here," she murmured.

Richard and Major Bowen both turned toward her. For the first time she noticed the man by the fireplace. She gazed at him, then took a faltering step toward him, holding out both hands.

"Charlie!" she cried, and fainted.

Chapter 15

Richard caught Miss Fell as she swooned. "Clara!" he cried.

"Rosalind!" cried the major, rushing forward.

They glared at each other.

"What," inquired Major Bowen icily, "is my cousin doing in your house?"

"Believe me," riposted Richard, "you cannot wonder more than I!"

At this point in the hostilities Mary darted in, having heard Miss Fell cry out, and found the two gentlemen eyeing each other furiously over the unconscious body in Richard's arms, "just like two dogs wi' but one bone," as she later described it.

"And what have you done to the poor dear now, Mr. Richard?" she stormed.

"Done to her?" caught up the major. "I'd like to know just what he has done up to now!"

"Don't 'ee be a fool, too," Mary advised him. She pushed Richard toward a sofa. "Tha's plannin' on holdin' her all day? Set her down, set her down, my poor young lady, such troubles as she's had."

By the time Lady Annabel and Lucy, hearing the commotion, came running down, Mary had the gentlemen organized. Richard had been ordered to send James with a note to Dr. Knighton. Charles had been set to chafing Miss Fell's hands.

"Since," as Mary said skeptically, "tha says as she'm thy cousin."

Neither gentleman was permitted to take time to discuss the situation. In fact, once they realized that they were quarreling while "Miss Fell" suffered, they hurried to obey the little maid's instructions.

Lady Annabel, Lucy and Richard, who had rapidly dispatched James, all entered the library at once.

"Charles!" exclaimed Lucy. "Whatever has happened?"

Lady Annabel, Richard and Mary all looked at him expectantly.

"It seems that your Miss Fell is my Cousin Rosalind," he said soberly. "How she came here, I cannot guess. Surely you can enlighten me?"

"I told you, Charles, how Richard and Tony found her on the moors, and she had lost her memory."

"If, as I gather, she recognized you, major, then she may have recovered and be able to tell us what happened," Lady Annabel pointed out.

Richard had displaced Charles at Rosalind's side and was gently bathing her brow with lavender water procured by Mary. Now her eyelids fluttered open. Her green eyes regarded him with puzzled distress, and moved to the others.

"Charlie," she whispered, "I found you. My head hurts so. What has happened?"

"To bed," pronounced Lady Annabel firmly. "Major Bowen, would you be so good as to carry her up to her chamber?"

Richard looked as if he would have liked to dispute her choice, but held his tongue. Miss Fell . . . no, Rosalind had not appeared to recognize him. She had appealed to her cousin, not to him. And she was in pain. He would not add to it with an argument. Suddenly he realized that his own headache had vanished, and he blessed Willett silently.

Lady Annabel instructed Lucy and Richard to remain in the library.

"Miss Fell cannot be questioned now," she said. "I shall give her a sleeping draft, I think, to calm her; and then we shall all meet here and pool our information, if the major agrees."

Major Bowen nodded, and she led him

upstairs with his cousin in his arms. Richard watched, frowning. Then he turned with a sigh to Lucy, who was bubbling with questions.

"Yes, Major Bowen came to offer for you, and no, I did not have time enough to turn him down, though I intended to. Miss Fell . . . no, what the devil should I call her now? Your major would not thank me for addressing her as Rosalind, I suppose."

"I think her name is Stuart, Richard. Charles has often spoken of her. They were brought up as brother and sister. Had he only described her appearance I might have guessed the truth. How silly men are! And what do you mean, you were going to turn Charles down?"

"Just that, Lucy. However, I suppose I must reconsider. I should find it difficult to forbid you to marry the cousin of the woman whose hand I have sought in marriage."

"You have, Richard? Oh, that is famous! Then Rosalind will be my sister as well as my cousin."

"You are too precipitate. She refused me," he admitted wryly. "Nor do I intend simply to give you permission to marry Bowen. You are young yet, Lucy. I should not be doing my duty were I to allow you to join yourself for life to the first man with whom you fancy yourself in love."

"I do not 'fancy' myself in love," objected Lucy indignantly. "If you will not forbid us nor yet give us permission, then what are you going to do?"

"I shall ask you to wait, and promise that if you are both of the same mind in six months, then I shall withdraw my objections."

"Six months! As well say forever!"

"You are only demonstrating your youth, Lucy. You may see him, correspond with him freely. Do you fear you cannot hold his love so long? If so, better to find out before the wedding."

"Charles and I trust each other absolutely. Very well, if you are determined to be disagreeable, I suppose we shall have to submit to your unjust decrees."

"Lucy, I do not wish to be disagreeable! I want what is best for you." There was pain in his voice that melted Lucy's stiff hauteur. She remembered that he was not as happy as she in his love. She hugged him.

"I know, Richard. I am sorry I spoke so. I will wait and be good, and I am sure Clara — Rosalind — will marry you in the end."

"She would not tell me why she refused me," he muttered hoarsely, his head buried in his sister's hair. *My face,* he was thinking, what woman would want a husband who looks like a Red Indian?

"I daresay, dearest," said Lucy wisely, sounding very like her mother, "that it was some reason that a gentleman would consider nonsensical. Only think, everything is changed now, so you may start all over again and woo her properly this time."

"I made a real mull of it, Lucy. I was so concerned about her lack of family, about not even knowing who she was, that I realized only very recently that I loved her quite desperately and did not care if her father was a carpenter."

"Then why should I care that Charles's grandfather was a nabob, and Rosalind's too, come to that?" she retorted.

"Cry truce, Lucy. I hear them coming. You will not tell mama what I have said? It can only distress her."

"Of course I will not tell, Richard, only I think mama knows a deal more than she mentions."

Lady Annabel and Charles appeared.

"She is sleeping," said Lady Annabel, "but her head is paining her excessively. I am worried, and I hope Dr. Knighton will soon come. Mary is watching her."

"If he is not here very soon, I shall fetch him myself," promised Richard. "Though I have less trust in the man since he recommended that Teutonic nincompoop. However, should he not rapidly effect a cure, we can call in someone else."

He and Charles were eyeing each other cautiously. Charles wondered what Richard had said to Lucy in his absence. It could not have been too terrible, he decided, or she would not be so calm. He resolved to do all in his power to win over this toplofty gentleman who, quite apart from his objections to his birth, seemed to have taken him in inexplicable dislike.

Richard made up his mind that he must learn to tolerate his future brother-in-law. Being honest with himself, he could find no good reason for his animosity. Perhaps it was simply because the man wanted to marry Lucy? And, dash it, the fellow was not only unconscionably good-looking but always appeared to be right! He must become better acquainted with him, he thought.

"Pray be seated, Major Bowen," he requested brusquely. Charles sat on the sofa beside Lucy.

"Now that you have found Rosalind

here, Charles, surely you will not want to post off to Northumberland, will you?" coaxed Lucy.

"No, indeed. I have told Bell to send the post chaise away when it comes to fetch me. I . . . it's a difficult matter to discuss, but I must tell you why I was in such a hurry to leave. It will explain Rosalind's flight from her home, at least in part.

"Her father and my mother were brother and sister. You must know that I was orphaned at an early age. Rosalind's parents brought me up as their own son, and my uncle ran the estate, Bennendale, which had been his father's until my nabob grandsire bought it. There are several reasons why I entered the army, including a youthful desire to win my spurs. And I did not wish to deprive my uncle of the land that should have been his. That was a consideration that weighed heavily.

"So I purchased a pair of colors, and, as you know, I was later posted to India. I was not displeased to become acquainted with the country from which my fortune proceeded.

"One of the disadvantages of a primitive society is, as you may guess, that the mails are often delayed, or even destroyed. I did not discover until very recently that my uncle and aunt had perished in an epidemic, a year since. Naturally, I at once applied for leave to come home to take care of my affairs and make arrangements for my cousin's comfort. I had thoughts even then of selling out, which my meeting with Lucy confirmed and brought to fruition. Unfortunately for me, as it turned out, General Frazer had a great victory shortly before my departure, and I was ordered to bring dispatches home with me. My voyage was speeded, but I have since been held kicking my heels in London when I should have been in Northumberland. Not that I can regret the weeks that I have spent in winning the love of my dear Lucy, yet my cousin had desperate need of me, of which I knew nothing.

"For the rest of this tale, I must rely on a letter I received yesterday from Lady Cressman, a close neighbor. It seems that my Uncle and Aunt Stuart were scarce in their graves when my Uncle Henry, my father's younger brother, arrived at Bennendale, bringing with him a Colonel Overton. He settled into my house and began to press my poor Rosalind to marry the colonel, to whom he owed a large sum of money. Rosalind has fifteen thousand pounds, and the dastard proposed to free himself of debt in this way.

"At first my cousin had considerable freedom, though she was constantly bullied. She saw Lady Cressman frequently, and wrote to me several times, letters which I never received. Gradually her visits ceased. As my uncle dismissed our old servants and hired his own, he gained more control over her even as he discovered her to be adamant in her refusal to marry his creditor. He had taken over the management of the estate and Rosalind's guardianship on the grounds that my survival was questionable. Either he destroyed my letters or they simply went astray, and no one thought to inquire at my regiment.

"Lady Cressman writes that she tried several times to see my cousin at Bennendale but was turned away by shockingly rough-looking characters. Her husband forbade her to do more. Sir Donald is a pacific gentleman who would go to a great deal of trouble to avoid trouble.

"The rest of the story was told to Lady Cressman by Rosalind's abigail, a few days past, so I have it at third hand. According to her, my uncle grew more and more impatient and unpleasant toward her mistress until at last he confined her to her room. This maid, Joan, was the only one to see my cousin apart from my uncle and the odious Colonel Overton. Imprisonment and a diet of bread and water, while undermining Rosalind's health, did not shake her determination. She was sure that I must return soon.

"One day, in late February, Joan caught sight of a letter on my uncle's desk. It was from myself, announcing my arrival in London. She told Rosalind, who unwisely taxed my uncle with the discovery. I think the man must have been partly insane by this time. His only response was to beat my cousin savagely, swearing that she would be wed before I could rescue her. The maid tried to prevent the beating, but was held fast by Colonel Overton. Her attempt, together with her revelation to her mistress of my return, led to my uncle imprisoning her in the same room.

"That night, Rosalind decided on a desperate measure. There is a huge old oak standing near the house, of which one branch reaches nearly to the window of her chamber. As I remember it, the branch is very narrow and weak and does not come within three feet of the casement. Certainly I never attempted the climb in my youth, and I was accounted an intrepid, nay, a foolhardy climber. My cousin had not seriously considered it before, because of the danger and because she had nowhere to flee. Now she was desperate, and she had only to reach London to find me.

"She escaped, of course. The maid was to follow, but was too terrified by the sight of my brave cousin swinging from the fragile branch to make the attempt. My uncle kept her shut up, that she might not inform on him, and only an oversight on his part allowed her at last, after nearly two months, to reach Lady Cressman, who wrote immediately to me.

"The rest of Rosalind's story, you know better than I."

"There!" exclaimed Lucy in triumph, "did I not say she was a heroine?"

The Carstairs were not the only ones to have listened to Charles's exposition with bated breath. In a very short time every servant in the house knew the whole story.

"Miss Lucy's right," was the general opinion. "A real heroine, right out o' one o' they romantical novels!"

Dr. Knighton was announced before any further discussion could take place. Lady Annabel took him to Miss Stuart's chamber.

"What shall you do about your wicked uncle?" Lucy demanded of the major.

"I shall consult my lawyer about legal remedies at once. Otherwise, I can do little for the present. I cannot leave London while Rosalind is ill."

"You shall stay here," said Richard, and then wondered if that was going too far. The beaming gratitude in Lucy's eyes persuaded him that it had been the right thing to say. He also enjoyed the look of astonishment on the major's face.

"Well," ventured that gentleman with caution, "it is most kind of you. I had thought to . . ."

"Of course you will stay here, Charles," Lucy stated firmly. "Rosalind needs you nearby. After all, she has only just found you after searching for two months! You know," she added reflectively, "I am inclined to think that Rosalind is very nearly as romantic a name as Clarissa. *As You Like It*, you see."

The gentlemen could not restrain their laughter, which released the tensions of the past hour.

"At least Shakespeare is a vast improvement over *Count Casimir's Castle*," wheezed Richard at last.

"Not only that, but you are quite correct, dearest," explained Charles. "*As You Like It* was my Uncle Roy's favorite play.

However, I cannot think he ever expected poor Rosalind to live up to her name."

Lady Annabel was heard bidding the doctor farewell. She came to the library directly.

"I am so happy to hear you laughing, my dears," she assured them, noting their guilty faces. "Rosalind would not mind, you know. She never relieved her own troubles by forcing them on the rest of us."

"What did Dr. Knighton say?" queried Richard with eager impatience.

"He can find nothing physically wrong. He approved my prescription," she said with some pride. "Miss Stuart was too drowsy to answer any questions and he says she is to sleep for twenty-four hours. If she should awake this evening and grow restless, she is to have another sleeping draft. He will come in the morning to see if anything more need be done."

The rest of the day passed slowly. They were all anxious to hear Rosalind's version of the story. Lucy was allowed to watch by her bedside for a while and was there when her friend awoke. Rosalind did not seem to recognize her, but she did not complain of any pain and soon fell asleep again.

When she roused again it was morning, and not long before the doctor was expected. Mary was sitting beside her, mending a torn hem. She had been warned that Miss Stuart might be confused and that she was not to say more than was absolutely necessary.

Miss Stuart looked at her in a puzzled way, and then closed her eyes. "Am I ill?" she asked. "My head hurts abominably."

"I'll get 'ee some breakfast, miss," said Mary. "Tha's not eaten proper in two days."

When she left the room, Rosalind's headache seemed to be ebbing, but when the maid returned, it came back in full force. She ate a little. Though she was hungry, it was too much effort to eat, nor could she summon up enough energy to think. She vaguely remembered seeing Charles, and willingly abandoned all her problems to him. If she had found him, she knew her uncle no longer had power over her.

When Dr. Knighton arrived, he asked Lady Annabel and Mary to sit on the far side of the chamber, where Miss Stuart could not see them, explaining that he did not want her attention distracted. After examining her and pronouncing her physically fit, he began to ask her a few cautious questions.

Though her head was much improved again, she said she had felt as if it were being ground between two millstones. With great care the doctor probed her memory, until he thought he understood the situation.

"You have had a shock, young lady," he told her kindly, "but there is nothing seriously wrong with you. I suggest you stay in bed today, read if you want to, sew, whatever takes your fancy. You must be sure to eat properly in order to regain your strength quickly. There is just one other thing I want you to do. If these headaches return, make a note of every circumstance surrounding the onset: who is present, what you are doing, the time of day, what you have eaten immediately prior, you understand the kind of thing? Very well. I shall drop by tomorrow, but I have every confidence that you will be happily up and about."

Lady Annabel kissed her brow and said, "I am delighted, my dear," then followed the doctor out. They went to the drawing room, where the others were awaiting the news.

"It is of the utmost importance," began Dr. Knighton, "that Miss — uh — Stuart should not be upset in any way. I have no fears for her physical health, you understand. Her mind is another matter. She is, so to speak, standing astride a mental abyss. She remembers with perfect clarity everything in her life up to the moment her horse threw her on the Yorkshire moors. The next thing she remembers is recognizing Major Bowen in a strange room."

"My library, in which she has often sat," said Richard thoughtfully. "So she did not know me when she looked at me in that odd way. Is that what you are saying, Doctor? That she does not remember any of us?"

"That is correct, my dear sir. It is possible that the memory of the past few weeks will return gradually as she sees you regularly. Indeed, that seems to be the most likely event. However, I do not want her to see more than one person at a time for the moment. I confess I am worried about the headaches. I should like to bring my German colleague to see her tomorrow."

"No!" cried Lady Annabel, with uncharacteristic violence. "I will not have that . . . that monster in the house."

"Yes, I understood that you had taken him in aversion, my lady, with good cause, I admit. Yet he is a brilliant physician in his field. Should you have any objection to my consulting him?"

"I suppose not," said Richard grudgingly, "as long as you do not try any treatment he may propose without full permission."

"Certainly, Mr. Carstairs, though it must lie with Major Bowen to give that permission. Good-bye, my lady, Miss Carstairs, gentlemen. I shall return tomorrow."

Lucy and Charles were all agog to hear about the "monster" to whom Lady Annabel objected so strongly. By the time the tale had been told, ending with the unforgettable quotation: "I mix up mine lenkvitches, iss all," they were all helpless with laughter.

"What a pity," remarked Richard, "that Miss Stuart will not be able to recall the incident. She described it much more amusingly than I can, having been present."

His comment sobered them all.

"If you do not object, Lady Annabel, I shall go and see my cousin," proposed Charles. "If she does not see me soon, she may believe she dreamed of our meeting. I hate to think what that would do to her memories."

After the doctor had left her, Rosalind's

headache came back again. Asking for a piece of paper, she wrote painfully:

Food — none

Drink — none

Time — (she consulted the clock on the mantel) eleven a.m.

Occupation — none

Present — no one

After a moment's consideration she scratched out the last and substituted "maid." Then she lay back with her eyes closed and prayed that the pain would go away. It faded, but every time she opened her eyes again, it returned, so she kept them shut.

Soon Charles came in and chased Mary out. "Miss Stuart is my cousin," he pointed out. "I wish to speak privately with her."

His presence seemed to banish the headache completely. Under his anxious interrogation she told him the full story of the dreadful year she had gone through.

"Oh, Charlie, if you had not come home at last, what should I have done?"

Horrified by her description, which was much more distressing at first hand than through the medium of Lady Cressman's letter, he soothed and comforted her. At last, clinging to his hand, she asked him doubtfully, "How did I come here, Charles? I rode and rode through the snow, it seemed like forever, but I cannot recall reaching London nor how I found you."

Charles was not sure whether, or how, he ought to answer. Rosalind seemed worried about it, so he decided it would upset her less to hear a part of the truth.

"You have been ill for some time," he explained gently. "You were found in Yorkshire by some very kind people who brought you here to me. This is their house, in London."

"Are they the ones who were in that room with us, where I found you? A lady and a girl and a tall dark gentleman?"

"Yes. They have been taking care of you." He debated telling her about his own love for Lucy. It seemed to add an unnecessary complication, so he left the news for later. Lucy had not told him of Richard's love for Rosalind, deeming her brother's confidence more important than her beloved's early enlightenment. She was sure it would all turn out happily in the end.

Thus Charles did not know the true reason for Richard's change of heart toward him. He could not call the demanded delay before their marriage unreasonable, considering that Lucy was not yet eighteen. Only two things remained to mar his happiness, Rosalind's imperfect health and memory, and the question of what to do about his Uncle Henry. The latter, at least, he could dismiss for the present.

"I must have been very ill," mused his cousin. "I do not feel as if I know them at all. Yet when I see them I feel a strange sort of tugging in my head. They must be delightful people to care for a complete stranger, Charles?"

She was shy but composed when they came in, one by one, to see her. Her head was bad again, so that she was unable to converse for long. She thanked Richard and Lady Annabel for taking her in and looking after her. It near broke Richard's heart that she looked on him as a stranger, until he considered that the alternative was to be regarded as a rejected suitor. Perhaps Lucy was right, and he would have a second chance, be able to start again with a clean slate and avoid all his mistakes. Then he remembered that the doctor expected her to regain the missing weeks gradually. There was no comfort for him whichever way he looked.

With Lucy, Rosalind had been able to talk a little longer, as her headache was not so severe at that time. She diligently noted its comings and goings and began to see a pattern. It seemed to disappear almost when she was alone or with Charles. Was she in some way sensitive to strangers?

Dr. Knighton was delighted when he saw her carefully kept record the next day. It confirmed his suspicions absolutely. He spoke to her only briefly, telling her she should leave her bed, though not her chamber. Then he hurried off to explain his theory, or rather Herr Doktor Holzkopf's theory. He was a little puzzled by the maid's appearance on the list, and bore her off with him, just in case.

His audience, gathered once more in the drawing room, was the same with the addition of a frightened Mary.

"See!" he cried, waving Rosalind's record at them triumphantly. "This confirms all my suppositions. Miss Stuart is in pain only when a Carstairs, or this young woman, is present."

"I wouldn't hurt her owt, sir, honest I wouldn't," sobbed Mary. "No more the others wouldn't neither."

"No, no, my good girl, I am not suggesting it is deliberate. You see, ladies and gentlemen, a part of her mind recognizes you, a part that is being suppressed for some reason. In fact, the part of the memory that deals with the last two months. The stimulus of your presence, any of you, brings the warfare in her mind into the open, so to speak, and gives her a raging headache." He looked round beaming, as if he expected applause, like a conjurer pulling a rabbit from a top hat.

Again, Mary was the only one to speak.

"Then why," she demanded suspiciously, "isn't James here? He went into t'room several times, to mend t'fire like, an' he tol' me he spoke to her, just to see if she were wanting owt. She knowed James when she were my Miss Fell."

"Aha!" exclaimed the great man, "you have inadvertently supplied the missing link, my dear young woman. You must have been very fond of Miss Fell, close to her?"

Mary nodded and sniffed.

"There we have it! James, I take it, is a footman. She would hardly know him in more than a casual way. She was only acquainted with Miss Carstairs for a week at the beginning, when she was very ill, and a few days at the end of the period. You will note that she records only mild pain in the presence of Miss Carstairs. Proof! This proves that the sight of anyone with whom she was intimate during the missing two months triggers these alarming headaches. Miss Stuart must go home!"

No argument would change his mind. The only totally efficacious treatment, he insisted, was to return to the place where nothing would remind her of the part of her life that she could not remember.

"It will be a blank, she will soon forget that it is there," he declared.

Lucy burst into tears. "But Charles and I are to be married!" she wailed. "How can he marry me if Rosalind and I may never meet?"

Richard could have voiced a stronger protest. He held his tongue. The doctor heaved a heavy sigh and raised his eyebrows in exasperation. It was so difficult to practice medicine efficiently with people around.

"When is the wedding to be? Not for six months? In six months anything can happen. She may recover her memory naturally. Or it may be dimmed by time so that it is no longer painful to her. In six months you have my permission to see her again. Today, off to Northumberland!" He took his leave.

After a great deal of discussion, it was settled that Charles and Rosalind should leave on the following Monday. Mary was heartbroken when she was at last convinced that there was no way she could go with her young lady.

Charles and Lucy were heartbroken to have to part so soon. Richard was heartbroken at the thought of losing Rosalind forever, though he did his best to conceal it. And Lady Annabel was heartbroken to see all the hearts breaking around her. It was a dismal party that sat down to luncheon, and only Lucy, her appetite quite unaffected by her emotions, made a good meal.

It was arranged that Charles should correspond with Lucy, and thus pass on news of Rosalind's health. For the moment, he reported that her headache had almost completely vanished, leaving only a slight nagging pain, which he attributed to her unfamiliarly familiar chamber.

None of them dared see her, even to say farewell. Sad faces looked down from the drawing-room window as Charles escorted her to the post chaise. He looked up and blew a kiss to Lucy, then they disappeared from sight inside the carriage.

A moment later the chaise turned the corner of the street and they were gone.

Chapter 16

Though it was mid-April, there was still snow on the high hilltops and in shaded hollows when the post chaise turned into the drive of Cressman Court. Rosalind shivered a little in the brisk breeze as Charles helped her alight.

He had decided to bring his cousin to Lady Cressman until he had discovered the situation at Bennendale. She seemed quite well, though apt to fall often into a brown study, but he did not feel that a confrontation with their uncle would be good for her health.

Lady Cressman welcomed them with open arms. A buxom lady with a soft Scots accent, she sent servants scurrying to provide refreshment for her guests, prepare a chamber for Rosalind, and fetch Joan. Rosalind had a damp reunion with her tearful abigail, who had been sure she must be dead.

From my lady's rambling chatter, Charles gathered at length that Uncle Henry was gone.

"Ran off just a day or two after Joan escaped, last week some time. And a good riddance to the rascal is what I say," declared Lady Cressman firmly. "The way he behaved to poor Rosalind, and Sir Donald says the land is quite gone to wrack and ruin, and that dreadful colonel . . ."

"Then we need not trespass on your hospitality," interrupted the major, knowing from long experience that if he did not do so he would never get a word in edgewise.

"Oh, you must both stay here," insisted Lady Cressman. "The man had no proper servants and from what I hear the house is all at sixes and sevens. I fear you will not find . . ."

"Do you know what became of our servants, ma'am?"

"I believe most of them went to their families. I daresay Joan might know more. If I were you I should . . ."

Joan and Rosalind's reunion was cut short and Charles questioned the girl while Lady Cressman took Rosalind above stairs to tidy herself. Presently Sir Donald came in, and the major was relieved to hear that the damage to his land was not as severe as he had feared.

"Take a bit o' hard work but you'll soon have it in good heart again," was Sir Donald's verdict. "Lavinia is quite right, you know, you'd better stay here for a few days. At least until you can get your staff together again. The house is a mess."

They had arrived early, so after a luncheon Charles and Sir Donald rode over to Bennendale to inspect matters. Rosalind would have liked to go, but Lady Cressman made her lie down for an hour or two.

"Charles . . . I suppose I should call him Major Bowen only that I've known him since before he was breeched, and you, too, of course, my dear, not that you were ever breeched, I do not mean . . . However, Charles says you have been ill for a long time and indeed you are a little pale, child, though I daresay it is only fatigue. Such a long journey, even if you did come slowly, and you had better rest a little, for we would not want you falling sick again when you are barely restored to us; and oh, Rosalind, I have been very worried about you these two months and more and I assure you I gave Sir Donald a piece of my mind, a regular scolding because he would not stand up to that *wicked* uncle of yours. And . . ."

"I am sure Sir Donald did what he thought proper, ma'am," broke in Rosalind gently. "I am very grateful for your concern. What should I have done without your support those early days after mama and my father died? And then you took in my poor Joan and wrote to Charlie at once. Indeed, no one could have done more."

Somewhat reassured, Lady Cressman pulled the curtains close, told her to try to sleep, and left her.

Rosalind was in fact a little tired after the long days of travel. Her headaches had stopped as soon as they left Cavendish Square, but she still felt disoriented. It bothered her that she did not know what had happened between her escape and finding Charles, and her dreams were full of a dark face to which she could put no name. Sometimes it smiled at her with warm eyes, at others looked at her with such haughty coldness that she awoke as from a nightmare, sweating and shivering. Waking, she could not remember its features.

Through the busy days that followed, the dreams faded. The servants were all found and happily returned to Bennendale. The house, a pretty brick mansion half hidden by trees in a dell that opened into a long vista to the south, had to be scrubbed from top to bottom. Chimneys were swept, closets full of rubbish turned out, the kitchen set to rights, and new curtains made for the several rooms in which they had been ripped. Charles returned each day from inspecting his fields to a home that was changing from a pigsty into the gleaming comfort he remembered. At last, he dared imagine inviting Lucy to set foot in his house.

The fields and pastures had suffered only from neglect. Every morning brought tenant farmers with new problems, and Charles was kept as busy as his cousin; yet every evening he found time to write to Lucy, and weekly he sent off long epistles. He was afraid she might be bored by the running account of his daily life; but her letters, which arrived regularly twice a week, often had shrewd comments on his work, and he realized that she must have learned a lot about managing an estate from Richard. No simpering miss, his beloved, he thought proudly, and the paragraphs describing overgrown hedgerows and weed-filled cropland were interspersed with tender endearments and words of longing.

Lucy was missing him quite desperately, she confided to her mother. True to her word to Richard, she continued to go to parties and meet eligible bachelors. The entertainments seemed flat and insipid; the beaux were dull and frippery fellows next to the memory of a certain stern-faced soldier with smiling eyes. If one of Charles's letters came a day or two later than expected, her anxious heart was assuaged only by Richard's ill-concealed impatience. He, for his part, was sure the delay betokened a relapse on Rosalind's part, which was preventing her cousin from writing. All in all, Lady Annabel was glad when the Season ended and they could return to Toblethorpe, where country pursuits, more to the taste of all of them, kept them almost as busy as were Charles and Rosalind, some eighty miles to the north.

In the middle of July, Charles left for London. The War Ministry needed him on some business connected with Lord Richard Wellesley's recall from India. Though he could hardly claim that it was en route, Toblethorpe was on his itinerary in both directions, and he was heartily welcomed. On his return journey he was pressed to stay for a week, and, with Lucy hanging on his arm with her begging puppy look, he could not refuse.

He and the Carstairs discussed their plans for the autumn, when, in Lucy's words, the "fateful six months" would have run their course. Charles reported that Rosalind appeared to have completely regained her health and peace of mind, and he would have no qualms about trying to arrange a meeting with the Carstairs again.

Richard had persuaded Tony to invite himself and his family to his Leicestershire estate, Disford Wood, at the beginning of the hunting season.

"And Harry shall invite Major Bowen and Miss Stuart," he had proposed.

"Dash it, Richard," the unfortunate Lord Denham had protested, "I know I said I'd decided I'm not the marryin' sort, but to be asked to entertain both the object of my affections and my rival is the outside of enough."

"Come on, Tony, you are a fine figure on the hunting field. Who knows but that you may win my sister after all?"

"Not at all sure that is what I want," Lord Denham had said frankly, then added complainingly, "Oh, very well. I see I have not a leg to stand on, and I am by far too lazy to argue with you. Consider it done."

Captain Lord Harry Graham had no objections to the plan. "Never met Charles's cousin," he had admitted, "but I hear she has a pretty little fortune. Might have a try there myself."

Richard's glower quickly dissuaded him and sowed the seeds of suspicion in the minds of both the Grahams.

"So that's the way the wind lies," Tony had commented thoughtfully to his brother. "I wondered, right from the moment we found her."

Harry, of course, demanded an explanation and had to be told Miss Fell's whole story, under seal of the strictest secrecy.

"Lord, it's just like one of those devilish romances the ladies are always reading!" he had remarked. "Well, if a Carstairs is after the wench, I can see she is above my touch." His grin was mischievous.

Richard's behaviour at Toblethorpe Manor awoke the major's suspicions also. He taxed Lucy with them and heard the whole tale as she knew it.

"And she refused him?" he asked thoughtfully. "When he offered her security, a family, a position in Society, and she had none of them, nor any hope of them. It does not sound to me as if he has much hope of winning her."

"Let me tell you what I think," begged Lucy. "I think she was being noble. Suspecting she might really be a governess or something, she did not want to involve Richard in a marriage he might regret. You know by now how Richard is about respectable birth."

"You are a true romantic, my love," Charles answered fondly. "I wish I could be so sanguine."

"Would you approve of such a connection, Charles? I cannot think of anything more delightful, but my brother has not always been kind to you."

"I have the greatest respect for Mr. Carstairs, and every expectation of calling him 'brother' in the not so far distant future. If Rosalind could like the match, I should be happy to see her settled. Otherwise, I daresay the pair of you quarrelling will drive me to distraction," he teased.

"No, we shall not!" cried Lucy indignantly. "Oh, you are bamming me. Indeed, Charles, Rosalind and I have never quarreled. She is the dearest creature, and whatever you say I am sure she will be my sister one day."

Richard's feelings were closer to the major's. He looked forward to the beginning of October with a mixture of longing and dread, uncertain whether to hope that Rosalind would know him or not. The worst possibility, he thought, was that she might once more develop the headaches, which must sunder him from her forever. The best he could imagine was the chance to woo her as a stranger, and he had no confidence that he would be any more successful this time than last.

Even as she watched Lucy bloom with the renewed assurance of Charles's love, Lady Annabel saw her son grow more and more silent and withdrawn. After Major Bowen's departure, he spent the greater part of every day out riding, and had to be persuaded to see any of their friends and neighbors. Unknown to her, he haunted the spot on the high moors where he had found the woman he had so painfully learned to love, torturing himself with remorse for the way he had treated her and wishing he could start over from that moment. Her grey-green eyes in her thin white face followed him about reproachfully and he found himself quite unable to imagine them smiling or laughing as he knew they had.

Had he confided in his mother, she could have reassured him that his behaviour to Miss Fell had been quite unexceptionable, indeed all that was kind and thoughtful. He did not, and Lady Annabel noted with anguish how his already spare frame grew thinner and his face almost haggard. Several times she had almost ventured to speak to him on the subject, but when Rosalind's name was mentioned, he would say calmly only that he was very pleased at her recovery and that it would be delightful to see her again in the autumn.

Whenever Lucy played upon the pianoforte, Richard would find some excuse to leave the room. At last Lucy was driven to protest.

"I know I do not play as well as Rosalind," she said crossly. "However, I think it most unkind in you to run away as soon as I sit down at the instrument. I have been practicing amazingly because Charles enjoys music, and the least you could do is sit still and listen."

"I beg your pardon," apologized Richard, smiling. "It is rude of me. Play me one of those lively tunes you perform so charmingly."

Mollified, Lucy complied.

Both Toblethorpe and Bennendale rejoiced in a busy social life. There were picnics, outings to places of interest, evening parties where as many as six couples might stand up to dance. Rosalind and Lucy had their rural admirers, and while Lucy blithely ignored their compliments and attentions, Rosalind was bound to consider them more seriously. Charles had at last dropped some hints that he was thinking of marrying, and she had heard too many tales of the dissension caused by two females in the same household.

Two gentlemen in particular seemed likely to offer for her hand. One was a pompously pious curate, a weedy young man with one eye firmly fixed on her fifteen thousand pounds. The other was a very respectable landowner of some forty summers who had been pursuing her for nearly six years. While she could dismiss the curate, Mr. Heathercot was another matter.

She did not love him, but she was on terms of great friendship with him. He had a comfortable income, and so could be acquitted of fortune-hunting. A personable gentleman, he was kind and reliable, and devoted to her if not wildly in love with her. All the neighbors said it would be an excellent match. He had proposed to her before, and she knew he would do so again. He would make a perfectly unexceptionable husband. Why, then, did she hesitate?

Mr. Heathercot had been absent during the months of her trials with her uncle, so she could not hold his nonintervention against him. He was intelligent and conversable; Charles liked him; his home was not far from hers. In every way he was suitable, and, sighing, she admitted to herself that she would probably have him in the end. In the meantime, she enjoyed herself flirting mildly with her unsuitable followers and wished that a prince on a white charger would come along and sweep her off her feet. For some inexplicable reason, the charger had always become a chestnut by the end of her fantasies.

There were several inexplicable things in her life. One was Charlie's reluctance to discuss with her his future bride. Another was the strange feeling that came over her whenever she played the piano, as if something or someone was hovering just beyond her grasp. The third was her unwillingness to mount a horse. Charles said it was natural, as she had been thrown and injured during her escape. She did not consider the explanation adequate, having been thrown before, but the reluctance was strong enough to make her walk or drive when she went out.

Thus it was that one hot day in late August she was returning on foot from taking lunch to Charles, who was directing the harvest. As she stepped over a stile, she heard a hail and saw Mr. Heathercot coming toward her. He turned back with her.

"You have hay in your hair," he said, after she had explained her errand. "Pray stand still a moment and I will remove it."

With one hand on her shoulder he carefully removed the straw, then equally carefully and gently kissed her lips.

"Rosalind, won't you marry me?" he asked, taking both her hands. "We should deal extremely well together, you and I. I have been waiting a long time for you and have never found another woman I want to be my wife."

"Ian, you have been very patient with me," she replied, looking up appealingly into his face. "I am almost certain I should say yes, but not quite. I cannot accept while I have doubts; it would not be fair to you."

"I cannot wait forever," he said roughly.

"I do not ask it. Only a few more weeks? Charles and I are going away in October and I am sure I shall know my own mind when we return. You see, Charles may be wed himself, and then . . ."

"Not a very flattering reason for marrying me," commented Mr. Heathercot dryly. "No, do not try to explain, I understand. As you wish, I shall await my fate when you return. Let us say no more until then." He proceeded to converse on a variety of topics, giving Rosalind time to regain her composure before they reached the house, where he bade her farewell.

The curate was not so easily dealt with. Impervious to snubs and to Rosalind's persistent efforts to avoid him, Mr. Borden was delighted, one rainy afternoon, to see her drive up beside him in a deserted lane. Common courtesy forced her to offer him a ride to his destination.

"Thank you, Miss Stuart," he panted after an undignified clamber into the dog-cart. He gave her an arch look. "Or may I call you Rosalind?"

"I do not think it would be at all the thing," she pointed out coldly.

Not a whit abashed, Mr. Borden pressed on. "We have known each other this age, have we not?" he queried tenderly.

"Oh, quite two years, of which I spent several months incarcerated."

The curate had the grace to look a little self-conscious. He had been conspicuous by his absence when Rosalind had been most in need of friends. He persevered, taking her hand. "I feel we are quite soul mates. The Lord has destined us for each other."

"Mr. Borden!" said Rosalind sharply, "if you do not let go my hand I shall lose control of the horses, and we shall be overset."

He hurried to comply, observing with displeasure that a dogcart was a vastly improper conveyance for a lady.

"When we are married you shall have a proper carriage and a coachman ready to take you about."

"We shall not be married, and my cousin's coach is always at my disposal. I prefer to drive."

"You would not go against the Will of the Lord?" cried the curate. "Woman was made to be a helpmate to her husband!"

"I am not your wife!" Rosalind was growing angry, the carefully schooled temper, of which her hair was warning, rising at his assumption of her acquiescence. "And believe me, I never shall be!"

"Ah, but you are already on the shelf," Mr. Borden remarked unwisely. "You will soon be an old maid, a most uncomfortable position for any female. I am sure a little prayer and penitence will soon make you see reason."

Rosalind pulled up the horses. "Get out," she said with dangerous calm. "Get out or I shall push you!"

"Well!" The curate was outraged. "What unladylike behaviour! However, I shall pray for you. I cannot believe you are serious, and I shall approach Major Bowen in the matter. I am sure he will bring you to your senses."

He was wise enough to climb down during this speech, and Rosalind was delighted to see him step in a puddle halfway to his knee. It so much improved her temper that she was able to say good-bye quite affably as she drove off, splashing him.

By the time she reported this incident to Charles, she was able to see its funny side and had him bursting with laughter.

"The impertinent toad!" he gasped. "Don't worry, I'll send him away with a flea in his ear."

"I am not even certain whether he means to complain of my indelicate behaviour, my improper vehicle or my refusal to marry him. I can only hope that the former has given him a disgust for the latter."

"We must hope so indeed. Rosalind," said Charles seriously, "you know I would not dream of permitting you to wed that nasty little man, but are you quite set against marriage? I had thought that Ian . . ."

"Ian proposed to me again. I told him I should give him my answer when we come out of Leicestershire. You need not fear that I shall stay when you are married, Charles."

"I did not mean such a thing," he protested. "My sweet Lucy is sure she will love you as I do, and there is no reason for you to leave. It is only that I am so happy myself in her love that I would wish the same for you, my dearest cousin."

"I doubt I am cut out for love, Charlie. Ian will suit me very well and we shall plan marriages between our children."

"You do not love him? No, I know that you do not." He sighed. "Well, we shall see. Perhaps it would be for the best."

Later, he told Rosalind about his interview with Mr. Borden. "He was up in arms about all your failings, Ros, and seemed to expect that I should come the heavy father and order you to marry him. Why he wants to when he has such a low opinion of you, I cannot guess. I tried to match his indignation, in your behalf of course, but was overcome with laughter. He was very much insulted and vowed he'd not enter our doors again."

"Darken our portals, you mean. Thank the Lord for small mercies! Oh no, the Lord is on his side. How delightful, I should say."

"Perhaps you will meet someone in Leicestershire whom you can love."

"Your friend, Lord Harry Graham, perhaps? I should catch cold, setting my cap at a marquis's son."

"Oh, a younger son, not at all high in the instep, and, after all, my junior in rank. A mere captain. No, I was not thinking of Harry. He is a sad rattle."

"His brother, then? Lord Denham?"

"Well, you never know, but I rather think not," said Charles cautiously. "I daresay we shall meet all sorts of people there."

"I shall be very happy with Ian." Rosalind closed the subject. "We dine with Sir Donald and Lady Cressman tonight. You had best get out of those muddy boots."

"Yes, ma'am," Charles submitted with a wicked grin.

The days grew shorter and leaves began to change color. Flocks of swallows gathered in preparation for their yearly flight to warmer lands. The fields were stripped bare, and crows competed with sea gulls for the last gleanings until the stubble was plowed under. The sheep on the high fells were growing thick new coats for the coming winter. Hedgerows filled with scarlet hips and haws, and thrifty house-wives sent their children gathering black-berries for pies and jellies.

The thoughts of all the gentlemen turned to hunting. Charles was very much envied that he was going into Leicester-shire.

"The best country there is," said Sir Donald, who had once hunted it in his youth. "Nary an acre o' humbug country. Ye'll be riding wi' all the London gentry, Corinthians and whatnot, I daresay. Well, ye're a fine rider, young Charles, ye'll not let our county down."

Charles did not dare mention that he was going to hunt a bride, not foxes.

Rosalind was a little nervous about going to stay with such exalted personages. Charles had given her a large sum, besides her pin money, to refurbish her wardrobe. When she appeared before him to show off a new evening gown of emerald green silk over a white satin underdress, cut simply in the way that best became her, he was stunned.

"You will be quite the belle of the ball,

Ros," he declared. "After my Lucy, of course."

"You do not think it too . . . too *flashy?* I am past the age of pastel muslins but I do not wish to appear fast. And it was shockingly expensive, Charles. None of my other gowns cost half as much."

"It is beautiful. It's past time you had some new finery, and we can well afford it. No, don't tell me how much. I might change my mind."

He had had new clothes made for himself also and hoped that Lucy would not mind that he was now a private gentleman. He could have worn his Reserve Army uniform, but he was uncomfortable with the colonel's epaulets, feeling he had done nothing to earn them. Looking at himself in the mirror, he thought he had avoided the excesses of the fops without becoming dowdy. Not being vain, he dismissed with a glance the blond hair and the face newly tanned by his active summer, merely deciding that he must send for the barber.

On a fine October day, with the bite of frost in the air, gold and russet leaves whirling around them, they set off.

Chapter 17

A kindly conspiracy had arranged that Rosalind should have a few days to become accustomed to her new surroundings before being called upon to face the Carstairs. Several other guests had been invited ("to provide cover for your goings-on," Tony told Richard), carefully picked to be sure none had met "Miss Fell" in London.

Major Bowen and Miss Stuart joined the party late one afternoon, after three days on the road. They were greeted by Lord Denham. Rosalind showed no signs of recognizing his lordship. She was introduced as the cousin of Lord Harry's friend.

"It is very kind of you to invite me as well as Charles," she said to him, immediately attracted by his cheerful, friendly manner and the twinkle in his eye.

"Delighted to see . . . meet you," he replied. "I've heard a great deal about you."

Rosalind looked a little surprised, but let it pass.

"Come and be presented to my aunt," continued Lord Denham. "She is acting as my hostess, you know." He led the way to a cosy salon furnished largely with comfortable leather armchairs. It appeared that he was more used to entertaining gentlemen than ladies at Disford Wood.

The major and Rosalind were duly presented to Lady Catherine, a plump, indolent widow as easygoing as her nephew, and were made acquainted with those of the guests who had arrived already. Charles found he knew several of them, including Captain William Denison and his wife. While Rosalind was chatting to Emma Denison, Charles asked his friend how he came to know Lord Denham.

"Lord, I've never met him before, Charlie," the captain replied, "though I've known Harry any time these ten years. To tell the truth, I was devilish surprised to receive the invitation. Nearly turned it down, too, what with the Corsican monster hovering just across the Channel, but his lordship mentioned that you'd be here, and Richard Carstairs also. Know him? He's some sort of distant cousin, been devilish good to all the family. Matter of fact, he just gave his home parish to m'brother Gerald. He and Lord Denham have been bosom-bows this age, so I daresay it's him we have to thank for the invitation."

Charles voiced agreement, though privately he wondered if Lord Denham had not rather been considering the comfort of Rosalind and himself. Whatever the reason for William's presence, it was exactly calculated to put both at their ease. Until it was time to dress for dinner, he told his friend about campaigning in India and heard in return an analysis of the unfitness of the troops in Kent to face any massive invasion from the Continent.

"Only the navy can save us this time," declared Captain Denison, "and since they let half Boney's fleet slip past them out of Toulon, they've been careering after Villeneuve over half the world."

"We'll all be murdered in our beds!" shrieked a young lady. Unnoticed by Charles and William, the room had gradually fallen silent, listening to their conversation.

"No, no, ma'am," soothed the captain hastily. "Lord Nelson and Admiral Collingwood have them locked in Cadiz, and the landing boats are still bottled up in harbour. I'd back Nelson against any man on the seas."

"Captain Denison would scarcely be here if he saw any immediate danger," pointed out Lord Denham, and calm was gradually restored.

The guests were all young people, friends of his lordship and his brother with their wives and sisters. The evening passed pleasantly in games of lotteries and speculation, much decried by the more dignified members of the party who, however, enjoyed themselves as much as anyone when overruled. Lady Catherine was persuaded to join in and won handsomely, to her evident delight.

When the tea tray was carried in, some bright spark suggested that the company might indulge in amateur theatricals during their stay at Disford Wood. The proposal met with general approbation and enthusiasm, and a delegation was deputed to drive into Leicester on the morrow in the hope that the bookshop might be persuaded to disgorge some suitable work.

Lord Denham was somewhat stunned by the way his hunting party had been taken over by what he freely stigmatized as "the nursery set." His usual guests were gentlemen of all ages who desired nothing more than to hunt and shoot all day and play billiards or gamble a little in the evenings.

"Just wait till Richard sees what he's got me into!" he said indignantly to Lord

Harry, when that young man arrived the next morning.

"I can't see Richard acting," grinned Harry. "You two aged gentlemen can watch and make disapproving comments while us young 'uns have all the fun. You had best join the Society for the Suppression of Vice." He dodged as his brother shook his fist at him.

A carriage had left for Leicester, escorted by three young gentlemen on horseback. Several others, including Charles and William, had gone riding. Rosalind, descending the main stairs, found her host and his brother in the hall and had Lord Harry presented to her. Lord Denham, noting Harry's wicked grin, was afraid he might tell her they had met before, but he merely asked her to go for a drive.

"You are just now arrived from London," Lord Denham pointed out. "Should you not take a nap to recover from your fatigue? Miss Stuart shall drive with me."

"Dash it, Tony, I came only from Leicester this morning."

"I thank you both," said Rosalind diplomatically, "but I am already engaged. Sir Peter Allington tells me that though it is frowned upon for a member of the Four

Hand Club to take up a lady, he feels sur
that an exception may be made in the case
of a private country party. He considers
that your grounds, Lord Denham, are of
sufficient extent and beauty that we shall
not need to leave them in the course of a
morning's drive. I believe he does not wish
to expose himself to the admiring gaze of
the populace with anything so . . . so
déclassée as a lady in his curricle."

Tony and Harry laughed.

"The man may be a top sawyer, Tony,"
grumbled Harry, "but what a chucklehead!
Why the deuce did you invite him?"

"On your urging, dear brother. You may
remember his sister?"

Harry pondered a moment. "Allington,
Allington . . . the blond one? Oh no, I remember, the little brunette. Pretty chit. I
find, however," he added in the grand
manner, "that I have developed a decided
preference for Titian hair."

Lord Denham raised his eyes to heaven
and sighed. "Do not heed him, Miss
Stuart. My brother is a sad rattle."

"The very words my cousin used!" cried
Rosalind in amusement. "Whatever have
you done, Lord Harry, to lead to such una-
nimity of opinion?"

"Alas," he replied mournfully, "I am

abused on every side by those who are jealous of my handsome face and winning manners. Come, Miss Stuart, will you ride with me this afternoon?"

Rosalind flushed, and Lord Denham glared at his brother.

"I do not ride, my lord," she apologized.

"And I spent all day yesterday on a horse. We shall walk around the gardens and admire the . . . the . . . What do you grow at this season, Tony?"

Lord Denham looked blank.

"Chrysanthemums, I expect," supplied Rosalind. "I shall be happy to join you. Perhaps Mrs. Denison might go with us? She is at present writing a letter to the sister who is caring for her children."

"William's wife? Certainly. You see, Tony, while you dither I have captured two beautiful ladies with whom to wander in the shrubbery."

A loud "Hi!" from outside drew their attention. Sir Peter had just driven up and evidently did not feel called upon to leave his magnificent greys in order to fetch the lady he was honouring with a ride behind them. Lord Harry escorted Rosalind down the steps, and as he helped her into the curricle, he whispered in her ear, "You need not fear for your safety with such a driver, Miss Stuart, only for your sanity."

Returning to his brother's side, he said, as they watched the vehicle sweep round the bend, "I find Miss Stuart no end of an improvement over Miss Fell."

"The poor girl was barely recovered when you saw her in London, and doubtless in a great worry over her future."

"She's turned out a devilish fine woman. I've half a mind to have a go at her myself."

"Lay off, Harry," warned Lord Denham. "You're to consider her Richard's territory unless or until we learn otherwise."

"As you say, brother mine," agreed Lord Harry, but there was a gleam in his eye.

By the time appointed for her walk with Lord Harry, Rosalind was ready to be entertained. She had been lectured for ten miles on the finer points of Sir Peter's team, the design of his curricle, and the qualities that distinguished a member of the Four Hand Club from a mere whipster. Sir Peter, who had seemed to admire her the previous evening, now reserved his admiration strictly for himself.

Rosalind had accompanied Charles into Leicestershire determined to have a last fling before settling down to a staid married life with Ian Heathercot. She had dismissed her fantasy prince on his charger, white or chestnut, to the back of her mind, hoping she had banished him forever; and she intended to flirt with as many young men as possible and enjoy herself thoroughly. If the thought of becoming Ian's wife did not exactly depress her, it did not excite her, and she foresaw the years ahead stretching monotonously into the future. She must seize a little excitement and gaiety while she was still free.

Lord Harry was the perfect foil. She did not for a moment take him seriously, but she found him amusing and was flattered by his attentions. For his part, he had decided that if Richard could not overcome a little competition, he did not deserve to win her. Accustomed to gallanting damsels more youthful, yet somehow more sophisticated, he found Rosalind's combined maturity and innocence enchanting. She had all the wit and poise of females his own age and none of the coyness or brash worldliness that so often accompanied them. With no thought of marriage in his head, he would be happy to indulge her with the flirtation to which she seemed as much inclined as he felt himself. He did wonder briefly whether he might not end by hurting her; but in spite of his words, he was not a vain man, and besides, both his brother and her cousin had warned her against taking him seriously. He looked forward to an enjoyable fortnight.

A half-hour strolling round Lord Denham's immaculate gardens gave neither cause for changed opinions. Emma Denison, who took Lord Harry's other arm, was a grave, quiet young woman who was evidently anxious about the welfare of her absent children. Far from ignoring her in favor of his more amusing companion, he was at pains to draw her out. He asked after little Billy, whom he had met recently on his first trip with his father to London to see the Tower. Rosalind was delighted with his courtesy and consideration.

They were soon joined by Charles and William, and Sir Peter's sister, Harry's "little brunette." She showed no disposition to believe herself ousted in his affections and would have clung to him had he not pointedly turned to Rosalind to inquire whether she should like to explore the birch woods at the end of the lawn. It was a decided brush-off, which made Rosalind revise her favorable impression somewhat, and Miss Allington looked decidedly discomfited. However, she soon turned her attention to Charles. William and Emma were deep in discussion, so Rosalind agreed that it would be pleasant to walk in the woods.

The birches and hazels were dressed in autumn gold, Michaelmas daisies abounded and they found a few late foxgloves. In the center of the wood they came across a small lake covered with wildfowl.

"They are so pretty," sighed Rosalind. "It seems a shame to shoot them."

"You will not think so when you have experienced Tony's cook's way with a wild duck," Harry protested. "It is the only reason I ever visit him here."

"Come, now, Lord Harry, I have heard you are a bruising rider to hounds, and is this not generally accounted the best country for hunting?"

"I have plenty of friends with hunting boxes in Leicestershire, but nary a one with a chef like Alphonse," laughed his lordship. "Nor one who has such charming guests. I hope we are friends, Miss Stuart. Will you not call me Harry?"

"If you wish. And you may call me Rosalind. After all, though we are newly acquainted, you have known Charles forever."

"And he is a major, while I am a mere captain. Shall I dare address the cousin of a superior officer by her Christian name?"

"Yes, for Charles is only a reservist now, and any corporal of the Regular Army may lord it over him."

"They would not dare, Rosalind. Certainly I should not!"

Rosalind blushed a little to hear him use her name, then remembered that this was her last fling. She had no intention of committing any improprieties, but she did not think allowing an old friend of her cousin to call her by her given name could be considered fast, merely a little forward perhaps.

"Should we not turn back, Harry?" she asked tentatively. "The party that went to Leicester must be returned by now and I should like to know what play they have found."

"By all means. Let me tell you the plot I have worked out whereby you shall play the heroine and I the hero."

"I have never acted in my life!" she exclaimed, but he overrode her protests, and all the way back to the house he whispered conspiratorially in her ear.

The delegation had found a melodrama with no less than five parts for the ladies and the same number for the gentlemen. As Harry had foreseen, there immediately arose an argument over who should play which part. All the ladies wanted to be the heroine, and none of the gentlemen wanted to be the hero, pronouncing him a regular slow-top. Rosalind and Harry watched in amusement, Lord Denham in disgust, as the squabble descended to the nursery level among the younger ladies present. At last Harry stepped forward.

"If none of you fellows will take the part," he said in tones of great self-sacrifice, "I feel it my duty, as your host's brother, to rescue the project by offering myself to play Sir Roderick. And pray note, young ladies, how unrewarding is the part of Patience Allgood. I find she has not a word to say until page thirty, while Lady Toplofty, the maid and the other two females never close their mouths. They offer far more scope for a display of talent."

He was heartily seconded by an assortment of young men anxious to see their sisters cease quarreling. Fortunately, there were precisely four aspiring actresses who quickly agreed on which role was whose. The remaining male parts were divided among those gentlemen least reluctant to make a cake of themselves. Finally, only the heroine was unchosen. Rosalind listened in amazed admiration as, without once mentioning her name, Harry persuaded the others that only she was suitable for the part. She accepted gracefully, her eyes laughing at Harry.

"Indeed," she declared, "I should hesitate to presume myself capable of taking any part less dull. I hope I shall prove adequate to this."

"You see," said a grinning Harry to her later, "was it not exactly as I predicted? These affairs are always the same, and I'd wager the plays are all written by the same hack with just such a party in mind. I must beg your pardon for insinuating that Patience Allgood could be played only by a lady of mature years who would not object to so uninteresting a part. You being the only unmarried lady over twenty it seemed the best way to direct them towards you."

"I felt I must be positively in my dotage," she replied. "Surely one of the married ladies might have liked the role."

"Ah, but I do not want a married lady for my heroine," pointed out Harry with a glint in his eye that made her blush. "If you are in your dotage now, I very much wish I could have seen you in your youth."

"I suppose that is a compliment?" inquired Rosalind. "A more involved one I have yet to hear. Come, we should be reading over our parts. Charles says you will be hunting tomorrow, so there will be no opportunity then."

All the gentlemen and most of the ladies followed the hunt the next day. Rosalind walked in the shrubbery for an hour with Emma Denison, and then she inquired of the butler whether there was a pianoforte in the house, as there was none in any of the rooms she had seen.

"Yes indeed, miss," replied the butler. "There is an Instrument in the Long Gallery. None of the Family being musically inclined, as you might say, nor yet most of our usual Guests, the Instrument was put there out of the way. However, I have made it my Business to see that the Instrument has been kept in order, and I venture to say that I think you will find the Instrument quite Adequate, miss, quite Adequate. If you will follow me, miss, I shall lead you to the Instrument."

The Long Gallery was a pleasant room on a sunny morning, with a long wall of windows facing east. Rosalind could see that at other times it would be extremely difficult to heat, and was not surprised that it was not in general use at this season. The Instrument proved to be in excellent condition, and she enjoyed several hours browsing through the collection of faded sheet music she found in the piano stool. She promised herself that the following day she would play the Beethoven she had brought with her. When Charles was in town in July, he had found her a whole book of sonatas by the great man.

The first part of the afternoon passed in reading and conversation with Emma, Lady Catherine and two or three other nonhunters. Towards four o'clock, feeling restless, Rosalind proposed a walk. None of the others showed the slightest inclination to leave their comfortable chairs by the cosy fire, so she decided to go alone. Lady Catherine assured her that she need not take a groom or her maid as long as she did not leave the park. Wrapping up warmly, she set off by herself.

She walked briskly, and hoping to catch sight of the hunt, which must surely soon be returning, she went rather farther than she had intended. When she turned back the sun was already low in the western sky, and the autumn trees blazed in its red light. She was barely half a mile from the house when she heard cantering hooves behind her and looked round.

Coming toward her across the level turf was a tall rider on a horse that glowed richly chestnut in the long rays of the setting sun. They seemed to be appearing straight out of her favorite dream, the prince on the charger who would sweep her off her feet and carry her to a glorious future. She caught her breath.

The rider did not gallop on, seizing her on his way. Instead, he pulled up beside her and dismounted. He looked at her with a question in his eyes, which was reflected in hers. She felt strangely sure she knew this man, though she did not recognize him, and she was startled when he said abruptly,

"Miss Stuart." There was a note in his voice that sounded to Rosalind like mingled disappointment and relief.

"Do . . . do I know you, sir?" she asked, looking up into his dark face.

"No, no. I . . . Charles has described you to me, that is how I recognized you. I am Richard Carstairs, his future brother-in-law." He still had a questioning look.

"Lucy's brother!" exclaimed Rosalind, reassured. "Are Lady Annabel and Lucy — Miss Carstairs — arrived then?"

"They are to spend the night in Nottingham and come on in the morning. I rode ahead." To see you, he ached to say.

"They will be here early, then. Lord

Denham did not expect you all till to-morrow evening. Charles will be so happy; he has missed Miss Carstairs dreadfully. I long to meet her."

"And she you. Are you out here quite alone, Miss Stuart? It is growing dark."

"I did not mean to go so far," she confessed. The sun had disappeared beyond the woods and the air was suddenly chill. She shivered.

Without thinking, Richard dropped Flame's bridle, took off his coat and draped it around her shoulders. She looked at him in surprise.

"Thank you," she murmured after a moment.

Richard had caught her expression and felt himself flush. He had not realized how hard it would be to treat her as a stranger. "Come," he said roughly, "I will walk with you."

He took up the reins, and Flame followed them as they headed toward the house. They had covered half the distance when Rosalind stumbled on some obstacle invisible in the dusk.

Immediately Richard's steadying hand was on her elbow. "Are you hurt?" he asked. She shook her head. "Take my arm. It is too dark to see where we are walking."

She obeyed, and the light pressure of her hand filled him with memories. Rosalind had none, yet though she could no longer distinguish his face, she sensed his emotion and wondered. They went on in silence and soon reached the house.

Chapter 18

"Rosalind!" cried Lord Harry as she entered the hall. "We were on the point of launching a search party."

"Oh dear!" Rosalind gazed with dismayed embarrassment at the agitated crowd. "I never thought that I had been gone long enough to worry anyone. But you will forgive me when you hear that I have brought an addition to our party. Mr. Carstairs has arrived. He has just taken his horse round to the stables."

Charles was beside her, his worried eyes searching her face. "Are you all right, Ros?" he asked anxiously. "How did you come across Richard?"

Thinking he was concerned about her long absence, Rosalind explained that she had met Mr. Carstairs in the park and had been delayed in conversation, or she would have returned before dark. Charles noted with relief that she did not appear at all unwell.

Lord Denham had managed to shepherd his guests into the drawing room. His brother joined the cousins.

"Much ado about nothing," he commented jauntily. "We all came home an hour ago, and my aunt would have it that you had gone to meet us. As we had none of us seen you, she decided to have the vapors, and everyone has been running around clucking since, driving poor Tony to distraction."

"I must go to Lady Catherine at once!" declared Rosalind. "And then I shall apologize to Lord Denham. Indeed, I did not mean to cause such an upset."

"Harry exaggerates," reassured Charles. "It is but half an hour since we all returned. Lady Catherine has clucked once or twice, Tony merely looks slightly harassed, and the rest are thoroughly enjoying what little excitement they can derive from your belated appearance. I am sure that Richard's arrival will drive all else from everyone's minds."

"Harry, you odious wretch!" Rosalind complained as Richard came through the door.

Charles's prophecy seemed to be entirely accurate. Mr. Carstairs was warmly welcomed, questioned about his family's whereabouts, introduced to those few he had not previously met, and told of the forthcoming performance. Miss Stuart missed most of this, as Lady Catherine had sent her up to her chamber to rest before changing for dinner.

At last all dispersed to their rooms, leaving Lord Denham, Harry, Charles and Richard standing before the drawing room fire.

"She didn't know you, then," said Charles to Richard. "I saw no signs of pain or distress, so all may be well. It seems that Dr. Knighton was right, that time was the key."

Richard had intercepted the laughing glance between Rosalind and Harry as he had entered the house and could not agree that all was well. "It is more difficult than I expected to act as a stranger," he admitted soberly. "I find I must constantly guard my tongue."

"I have several times near come to grief," agreed Lord Denham, "and I did not know 'Miss Fell' half so well as you."

"Not I," asserted Harry. "I find no difficulty in treating an exceptionally delightful female as she deserves."

"So I have noticed," said his brother dryly, and Richard gave him a black look. Charles was rather amused. As far as he was concerned, both gentlemen were equally eligible, and so was Mr. Heathercot, who would wed his cousin if neither came up to scratch, or both were rejected. He looked forward to an enjoyable two weeks, reunited at last with his Lucy, and entertained by Richard and Harry fighting over Rosalind.

The evening that followed fulfilled his expectations. Lord Denham had seated Richard and Rosalind together at dinner and placed his brother at the far end of the table, but an adroit maneuver by Harry put him just where he wanted to be. Charles, seated opposite the three, had a perfect view. Rosalind correctly divided her time and attention between the two gentlemen. Harry was his usual charming self, while Richard, never at ease in a large company, managed to converse only in commonplaces with Rosalind and completely ignored the unfortunate damsel on his left.

When the gentlemen joined the ladies after passing the port and brandy and discussing the day's hunting, Sir Peter Allington managed to seat himself on the chair beside Rosalind. He was speedily ousted thence by Lord Harry, who claimed he had to study the melodrama with her.

Richard watched moodily from a distance, quite unconsoled by the fact that

Miss Stuart frequently glanced at him. He saw no warmth in her green eyes, only puzzlement. In her presence, all the plans he had worked out for wooing her seemed cloud castles. Unless he could speak to her alone, he could not even attempt to carry them out.

At last, unable to bear watching her laughing with Harry, he approached. "Miss Stuart," he ventured, "Charles has told me that you are a superb pianist. Might I have the pleasure of hearing you play? I expect you have discovered that Tony keeps his pianoforte hidden away. None of the Grahams are at all musical."

If he had expected thus to oust his rival, he missed his mark. Harry managed to convert his proposal into a general scheme, and quite half the company followed as Richard and Rosalind led the way to the Long Gallery. As they went, she described how the butler had presented the Instrument to her, and he laughed. His face was transformed, and Rosalind felt her heart jump at the sight. How strange, she thought. Why should such a little thing affect her so?

At least three other young ladies were anxious to display their talents. Rosalind was inclined to let them perform before her, but Harry would not permit it. He opened the pianoforte while she and Richard sorted through the music. Richard found her Beethoven, which she had left there.

"Will you play some of this, Miss Stuart?" he started, then paused and looked at their companions. "No, not now. Perhaps you would play it for me, say, sometime tomorrow?"

"Why, of course, Mr. Carstairs, if you wish. You know Herr van Beethoven's work? I agree that it is not suitable for this company."

They smiled at each other, in perfect sympathy.

Harry felt an unexpected dart of jealousy. "Have you chosen something, Rosalind?" he interrupted. "I confess I have no great ear for music, but I like a good tune, and there is no sight so picturesque as a beautiful girl seated at the pianoforte."

Rosalind laughed. "I shall play a sonata by Corelli," she told him. "I hope you will think it a 'good tune,' Harry, though that is not how I should describe it." She looked up at Richard. "Will you turn the pages for me, sir?"

Harry had to admit that Richard had won that round, as his rueful look acknowledged. He went to sit with the rest of the audience and bore the performance with what patience he could muster. When the piece was finished, there was a scattered round of applause in which he joined enthusiastically. Rosalind did not notice. She was listening with bowed head to Richard.

"Charles did not exaggerate," he said warmly in a low voice. "I suppose we must give the others their turn now. Until tomorrow?"

She raised her eyes to his. "I think you are a true music lover, Mr. Carstairs. Until tomorrow. Do you join the hunt?"

"No. I shall not go out, as my mother and Lucy should arrive early. After breakfast, Miss Stuart? We are as likely to have peace then as at any time." And with any luck at all Harry will be chasing a fox around the countryside, he thought savagely.

Rosalind agreed to his suggestion. As they talked they had been ceding their places to the next performer. Somehow Rosalind found herself sitting next to Lord Harry, while Richard was forced to find a seat on the other side of the room. How the devil did Harry do it? he wondered.

The performances that followed were

uniformly mediocre, and received just as much applause as Rosalind's. The last in line played a lively polka with a verve that reminded Richard of Lucy, though his sister had by far more accuracy. He caught Rosalind's eye, and she directed his gaze at Harry's foot, which was tapping in time to the music. Their eyes met again, and they exchanged looks of amused despair and hardly perceptible shrugs.

Richard retired to his chamber far from dissatisfied. Considering that Harry had had two days advantage and that, as far as she was concerned at least, he had only known Rosalind a few hours, he felt he had made progress. And he had an assignation in the morning.

Rosalind went to bed perplexed. Everything indicated that she had never previously met Mr. Carstairs, yet she felt a curious bond between them, had felt it even before being attracted by his smile and his evident appreciation of her playing. Her last fling promised to be even more interesting and exciting than she had expected. She looked forward to the morning.

The next day, Lord Harry proved recalcitrant. His brother tried to send him off to the hunting field, even offering him one of his own hunters when he protested that his own horse needed a day of rest.

"Dash it, Tony, you cannot expect me to go out every day!"

"Why not? You usually do."

"You do not usually provide such devilish attractive entertainment at home. I must study my part. Sir Roderick must be word-perfect," declared Harry.

"Then here is Miss Davis to study with you. And I believe she mentioned a wish to go into the village later to make some small purchase, did you not, Miss Davis? There, Harry, you may escort her," proposed Lord Denham, smugly. He did not often exert himself to outwit his brother and succeeded still less often.

Harry had no choice but to submit gracefully and watch in annoyance as Richard and Rosalind left the breakfast room together.

The omniscient butler, who had miraculously provided a roaring fire in the Long Gallery the previous evening, had done likewise today. It was a chilly, grey day, and Richard and Rosalind were glad of its warmth. The keys of the Instrument were icy, but a few minutes' practice loosened Rosalind's stiff fingers.

"What would you like me to play?" she

asked shyly. This morning Mr. Carstairs seemed a complete stranger once more.

"You know the *Pathétique*? That has a slow start, to let you warm up." He smiled at her, which did more to warm her than any amount of playing could have. He found the place in her book and moved his chair close beside her so that he could reach to turn the pages.

"I know it well, sir," she said hurriedly. "I do not need the music." He realized that his nearness, when they were alone together, disturbed her.

"Then I shall be able to listen without distraction." He took a seat at a little distance. "I believe this will be the best place to hear the Instrument to advantage." And to see the performer.

She played brilliantly. Absorbed by the music, he forgot to watch her. The sonata came to its dashing conclusion and there was silence. Rosalind, with no false modesty, knew she had played well and accepted the silence as a tribute more meaningful than any number of words.

Richard sighed. "Thank you," he said simply.

"One wishes it did not end so soon, does one not? Shall I play something more? It is a difficult piece to follow."

"There is a piece by Mozart of which I am very fond," he suggested hesitantly. "Quite different in character. I forget its name but if I hum it, perhaps you will recognize it." It was the dainty minuet she had been performing the first time he heard her play, when he had arrived at Toblethorpe from London to fetch her.

"Of course,"' agreed Rosalind, "it is the very thing to come after Beethoven's grandeur. I have not played it for some time, but I think *I* remember it well enough."

Nothing distracted Richard's attention from her face this time. The glint of firelight on her hair seemed an attribute of the music. Thinking back to that evening, he recalled the delightful days that had followed it, marred only by "Miss Fell's" discovery that she could not ride his horse.

At the end of the Mozart, he applauded. "I have heard that piece many times, Miss Stuart," he commented, "yet never so well played. The way your performance transforms it from the commonplace is as great a testimony to your talent as any more difficult music. May I ask who was your teacher?"

"I studied in Edinburgh under a French émigré, Monsieur Rameau. A descendant of the composer, he claimed. At any rate, he made me play so much Rameau that I never touch his music now!"

"You spent a great deal of time in Edinburgh?"

"Oh yes. That was where I made my début in Society. My Grandfather Stuart supported the cause of Prince Charles and would not hear of any of the family going to London. He died long before, but my father was acquainted with everyone in Edinburgh, so we continued the custom."

"It is much closer to your home, also." They were discussing Edinburgh's social life and musical activities when Charles joined them.

"Had a devil of a time escaping that Allington wench," he announced cheerfully. "Richard, I hope you will allow Lucy and me to make our betrothal public at once, or I shall be constantly fighting her off."

"Hark, what modesty!" jibed Rosalind. "Mr. Carstairs, you must know that Charlie finds he is irresistible to a certain type of coy, empty-headed young female that he cannot abide."

"Perhaps that is why I fell under the spell of Lucy," pondered Charles. "Like you, Ros, she has no trace of coyness in her. When are we to expect her, Richard?

Did you not say they stopped in Nottingham? That cannot be above twenty-five miles."

"As the crow flies," Richard replied. "However, the way is mostly by narrow, winding lanes. Nor do I think they would have started early. It is not so far from Toblethorpe, and we spent two days on the journey, but the roads were appalling. My mother was greatly fatigued yesterday when I left them. I was on horseback most of the way and escaped the worst of the jolting. I'd not look for them before midday."

"Patience, Charles, patience," counseled Rosalind. "And that reminds me. If I am to play Patience Allgood well enough to preserve my self-respect, I really must make a start on learning my part. Charlie, will you hear me in a while?"

"Not if Lucy is here," said her cousin ungallantly.

"Well, I daresay I should try it over with Harry," admitted Rosalind, before Richard could offer his services. "Pray excuse me, Mr. Carstairs."

"You will play for me again?" Richard begged hurriedly.

"I am always happy to play for a truly appreciative audience." The warmth of her smile denied the impersonality of her words.

Richard looked after her wistfully as she left, then turned to Charles. "You have known Harry a long time, have you not? Has Miss Stuart met him often?"

"Only very briefly, in London, just before I found her at your house. She did not remember him when we came here." He took pity on Richard's long face. "I do not believe there is anything serious between them. I've never known Harry dangle after any female for longer than three weeks, and Rosalind . . . I am not at liberty to discuss her position, but I think I may tell you that she has come into Leicestershire determined upon enjoying herself. She is not hanging out for a husband."

"I see Lucy has been talking." Richard was poised between gratitude and annoyance.

"She is a little chatterbox, but she told me nothing I had not already guessed," Charles defended his sweetheart.

"Am I so obvious?" asked Richard with some bitterness; then added grudgingly, "If you and Lucy are still of the same mind when we leave Disford Wood, you had better come straight to Toblethorpe and be married. I'd prefer that you do not announce the engagement until Lucy has had a chance to reconsider. She has seen so little of you since the spring, and she is still very young."

"Richard, you cannot suppose that I should hold Lucy to a match that had become distasteful to her! Not that I think for a moment that she will have changed. You do not understand what it is to have the certainty that the one you love loves you as much as you could hope or desire."

"I have not had the experience. Charles, have I any chance of winning Rosalind?"

"Who can tell? There's no understanding women!"

With that sentiment Richard was forced to agree.

Only a few dedicated souls had ridden out with the hunt that day, so most of the party assembled at the luncheon table. They had scarce sat down after filling their plates at the buffet, when a footman entered and murmured something to Lord Denham, who rose.

"Richard, Charles — Lady Annabel and Lucy are arrived. Do the rest of you excuse us, please. No, Aunt Catherine, do not bestir yourself. I am sure Lady Annabel would not wish to interrupt your meal."

A glance of appeal from Charles brought Rosalind to her feet to accompany the three gentlemen. Harry, seated beside her, would have followed if he could have thought of an excuse to leave the other guests.

The butler was ushering the ladies into the hall as they reached it. Lucy uttered a squeal, dropped her muff, and flung herself into Charles's arms. Rosalind decided with amusement that it would be some time before she could be introduced to her future cousin-in-law.

Lady Annabel was looking far from well. Richard hurried to her side.

"Mama, are you ill?" he asked anxiously.

"No, dearest, but very tired." She managed a faint smile. "The wretched inn last night was excessively noisy, and after the shocking roads from Yorkshire I fear it has given me the headache. Lord Denham, how delightful to see you again." She carefully did not greet Rosalind.

"I am sorry you are not in good frame, Lady Annabel," said Tony. "Your chamber is prepared. I expect you would like to rest for a while."

"Thank you, I should, if Lady Catherine will forgive me."

"Let me present Miss Stuart to you," his

lordship suggested, "as Charles seems to have quite forgot his duty. Charles's cousin, ma'am. Miss Stuart, this is Lady Annabel Carstairs."

Lady Annabel, in spite of her headache, wished she could embrace Rosalind. She had every expectation of being as fond of her as she had been of her *alter ego*, Clara Fell. Rosalind's first words confirmed her expectations.

"Charles has told me how kind you have been to him, my lady. Pray do not let me keep you from your rest. May I take you to your room and see that you have all you need? Lord Denham will not mind if I act as Lady Catherine's deputy."

Richard gave her a look of gratitude. "Shall I help you upstairs, mama?" he queried.

"Miss Stuart will assist me, thank you, Richard. I shall be quite well after a rest."

As she supported Lady Annabel up the staircase, Rosalind said to her, "I trust you will not think me forward, ma'am. Miss Carstairs was so very . . . occupied, and I hope soon to be your niece-in-law, if such a relationship exists. I daresay your maid is busy with the luggage."

"Oh, Vane is useless when one is not feeling quite the thing. She tends to dissolve in tears." Lady Annabel wondered nervously whether the abigail would remember her strict instructions in regard to Miss Stuart. "Indeed, I shall be happy to gain a niece as well as a son when I lose my daughter."

"Here is your chamber. The maid is not here yet. Let me make you comfortable." Rosalind helped Lady Annabel divest herself of her outer clothing and slip into the ready-warmed bed. "Should you like a glass of wine, or something to eat? It is so difficult to take proper meals on the road; your headache may be partly due to hunger, may it not?"

Lady Annabel already felt better. She was sure that worry over the effect on Rosalind of seeing the Carstairs again had been responsible to some extent for her discomfort.

"I expect you are right," she acknowledged gratefully. "Perhaps a cup of tea and a snack. Won't you join me? I should like to become acquainted with my new niece."

Rosalind rang the bell and ordered a light luncheon. She also sent for her own maid, since Vane had not yet appeared, and asked her to fetch some lavender water, with which she bathed Lady Annabel's forehead.

Vane at last arrived, followed by two footmen bearing a trunk, which she would have had them carry into the chamber had Rosalind not instructed them to leave it in the passage for the present. Lady Annabel sent her servant to find herself a meal.

"Miss *Stuart* is looking after me, Vane. I will ring if I need you," she told her. She and Rosalind settled down to a comfortable cose over their luncheon. By the time Lucy ran in, a couple of hours later, she felt quite herself again.

"Are you better, mama?" cried Lucy. "I'd have come before but Charles said I would only fuss you and Rosalind would care for you better. You do not mind if I call you Rosalind?" she asked. "We shall soon be sisters, nearly."

"Not at all," answered Rosalind smiling. "Since Charles always calls you Lucy, I never think of you as anything else. It will be delightful to have a sister."

"Will it not? I have always wished for one. Charles says . . ." She chattered on until Lady Annabel stopped her.

"I cannot think how Charles ever manages to say anything," she declared. "Hush, child. Miss Stuart will think you a veritable rattlepate."

"Will you not call me Rosalind, too,

402

ma'am?" asked Rosalind shyly.

"If you wish it, my dear. Now I shall get up and come down to meet the rest of the company. Lucy, ring for Vane, please. I shall see you both in half an hour or so."

Rosalind found the company dispersed about the house. It had begun to rain heavily and even the most enthusiastic huntsmen had returned. She looked for Richard to tell him of his mother's recovery, and found him playing billiards with Lord Denham. Well coached by her father and her cousin, she waited in silence until he had finished his shot. He saw her as he straightened up, and the glad welcome in his eyes made her forget her errand for a moment.

"How is Lady Annabel?" asked Lord Denham.

"Oh, she is quite well again. I think she was only tired, Mr. Carstairs, and soon revived. She is coming down shortly."

"Thank you for looking after her, Miss Stuart," said Richard warmly. "It was most considerate of you."

Rosalind blushed and uttered a hasty disclaimer.

"I did not feel Lucy could be relied on to do her duty at that moment," she added dryly.

"I'm afraid not. You have met my sister?"

"Yes, she came up to Lady Annabel's room. What a charming child! Charles is lucky indeed to have found such a bride with such a family."

"I am glad you think so, Miss Stuart." Richard wondered if he was included in her encomium, but before he could think of a way to find out, Harry came into the room.

"Rosalind!" he exclaimed, "Lucy told me where to find you. I need your help with Sir Roderick. Come, let us find a quiet corner and rehearse."

"Oh yes, Harry!" she replied gaily. "I learned a few speeches this morning and hoped we might hear each other recite. Miss Patience Allgood seems to spend a great deal of time bewailing her fate."

"Sir Roderick to the rescue!" cried Harry, and cast a mocking glance at Richard as he ushered her out.

"I do not wish to interfere," said Lord Denham cautiously, "but I feel it would be a good move on your part to get on first-name terms with Miss Stuart. With that dratted brother of mine running around calling her Rosalind at the top of his voice, the contrast is quite painful."

"Believe me, I have noticed it," answered Richard ruefully. "I had not wanted to push matters too fast. After all, she met me for the first time yesterday. Though, indeed, she met Harry only two days ago."

"It should not be difficult now that Lucy is here. It seems she has already managed it, and if Miss Stuart is to be, more or less, her sister-in-law, then you are nearly Miss Stuart's brother."

"Dammit, Tony, I do not wish to be Rosalind's brother!"

"She may have both of us for brothers if you do not watch out. I've never known Harry remain interested in a female when it meant fighting off a rival. It's always been easy come, easy go with him. It's my belief he's been hooked, even if he doesn't know it yet himself. And since your little puss turned me down, he's a fair chance at being a marquis one day."

"Miss Stuart would not fall for a title," said Richard coldly.

"How can you be sure? And, anyway, there's no saying she won't take a liking to him, the ladies often do. There's no understanding women."

"That's what Charles said," Richard affirmed gloomily, and they went back to their game.

Harry had never had any difficulty in understanding women. The only thing that puzzled him about Rosalind was the reason behind her frivolous behaviour. He was certain that it was not her usual manner and that there was a definite cause. He knew equally well that she found him attractive and amusing, enjoyed his company, and looked no further, and that she was fighting a much stronger attraction toward Richard for which she could not account to herself.

He was far less certain about his own feelings. The pang of jealousy that had shot through him when he saw Richard and Rosalind in perfect accord at the pianoforte had taken him by surprise. Until that moment he had considered her an unusually pleasant companion with whom to while away the hours. Suddenly she had become something less easy to define. For the first time in his life he found himself contemplating matrimony, and he hastily pushed the thought away. Tony was the heir, it was his business to continue the family. Rosalind was a delightful woman, and he firmly intended to spend every possible moment of the next couple of weeks in her company, after which Richard could have her with his blessing.

If she wanted him, which he rather hoped she did not.

Chapter 19

Lady Annabel renewed her acquaintance with Lady Catherine Graham. They had both come out in the same Season, and though they had never been intimate, they had many memories in common. Both had been married and widowed, and while Lady Catherine's marriage had been childless and far from ideal, their experience was another bond between them. They spent many happy hours reminiscing.

Charles and Lucy joined the hunt regularly and as regularly lost it a few hundred yards after the start. Had they ever noticed where they were going, they would have been able to describe half Leicestershire in detail. When they were not out riding together, they managed to find an amazing number of private nooks and crannies in Lord Denham's house and gardens. After three days, an envious Richard agreed that they might announce their betrothal, which came as no surprise to anyone. Lord Denham, as always philosophical, produced champagne.

Reflecting on his usual hunting parties, Lord Denham could not approve of the course this one was taking. Only the thought that he was doing it for Richard stopped him saying so at frequent intervals. At all hours of the day and night, he would come across actors loudly declaiming their lines, singly, in pairs or in groups. Half his staff seemed to have been co-opted, either to build a stage at one end of his small ballroom, or to sew elaborate and fanciful costumes. Even those of his guests who were not directly involved in acting were busy designing and painting scenery, collecting props, or coaching.

On the days that the local hunt met, he usually managed to muster four or five gentlemen and two or three ladies, but for this he could not even count on Richard, whose detestation of the thespian world was quite equal to his own.

Richard had considerable difficulty in extricating Rosalind from the constant rehearsals Harry seemed to find necessary. However, she was fundamentally far more interested in music than in amateur theatricals, and she played for him every day. Lady Annabel often joined them, and occasionally Charles and Lucy or one or two of the others would drop in to the Long

Gallery and listen for a while. One sunny day when no one else was with them, Richard seized his chance.

Rosalind had just finished playing. She turned to him and said gaily, "It is a beautiful day, Mr. Carstairs. Are you going to ride out today?"

"I should like to do so if you would join me, Miss Stuart. Do you never ride?"

"I was used to," she replied hesitantly. "I had an accident — Charles may have mentioned it — and since then I find the thought of riding makes me very uncomfortable."

"When you learned to ride, did your instructor always make you mount again immediately when you fell off?" he teased gently.

"Oh yes. You see, I was unable to do so for some time, and I suppose my aversion became settled."

"Do you think it too late to try again?" Richard asked. "I should gladly do all in my power to help you. Lucy brought two horses. One is a very quiet mare. You might start with her."

"It would be very pleasant to ride again," Rosalind said wistfully. "It is too muddy for walking, and driving is no exercise. You really think I might overcome my fear?"

"You are not lacking in courage, Miss Stuart. Will you not make the attempt?"

"I will," she answered decisively. "Pray let us go immediately, before I lose my nerve. Oh, I did not bring a habit with me!"

Richard brushed aside this frivolous feminine objection. "I shall take care that no one is around. Can you not wear a walking dress?"

Rosalind admitted that perhaps she could.

"Very well. Come, do not look so agitated. I'll not force you to mount, you know. I shall meet you at the stables as soon as you can be ready."

Richard had had just this eventuality in mind when he had suggested that Lucy bring old Whitesocks as well as her hunter. When Rosalind entered the clean-swept cobbled stableyard twenty minutes later, he had had the mare saddled and sent the grooms about their business.

"Come and talk to her," he called.

She had no fear of petting the horse. In fact, she had frequently driven herself about during the summer with no qualms. It was just the idea of actually sitting in the saddle that she could not face.

Richard would not let her back out

easily. "You see how small she is. I bought her for Lucy on her twelfth birthday. She was always the gentlest creature, and she is tethered to the rail. Let me lift you up, and I will hold you."

"You'll not let go?"

"Not as long as you need me, I promise. Are you ready?"

He placed her securely in the saddle and stood with his arm around her waist. He could feel her tension. She was trembling slightly and her face was pale. Her eyes were fixed on her hands, which held tight to the pommel. Richard spoke to her soothingly, as he would to a frightened horse. She did not relax, but sat there for a minute, then turned to him.

"I want to get down," she said very softly, with a catch in her voice.

In an instant she was on the ground again, and, seeing that she could support herself, he reluctantly withdrew his arm.

"Brave girl," he approved.

"You make me feel like a small child, Mr. Carstairs." Her face was still pale, but her eyes were dancing and she managed a shaky smile.

"It is the irrational, childish fears which are hardest to overcome," he pointed out seriously. "One cannot argue against them.

411

Will you try again, a little later?"

"Yes, if you will help me. I could not bring myself to do it alone. With you I feel safe and can almost believe I may ride again."

"I do not doubt that you will do so. However, now I should like to take you for a drive, if you will spare me another hour?"

"A reward for being a brave girl? That will be delightful, Mr. Carstairs." Her teasing smile emboldened him, and he caught her hand.

"Miss Stuart, will you not call me Richard? After all, we are soon to be cousins, are we not?"

"Then I should call you Cousin Richard, and you may call me Cousin Rosalind. A nice distinction between impropriety and informality."

"You are a shocking tease, Rosalind." He kissed her hand. "Come, let us have the horses put to, cousin. I believe the only vehicle left to us is a gig, but you will not mind that. Where would you like to go?"

"Should you object to taking me into the village? There are one or two things I must purchase for the play. Miss Patience Allgood is disguised as a maid for the first part, you know, and I am determined to wear the biggest mobcap I can find."

"You are thoroughly enjoying the theatricals, I think."

"Oh yes! I have never done such a thing before, and I daresay I never shall again; but I confess I cannot see the harm in it, and it is excessively amusing."

"I believe you are too sensible to allow your emotions to be affected. Yet do you not think a young girl might become so caught up in her role as to let it overset her common sense?"

Rosalind did not answer immediately. As Richard helped her into the gig, she considered his remarks with mixed feelings. It was a compliment of sorts to describe her as sensible. However, Richard had pronounced it in a tone of hopefulness, rather than certainty. On the whole she was inclined to resent his implied assumption of the right to criticize her behaviour, though his words had been unexceptionable. She was left feeling slightly uneasy and wishing she had not so blithely agreed to an exchange of Christian names.

"I see no harm with adequate chaperonage," she said shortly.

Richard was far from sure how he had offended, but it was plain that she was displeased. With a sinking heart, he dropped the subject and vowed to keep a tighter rein on his jealousy, which he recognized as being the instigator of his comments.

As they drove out of the yard and down the lane, he exerted himself to please her. He had rarely in his life felt the need of such exertion, being in the habit of disregarding as beneath him the disapproval of the greater part of the world. Despite his lack of practice, he succeeded tolerably well, and by the time they reached the village Rosalind was once more in perfect charity with him and conversing happily.

Richard, while finding himself more and more in love, could not help contrasting the late Miss Fell with the present Rosalind. Miss Fell had had a delightful sense of humour, but her constant awareness of her anomalous situation had suppressed true lightheartedness, whereas Rosalind was free to indulge in it. Miss Fell had been an invalid for almost the entire period of their acquaintance. He had found beauty in her eyes and in her glorious hair, as he still did in Rosalind. Yet what a difference in this blooming creature sitting by him, not a classical beauty, perhaps, but glowing with life and health. And that was the biggest contrast, he thought despondently. Miss Fell had needed him. Rosalind manifestly did not.

Rosalind, meanwhile, was comparing not past and present but Richard and Harry. The greatest difference, she decided, was that while both were amusing, with Richard she could also discuss serious subjects that never seemed to have crossed Harry's mind. He was well-informed about everything that interested her and always ready to listen to her opinions.

On the other hand, in spite of his evident admiration and occasional compliments, she could not flirt with him as she did with Harry, whose compliments grew more outrageous daily. After all, she reminded herself, she had come here to enjoy herself. She would have plenty of time for serious matters when she was married to Ian Heathercot.

The other contrast between the gentlemen in question was their appearance. Harry's fair, cheerful good looks and fashionable apparel, when he was not in regimentals, were a far cry from Richard's usually somber face and restrained elegance. She knew that several of the young ladies in the party regarded the latter's dark complexion with abhorrence. Hoping that she had too much discrimination to be swayed by outward appearances, she also realized that far from being shocked at her

415

first sight of him, she had felt a kind of inexplicable recognition, almost as if she had expected his swarthiness. Now, of course, she saw not the color of his skin but the expression on his face and in his eyes.

And they, she thought crossly, generally held altogether too much warmth for her peace of mind. After all, she had known the man only a week.

The day of the performance was drawing close, and Rosalind found more and more of her time occupied in rehearsing. She still played the piano daily for Richard, and once or twice a day they would seize a few minutes to slip down to the stables for a riding lesson. Rosalind was soon able to stay on Whitesocks's back while Richard led the mare around the yard. However, she had no time for driving or walking with him, or trying to ride farther, and even their conversations were curtailed. Richard longed for the performance as fervently as any of the actors.

It was due to take place on a Friday evening — the day after was the date of the Hunt Ball, and the following Monday Lord Denham's party was to break up. Lady Catherine had roused herself to veto vigorously any suggestion of inviting the neighbors.

"Most ineligible!" she exclaimed to her disappointed younger nephew. "Why, Harry, that would make it almost a public performance. You cannot be serious!"

Harry had been serious, but accepted his aunt's disapproval, with a good grace. The audience was to be composed of the non-participating guests and those of the servants who could be spared from their duties.

The cast kept their costumes a closely guarded secret from those who had no hand in their making. It was known that the attic had been raided and had disgorged trunks full of the fashions of the last century, including even wigs. More than one young lady was hopeful of dazzling the eyes of certain members of the audience.

The plot, disclosed to Richard by Rosalind with much giggling, concerned a villain who, for unspecified reasons, had stolen the infant Patience Allgood and had her brought up as a maid by his sister, Lady Toplofty. This starchy matron had two daughters whose hands were being sought by a pair of suitors, one of whom was Sir Roderick Lebeau, to be played by Lord Harry. Sir Roderick was to fall in love with Patience, in her guise as maid. After many vicissitudes, Squire Allgood, Patience's father, arrived to claim his daughter, whereupon Sir Roderick asked for her hand, to the discomfiture of the villains.

As Harry had pointed out, the heroine's role was minor. Until the last scene Rosalind spent most of her time wringing her hands while the other female parts, not excepting the maid, strutted and preened and gave her orders.

On the gentlemen's side the situation was reversed: The hero had the weightiest part, with a great many declamations and soliloquies. Harry was in his element. Wildly overplaying his part, he led the rest of the cast on to efforts they had never dreamed of. He had the audience in gales of laughter, which generally concealed the necessity of frequent prompting.

The last scene before the denouement was a tender love scene between Sir Roderick and Patience. Rosalind, in a black dress, starched white apron, and huge chartreuse mobcap, was taken aback to find that Harry, abandoning the manner of their rehearsals, was playing his part with passionate sincerity. She could only attempt to do likewise. The sole laugh came when, in the middle of a long speech,

Harry seized her headgear and cried unexpectedly, "I cannot possibly make love to you in that ridiculous cap!"

By the time Patience had renounced Sir Roderick's hand forever on the grounds of not being worthy of him, several maids in the back of the hall were sobbing openly, and even Lady Catherine was seen to dab at her eyes with the corner of a dainty lace handkerchief.

For the final scene, Rosalind had been persuaded, with some misgivings, to wear a gorgeous court dress of the 1760s. Her hair was hidden under a tall powdered wig and paste diamonds sparkled at her throat and wrists. She swept onto the stage with her usual queenly bearing, and looked so *grande dame* that Richard barely recognized her. She would make a superb marchioness, he thought with a pang.

Lord Harry was thinking much the same. If he could have found a private moment with her, he would have proposed immediately, but in the excitement of applause, congratulations and discussions of the performance, it was quite impossible.

Rosalind was relieved that it was all over. Acting in front of people, however well she knew them, she found to be very different from rehearsing in private. She had felt little stage fright, but had been embarrassed by the penultimate scene. Extremely annoyed with Harry for changing the character of his role so drastically at that moment, she held him largely responsible for her embarrassment. She was inclined to think that possibly Richard was right, though, that acting was not at all a suitable pastime for well-bred young ladies.

She was annoyed with Richard for proving correct. When she managed to seize a few minutes for quiet reflection, she was inclined to exonerate Harry from much of the blame. Everyone knew he was incurably frivolous and surely would not think any impropriety attached to her listening to his passionate declaration in public. It was only acting. When Lady Catherine congratulated her on her thespian talents, she was sure that her behaviour had been unexceptionable and was able to meet Richard's eyes calmly, though with a certain feeling of defiance, which she resented. What business had he looking so miserable?

"You looked magnificent in the last scene," he told her, "though I prefer your natural hair to any wig." He found himself quite unable to praise her acting and turned away quickly, hoping she had not noticed his hurt.

Exhausted, Rosalind went to bed early and arose late. She breakfasted in her chamber, and then tried on her new ball gown of emerald silk, which she intended to wear for the first time at the Hunt Ball.

While her abigail was placing a few pins to mark last-minute alterations, Lucy knocked and entered.

"What a beautiful dress!" she cried. "That is precisely the color for you, Rosalind. Why do you not wear it more often?"

"It would not then have half the impact," laughed Rosalind. "What do you mean to wear tonight?"

"Oh, I don't know. Something blue. Charles likes me in blue. Ros, look what he has given me." She held out a pair of sapphire earrings. "And he says he will find me some blue flowers to wear. I can't think what, at this time of year. He says blonds with blue eyes usually wear blue to enhance the color of their eyes, but my eyes need no enhancement. Is that not pretty?"

"Yes indeed, and I cannot think of any precious stone that is as brown as your eyes."

"Well, no, though I am sure that if there were one, Charles would find it for me. He is quite the dearest person in the world. Rosalind, I am so happy I could burst!"

"Pray do not do anything so shocking in my chamber, Lucy! How should I ever explain it to Charles? Yes, he is a dear, and I am lucky to have had him as a brother."

"Ros, I have been wanting to ask you for some time, only you have been so busy. Will you be my maid of honour? Mama says it will be quite unexceptionable, for my cousins, you know, may be my bridesmaids."

"My dear, I shall be honoured, if you truly think your eldest cousin will not feel slighted."

"Oh, Jenny will not care, and I am sure Richard would much rather squire you than my cousin."

Rosalind blushed. "I had not thought, will not your brother give you away?"

"Yes, but he will also be Charles's best man, as it is to be a quiet family wedding, and the best man always escorts the maid of honour, you know."

Charles had maliciously considered asking Lord Harry to be his best man, then decided that making Richard miserable would hardly enhance his own wedding. He had no idea how Rosalind felt toward the rivals, but she seemed to be enjoying herself and showed no signs of being troubled by errant memories, so he relaxed in his own happiness and left her to sort out her suitors for herself.

He knocked at her chamber door just as Joan was carefully removing the green gown.

"One moment," called Lucy, seizing a wrap and casting it round Rosalind's shoulders. "It's Charles, I'm sure," she added to Rosalind. "He has something for you, too."

Rosalind quickly made herself decent, and Charles came in.

"I've a gift for you, Ros," he explained, confirming Lucy's words. He handed her a velvet box. "I bought the stone in India, very cheap I may say, but it had to be set. There hasn't been a suitable occasion for giving it to you, until now. I thought you would not wish to wait until Christmas or your birthday."

Rosalind opened the box and gasped.

"Charles! It must have cost a fortune! Oh, it is truly beautiful." She drew from its velvet nest a single square-cut emerald on a simple gold chain. "Should not Lucy have it? It will be an heirloom."

"I bought it for you, before ever I met Lucy. And do not think I squandered a fortune on it, even for you, Ros. I suspect it was stolen from the hoard of some long-dead maharajah, for I paid only about one-tenth the going price, and such things are far less expensive in India than in London to start with. I daresay I should rather have turned the peddler over to the authorities; but he was brother to one of my men, and besides, I always thought you should wear emeralds."

Rosalind threw her arms around his neck and kissed him on both cheeks. Lucy laughed as he blushed.

"Oh, you are the best and dearest of cousins, Charlie. I shall feel like an Indian queen in it. A maharani, is it not?"

"Cupboard love," growled Charles. "I missed you, Ros. Come, Lucy, if we are to ride before luncheon, we must go."

Lucy kissed Rosalind and followed her betrothed. Rosalind sat down on her bed and wept a little. For the first time, she considered the possibility of living at Bennendale with her cousin after his marriage. She knew she would be welcome and could continue to regard it as her home. Then she rejected the comforting thought. It would not be fair to Lucy, would not give her a chance to make it into her own home. She must marry Ian and be thankful she had that choice.

Descending below stairs for luncheon, Rosalind was pounced on by both Richard and Harry. They escorted her to the breakfast room, where a cold collation had been laid out, hovered over her while she chose her meal, and both managed to sit beside her. Both had plans for her afternoon. Harry was determined to be alone with her, Richard equally determined not to let her out of his sight.

In the end, they all three went walking. Several days of dry weather had cleared the worst of the mud, and the gusty wind with its hint of frost was invigorating in the golden sunshine. They strolled into the woods. The two gentlemen forgot their animosity and behaved like schoolboys, catching falling leaves before they touched the ground and presenting them to Rosalind with a promise of a month's good luck for each. They climbed trees for nuts, ate blackberries by the purple handful and dropped the fruit berry by berry into her mouth so as not to stain her fingers with the juice. If both longed to kiss that mouth they kept the longing to themselves and argued amicably over the best way to weave a garland of Michaelmas daisies for her hair. Rosalind, in her long skirts, could not climb trees, but she gathered her gown in her hands and ran rustling through drifted heaps of dead leaves while her lovers threw great armfuls of them at each other. When at last she took an arm of each and they turned homeward, she crowned with daisies, they with leaves in their hair, she felt that she had not so enjoyed an afternoon since she was a child playing hooky with Charles.

In the hall they met Lady Annabel and Lady Catherine, who stared with horror at their disarray.

"Harry," said his aunt in minatory tones, "you have leaves in your hair."

"Don't scold, ma'am," he answered pacifically, "I gave as good as I got. Look at Richard."

"Well, dearest," said Lady Annabel, "I cannot imagine what you have been doing, but it is just as well you have brought Rosalind back, for I daresay she will wish to lie down for an hour before dressing. We are to dine early, as it is near an hour's drive to the ball."

Harry and Richard were both about to claim the honour of driving Miss Stuart to Haddesdon Hall. They caught each other's eye.

"Cry truce, Harry," proposed Richard

resignedly. "Rosalind, Harry and I beg to be allowed to escort you to the ball. Lord knows what vehicle will be available but we shall have to find one that will carry three."

"Not at all," grinned Harry. "It will be much warmer if we are a little crowded."

Rosalind blushed. "You will not wish to crush my new gown, Harry! I shall be happy to accompany you, gentlemen, if it fits in with the plans of the rest of our party."

"I'll have a word with Tony," said both gentlemen simultaneously.

"I beg you will not speak in chorus all evening," protested Rosalind, laughing. "I'd as lief you took it in turns to address me on behalf of both."

"We shall require a minimum of a waltz and a country dance apiece," declared Harry. "And I suppose we shall have to share supper between us."

"As long as I get something to eat, you may share supper between you," promised Rosalind. "And now I shall take Lady Annabel's advice and rest a little."

When Rosalind reached her room, she found an elaborate posy from Lord Harry and a simple spray of copper-colored beech leaves from Richard. She would gladly have worn the latter, which exactly suited her taste, but the last thing she wanted to do was to spoil the newfound and, she suspected, fragile accord between the two. Taking the circlet of wilted daisies from her head, she wished she might wear that.

She read for a while, and then rang for Joan. It took her some time to dress, as she had decided to try her hair in a new style. Usually she wore it pulled gently back into a knot at the nape of her neck. Now the maid wove it into braids that softly framed her face and rose to circle her head in a coronet of shining copper. Gazing into the looking glass, she wondered why she had not experimented before.

"I think it suits me, do not you, Joan?" she asked.

"Oh yes, Miss Rosalind. When you are all ready, you'll be as fine as fivepence, and no mistake."

"How did you learn to dress hair like this? I'd no idea you could do such beautiful work."

"Lady Annabel's maid condescended to give me a few tips, miss. She've taken a rare liking to you."

"How strange. I don't believe I have spoken to her above twice. I must thank her for coaching you. And thank you, Joan, for taking the trouble to learn."

"I'm happy as you like it, Miss Rosalind. It's a pleasure to work with hair like yourn. I've taken those tucks in the gown. Will you put it on now?"

"Yes, I am ready. You know, it is a long time since I have been to such a grand ball. I feel quite fluttery."

"There'll not be a lady to beat you, miss. I just wish I could see you dancing, a proper picture you'll be."

"I wish I could take you, Joan, if it would please you. You'll not wait up. I've no notion how late we'll be."

"Oh, we're to have a bit of a fling in the servants' hall, miss. I 'spect I'll still be about."

"Enjoy yourself, my dear. I'll wager you'll look as pretty as a picture yourself. There, just the necklace and I'll be ready to go down."

The abigail fastened the chain, and the huge stone lay glowing on her breast. She looked at it in the mirror, a little awed, and thought of Charles with sudden tenderness. How kind he was to think of her at such a time.

When she entered the salon, the reaction was all she could have desired. Richard and Harry came swiftly to greet her, and she read in their faces that she was beautiful.

"What a magnificent stone!" exclaimed Harry. "Yet your eyes are more brilliant by far, and the copper of your hair is more precious than any gold chain."

"Very poetic," declared Rosalind, laughing at him. "Now make it rhyme."

"Lucy told me Charles was giving you a pendant," Richard said. "A princely gift indeed! No brother could be more generous and thoughtful."

"He was always loving and considerate," Rosalind assured him softly. "You need have no fears for Lucy."

He smiled at her with gratitude, and spoke in a voice as low as hers. "You are right. I think if I had to pick any one quality I should most require in a husband for my little sister, I should choose kindness. I shall put away my doubts."

Rosalind would have replied, but Harry, who had been hovering impatiently, trying not to eavesdrop, interrupted.

"Come, Rosalind," he cried gaily, "we are agreed to share your time fairly tonight, and you must promise to favor neither. Tomorrow is Sunday. You would not have us fight a duel on the Sabbath?"

"No, nor any other day. If I thought you contemplated such a shocking action, I should have no hesitation in informing the nearest magistrate and having you both clapped up in jail," said Rosalind with mock severity.

"You would catch cold there, for Tony is a justice and would free me at once."

"Whatever makes you think so?" asked Lord Denham, appearing at his brother's elbow. "Miss Stuart looks a very queen. If she commanded it, I should undoubtedly ship you to Botany Bay on the next transport!"

"Oh, unnatural brother!" Harry groaned and clutched his head.

"You see, Rosalind," Richard pointed out with a twinkle in his eye, "you must be a very paragon of fairness this night, or you will be responsible for fratricide at the least."

"I think it will be much easier if I simply refuse to speak to either of you," suggested Rosalind.

Both gentlemen cried out upon this, and they went in to dinner laughing.

To Rosalind's surprise, the truce continued throughout dinner and the drive to Haddesdon Hall. She stood up for a country dance with Harry, and then was partnered by Charles, Lord Denham and William Denison in turn. The orchestra struck up a waltz next, and Richard claimed her hand.

She had felt his arm around her before, but her memory was only of the times he had supported her as she learned to ride again. She had been too agitated to notice anything except the task before her. Now it made her slightly breathless, and she was constantly conscious of the light pressure at her waist as they spun about the room. They did not speak. They floated in a dream, seeing only each other's eyes, dark gazing down into green, oblivious of all else.

The music ended. Rosalind stood a moment within the circle of his arm, then gave a tiny sigh and pulled away. He kept hold of her hand.

"Rosalind . . . ," he began urgently, and there was Harry bearing down on them.

"Suppertime," he announced. "Come quick or someone will snaffle all the lobster patties."

They joined Charles and Lucy and several others of Lord Denham's guests in the supper room. Nothing seemed quite real to Rosalind. She ate a little, drank some champagne, talked and laughed, and politely acquiesced when Sir Peter Allington reminded her that she had promised the next dance to him.

Somehow she found her way through the figures of the dance, and then found herself waltzing with Lord Harry, a splendid figure in his regimentals and slightly tipsy on champagne. His extravagant compliments soon brought her back to earth, and between laughter and exercise, she began fanning her hot face vigorously when the dance ended.

"Come out on the terrace for a minute or two," suggested Harry. "There is a full moon, you know."

They stood by the stone parapet for a moment. Rosalind admired the golden harvest moon, hanging huge and low over a glittering lake. Harry was admiring her.

"What, struck dumb?" she mocked, laughing. "I did not know you ever lost your tongue."

Suddenly Harry was sober. "Rosalind!"

She turned her laughing face to him.

"You don't take me seriously, do you?" he asked with abrupt bitterness.

His tone chased Rosalind's mirth. She was silent for a moment. "No, Harry," she answered gently.

"Richard?"

Again she paused before replying. "I take Richard seriously."

"I thought so." Harry recovered his gaiety with an effort. He seized her hands. "I shall leave for London in the morning. Kiss me good-bye?"

She turned her face up to his and their lips touched briefly.

"Good-bye, Harry," she murmured.

Richard was beside them, his face unreadable even in the bright moonlight. "My dance, I think, Miss Stuart." His voice was expressionless.

Harry watched as they walked silently back to the crowded ballroom.

Rosalind had been taken by surprise, or she would have asked for a word in private and explained the apparent breach of her promise. They were taking their place in the set before she could do so. Even then, had Richard seemed angry, she would have insisted on an explanation later. However, when his eyes briefly met hers, there was no anger in them, only a deep hurt.

It made her feel guilty, and from guilt her feelings quickly moved to an anger of her own. What right had he to look at her like that, to make her feel ashamed of an act that, while perhaps a little fast, she could not think improper in the circumstances? He was not her brother, to watch over her conduct, nor had he any other claim on her. She resolved to show him that she did not care what he thought of her.

The movements of the dance rarely presented opportunities for conversation, and neither seized those that were offered.

When Rosalind's next partner claimed her, Richard bowed curtly, carefully avoiding her eye. She felt inexplicably fatigued and begged the very youthful gentleman to excuse her.

"To tell the truth, ma'am, I'm not much of a hand at dancing. I shall be happy to sit it out," he confessed ingenuously. "Should you object to telling me a little about Major Bowen's adventures in India?"

"So I owe our acquaintance to my cousin, do I?" she teased.

He blushed. "I am hoping to enter the army myself, you see," he stammered. "I thought you looked kind as well as beautiful, so I wangled an introduction."

Rosalind took pity on him, and related all the most exciting parts of Charles's tales, hoping she was retelling them correctly.

She drove home from the ball with Lucy and Charles and Lady Annabel, both her cavaliers having deserted her. She quite understood Harry's defection, but Richard's annoyed her intensely. *I was only* comforting *poor Harry,* she thought bitterly. Anyone would think she had run off to Gretna Green with him.

She cried herself to sleep.

Chapter 20

Harry was gone before most of his brother's guests roused the next morning. A few gentlemen straggled down to breakfast, and several ladies dressed in time to attend church in the village, but the majority were not seen before luncheon.

Richard had ridden home after his last dance with Rosalind, and retired to his chamber with a bottle of his host's best brandy. He woke after noon with a mild hangover, his first since the spring, and cursed the day he had found Miss Fell on the moors. He drank a cup of coffee, dressed, and went out for a long and solitary ride in spite of the heavy drizzle.

Rosalind did not see him all day. Her low spirits went unnoticed in the general depression caused by the weather and the approaching end of the party. When he entered the salon where the company was gathering before dinner, she thought he looked unwell. She would have been glad of a chance to talk to him, but he did not look at her, going straight to Lady Annabel and remaining in conversation with her.

Lord Harry's disappearance had been remarked on during course of the day. Now Rosalind saw that Miss Allington and one of her cronies were whispering and giggling behind their hands and casting frequent glances in her direction. She was sure that they were discussing the loss of both of her admirers, and her anger against Richard, which was dying, reanimated. How dare he expose her to the impertinence of a pair of schoolroom misses! She tried to ignore them, and continued her conversation with Emma Denison, wishing that on the morrow she would be setting out not for Toblethorpe but for home and Ian. She would like to show the arrogant Mr. Carstairs how little she needed him!

At last he came to her side. He bowed and muttered something about making an early start in the morning. At that moment the butler announced dinner, and once more she had no chance to speak with him. They were seated at opposite ends of the table and on the same side, so she could not even see him.

She eagerly awaited his appearance in the drawing room when the gentlemen joined the ladies. Lord Denham made his way to her.

"Richard asked me to present his excuses, Miss Stuart. Captain Denison challenged him to a game of billiards. I believe they wish to discuss his brother at Toblethorpe."

"I was not expecting Mr. Carstairs," announced Rosalind brightly. "I have a slight headache, and in view of the journey tomorrow, I shall retire very soon." She went on to thank him for the delightful visit and his kind hospitality.

When she left in search of Lady Catherine, Tony shook his head and sighed. Richard had asked him to arrange the party to provide an unexceptionable meeting place for Charles and Lucy, but he had really done it for Richard himself. It looked as if it had all been in vain, he thought, watching Miss Stuart's straight back and the proud tilt to her chin as she passed the malicious Miss Allington. She would have been good for his friend; she brought him out of his shell. He wondered what had caused the split, hoped it was not his mischievous younger brother, and then remembered that Richard would have several weeks in Yorkshire to try again. He decided to drop a hint that Miss Stuart was looking unhappy, and feeling more cheerful, made the rounds of his departing guests, most of whom he would be delighted to bid farewell.

Monday dawned blustery and grey. However, the rain had ceased, and it was generally agreed that it looked to be a reasonable day for travelling. Shortly after eight o'clock, carriages and chaises began to pull up before the front door as those with long journeys ahead of them prepared to depart.

At the last minute, Lady Annabel had declared that she simply could not face driving again over the dreadful roads between Nottingham and Leeds.

"They will be even worse after this wet weather," she explained to Richard. "I know it is farther, dearest, but could we not take the Great North Road? Besides, I should very much like to stop at Arnden and make Charles properly known to Geoffrey and Blanche. It will be so confusing for the poor boy to meet all his new relatives only at the wedding, and you know in London he was introduced as a mere acquaintance."

"Of course, mama," replied Richard. "I should not dream of subjecting you to such discomfort. I had not properly considered the matter."

"You have a great deal on your mind, do

you not, Richard?" queried Lady Annabel hopefully. Richard was not to be drawn out.

"Nothing more important than my dear mama's wishes," he said lightly but firmly. "I shall send a message to Arnden at once."

Lady Annabel, Lucy and Rosalind traveled in the Carstairs carriage, the two abigails and Richard's valet, Willett, in Charles's chaise. The gentlemen announced a preference for riding alongside, and would take turns in the carriage. In fact, though Charles joined the ladies quite frequently, when they stopped for a late luncheon in Newark Richard had been on horseback the entire way.

He was scrupulously polite to Rosalind, and completely formal. Taking her cue from him, she was equally constrained, and their mutual coolness cast a pall over the other three. Lucy decided to ride with Charles for a while in the afternoon and Lady Annabel seized her opportunity.

"Rosalind," she said hesitantly, "have you quarreled with Richard? I do not mean to interfere, only if there is some misunderstanding, perhaps I may help."

"We did not precisely quarrel," Rosalind answered. "He . . . he saw me kiss Lord

Harry and gave me no chance to explain that I was just saying good-bye. I . . . Harry needed comforting, you see. I cannot say more."

"I think I understand," Lady Annabel assured her. "Perhaps I should tell you a little about Richard so that you do not misinterpret his behaviour. I am afraid he often appears arrogant, even cold, when he is trying to avoid being hurt." She described to Rosalind his painful school-days and his subsequent inability to trust anyone with his feelings.

"And all because of his darkness?" asked Rosalind wonderingly. "What horrors little boys are! Lady Annabel, you should not be telling me this. Mr. Carstairs has been as kind to me as if I were truly his cousin, but I have no right to know of such personal matters."

"My dear, I had hoped . . ."

"Mr. Carstairs has given me no reason to think he looks on me as anything other than a cousin. That is why I was angry when he enacted a Cheltenham tragedy after seeing me and Harry. I only wanted a bit of fun before I go home and marry Ian Heathercot." Rosalind started this speech firmly. By the end, she was wailing and she burst into tears. Lady Annabel took her in her arms and patted her soothingly.

"Hush, child, hush. I did not know you were already betrothed or I would never have. . . . Oh dear, what a coil!"

"I am not betrothed," hiccupped Rosalind. "I told Ian I would give him my answer when I return to Bennendale. If I had been already promised, I'd not have behaved so, and none of this would have happened."

"You are not . . . ? I declare I am growing quite confused. Well, then, we must hope that Richard will climb down off his high horse, and we may all be friends again. Come, dry your eyes, my dear. I am sure everything will work out for the best."

Meanwhile, Lucy was attacking her brother. "Richard, how can you be so odious to poor Rosalind! You are making her quite miserable."

"*I* making *her* miserable!" he exclaimed with bitterness.

"Did something happen at the Hunt Ball?" asked Charles curiously, adding in haste, "No wish to pry, old man, but it seemed to me that until then you were contriving admirably."

"Come, tell, Richard," coaxed Lucy. "It will quite spoil my wedding if you and Rosalind are both full of megrims."

"Well, if you must know, I saw her kissing Harry Graham."

This news struck Lucy dumb, but Charles was equal to the occasion.

"And the next day Harry left before dawn," he pointed out sapiently. "Do you think my cousin has the air of a girl concealing a secret engagement?"

"N-no," admitted Richard. "But if she was just saying good-bye to him, why did she not explain to me?"

"Did you give her a chance?" asked Lucy. "Anyway, have you given her any reason to suppose that you have a right to an explanation? You are not *her* older brother, you know, and if you go on this way, you will never be her husband, either."

"Lucy!" reprimanded Charles.

She flushed but objected. "It's true! I beg your pardon, Richard, but I do not want you to ruin your life because everyone is too mealymouthed to tell you when you are being chuckleheaded."

Charles laughed, and even Richard smiled.

"I assure you," he said to Charles, "that my mother has done her utmost to teach Lucy to speak like a lady. However, I daresay she is right," he added painfully. "I find it difficult to keep in mind that Rosalind does not remember . . . what I said to Clara Fell."

"Clarissa!" maintained Lucy.

Richard had no idea how to go about mending the breach. He wished he could invite Rosalind to ride with him. Failing that, he decided to wait until they reached Doncaster, where they were to spend the night, and attempt to speak to her privately at the inn.

In the meantime, the reminder of the late Miss Fell brought another problem to mind. "Oh, the devil!" he groaned. "How are we going to introduce Rosalind to Aunt Florence?"

"Oh dear," gasped Lucy, "I had not considered! And what is more, Rosalind must not hear whatever we tell her, Richard, or she will know the whole."

Charles demanded an explanation, which his betrothed supplied. He then demanded an explanation of the explanation from Richard.

"I see," he said at last. "Of course, I do not know your aunt, but surely it would be best to lay the whole business before her."

"Never!" cried Richard and Lucy with one breath. "I cry craven," admitted Richard with a grin. "Besides, my mother is involved in the deception, also. In fact it was she who invented the story about her old school friend."

"Then we shall have to leave the school friend intact," mused Charles. "That leaves only the change of name to be accounted for."

"And the sudden demise of the school friend," Richard pointed out.

"I think she must have died quite some time ago," suggested Lucy, "and mama simply forgot to mention it to Aunt Florence."

"I suppose so," agreed Richard dubiously. "Wait a bit! Rosalind said something about her Grandfather Stuart having a strong distaste for London. Perhaps we might build a tale around that?"

"I have it!" cried Charles in triumph. "Listen! Rosalind's mama died, oh, say eighteen months ago. We might as well stick as close to the truth as possible. After a year of mourning, as I was in India and showed no signs of coming home, Lady Annabel invited her to spend some time with you in London. Now, here is her grandfather's will: No member of the family was ever to grace the metropolis with his presence. The lawyers agree that the provision is unreasonable and suggest an alias as a way of avoiding it. And there we have Miss Fell."

"Charles, you are so clever," murmured Lucy admiringly.

"It looks all right to me," assented Richard. "And I know why Aunt Florence is not to mention the matter to Rosalind. Miss Stuart is wretched about deceiving her and she will do her a kindness by not bringing it up or appearing to have known her before."

"That last is a little weak. And I thought you said Miss Carstairs was a very Gorgon," objected Charles. "Why should she be so considerate of my cousin?"

Lucy looked a little guilty. "Aunt Florence is only terrifying to gentlemen and *young* ladies," she admitted. "Mama thinks her perfectly amiable."

"I believe she became quite fond of Miss Fell," added Richard. "Mama will have to tell her all this. She will not question her."

"And mama may tell her she did not disclose the whole before because she respects Aunt Florence's dislike of gossip. Then she will be quite unable to ask anything further!" declared Lucy triumphantly.

"Now all we have to do is to persuade Lady Annabel to present this farrago to

447

Miss Carstairs," said the practical Charles.

"I shall leave that to you two," Richard told them. "You may disclose the whole to her in her chamber at Doncaster, and I shall distract Rosalind so that she does not suspect what is going on."

Charles and Lucy exchanged looks and agreed.

On arriving at the Angel, the ladies went to their room to rest before dining. Lucy and Rosalind were sharing a chamber. They sat by a glowing fire, the curtains pulled tight against the dusk outside, and chatted in a desultory way. Rosalind was inclined to be thoughtful and spent some time gazing absently into the flames. After a while, Lucy announced that she was going to dress for dinner.

"I expect Vane is with Lady Annabel," said Rosalind. "I shall ring for Joan, and she may help us both."

It did not take them long to prepare themselves. Lucy led the way out of their room as if to go below to their private parlour.

"I must speak to mama for a moment," she told Rosalind. "Do you go on down and I shall join you presently."

Rosalind continued down the stair, shivering in the icy blast from the open front door of the inn. A potboy directed her to the parlour. When she entered she was taken aback to find only Richard there, standing at the window looking out into the dark street. He turned and came toward her.

"Come by the fire," he said, taking her hand. "The corridors are decidedly chilly, are they not?"

"Yes," she murmured, looking at him questioningly.

"Miss Stuart, I believe I misunderstood something I saw." Once he had started, the words rushed out. "I beg you will forgive me for behaving like a sulky child. I thought . . . I thought . . ."

She placed a finger to his lips. "No matter what you thought if you do not think it now. I am not over pleased with my own behaviour," she confessed wryly. "I hope you will overlook it and we may be friends again. Is it not mortifying to find it so easy to indulge in schoolroom sullens?"

Richard kissed her hand. "I cannot imagine that you were ever a naughty child, Rosalind."

"Oh, can you not?" She proceeded to regale him with tales of the horrifying exploits undertaken by herself and Charles in their tender youth, and Richard recipro-

449

cated. When the others ventured to join them, they were both laughing as helplessly as any pair of schoolchildren.

Lady Annabel, much against her will, had agreed to approach Miss Florence. She had, however, posed a difficulty that the conspirators had somehow overlooked.

"My dears," she had said, "it is not just Florence who must have an explanation. The whole family met Miss Fell. I cannot imagine how we came not to remember it before."

It was decided that Richard must ride ahead to Arnden in the morning, a distance of some thirty miles, and disclose the whole to his Uncle Geoffrey. That gentleman would be left to determine how to present the matter to his family and to coach them in their roles before the others arrived.

"We must arrange it so as to arrive at about two o'clock," Lady Annabel proposed. "Florence always takes a nap at about that time, and I shall be able to see her privately. Oh dear, what a complicated business."

They spent a delightful evening in conversation, and if her companions were at times somewhat distrait, Rosalind did not notice it. She was looking forward to the next month, to seeing Charles happily wed, and was determined to look no further.

The following day, all went without a hitch. Mr. Geoffrey Carstairs, a genial gentleman but one accustomed to being obeyed, simply ordered his family to forget that they had ever seen Miss Stuart before. Lady Annabel, with a more trying mission, caught Miss Carstairs when she arose from her forty winks, and stumbled through an explanation.

"So you see, Florence," she ended airily, "I did not wish to bother you with the details, knowing how you abhor tattle-mongering. However, the poor child is sadly afraid that you will be offended with her. She would take it as a kindness if you would act as if you have not met her before."

"Odd!" commented Miss Carstairs. "If that is what she wishes, of course I shall do so, Annabel, but what of the children? They also met Miss . . . Stuart before."

"Geoffrey is dealing with them," explained Lady Annabel. "Our only aim is to avoid any possible embarrassment to dear Rosalind." She hesitated. "I daresay should not tell you this, Florence, but I have some hopes that Richard and Rosalind may make a match of it."

"A sensible and charming young woman, as I recall. You would be glad of the connection, I take it."

"Oh yes, especially as I am to lose Lucy. We are already agreed that she is to be my niece-in-law but that will not keep her by me, and it would be delightful to have her as a daughter."

"And good for Richard, no doubt," declared Miss Carstairs magisterially. "You may depend upon it that I shall do nothing to make Miss Stuart uncomfortable."

She was not so sparing of Richard, greeting him with a look of disapproval and announcing that he might have better taste in clothes than his Cousin Edward, but she doubted that he had any better sense. Since he had not seen her in several months and could not imagine on what grounds he was being attacked, he was speechless, casting a long-suffering glance at Lucy, who came off only slightly better.

"So you have caught yourself a husband," commented Miss Carstairs acidly. "Good luck to you, niece!"

To Charles's astonishment she was perfectly good-natured when Rosalind was presented to her, even going so far as to say kindly,

"I am happy to make your acquaintance, Miss Stuart."

Rosalind, alarmed by her treatment of her nephew and niece, blushed at this condescension, which Miss Carstairs put down to quite other causes.

Charles was even more surprised when the formidable lady turned to him with something close to approval.

"A military gentleman, I understand," she said. "You shall tell me about India." Lady Annabel had quite forgotten that Florence had always had a soft spot for a soldier.

They had intended to stay at Arnden for only one night, but Blanche easily persuaded Lady Annabel that Lucy should shop for bride-clothes in nearby York.

"You say they are to be married as soon as the banns have been put up, Annabel? You cannot possibly find all the necessary in that time. Toblethorpe is very isolated," she pointed out. So they stayed for several days. In spite of Lucy's impatience, she was dragged on daily expeditions round the shops of York, which her envious cousin Jenny enjoyed far more than she did.

Rosalind found the family friendly and hospitable. She was as amused by Edward's costume at their second meeting as she had been at their unremembered first. He was indeed more spectacular in a country setting, where he had no competition. After a few conversations with him she could not understand how Miss Carstairs could have compared Richard to him with regard to sense. She did not think he had any whatsoever.

While they were at Arnden, news came of the Battle of Trafalgar. The French and Spanish fleets were destroyed and Admiral Lord Nelson had won another great victory, this time at the cost of his life. Everyone seemed to feel that the loss of England's hero outweighed the end to the Emperor Napoleon's threat of invasion, and there was no rejoicing. In fact, the news seemed to have no impact whatever on their way of life. Lucy went on shopping, Richard continued to guide Rosalind's daily rides, and Edward continued to wear his shocking pink waistcoat with the purple butterflies.

Rosalind was now able to ride without Richard leading her horse, but she still needed him next to her and would not go above a trot. She graduated from Whitesocks to a dapple grey hack of Jenny's, and had a new habit made up in York. The two of them explored the fields and woods around Arnden and once rode into York so that Richard could show Rosalind the Minster and the old city walls.

More than once he nearly asked her to marry him, then decided the moment was not quite right. He was far from sure that it would be honest to do so when the greater part of their relationship was a blank to her. Suppose she remembered everything after they were wed, and it changed her feelings toward him. Yet he could think of no way to remind her without risking her health. Uncertainty was a constant shadow over his enjoyment of her company.

Rosalind was aware that all was not well. She could not remain ignorant of Richard's love for her and could not understand what held him back from declaring himself. Knowing that he was very dear to her, she was still not sure what her answer would be if he did actually ask for her hand. She had known him for such a short time, and most of that time she had been equally involved with Harry. She became more and more conscious that only a little over three weeks remained before she must give Ian Heathercot a final answer. In that short time she must get to know Richard well enough to decide between them. And she could not tell him of her deadline, so even if she did love him enough to marry him he might not ask her in time.

They spent every possible moment together.

The day came when they must go on to Toblethorpe or postpone the wedding for another week. With the long climb up into the Pennines ahead of them, they left immediately after breakfast. The children ran down the driveway after them, waving.

"See you in a few weeks, Aunt Annabel," they hallooed.

"Don't forget, you promised I could ride Flame," called Christopher.

Their last sight was of Anna and Lydia dancing in a ring and chanting. "I'm going to be a bridesmaid, a bridesmaid, a bridesmaid!"

Charles and Richard again rode most of the way. About five miles from home, Lucy decided to join them, and Richard tactfully retired to the carriage. Rosalind was commenting on the similarities between Toblethorpe's surroundings and her own home country.

"The hills are very like those around Bennendale," she told them, "except ours are greener. We have more bracken, where you have heather and gorse." She and

Richard discussed their relative merits as sheep fodder.

As they drove through Toblethorpe village, Rosalind fell silent. The weary team pulled steadily up the hill and they passed through the gates, greeted by old Matthew. Toblethorpe Manor appeared before them. Rosalind put her hands to her head and closed her eyes.

"I feel strange," she said unsteadily. "I cannot think what is the matter with me."

Richard and his mother bent toward her anxiously. The carriage pulled up at the front door.

"Take her inside quickly, dearest," instructed Lady Annabel. "She had better lie down at once. Rosalind, dear child, I shall be with you directly."

Richard helped Rosalind from the carriage, half supported her up the steps and into the house. She was breathing rapidly, unevenly, and the hand that was not on his arm was still at her head, but her eyes were open and she was looking around her in a puzzled way. There were several servants in the hall, and her gaze fixed on one of them.

"Mary?" she asked uncertainly.

"Oh, miss!" cried Mary, running forward with tears in her eyes. "I knowed tha'd not forget me."

Rosalind held out her hand. "Of course not, Mary," she assured her. She looked up at Richard, her face very pale.

"Come and sit down." He led her gently into the drawing room and she sank into a chair. He pulled up a footstool beside her and took her hands in a reassuring clasp.

"I'm not going crazy, am I?" she whispered. He shook his head. "Then what is happening? I am so confused. I seem to see everything twice. What is happening to me, Mr. Carstairs? Richard?"

"You are simply remembering things you had forgotten," he told her gravely. "I will tell you what occurred and I hope it will help you sort things out in your head.

"You ran away from your uncle. You remember that?" She nodded. "You rode all the way from Bennendale through the snow until you reached the moors near here. There your horse threw you and kicked you on the temple. That made you lose your memory. I — well, Lord Denham and I — found you and brought you here. We had no idea who you were or where you came from. We called you Clara Fell, for want of a better name, and my mother nursed you. You were very ill, we feared you would die.

"When you recovered you went to

London with us, and there, after some weeks, you met Charles. The shock made you forget your time with us, and you remembered all your previous life."

"Why did you not tell me all this long ago?" Rosalind gripped his hands tightly as she struggled to straighten out the sudden rush of memories. Lady Annabel had come into the room, but seeing that they were talking quietly, she did not interrupt.

"I . . . we wanted to, Rosalind. After meeting Charles, you started getting terrible headaches whenever you saw any of the rest of us. The doctor said you must go quite away from us, and not be reminded of us in any way. I was afraid I might never be able to see you again. Disford Wood was an experiment. When you did not recognize us, nor suffer any apparent ill, we never thought that returning here might be dangerous."

"Not dangerous," said Rosalind slowly. "I have no headache. I think I need time to adjust to this. I should like to be alone for a while, Richard, if you do not mind."

Lady Annabel intervened. "Bed!" she declared firmly. "Richard, you may carry Rosalind upstairs. I daresay it will make her feel quite at home. You shall have your dinner on a tray, my dear, and need not come down until you feel quite ready to face everyone."

"I can walk," protested Rosalind, with tolerable composure, but after a few shaky steps she was glad when Richard lifted her unceremoniously in his arms. Surprised at how natural it felt, she laid her head back trustingly against his shoulders and closed her eyes.

When they reached her room, the same one as before, they found Mary and Joan arguing about who was to wait on her. Lady Annabel shooed them both out, and Richard, too.

"I'll help you into bed and then leave you in peace. I am sure you need a quiet period for contemplation, my dear, and no one shall disturb you."

An hour or two later an unknown housemaid brought her a tray loaded with delicacies. She recognized Monsieur Pierre's artistry, and more pieces of the complex puzzle that was her memory clicked into place. Lying quiescent, she let faces and scenes float by her mind's eye and gradually everything came into focus. She fell asleep with a smile on her lips.

Lucy and Charles had taken a long way round to the manor. By the time they arrived, Rosalind had been in bed for half an hour. Charles was horrified to hear what had happened and wanted to rush to his cousin's side. Lady Annabel had great difficulty in dissuading him.

"She needs time," she insisted. "I will send for Dr. Grimsdale if you will have it so, but I do not think it necessary. Rosalind will call for us if she wants us."

Richard agreed with her. "Don't worry, Charles," he said soothingly. "The first shock was very agitating but her nerves were not overset and she very quickly grew calmer. She asked to be alone, and I do not believe anyone should try to see her until tomorrow."

In spite of his reassuring words to Charles, Richard was far from tranquil himself. He spent the greater part of the evening pacing up and down, looking up eagerly every time a servant entered the room. In his dreams that night he proposed to Rosalind again and again, and every time she told him she did not know who he was.

Morning brought a warm, moist wind from the west, like a last breath of summer. After breakfast, Richard retired to the library, ostensibly to go over his accounts. Rosalind found him there, once more pacing up and down.

"Richard, would you take me up on the moor, where you found me?" she asked shyly. "I can't explain why, I just feel a need to see the place."

They were soon riding up the lane and turning onto the bridlepath. Rosalind was silent, so Richard did not speak until he recognized the spot where he had seen that limp bundle so long ago.

"It was there," he pointed, "behind that gorse."

"You remember the very bush?" she asked wonderingly.

"I spent a great deal of time looking at it last summer," he admitted wryly, "for want of you to look at."

She blushed. "Help me down," she requested. "I want to go over there."

Richard dismounted and lifted her down. Her closeness intoxicated him, and suddenly forgetting all his good resolutions, he drew her to him and sought her lips with his. After a moment of startled protest, she turned her face up to him and ceased to push against his chest.

A group of interested sheep raised their heads and watched in apparent fascination. The embrace was so protracted that after a while they returned to cropping the short wiry grass.

At last breathlessness forced the pair to draw apart a little, though Richard kept his arms firmly around Rosalind's waist.

"I love you so much," he murmured. "You will marry me, won't you?"

"But I was planning to go home and marry Mr. Heathercot," objected Rosalind demurely.

"Whoever Mr. Heathercot may be, I am sure he would never condone your behaviour at Disford Wood."

"Ah, but I should not tell him."

"Mr. Heathercot does not have a mother who loves you as a daughter and needs your companionship. At least, I trust he does not."

"I have never met Mr. Heathercot's mother. I have heard she is delightful."

"Well, I have an ace up my sleeve. My heir."

Rosalind looked up at him inquiringly.

"Only consider that if you do not become my wife, I shall never marry and Cousin Edward will inherit Toblethorpe!"

Rosalind, her eyes dancing, put her arms around his neck.

"You leave me no choice," she murmured. "Besides," she added practically, "I may have temporarily forgotten it, but I have been in love with you ever since the first time you smiled at me."

"Then why did you refuse me, my darling?"

"I feared that I might turn out to be a butcher's daughter, and you would regret having married me."

"Once I had discovered that I loved you, I would not have cared if your father was a transported convict!"

"But you did not say that you loved me, only that you admired me and wished to protect me."

"I did not? I am sure I meant to, my poor sweetheart. I was not altogether *compos mentis* at the time. I shall have to make up for my omission. Rosalind, my dearest love, will you marry me?"

"I thought I told you already, Richard."

"You said I left you no choice. I want a plain answer. Once more, will you be my wife, beloved?"

"Yes, my darling," she answered, and had the sheep been watching, they would have seen a repeat performance.